Praise for
GOODBYE TO ALL THAT

"GOODBYE TO ALL THAT is for any woman who has picked up that last pair of shoes or done that last stack of laundry and wanted to walk—or run—out the door. Written with wit and compassion, Ruth's story of revival and rediscovery is simply one of the best books of the year. A must read!"
—*Jill Barnett,* New York *Times* Bestselling Author

"Every character is real and rare, people you already know. You hurt for them . . . and love for them. A joy of a book—witty, wonderful and wise."
—*Jennifer Green, USA Today* Bestselling Author and winner of RWA's Lifetime Achievement Award

"With surgical precision, Judith Arnold dissects the strands of family and relationships, giving voice to the often unspoken desires felt at any age. Warm, witty and unflinchingly honest about the depths to which our families shape us, GOODBYE TO ALL THAT was one of the best books I've read all year."
—*Kristan Higgin,* New York *Times* and *USA Today* Bestselling Author, and two-time winner of the RWA Rita Award.

"Judith Arnold's sly, perceptive look at a family resisting change is a delightful, often humorous, read, with characters you won't stop thinking about after you turn the final page."
—*Emilie Richards, USA Today* Bestselling Author.

Goodbye To All That

by

Judith Arnold

Bell Bridge Books

This is a work of fiction. Names, characters, places and incidents are either the products of the author's imagination or are used fictitiously. Any resemblance to actual persons (living or dead,) events or locations is entirely coincidental.

Bell Bridge Books
PO BOX 300921
Memphis, TN 38130
Print ISBN: 978-1-61194-093-0

Bell Bridge Books is an Imprint of BelleBooks, Inc.

Copyright © 2012 by Barbara Keiler writing as Judith Arnold

Printed and bound in the United States of America.

We at BelleBooks enjoy hearing from readers.
Visit our websites – www.BelleBooks.com and www.BellBridgeBooks.com.

10 9 8 7 6 5 4 3 2 1

Cover design: Debra Dixon
Interior design: Hank Smith
Photo credits:
Photo (manipulated) C Richard Thomas | Dreamstime.com

:Lagt:01:

exotic people, people with actual lives, got to wean themselves from booze, cocaine, cigarettes and compulsive sex. Jill was trying to wean herself from Diet Coke. She didn't want to analyze what that said about her.

Taking a swig, she savored the fizzy burn of the carbonation across her tongue and up into her sinuses. She hoped the caffeine would give her brain a needed jolt, like those paddles doctors used to restart the hearts of patients in cardiac arrest. Jill was in mental arrest; she needed her brain shocked back to life, *stat*, as they said in medical dramas on TV. Geoffrey needed the shantung-scarf copy by five p.m. Which meant she had to get it written and emailed by three. Once the kids got home, Jill's time, like her language, was no longer her own.

Geoffrey Munger, the editor of the Black Pearl catalog, favored what he called "nature-based yet sensuous metaphors" in the copy describing the company's offerings. Lois Foreman, the editor of the Prairie Wind catalog, had a strong preference for "bright and breezy." Sabrina Lopez, the editor of the Velvet Moon catalog, preferred "edgy and erotic." Jill appreciated how lucky she was to be writing catalog copy for three different companies—not just because the money was three times better than writing for only one but also because the three different commissions offered her creative variety. She only had to remember which catalog she was writing for on any given day.

She also had to try not to let the catalogs' refusal to describe colors by their actual names distract her. "Blue" didn't exist for any of the companies that employed Jill. A customer could buy a garment in periwinkle, navy, aqua, royal, sky, tiffany, ocean, peacock, azure, powder or indigo. Not blue. Never blue.

Another hit of Diet Coke and she was back at her desk, shoving the blues to a remote corner of her brain and reminding herself that today she was writing for Geoffrey Munger at Black Pearl. If she sent him edgy and erotic text instead of natural yet sensuously metaphorical text—if, for instance, she described the shantung scarves as being ideal for lashing one's lover to a four-poster—he'd probably keel over.

She stared at her computer monitor so long her eyelids synchronized their blinks with the pulsing cursor. A sharp shake of her head broke her trance, and she took another stab at describing the scarf Black Pearl hoped to entice thousands of women into purchasing. *More refreshing than a waterfall, lighter than a breeze, perfect to protect bare shoulders during a romantic evening stroll. Our shantung silk scarf is available in every color of the rainbow. Be playful in persimmon. Lyrical in lemon. Mysterious in midnight. This scarf is available in a wide array of hues to match your wide array of moods.*

The phone rang.

"Shit," Jill said.

She supposed she could ignore the phone and let the caller leave a message. But before the machine picked up, she'd have to listen to four more rings, which would shatter her concentration. As if one ring hadn't already shattered it.

She allowed herself a brief fantasy of setting up her catalog copy business in a real office rather than a corner of the kitchen—an office with a separate phone number, just for her. She imagined commuting to her office every day . . . in bumper-to-bumper traffic, in blizzards, in flooding downpours and tornado-like microbursts.

No. She'd settle for an office right here in the house, but soundproofed so she wouldn't hear the family phone when it rang. In the unfinished part of the basement? Too dark, and there were spiders. In the attic? Too hot, and there were spiders. Maybe she could hire a contractor to build an extension off the back of the house. An office suite, spider-proof, with a private bathroom and kitchenette to go with the private phone line. It would only cost about twice what she earned in a year.

The phone rang a third time. Two more rings and the machine would pick up.

Her caller might be one of the kids. Or the school nurse, informing her that Noah had puked his lunch all over the floor in gym, or Abbie had gotten her period and needed Jill to bring her some clean panties and jeans. That very disaster had occurred last spring, and for the following week Abbie had moped around the house, whining that the humiliation had been so awful she wanted to die.

Jill was a Good Mom. How could she ignore her ringing phone when the caller could be her daughter, wanting to die?

She shoved away from the desk, mumbling a few therapeutic curses, and strode around the center island to reach the phone. "Hello?"

"Jill? It's your mother."

As if, after thirty-six years as Ruth Bendel's daughter, Jill wouldn't recognize the woman's voice. "Hi," she said.

"Have you got a minute?"

Jill sighed. Her monitor glared at her, the cursor flashing imperatively, a computer version of a nagging, wagging finger. "I really don't," she said.

"I'll be quick," her mother promised. "I want you to invite your

Acknowledgements

My huge thanks to the team at Bell Bridge Books: Debra Dixon, Deborah Smith, and my wonderful editor, Pat Van Wie. I am also grateful to Lisa Gardner, Jennifer Greene, Kathryn Shay, the Romexers, the Bunnies and my BHS buddies for inspiring me, encouraging me, listening to me whine and celebrating with me. Finally, thanks to Ted, who has always had more faith in me than I have in myself, and our two glorious sons, who keep my life in balance and remind me of what's important. I love writing about families, because in my own family I am truly blessed.

Chapter One

It was perfect.

All right, it was small. Three rooms, the ad claimed, but Ruth would hardly call the kitchen—an L-shaped configuration of Formica counters with painted metal cabinets above and below, a stove that had cooked at least twenty years worth of meals, a stainless-steel sink that wasn't stainless and not even enough space for a table and chairs—an actual room. A cooking alcove, maybe. A galley. An applianced hallway. She could probably jam a small, square table into the corner, with one chair. Pushed all the way in, the chair wouldn't block the doorway into the entry, at least not much. A second chair would interfere with the refrigerator.

Ruth didn't need a second chair.

According to the rental agent, an unnaturally perky woman in a polyester suit that struck Ruth as a little too formal for the occasion, the living room was eighteen by twenty feet. Ruth would bet the diamond earrings Richard had given her for her fiftieth birthday that the agent was exaggerating by a few feet. And the carpet—it wasn't quite shag, but the nap was longer than it should be. It reminded Ruth of how the front yard looked in the rainy early days of summer when the lawn service skipped a week of mowing because the ground was too wet. Ruth might not have minded the carpet's uncut-grass length if it was also uncut-grass green. But it was a dull neutral shade, somewhere between taupe and khaki.

"It matches with everything," the rental agent boasted.

It matches with nothing, Ruth thought.

The bedroom was small, too. Like the living room, it overlooked the parking lot. Beyond a hedge of yews bordering the lot was a broad four-lane avenue, and on the other side of the avenue was a strip mall with the First-Rate convenience store where Ruth would begin working next week.

Imagine: Ruth Bendel, a college graduate who'd written her honors thesis on Arcangelo Corelli's use of suspended seconds, running a cash register at First-Rate.

Cash registers were complicated, she reminded herself. And even without having to master the buttons and scanners and "enters" and "deletes" on the cash register, Ruth would find the job challenging. The rituals, the responsibilities, the schedule, the social environment—everything would be different. Unfamiliar. A whole new way of life.

A double bed would just about fit inside this room, she thought as she surveyed the bedroom. Only one closet, but it was wide and she didn't have to share it with anyone. The apartment also had a coat closet in the entry and a walk-in closet adjacent to the bathroom, as well as access to its own locked storage cage in the building's basement.

That would be enough, she assured herself as she did a mental calculation of just what she was planning to bring with her and what she would leave behind. She wouldn't need that many clothes, really. At First-Rate she'd be wearing an official red apron over her outfit to identify her as a store employee. So there was little point in filling the apartment's closets with chic ensembles.

Not that she'd ever been particularly chic. Once Frugal Fannie's had gone out of business, she'd cut way back on buying trendy clothes. She couldn't see spending a fortune on a fancy garment so distinctive she might only wear it once. Good, solid, clothes, classic styles that lasted forever—that was her preference, especially when they were on sale.

So she'd pack some slacks, a few skirts, a few sweaters and move them here. With her red First-Rate apron covering everything she had on under it, why knock herself out?

The closet would do, she decided as she shut its hinged panel doors and surveyed the room once more. A double bed, a dresser, a night table . . . It would all fit in somehow. And she could buy a couple of plastic bins and stash them under the bed. They were good for storing linens and sweaters.

Better yet, she could buy a platform bed with drawers built into the frame. She'd always thought platform beds were amazing. Such a smart use of space, and they seemed so . . . Swedish. Sweden was an idyllic country, politically progressive, with excellent health care and maternity-leave policies. The word *Eden* was tucked inside Sweden. That had to mean something.

Richard had always been opposed to platform beds. "A bed should consist of a mattress and a box-spring," he'd insisted. "A platform topped with foam padding doesn't offer the proper support." Since he was a doctor, she was supposed to accept his opinion as scientific.

But all those Swedish people didn't seem to be hobbling around like cripples. They were too busy skiing and playing hockey to kvetch about their bad backs. Platform beds were probably as orthopedically sound as any other bed. And extra storage space never hurt anyone.

What did Richard know, anyway? He was a cardiologist. Since when was he an expert on the subject of back support?

"There's a laundry room in the basement," the rental agent noted, hovering near the window as if she wanted to draw Ruth's attention back to the spectacular view of the parking lot. "Very well lit, very safe. The buildings are secure. We've never had a problem here."

Well, there was always a first time. Ruth had enough Russian blood in her to expect the worst. But how much more dangerous was this apartment than the house? Richard had installed an alarm system shortly after they'd moved in, and Ruth had screwed it up so many times, pushing the wrong buttons or the right buttons in the wrong order and accidentally summoning the police, who would then bill her a hundred dollars for the false alarm, that Richard had wound up having the system removed. What a waste. Ruth had never felt safer with it.

"This particular unit," the rental agent said, "gets a lot of sunlight. It's really a very bright unit."

Ruth wished she wouldn't call the apartment a "unit." It was a residence, a dwelling. A home.

Not a home like the house where her children had grown up and where Richard still lived. Not a spacious colonial with rhododendrons and daffodils and spirea that Ruth herself had planted, and ancient pines bordering the backyard and towering above the roofline. Not a house with a kitchen big enough to prepare a Thanksgiving feast or a Seder for the whole family and a finished-basement rec room with a ping-pong table, and a formal living room that always looked pristine because it was so rarely used. Not a house with an elegant master bedroom suite, with two walk-in closets and a sleek fiberglass tub in the bathroom.

This place—this *unit*—was very bright. That would be enough.

It would be perfect.

Chapter Two

Like a silken waterfall, our shantung scarf will leave you feeling caressed and refreshed as it spills over your skin. Drape it around your arms like a stole or fling it dramatically over one shoulder. Loop it in a sassy sash around your waist. Wrap it multiple times around your neck, stand on a chair, tie the end to a tree limb and jump.

With a groan, Jill shoved away from what she euphemistically called her desk. It was in fact just an extension of the kitchen counter, beige laminate atop a cabinet of drawers crammed with scissors, rolls of tape, unsharpened pencils and other school supplies. Her printer sat on the floor underneath the counter in the space where her feet were supposed to go, forcing her to straddle her chair with her legs spread wide enough to facilitate childbirth.

Geoffrey had emailed her several photos of the scarf, which she'd printed out, spread across the counter and stared at for the past two hours, hoping for inspiration. Unfortunately, the scarf didn't have much going for it. It looked nothing like a waterfall, silken or otherwise. And the Black Pearl catalog refused to refer to the available colors in ordinary language. There was no red scarf, although it could be purchased in "cherry" and "persimmon." No green scarf, but customers could choose from "lime" or "mint." Not purple but "grape," "plum" and "eggplant." Not brown but "chocolate," "mocha" and "taffy." Not black but "licorice."

The hell with flinging the scarf over your shoulder. You might as well eat it.

Or use it to hang yourself.

"Shit," Jill muttered. She could curse out loud because Abbie and Noah weren't home from school yet. Once they got home, she had to be a Good Mom. Good Moms didn't say "shit" within range of their children.

She shoved away from her computer, crossed to the refrigerator and pulled a can of Diet Coke from the bottom shelf. She'd managed to cut back to only two cans a day and intended to wean herself completely before Abbie's bat mitzvah, eight months from now. Interesting people, brother and sister to your house this weekend. Saturday afternoon would work. No need to fuss."

Jill was a Good Daughter as well as a Good Mom, so she refrained from cursing—just barely. "You want me to host a family gathering?"

"I'd host it, but I think it's better if everybody isn't at my house."

"Why do they have to be at *my* house? What do we need a gathering for? And so last-minute. We're all busy, we all live hectic lives—"

"I know, but this is important. And it's better we get together to discuss it. It's not something I want to talk about over the phone."

Jill suddenly felt wobbly. She gripped the kitchen counter and swallowed. "What is it, Mom? Is Dad sick?"

"No."

"Are you?"

"Everyone is healthy," her mother said, sounding vaguely annoyed, although Jill failed to see anything annoying about good health. "Just call your brother and sister and invite them to your house. One o'clock? Two? Whatever is easier for you."

What's easier for me is not doing this, Jill thought glumly. "Why can't Doug host this gathering?" she asked. No point suggesting that Melissa might handle the hostessing duties. Melissa lived in Manhattan and the rest of the family lived in the suburbs west of Boston. Besides, Melissa was ditzy and disorganized and couldn't be counted on to do anything useful.

"You know Doug," her mother said.

Yes, Jill knew her brother. He was like her father: brilliant, a doctor, with an ego the size of Antarctica before global warming had reduced its glaciers. Doug's wife loved to entertain, though. "I'm sure Brooke—"

"Don't start with Brooke," Jill's mother said. "She'd turn it into an affair, with catering and a music ensemble and a bartender mixing drinks on the three-season porch."

A bartender sounded good to Jill.

"She's so . . . elaborate," her mother continued. "She's wonderful, I love her like a daughter, but . . ." A long, deep sigh. "You know Brooke."

Jill knew Brooke well enough to know Brooke might indeed hire a bartender, which made her the ideal person to host this gathering. "Mom, you're asking us to turn our schedules upside-down. Abbie and Noah have soccer games Saturday morning, and I'm supposed to put together a family reunion in the afternoon?"

"They shouldn't have games on a Saturday morning. It's not fair to the Jewish kids."

As far as Jill knew, none of the Jewish players in the town's soccer league—including Abbie and Noah—were the least bit bothered about missing Saturday morning services to play soccer. "I don't see why you can't tell me what this is about," she said. "You're asking us to rearrange our lives. Doug plays golf with Dad on Saturday afternoons. Brooke probably spends the entire day getting a facial or something. Melissa has to schlep all the way up from New York. What's the big mystery?"

"It's not a mystery." Ruth's tone was tart. "It's just not something I want to discuss over the phone."

"So we have to have a party?"

"Not a party. A get-together." Her mother sighed again. "If you don't think it's important when your parents are going through something . . ."

"What are you going through?" Jill asked with forced patience. "We've already established that no one's sick."

"I'll tell you on Saturday. You said you didn't have any time to talk, so I'll say good-bye. I'll see you this weekend. Give me a call, let me know what time."

Right. As the hostess, as the person who had to telephone her siblings and organize this stupid party—correction: get-together—and run out to stock up on gourmet coffee because Doug wouldn't drink the stuff that came in a can, and organic herbal tea for Melissa, assuming she was still on *that* kick, and the sticky honey rugelach her father loved, and she'd have to vacuum because her mother would notice if she hadn't, and Gordon would crab about how her mother was too demanding and she really ought to develop enough backbone to say no to the woman every now and then, Jill would get to decide what time this affair would take place.

Through the window she heard the low-pitched rumble of Abbie's school bus chugging past the house. The bus dropped Abbie off at the corner, and it took her anywhere from five to fifteen minutes to walk the half-block home, depending on how much she and Caitlin Orensky had to discuss in person before they parted ways, entered their own homes and started texting each other.

In any case, Jill didn't have time to prolong this conversation, let alone decide whether lemon, as in "lemon shantung scarf," was actually a lyrical color—whether *any* color could be lyrical, although she did like the alliteration. She wasn't going to get the catalog copy done by three, damn it. She might not get it done by five. Geoffrey would fire her, and all because her mother was being not just demanding but ridiculously cryptic.

"Just tell me what's going on," she said, deciding she could be demanding, too. "Tell me, or I won't host this thing."

"I really don't want to talk about it on the phone."

"Why? Do you think the NSA has my line bugged?"

"What's the NSA? One of those spy things?" A pregnant pause. "All right, Jill. I'll tell you. But please don't tell Doug and Melissa. Let Dad and me tell them in person."

Jill hadn't realized this was a question requiring a response until her mother's silence stretched several long seconds. "Okay," Jill agreed. "I won't tell."

"Your father and I are getting a divorce."

Jill almost gasped. Almost laughed. The very idea was so shocking it was hilarious.

She wasn't naïve. She was aware of the statistics—half of all marriages and blah-blah-blah. She counted among her acquaintances a fair share of divorced people. Two of her closest friends from college were divorced. Connie and Bill McNabb from down the street got a divorce last year and sold their house at a loss. Everyone in the neighborhood had seemed more upset by the puny price they'd accepted for their four-bedroom contemporary than by the news that the McNabbs were splitting up. Their divorce might not have threatened the other married couples on the street, but it did threaten their property values.

Divorces didn't happen in Jill's family, though. The marriage of her grandparents on her mother's side had survived World War II, most of which Grandpa Schwartz had spent in a cold, damp trench somewhere in Belgium while Grandma Schwartz collected tin cans and grew vegetables in a ten-by-twenty-foot plot behind their three-decker in Roxbury. Then Grandpa Schwartz had come home and their marriage had survived a move to Brookline, Grandma Schwartz's frequent spasms of hysteria, and Grandpa Schwartz's fondness for schnapps. It had survived financial ups and downs and passionate fights and their son Isaac eloping with a shiksa. Grandpa Schwartz was gone now, his butt no doubt planted firmly on a bar stool somewhere in heaven, and Grandma Schwartz was missing about half her mind, but the remaining half seemed to be coping well enough, supported by the competent staff at the assisted-living facility she'd moved to last year. The Schwartz grandparents had stayed together until Grandpa Schwartz shuffled off his mortal coil.

The same with Jill's paternal grandparents. The Bendels had been a perfect match, both of them slight and pale and meek. Grandpa Bendel had been bald, Grandma Bendel had had breasts, but other than that they'd been more or less interchangeable.

So neither of Jill's parents had come from broken homes. And until a minute ago, Jill hadn't come from a broken home, either.

"How can you get a divorce?" she wailed. For some reason, her mother's announcement seemed like a personal affront. What Jill had really wanted to shout was, *How dare you?* Which didn't make sense. It was her mother's divorce, not hers. Her mother's and her father's. "You've been married for forty years."

"Forty-two, but who's counting? We can talk more on Saturday. I know you're busy. You're working on one of those catalog jobs? I shouldn't keep you."

Don't do this, Jill thought, unsure of what *this* was. *Don't guilt-trip me about my work. Don't dump a bombshell on me and hang up.*

Don't get a divorce.

"What happened?" she asked. "Did Dad . . . do something?" She couldn't imagine her father doing anything divorce-worthy. Sixty-four years old and the man had never even gotten a speeding ticket. The idea of his having an affair, or visiting porn websites, or . . . *what?* Switching his voter registration to the Republican party? Jill's mother would probably kick him out of the house for that.

"It's not any one thing, Jill. It's nothing I can explain when you haven't got any time to talk."

"Try."

"You haven't got time," her mother reminded her. "We'll talk later. Call and let me know when we should come on Saturday."

Before Jill could argue with her, before she could insist she *did* have time even though she didn't, before she could plead with her mother, and cry and stamp her feet and declare that if her parents did this stupid thing she'd hold her breath until she turned blue and passed out, her mother had hung up the phone.

Jill didn't have much choice but to hang up, too.

She crossed back to her desk, weak and dizzy. What could have precipitated such a drastic move by her parents? What could her father have done to drive her mother away?

What if it was Jill's mother who had done the doing? What if Ruth had fallen in love with someone else? A neighbor. Someone from her synagogue. A younger man. A younger *woman*. What if she'd suddenly discovered she was a lesbian?

What if she'd decided to join the Republican party?

Jill couldn't imagine that. Lesbian, maybe. Republican, never.

Words swam before her on the computer monitor: *romantic, rainbow, midnight*. Forty-two years, she thought. It wasn't being the child of a broken home that upset her; it was the idea that something she'd depended on, something that had lasted longer than her own life, something she'd had such tenacious faith in, could suddenly stop existing.

If she could misread her parents' marriage so totally, how could she trust her judgment on any other issue? If Ruth and Richard Bendel could get a divorce after all these years, why shouldn't Jill also assume that gravity didn't exist, and chocolate-chip cookies lowered your cholesterol, and Abbie didn't need a bat mitzvah, and the shantung silk scarves being peddled by Black Pearl actually felt more like sandpaper than a waterfall against one's skin?

The back door swung open and Abbie swept in, her eyes bright, her hair windblown and her backpack dangling heavily from one shoulder. "I hate pre-algebra," she announced with operatic grandeur. "Three worksheets are due tomorrow. *Three*. And Mr. Parshna *knows* it takes, like, a half hour to get through a worksheet. He said so, he said he expects us to spend, like, a half hour on a worksheet, and then he gives us *three* and says they're due tomorrow. Like I don't have anything better to do."

Jill should say something. Something sympathetic about the work sheets, something supportive of Abbie's math teacher, something about not dumping her backpack on the kitchen table if she was planning to eat a snack, because the during the trip home from school the backpack had probably been sitting on the floor of the bus, where it would have picked up enough germs to poison the population of a small nation.

But her lips refused to move. If she spoke, she might say something about her parents' divorce. And she couldn't tell Abbie about that. Abbie adored her grandparents. She would be devastated to think they no longer adored each other.

Of course they adored each other. Forty-two years of love didn't just evaporate overnight. The whole thing was absurd.

On Saturday, the Bendel family would converge at Jill's house and she would work this thing out. She was the fixer, the solver, the person who held her loved ones together. The Bendel everyone depended on.

She'd make this right.

"Are you okay, Mom?" Abbie asked.

"Sure," Jill managed. She turned from her daughter, her beautiful daughter, whose blondish-brown hair looked a lot more like a silken waterfall spilling down her back than Black Pearl's silk scarf ever would. "I'm just a little distracted, that's all. I've got to write this copy before Noah gets home." The middle-school bus dropped Abbie off a half-hour before the primary-school bus dropped Noah off. In thirty minutes, maybe Jill could spew out some text for the catalog.

"Once he gets home," Abbie said, sounding far too wise for her years, "life as we know it comes to an end. Can I bring an apple to my room? I've got to get started on these stupid math sheets."

Jill usually banned food from the kids' bedrooms, especially food that could drip juice onto the carpet. But she needed to be alone right now as much as Abbie needed to do her math sheets. "Go ahead," she said. "Just be careful."

"Oh, darn. I was planning to be careless," Abbie said sarcastically as she swung open the refrigerator door. "Yay, you bought Granny Smiths. I love Granny Smiths." She waved a round green apple in her mother's direction. "I don't know why Daddy and Noah like those Cortlands so much. These are much better." She took a bite, grinned and tore a square of paper towel from the roll next to the sink. "Any apple they name after a grandma has to be the best," she said before scooping her backpack off the table and prancing out of the kitchen.

Abbie idolized her grandmother. What would she think if she knew her grandmother was planning to divorce her grandfather? What would she do? Abandon Granny Smith apples for Cortlands?

Jill wanted to cry. She wanted to be a Bad Mom and curse. She wanted to be a Bad Daughter and call her mother back and accuse her parents of being idiots.

Instead, she guzzled some Diet Coke and typed, "Our new shantung scarf will wrap around you like a fresh breeze." The hell with alliteration. And waterfalls.

Chapter Three

Doug steered his car up the winding driveway to the house. The car was a Mercedes, the house a sprawling twelve-room multi-story featuring abundant quantities of fieldstone and glass and surrounded by landscaping that had cost something on the far side of twelve Lasik procedures. Behind the house, a free-form pool was imbedded in the slate patio, its contours curved to accommodate a hot tub.

Thirty-eight years old and Doug had everything he could possibly want: a showcase house, a luxury car, a thriving eye surgery practice, a beautiful wife and a set of six-year-old twin daughters. His hair showed no signs of thinning, his waist no signs of thickening. Brooke had booked them for a week next February in an ocean suite at the Four Seasons Resort in Nevis. Just the grown-ups; his parents had volunteered to take care of Madison and Mackenzie for the week.

Five months from now, he'd be schtupping his beautiful wife silly in a tropical paradise. He and Brooke would lounge on the beach all day sipping exotic neon-hued drinks, they'd have sex all night, and they'd return home a week later tanned and relaxed, toting cute little shell necklaces and T-shirts that said "Nevis Land" for the girls. He worked hard for such indulgences. He'd earned them.

He punched the button on the remote control to open his garage door and steered the Mercedes into the bay between Brooke's Audi wagon and the Land Rover he'd bought for the two days every winter when the snow plows didn't get the job done and the roads were a mess. As an ophthalmologist specializing in corrective laser surgery, he rarely dealt with emergency calls—in fact, he couldn't remember the last time he'd been summoned on one—but you never knew. If someone suddenly suffered a life-threatening stye in the middle of a blizzard, he'd be there.

Inside the garage, he pressed the remote button again and listened to the motorized door hum shut behind him. He leaned back against the Mercedes's contoured leather upholstery, his hands resting on the steering wheel, his tie loosened around his neck. Four consultations today, two post-ops, two surgeries. Busy, always busy, but he couldn't complain. If there weren't so many people who despised eyeglasses and contact lenses, he wouldn't have been able to afford this house, or this car, or the trip to Nevis. Or his beautiful wife, probably.

After a deep, cleansing sigh, he straightened and swung out of the car. The garage wrapped him in its cool, musty atmosphere. He pulled his white medical coat and briefcase from the back seat, then climbed the three steps to the inner door that led into the house.

Brooke stood by the cook-top in the kitchen's center island, a glass of white wine in one hand and a stirring spoon in the other. How a woman could look so enticing while stirring marinara sauce was beyond him. He wasn't in the mood for spaghetti, but the girls loved it. Brooke did, too, even though she ate at most a dozen strands because she was always watching her carb consumption. Spaghetti was easy to make, she said. Boil water, dump in the pasta, heat up a jar of sauce and *voila*.

Still, he wished the kitchen—a monumental room teeming with the latest gourmet equipment, from a Viking range and a Sub-Zero fridge to engineered stone countertops—didn't reek of pureed tomatoes and garlic. He wanted to smell Brooke. He wanted to bury his nose in her glossy blond hair and inhale her perfume. He couldn't recall the name of the scent she wore, but it was obscenely expensive.

And worth every penny, he thought as he studied her from the mudroom doorway.

She glanced up from the stove and smiled. "Hi, honey. I hope you don't mind." She gestured toward the saucepan with her long-handled cooking spoon, and then at the large pot sitting on an adjacent burner. "The girls had a play date after school, and by the time we got home . . ."

"No problem," he assured her, silently ordering himself not to be a prima donna about dinner. The girls had had a play date. Brooke couldn't be expected to throw together a gourmet feast. Cooking wasn't her forte, even when the girls didn't have a play date.

He started toward her, thinking again about burying his nose in the soft, silky blond locks of her hair and gathering her to himself. But before he got close enough even to take her hand, she told him, "And you have to call your sister. As soon as you get home, she said."

So much for kissing Brooke. So much for pulling her slim, dozen-strands-of-spaghetti body against him. So much for a calm, private minute with his wife before the girls—or, in this case, his sister—barged in. "Damn. What did Melissa do now?"

"Not Melissa. Jill," Brooke corrected him, stirring the sauce as if she actually had to do that to make it cook properly. "She called earlier and said she needed you to go to her house on Saturday afternoon. I told her you'd be playing golf with your father then, and she said no you wouldn't."

Frowning, he turned from Brooke and veered around the island to the cordless phone. He and his father played golf every Saturday afternoon. If his father spent his Saturday mornings at synagogue, Doug didn't know. He didn't ask. Fortunately, his father didn't ask him, either. The only time Doug entered a synagogue lately was if someone was getting married or bar mitzvahed. Funerals, most people opted for graveside services these days. Sometimes a memorial at a shul a month later. Doug didn't know too many dead people, thank God.

But just about every Saturday between late April and early October, he and the old man golfed eighteen holes at Sandy Burr. It was their routine, their manly celebration. Men were outnumbered by women in the Bendel family, and throughout Doug's life his father had always come up with activities for just the two of them, official testosterone rituals. Boy Scouts, Little League, fishing at Quabbin Reservoir. Hikes through the rolling hills near Amherst during Doug's college years. And now golfing. Doug's father wasn't particularly skilled at swinging a club, but they didn't play to win. They played for the excuse it gave them to stroll a few miles around gorgeous, manicured lawns and talk about things that had no real importance in their lives: the Red Sox pitching staff, some article on arrhythmia in the latest issue of the *New England Journal of Medicine*, the qualitative differences between this and that brand of golf ball.

Doug couldn't imagine his father canceling their regular date at the club—especially when they had only a few good weeks of golf left before the weather turned cold—just because Jill, of all people, was making demands. Jill never made demands. Melissa was the one always frantic, always frenzied, in desperate need of guidance or assistance.

He punched in Jill's speed-dial number and wandered into the pantry while the phone rang on the other end.

Jill answered on the third ring. "Hello?"

"Hey, it's me," Doug said, his gaze roaming over the glass-fronted cabinets that lined the pantry's walls. On the other side of the glass stood neat stacks of Brooke's special-occasions Wedgwood china, as well as cookbooks and implements—an electric skillet, an ice-cream maker—that he'd never seen her use. "What's this crap about Saturday? Dad and I are playing golf."

"No you're not," Jill said in an officious voice. It was the same voice she used to trot out when they were all little and he and Melissa would get into a fight. Jill, the noble middle child, the mediator, the one who insisted on their forging a truce before Mom and Dad barged in and started handing out punishments, would always get that I-am-the-only-sensible-person-in-this-room voice. She might be twenty-five years older today, but her tone of voice hadn't changed at all. "Everyone's coming to my house. One thirty. Dad will be here, too."

"Why?"

"I can't tell you."

It took him a moment to remember his birthday was in March. Jill couldn't be planning a surprise party for him—although a birthday party six months early would sure as hell be a surprise.

He didn't like surprises, birthday or otherwise. If Jill had suggested a surprise party in his honor, Brooke would have vetoed the plan. She would have insisted on hosting the thing herself, and she would have conferred with Doug on the choice of caterer, the menu and the decorations. She would have chosen a theme for the party. He didn't understand her obsession with themes, but her parties were always classy, and according to her, classy parties had themes. Last June, the twins' birthday party had had a circus theme, complete with a calliope, a clown who juggled bowling pins and a tightrope set six inches above the ground that all the children got to walk across while clutching Brooke's and Doug's hands. The theme of the party she'd thrown for Doug to celebrate the opening of his corrective-eye-surgery clinic was—no surprise—*vision*. She'd decorated the rooms with oversize plastic eyeglass frames and posted eye charts on the walls, and served hors d'oeuvres on round glass plates shaped like gigantic contact lenses. His parents' fortieth anniversary party a couple of years ago had featured a jukebox filled with rock songs that had been popular during their youth. All the guests had been required to dress like hippies.

His family knew better than to attempt to trump Brooke when it came to entertaining.

So why did he have to go to Jill's house? Obviously not for a party. A family pow-wow of some sort. Maybe Grandma Schwartz was deteriorating—although that certainly shouldn't entail a Bendel summit meeting. The woman was ninety-four. She wore diapers and sang unrecognizable melodies most of the time. She seemed happy enough when Doug visited her at her assisted-living community.

"I don't like secrets," Doug told Jill.

"I don't either, but Mom made me promise."

And you're Mom's favorite, Doug almost retorted, but that wasn't really true. Their mother loved all her children equally, or so she often insisted. And since Doug was clearly their father's favorite, he supposed he was ahead by half a length. "Tell me what's going on, or I won't come," he tried. Sometimes ultimatums worked.

Jill made a sound that was halfway between a sigh and a groan. The asthma of frustration, he diagnosed it. "I can't, okay? It's just . . ." Another little wheeze. "It's a mess, and the whole family needs to get together and sort it out. Melissa's coming up from New York, too."

Doug frowned again. Melissa created messes. She didn't sort them out.

"Look," Jill continued, her tone now conciliatory. "You'll come, Dad'll be here, and if everything goes well, you and he can leave and play golf. I don't care. I don't want any of this."

"Then why are we doing it?"

"We have to help Mom and Dad."

Shit. Were they having financial problems? Doug's father's income was lower than Doug's; preventing patients from dying of heart ailments clearly wasn't worth as much as reshaping their corneas. Still, his father did very well.

But he was getting older. He might have another five years of practice left in him, maybe ten if his patients didn't mind having their heart palpitations monitored by a septuagenarian. Once the old man was retired, though, how well were the folks set up? They had equity in their house, and Doug was sure his father's practice had established a 401K plan for their staff. His parents weren't extravagant. They didn't take world cruises. They didn't drop thousands of dollars at the casinos. Unlike Brooke, Doug's mother wasn't a big fan of manicures and overpriced perfume.

Where could their money have vanished to?

If they were facing destitution, of course, Doug would be expected to kick in the most to help them out. He had the most to kick in. As an associate with a New York law firm, Melissa earned a generous income, and if she made partner that income would rise. But she lived in Manhattan, and whatever part of her salary didn't get devoured by rent was spent on sprees at, as she called it, "Cousin Henri's." Brooke had had to explain to Doug what Henri Bendel was. Pricey store, no relation.

"What time is this gathering?" he asked Jill, toying with a dish towel that hung over the knob on one of the drawers. Where had that come from? And why did it feel so soft? Like suede.

"One-thirty," Jill said.

"Make it one o'clock. If we finish early, Dad and I can still get in eighteen holes."

"One-thirty, Doug. Don't give me a hard time, okay? I don't like this any more than you do, and I'm not even a golfer."

She might not like it, but at least she knew what was going on. Doug was the eldest. And not to get sexist about it, but he was the only son. It wasn't fair that Jill knew things he didn't know. "Jill," he said in his sternest older-brother voice. "You have to tell me what this is about."

"I promised Mom."

"Mom put you in an untenable position. We're sibs, right? United we stand. I covered for you when . . . well, you never did anything wrong, so maybe I didn't cover for you. But we both covered for Melissa a million times. And I got you through that stupid biology course you took in college."

"I shouldn't have signed up for that class," Jill admitted. "My advisor kept telling me I wasn't well-rounded and I needed science in my schedule."

"If it hadn't been for me, you wouldn't have made the Dean's List that semester. I was there for you, Jill. I had your back."

She fell silent. He imagined guilt and indebtedness simmering through the wires between them. "All right," she said finally, reluctantly. "But you can't tell anyone."

"Fine."

"Not even Brooke. I mean it, Doug. Mom made me promise—"

"I won't tell Brooke. What?"

"They're getting a divorce."

Doug scowled. "Who?"

"Mom and Dad. Don't tell anyone. They want to tell us all in person. Except that I made Mom tell me. And now I've told you." Jill's voice wavered, as if threatened by a sob.

"All right, all right," he said, too focused on calming her down to digest what she'd just told him. "It's going to be all right. I won't tell anyone."

"Not even Melissa."

"Especially not Melissa." *Why the hell not Melissa?* he wondered, then answered his own question: because Melissa would freak out.

Not like him. He had nerves of steel. He made microscopic incisions in people's corneas several times a day. He could handle this.

A divorce? A fucking divorce? His parents?

"And you have to act surprised," she added. "When Mom and Dad tell us, you have to act like you didn't know."

"Right." Jill's news was beginning to sink in. Jesus Christ. A divorce. Mom and Dad. Ruth and Richard Bendel, who'd been together so long their names had merged. RuthandRichard.

He heard his daughters' voices chirping down the hall as they approached the kitchen. They were chattering about something, both speaking at once, as they frequently did. For some reason, they could talk and listen simultaneously, only with each other and usually in such a way that no one else could begin to absorb their words. Maybe they'd developed that talent in utero.

"I've got to go," he said, peering down the in the direction of the family room. "I'll see you Saturday."

"One-thirty," Jill reminded him.

"Right."

"And don't tell anyone."

"Right." He thumbed the disconnect button and stifled a groan. A divorce. How? Why?

Son of a bitch. A faint smile caught his mouth as he considered the most obvious *why*. His father—that old fox—must have something going on the side. A patient, maybe. Someone whose life he'd saved with a well-placed stent who simply had to show her gratitude to him. Or a lusty young nurse. Doug had never met the sort of nurses he used to read about in girlie magazines when he'd been in high school, but maybe they existed. Maybe his father had crossed paths with one.

Doug wished more than ever that he'd be hitting the links with his father on Saturday. The old man wouldn't open up about his extracurricular activities in front of Jill and Melissa. And of course he wouldn't feel comfortable discussing his peccadilloes in front of his wife. But he and Doug, man to man, somewhere around the fourth hole . . . He'd love to hear what the senior Dr. Bendel was up to.

His amusement was instantly replaced by a remorse-tinged flare of indignation on his mother's behalf. If the senior Dr. Bendel was performing pelvics on some lusty, busty young nurse, Doug might have to chew him out. He might have to lecture him to shape up, to show some respect for the woman who'd borne his children. For God's sake, Doug's father was too old to be having a mid-life crisis.

Of course, if the nurse was *really* hot . . .

Shaking his head, he returned to the kitchen and set the phone back in its cradle to recharge. Brooke had moved to the sink and was hunkered down so she could view the girls at eye level while they blathered at her about something they'd just seen on television. Something utterly hilarious, given their shrill giggles and breathless descriptions.

He hovered near the cooking island, watching them through the plumes of steam that rose from the pot of boiling pasta. Madison wore a striped jumper and Mackenzie had on pink overalls. They refused to dress identically, which made life easier for their teachers and friends. They no longer looked identical to him, either, but that was because he was their father and knew them so well. He knew Madison liked to suck on her hair and Mackenzie tilted her head when she wanted to ask a question. When Madison was excited, she tended to hop on one foot, whereas Mackenzie preferred to bounce on both feet.

Right now, they were so involved in describing the show they'd been watching that they didn't even notice their father's arrival in the kitchen.

Brooke didn't notice him, either. She looked slightly blurry through the fog rising up from the pot, nodding and smiling and managing to sneak a sip of her wine as the girls twittered and fluttered like baby birds attempting to fly.

He didn't understand a word they said. Watching them was like watching a foreign film without the subtitles. He observed, admiring his girls, his beautiful girls, all three of them, all of them his. He observed and wondered what Brooke would think when he told her about his parents.

Chapter Four

One bedroom with big closets, or two bedrooms with small closets? The truth was, Melissa needed more space for her clothes than she did for herself.

What would she do with a second bedroom, anyway? She wasn't about to turn it into a nursery. She wanted kids, but she also wanted to make partner at the law firm, and she figured she ought to secure a partnership first. Plus, she probably ought to get married, although that wasn't a necessity. Lots of women had babies without getting married. Professional women. New York-type women.

On the other hand, having a husband as well as a baby meant that in the two-tenths-of-a-percent of your life that wasn't consumed by changing diapers and nursing the kid and trying to keep your career from flat-lining, you might be able to squeeze in a little sex. Without a husband, you'd have to go out and find a guy, and who'd have the time or the energy for that? Or else use a vibrator, which seemed kind of desperate to Melissa and also potentially hazardous with a child in the house.

She glanced over at Luc and tried to assess his husband potential. She'd known him only a few weeks, so it was hard to say. He did have a lot going for him. He was an amazing hair stylist, a creative cook, a good dancer. He dressed well. Football bored him. He was practically gay, except in bed, which made him damned near perfect.

Plus, he'd gotten access to this car, which meant she could travel to Jill's house in style. Well, not exactly in *style*; the car, which belonged to his roommate, resembled a chop shop reject. The CD player wasn't working. The vinyl upholstery was faded and cracked, and a patch of duct tape bandaged one part of the back seat. The ceiling fabric was held up by thumb tacks, the floor mats had gone so long without a cleaning that Melissa couldn't guess their original color, something rattled in the trunk every time they hit a pothole, and a set of red plastic rosary beads swayed from the rear-view mirror, as if a few prayers were all that kept the car from stalling right in middle of the Cross-Bronx Expressway.

But even a crappy car was better than the bus, so Melissa wasn't complaining. She usually took Greyhound instead of Amtrak when she visited her family, because the bus terminal was closer than the train station to where everyone lived. She hated that on the bus, you couldn't stand and stretch your legs during the trip, and the little lavatory across from the back seat emitted putrid odors, and you usually wound up sitting next to someone who snored or had dirty fingernails, or who was so fat his blubber oozed under the armrest and into your territory.

Of course, you could get stuck sitting next to a fat, dirty snorer on the train, too.

She'd been willing to tolerate the bus trip this weekend because Jill had insisted that her attendance at this all-of-a-sudden family shindig was essential. "I know it's a schlep for you," she'd said, "but Mom and Dad really need you here on Saturday. We all do."

Melissa and Luc had already made a plan for the weekend. She'd intended to spend the morning checking out a few apartments for sale, and then in the afternoon she and Luc had figured on taking in a movie—another terrific thing about him was that he didn't mind chick flicks—and dinner, and maybe some club-hopping followed by a night in bed. He often worked on Saturdays, either seeing clients in the salon or doing hair for a bridal party at this or that hotel. Lots of women got married in New York every weekend. Maybe someday Melissa would be one of them, and she'd get a stylist from a salon like Nouvelle to come to the hotel and do everyone's hair. Expensive, but given the total cost of a Manhattan wedding, who'd even notice? Hair was at least as important as the flowers. Maybe even as important as the dress.

But Luc happened to be free this weekend, and she'd been looking forward to their first Saturday afternoon together until Jill had phoned and summoned her home. Melissa had whined and fumed, to no avail. She'd attempted to find out what was so freaking essential that it required her to drop everything and come running, also to no avail.

Jill could be outrageously bossy.

Wallowing in disappointment, Melissa had phoned Luc to break the bad news to him about their thwarted weekend plans, and he'd told her to hang on a minute, and when he'd come back to the phone he'd announced that his roommate didn't need his car that weekend. Luc would have to do all the driving—Alan didn't trust just anyone with the keys to his precious wreck of a car—but driving to Massachusetts with Luc would sure beat spending four hours each way on the bus seated next to a filthy, obese snorer and inhaling rancid fumes from the lavatory.

She'd already told Jill she would be taking the eight a.m. bus and promised to call when it was about fifteen minutes away from the terminal so whoever was going to pick her up could time the short drive. She probably should have phoned Jill back and informed her of the change in transportation plans, but she hadn't. She'd been pissed off by Jill's imperiousness. So she and Luc would show up unannounced at Jill's front door, and Jill would deal with it. Jill was a whiz when it came to dealing with things.

Melissa and Luc had packed overnight bags, figuring they'd spend Saturday night in Massachusetts and drive home Sunday. If Jill didn't want to put them up at her house—and Melissa could respect that; Abbie was twelve years old, and Jill might not want her spending the night under the same roof as an aunt engaging in premarital sex—then they could stay at Doug's house. It had a zillion rooms, and the twins were too young to care who stayed in which room with whom.

Or, if necessary, she and Luc could stay at her parents' house. They hadn't turned her bedroom into a study or a sewing room or a second den. Melissa's childhood bedroom remained intact, the décor unchanged from the day she'd left for Brown University thirteen years ago. French provincial furniture, pink Swiss-dot curtains, rose-hued carpeting, a canopy bed—the room was a shrine to girlie-girl taste. One of these days Melissa would drop by and reclaim her stuffed animals. For her future children, of course, not for herself.

If worse came to worst, she and Luc would get a room at a motel for the night. A bed-and-breakfast would be more romantic, but the autumn leaf season was in full swing, and most of the B-and-B's in New England had been booked a year ago. She consoled herself with the thought that a motel would be cheaper. She really had to save money if she was serious about buying an apartment.

Traffic was heavy on the Cross-Bronx—as if that was anything new. Cars, cabs, vans and eighteen-wheelers inched along, brake lights flashing like electrified rubies. Luc fiddled with the radio dial, gliding from one burst of static to the next. Apparently the radio didn't work any better than the CD player. Melissa could attempt a conversation with him, but he didn't look interested in chatting, so she focused instead on the folder of print-outs in her lap, each page describing a condo or co-op for sale. Kathy, the broker she was working with, had faxed them to her yesterday.

One bedroom or two?

Assuming she did wind up having children . . . and she really hoped she would in the not too distant future. She was already thirty-one years old and didn't want to be one of those forty-something moms contending with colic and hot flashes at the same time. Plus, she wasn't sure she should raise her offspring in the city. City-bred kids were so hard, so tough, so jaded, and you had to pay a fortune in tuition for a decent private school. So investing in an apartment big enough to include a nursery seemed pointless. Closets were far more practical.

Still, it bothered Melissa that a one-bedroom apartment could cost as much as a two-bedroom. She compared two of the units Kathy had recommended, holding their sheets side by side on her knees. Both apartments were located in buildings in the same borderline neighborhood—not quite the Flatiron District, not quite Grammercy Park, not quite the northern edge of Greenwich Village. Closets were important, but did two huge closets equal one bedroom? And bottom line, did she want to spend close to seven figures for an apartment that wasn't actually in a neighborhood?

Setting those two pages aside, she lifted the next one from the pile and tried to read it as the paper trembled in her hand, picking up the car's vibrations. Clinton—at least that was a real neighborhood, and nowadays Hell's Kitchen, which overlapped with Clinton, was almost chic. Two bedrooms but tiny, tiny, tiny, if Kathy's notes about the square footage were accurate. The second bedroom could easily pass for a walk-in closet. Melissa could move an armoire in front of the window. No one would have to know it was an actual room.

She was so damned tired of renting. And if she bought an apartment, it would give her an excuse to move out of her ugly, boxy Upper East Side studio apartment, which cost an alarming amount in rent even though it had so little closet space she'd had to buy a coat tree for her jackets and raincoats.

She glanced over at Luc, who'd landed the dial on a station playing an overblown metal song she didn't recognize, which, while awful, was an improvement over the static. He looked dashing in his sunglasses. Slightly bored, perhaps a little too highly buffed, but gorgeous enough to spark a tremor of excitement low in her belly, a response which made her realize that taking a motel room tonight would be a wise move. Even in Doug and Brooke's enormous house, Melissa wasn't sure she and Luc would have enough privacy for her to feel comfortable jumping his bones.

She wondered what her family would think of him. She wondered if this was an optimal time to invest in real estate. She wondered if she'd be able to push through a settlement with the purse counterfeiter her client had brought a suit against before their trial date, which was ten days away. It was a stupid case; the counterfeiter didn't have a prayer of winning. But he kept balking at a settlement because settling would mean shutting down his business, and as long as he could delay that fateful step he could continue making money selling made-in-China rip-offs of her client's expensive bags from folding card tables on street corners. It was going to take a judge's order to force him out of business, which meant it was going to take a trial.

Ten days. Shit.

Forget about it, Melissa ordered herself. *Forget about everything: the city's real estate market, the looming trial, the sour aroma of truck exhausts, the fact that we still haven't reached Connecticut because the traffic is moving so slowly*. What the hell were so many long-haul truckers doing on the highway on a Saturday morning, anyway? Didn't they get weekends off? The rig in front of them had license plates from Tennessee, West Virginia and Arkansas. She'd bet the driver was chewing tobacco and listening to a CD of some nasal-voiced singer with two first names.

"What time do you think we'll get there?" Luc asked.

"If the traffic ever thins out, we might be able to do it in three and a half hours."

Luc made a face. Even pouting, he was adorable. He wore a black T-shirt that fit him just loosely enough not to be obscene, jeans faded to powder blue, a slate-gray blazer and tooled cowboy boots with silver tipping their toes. His black hair was short but well styled, his cheeks darkened by a stubble he'd trimmed to just the right length using a hair clipper. Melissa had always assumed guys got that kind of stubble by not shaving for a day. She hadn't known they could actually create a day-old stubble with a grooming tool.

She'd learned so much from Luc. She'd learned the importance of mixing lowlights with highlights to give her hair dimension, and she'd learned about a fantastic serum that cost eighty dollars an ounce but kept her hair from frizzing like nothing else she'd ever tried, and she'd learned that she did, indeed, have a g-spot.

"You sure my being there isn't going to be a problem?" Luc called over to her.

"They'll love you," she said, hoping that uttering those words with conviction made them true. She hadn't told anyone in her family about Luc, not because her social life wasn't their business but because she didn't want their input. She'd learned that if she mentioned she was seeing someone, they all inputted like yentas on meth.

She'd met him in August when she'd splurged on a cut and color at Nouvelle Salon and Spa. Her friend Emily had recommended the place, and Emily's hair always looked fabulous, so Melissa had thought, what the hell, it's only money. Three hundred bucks of money, as it had turned out, but worth every penny. The stylist she'd been assigned to, a sexy guy with a sexy name—Luc, not Luke, because Lucas was spelled with a "c" and no "e," as he'd explained to her once they'd reached that level of intimacy—and black hair and eyes the color of blue Curacao and a well-honed physique barely hidden by a dark T-shirt and jeans—much like the outfit he had on now, she realized—had whisked her into a chair and asked what she'd like him to do for her. She'd stared at his reflection in the mirror as he hovered behind her, staring at *her* reflection. *God,* she'd thought, *he's gorgeous.*

"Make me a new woman," she'd said.

And he had.

"So," he said, inching Alan's car close enough to the hillbilly rig for her to read the words *fuck you* which someone had rubbed into the layer of road dirt between the tail lights, "tell me about who's going to be at this thing."

"My sister Jill, of course," Melissa answered. "Our hostess. She's very nice. Very calm and undemanding." When she wasn't busy bragging about how she was the only calm, undemanding member of the family. "You know how some people always make waves? She's like oil on water. She calms the waves." Even if she sometimes treated Melissa like a toddler. Actually, she also sometimes treated Doug, who was two years older than her, like a toddler.

"Her hair could use some work," she added, wondering if Luc might have an opportunity to assess Jill's bland brown mop and come up with a few suggestions. A trim here, a snip there, move the part. Highlights. Lowlights. He could transform Jill from a dowdy housewife into a less dowdy housewife.

And then Jill would love him. That would be one vote in favor.

"Jill writes catalogue copy."

"Huh?"

"The descriptive little blurbs that accompany the photos of clothing in catalogues. Someone has to write those things, and she's that someone. She's married to Gordon, who's a high school English teacher," Melissa continued, "and they have two children. Abbie's twelve and Noah's almost ten. Abbie's bat mitzvah is coming up next spring. That's kind of a big deal."

Would she and Luc would still be together next spring? Would she get to show up at the bat mitzvah with the most handsome man she'd ever dated hanging off her arm? If he accompanied her, she would have to buy a new dress for the occasion. She'd probably have to buy a new dress, anyway, but it would be fun to blame the extravagance on Luc.

"How big a deal?" he asked. "Should I congratulate her or something?"

It occurred to Melissa that he might not know what a bat mitzvah was, other than in the most general sense. He did all those bridal parties, sweeping into the Waldorf-Astoria or the Pierre to create magnificent coiffures for the bride and her attendants, but bat mitzvahs didn't generally call for private sessions with a hair stylist. Frankly, she couldn't imagine Abbie wanting anyone, professional or otherwise, messing with her hair. As far as Melissa could tell, Abbie considered winning a soccer game more important than looking beautiful.

"No congratulations until after the bat mitzvah. I just thought I'd warn you—whenever the family gets together, that subject usually comes up. She's the oldest grandchild, the first one. My parents are pretty excited about it."

"Okay." Luc nodded.

A jangle of clashing guitars blasted through the speakers, and Melissa turned down the radio's volume. "Then there's my brother Doug, who's brilliant and arrogant. He does laser surgery on eyes. He has his own clinic and he's mega-rich. A lot of people want perfect vision without glasses."

"I wouldn't want to wear glasses," Luc said. Of course he was wearing sunglasses, but that was different. Sunglasses you could hide behind. They were optional. Regular glasses were just plain dorky.

Melissa knew this from personal experience; she'd replaced her glasses with contacts when she was sixteen. She'd love to have the corrective surgery done on her own myopic eyes, but it was expensive and she had to save for a down payment on a co-op or condo. She'd once asked Doug if he'd Lasik her eyes, figuring he'd give her a huge discount or maybe even do the job for free, but he'd said smart doctors never operated on their loved ones and he'd be happy to pass along the names of a few colleagues whose success rates he could vouch for. His colleagues would have charged her the usual fee, so she'd let the subject drop and tried not to resent him.

He ought to do her eyes for her, though. He wasn't *that* smart.

"Doug is married to Brooke, who's the sort of woman you'd expect to be married to a brilliant, arrogant doctor who earns tons of money."

"What does that mean?" Luc asked.

Melissa shrugged. "When you meet her, you'll know. She's just . . . very polished. Polite and poised and kind of presumptuous. She takes things for granted." Actually, she was probably like the majority of his clients at Nouvelle, the regulars who waltzed in every week and handed over hundreds of dollars to have him clip two or three wisps of hair when they were done with their facials and paraffin treatments.

Fortunately, Luc didn't subscribe to Doug's theory about people not operating on their loved ones. Now that he and Melissa were a couple, he did her hair without charging her, although she had to pay for the coloring products and conditioners, which weren't exactly cheap.

"Doug and Brooke have twin daughters," she went on. "Mackenzie and Madison. They're six years old. No imminent bat mitzvahs for them, but let me tell you, once they reach the right age, *nothing* will be spared. Doug and Brooke'll probably rent the entire Ritz-Carlton. Or maybe Symphony Hall. Or the U.S.S. Constitution. It will be an event, I promise you."

Luc nodded.

"And then there are my parents. Ruth and Richard Bendel. They're . . ." She hesitated. What could she say about her parents? They simply *were*. They loved her. They drove her crazy. They were strict. They were lenient. They could spend hours describing a ten-minute trip to the drug store. They thought rock and roll had peaked with the Beatles, or maybe Elton John, and had been on a long, sad decline since 1973.

"They're nice," she finally said, then realized that was hardly adequate. "My father's a cardiologist and my mother's a housewife. They finish each other's sentences. My mother knows when my dad wants her to pass him the salad dressing before *he* knows."

Luc said nothing. A couple of weeks ago, after they'd made loud, sweaty love at her apartment—they couldn't do that at his apartment because Alan was there most of the time—she'd pestered him to tell her about his childhood. She'd figured she was entitled, after loud sweaty sex. Luc hadn't been overly forthcoming, but he'd told her his parents had divorced when he was eight and his father had eventually moved to Las Vegas. Throughout his youth, Luc had visited his father every summer, and he'd seen shows featuring scantily clad dancers in rhinestone bras and feather headdresses and sneaked a few chips into the slot machines when the pit bosses weren't watching. His mother had remarried and his step-father was "okay," a word he'd said with a shrug, so Melissa wasn't sure just how "okay" the guy was.

In any case, Luc's childhood clearly hadn't fit the nuclear-family cliché like Melissa's, with a nice house, a new car every few years and grandparents nearby. She and her siblings had all gone to the same high school, and all three of them had gone to college in New England. Now Doug and Jill both lived within ten miles of their parents' house in the cozy suburbs west of Boston. To Melissa's family, New York City was a foreign country, as alien as Las Vegas must have seemed to Luc the first time he'd visited his father there. "Yankees territory," her father often muttered about Manhattan. The Bendels were, by birth and by blood, a Red Sox family.

Melissa had moved to New York because she'd thought it would be more glamorous than Boston—which it was. The law firms were bigger there and the pay was higher, even if her paycheck magically disappeared every month, absorbed by rent, her MetroCard and the ridiculously high price of dirty martinis at marginally fashionable bars. Dinner out with friends? Bye-bye, eighty bucks. Tickets to a concert? Sayonara, a hundred. Even the museums cost too much money. And a woman needed clothes, for God's sake. Especially if she was bucking for partner at a major law firm.

But she probably would have moved to New York anyway, just to put a little distance between herself and her family. Just so she wouldn't have them all nosing into her business. Just so she could get away from a place where high school teachers used to tell her, "You're smarter than your sister, but she was better behaved."

At last, they'd reached Connecticut. Melissa always expected something magical to happen when she crossed from one state to another. At the very least, she expected to see a heavy black line painted across the ground, denoting as clearly as a map where one state ended and the next began. Instead, most state borders were marked by a billboard not much more appealing than a highway exit sign saying, "Welcome to Whatever State," with the governor's name printed below. Sometimes the road's pavement would change color at the state line, because God forbid New York's highway budget should pay to resurface even an inch of Connecticut's turf, and vice versa.

Connecticut was progress, however. They were one state closer to their destination.

She reopened the folder that had been resting in her lap. "What do you think makes more sense?" she asked. "A one-bedroom with lots of closets, or a two-bedroom that skimps on closets?"

"Closets are good," Luc answered.

"If you were buying an apartment, you'd go for the one bedroom with lots of closets?"

"If *I* were buying an apartment, I'd want a huge, gorgeous bathroom with lots of mirrors and primo lighting."

Of course he would. After all, a hair salon was really just a glorified bathroom with lots of mirrors and light, sculpted sinks, sleek counters and no visible toilets. She'd been so focused on the closet situation, she hadn't really considered the bathrooms in the apartments Kathy had recommended. She'd be willing to bet that, despite their astronomical prices, the apartments wouldn't have bathrooms that were huge and gorgeous.

That thought depressed her. "Do you think the extra bedroom is a good idea?"

"I don't know. It's up to you." He shrugged. "I'm not buying any apartments in the near future. Not unless I hook up with a really rich chick." He sent her a mischievous smile and added, "A sugar mommy."

Swallowing her uneasiness, Melissa smiled back. She never knew how serious he was when he made jokes like that. If he was looking for a sugar mommy, she sure wasn't it. Her salary was a hell of a lot higher than his, but she had expenses. And he got tips.

She consoled herself with the understanding that he came in contact with dozens of really rich women every week. He wouldn't have chosen her if he'd wanted a girlfriend with a huge bank account. And he wouldn't have offered to drive her all the way to Jill's house if he didn't at least like her.

Of course he liked her.

And she wasn't going to think about real estate for the rest of the drive.

THEY REACHED JILL'S HOUSE at a little before noon, right around when Melissa would have been phoning Jill to announce her imminent arrival at the bus terminal. She'd lived in New York City long enough that the suburban tranquility of her sister's neighborhood unnerved her. All those fat maple and sycamore trees, their leaves burning with fall color. All those shrubs. All those tidy lawns. All that sky. She felt as if she'd made a wrong turn and wound up on the set of a sit-com, or maybe a Disney movie. She half-expected plump little bluebirds to flit out of the foliage, trailing satin ribbons.

She'd grown up in a neighborhood much like this, so it ought to feel like home. But as she pointed out Jill's driveway to Luc, she felt distinctly like a guest. Especially because she had Luc with her.

She hoped her family would like him. He really was likeable. He'd freaking *driven* her here. How much nicer could you get? Even though he'd admitted as they'd approached New London that he loved driving and didn't get to sit behind the wheel often enough in New York, and if they hadn't made this trip he probably would have borrowed Alan's car anyway and just cruised up and down the Henry Hudson Parkway. Maybe someday, if he ever got sick of doing hair—an eventuality he couldn't imagine right now—he'd become a cab driver.

A Mercedes was parked in the driveway—Doug's car—and Luc pulled up behind it and yanked on the parking brake, which gave a metallic croak. Melissa hoped it held.

Luc didn't seem overly awed by Jill's house. It wasn't spectacular, just a nice, ordinary colonial with a farmer's porch. Three bedrooms, finished basement, deck off the back. Pretty much what you'd expect a high school teacher and his family to live in.

They strolled up the walk to the porch. Melissa rang the bell and gave Luc a reassuring smile. He didn't look as if he needed reassurance. His stance was relaxed, his jacket open and his hands tucked into the front pockets of his jeans. Maybe she should have told him to wear khakis—although if he owned a pair, she'd never seen them. Every time they'd gotten together, he'd had been wearing either blue jeans or black jeans. Or no jeans at all.

Jill opened the door, and her smile faded into a near-grimace as she took in the couple on her porch. Then she forced her mouth back into a smile. Melissa could see her cheek muscles exerting themselves. "Melissa!" she said. "I thought you were taking the bus."

"Hello to you, too," Melissa retorted, then swallowed her resentment. Jill looked like shit, her cheeks wan and drawn, her hair gathered into a scrunchy at the nape of her neck, her long-sleeve white T-shirt stained by something pale and pink. A splash of wine, Melissa thought hopefully. She could use a glass of wine. Or a margarita, but that stain definitely didn't say margarita, and Jill's pinched appearance implied that nothing even remotely festive was being consumed inside the house.

Jill's gaze shifted to Luc and her smile grew brittle.

"This is Luc Brondo," Melissa introduced him. "Luc, this is my sister, Jill."

Doug abruptly materialized in the doorway next to Jill. Unlike her, he didn't look bedraggled. But then, he never looked bedraggled. He had on a cotton polo shirt—complete with a horseback-riding polo player stitched onto the chest pocket—and pleated twill slacks. His hair was parted and his eyes—eyes that had undergone a Lasik procedure; Melissa wondered if the colleague who'd done the job had charged him for it, not that he'd have had any difficulty coming up with the money—were bright. He didn't even attempt a smile. "Who the hell is this?" he asked, jabbing his index finger in Luc's direction.

"And that's my charming brother, Doug," she said to Luc. To Doug, she said, "He was kind enough to drive me here."

"Great. That was very nice of him. Maybe he can wait for you at Starbucks until we're done here."

"Doug," Jill scolded. "He's not going to wait at Starbucks. He's Melissa's friend. Please come in," she belatedly welcomed Luc. "I'm sorry, but things are a little frazzled here."

"Things are not frazzled," Doug argued, although he stepped back, allowing Melissa and Luc to enter the house. "This isn't a party, Mel. You weren't supposed to bring a date."

"He's not—I mean—"

"I could leave," Luc offered.

"No, no, of course not," Jill said, transforming from stressed-out sister to gracious hostess. She hooked her hand around Luc's elbow and ushered him further into the hallway. "It's just that we're in the middle of a family crisis."

Melissa had figured something was up, given the way Jill had demanded her presence in Massachusetts that weekend. "What crisis?" she asked.

"Nothing," Jill and Doug said in unison, then exchanged guilty glances.

Before Melissa could question them, she heard a chorus of giggles accompanied by the squeak of sneakers on hardwood. "Aunt Melissa's here!" the twins shrieked as they barreled into the hallway.

Finally, some relatives behaving normally.

Melissa hunkered down and gathered one twin in each arm. "Madison!" she greeted Mackenzie.

"No, *I'm* Madison," Madison shrieked.

"*You're* Madison? Then are you—? No, you can't be Mackenzie!" It was a game she played with the girls, one they hadn't yet tired of. She was pretty good at telling them apart, but she always pretended to mix them up and they had a grand time setting her straight, snickering and chattering and jumping up and down with excess energy.

"Your hair looks so pretty, Aunt Melissa," Mackenzie said, once the which-twin-are-you game wound down.

Mackenzie was now Melissa's favorite family member, followed closely by Madison, who echoed Mackenzie's compliment. Jill and Doug could screw themselves. She'd stick with the girls, who knew a beautiful hairstyle when they saw one. "Do you like it? Thanks!" She shot Luc a grateful smile, then straightened up and presented him. "These are my nieces, Mackenzie and Madison. I'm not sure which one is which."

They erupted in fresh peals of laughter and high-pitched explanations of who they were. Luc seemed mystified.

Melissa turned her attention back to her siblings. The hall had gotten quite crowded while she'd been hunkered down. Gordon had joined the mob, and he even managed to give Melissa a brotherly hug—more than her own brother had done. Noah lurked at the end of the hall, scuffing the toe of his sneaker against the runner rug and looking bashful. Brooke and Abbie hovered in the arched doorway to the family room, their gazes fixed on Luc. Not that Melissa blamed them. He was the most interesting thing to look at in the hallway, far more interesting than the mail table and the mirror and the stairway up to the second floor. Much more beautiful than her new hairdo.

"All right. I'm sorry, but we have to talk." Jill clamped her hand on Melissa's shoulder—one of Melissa's great regrets in life was that now that they were all done growing, Jill had wound up taller than her—and steered her toward the powder room. Melissa cast a backward glance at Luc, but he was being led down the hall by the twins, each one clinging to one of his hands as they delivered him to their mother and both of them yakking at him nonstop.

The powder room was crowded enough with Melissa and Jill in it, but somehow Doug wedged himself in, too, closing the door and shutting them inside. He took a post by the pedestal sink, Jill stood in front of the toilet, and if Melissa suffered from claustrophobia she would have started screaming. She was tempted to scream, anyway, just on principle.

"You shouldn't have brought that man here," Jill said in a near-whisper.

"Well, duh. You've made that pretty clear." Melissa backed against the wall to give herself a little room and bumped her foot on the wicker trash can. The air smelled flowery, thanks to the air freshener plugged into the wall socket beside the sink. "You said this was a family party."

"I never used the word party," Jill argued.

"And he's not family," Doug pointed out.

"Gordon and Brooke are here," Melissa defended herself, pushing up the sleeves of her sweater. The density of the bodies in the room made her uncomfortably warm.

"Well, *duh*," Doug mimicked her. "We're married to them. That makes them family."

"Which is neither here nor there," Jill said, using her peace-maker voice. Obviously, there was no time for arguments. They had a crisis. "This is an awkward situation, Mel," Jill went on. "Mom and Dad'll be here any minute, and—"

"So what's going on?" Melissa asked.

"Nothing," Jill and Doug chorused, this time deliberately avoiding each other's gazes.

"Oh, come on!" Melissa heard the whine in her voice, the wail of the baby sister getting ignored. They used to leave her out of their games, out of their trips to the movies or the mall. They'd soared into adolescence years ahead of her, abandoning her to the games and toys they could no longer be bothered with once they'd succumbed to hormones. She'd always felt like a stupid afterthought of her parents. Her parents insisted she was very much wanted, but that was what parents were supposed to say. She was the accident, the oops, destined to be left behind by her older siblings.

Now Jill and Doug were leaving her behind again. They knew something she didn't, and if she had to be trapped in this tiny powder room with the two of them, inhaling that cloying lilac scent while the toilet paper roll poked her hip, they'd damned well better not treat her like a baby. "Tell me what's going on."

Jill eyed Doug, who shook his head. It wouldn't take much effort for Melissa to kick his shin. She was wearing ankle boots, not as pointed as Luc's cowboy boots, but she could probably leave a small bruise. Or at the very least a smudge of dirt on his crisp khakis.

"None of us is supposed to know anything," Jill said.

"But you and Doug know something and I don't."

"But we're not supposed to."

"Oh, for God's sake," Doug grumbled.

"*What?*" Melissa bellowed.

Doug and Jill both looked at the door, as if they expected the rest of the party to storm into the bathroom to see what the shouting was all about. After a moment, Jill sighed and said, "Mom didn't want to tell me, but I said I wouldn't have everyone over to the house unless she did. She swore me to secrecy."

"But you told Doug," Melissa said.

"And I was sworn to secrecy," Doug informed her.

"Fine. Swear me to secrecy, too." Melissa held up her right hand, willing to take an oath.

"They're getting a divorce," Jill said.

"Who?"

"Mom and Dad."

"*What?*" Impossible. Absolutely impossible. Not her parents. Not Ruth and Richard Bendel. No way.

"They wanted us all here so they could tell us in person," Jill explained.

"Without any boy-toys to share the celebration," Doug added dryly.

"He's not a boy-toy," Melissa snapped. "He's my age." At least she thought he was. Next time they had loud sweaty sex, she'd ask him.

In the meantime, she had to deal with the notion that her parents, the two steadiest, sanest, most dependable people in her entire life, were planning to do something totally bizarre. Totally surreal. Totally unlike them.

"They can't be serious," she said.

"I hope they're not," Jill agreed. "Whatever is going on with them—"

"Is Daddy cheating on her?"

"Why do you assume it's Dad's fault?" Doug said indignantly, although he looked a little sheepish.

"Because Mom wouldn't cheat. She just wouldn't."

"Neither would Dad," Jill said.

"Dad's a guy," Melissa pointed out. "He's got one of those little guy-brain things between his legs."

"Eeuw!" Jill closed her eyes and shuddered.

"All right, all right. It's just, I've known more guys than you have." That was one thing Melissa had on her older sister, who'd met her husband in college and gotten married shortly after she'd graduated. "They all have those little guy-brain things."

"Can it, Melissa," Doug scolded. "Stop being such a sexist."

"Oh, right. *I'm* the sexist."

"We don't have time for this," Jill said, holding her hand up like a traffic cop. "Mom and Dad will be here any minute. Now remember, Melissa, you aren't supposed to know about the divorce. Neither is Doug."

"Right."

"I mean it. I promised Mom I wouldn't tell."

"Okay," Melissa said impatiently.

"We'll act calm and sympathetic, and hopefully we'll be able to work this out so they won't get a divorce."

"Fine. We'll act calm and sympathetic," Melissa said. A wave of sorrow rushed at her, and she felt her knees wobble. "A divorce? I don't want them to get a divorce."

"None of us do."

"I mean, it's terrible." She thought of Luc flying out to Vegas to gawk at showgirls with his father. She thought of everyone she knew who came from broken homes. Her friend Lindsay, who had to pass messages between her parents because they refused to talk to each other. Her friend Natalie, whose father had celebrated his fiftieth birthday by dumping her mother and marrying a twenty-year-old waitress. Her colleague Garth, whose father liked to trade in for a new model every year and whose mother now lived with four cats.

Oh, God. The thought of having of a twenty-year-old stepmom and a mother who was a cat lady brought Melissa to the brink of tears.

The doorbell rang. "That's probably them now," Jill whispered. "Remember, calm and sympathetic, and none of us knows what this is about."

Melissa and Doug nodded. Gordon's voice sounded muffled through the bathroom door as he said, "Hey, Ruth and Richard! Come on in."

"Calm and sympathetic," Jill repeated.

Melissa hardly heard her. She burst out of the bathroom and charged down the front hall, screaming, "Mommy, Daddy, you can't get a divorce!"

Chapter Five

It took Jill a good fifteen minutes to herd the family from the hallway to the dining room. Parents and siblings only; Gordon was charged with steering Brooke, Melissa's studly chauffeur and the kids, whom her parents had greeted as if nothing was wrong, back to the family room.

In the midst of embracing, kissing and fussing over her assorted grandchildren, Jill's mother had sent her a lethal look. All right, so she'd told Doug and Melissa about the divorce. She wasn't going to apologize. Siblings had certain bonds that superseded the promises a person made to her mother, especially if those promises were made against her will. Wasn't there some legal thing about contracts signed under duress being invalid? This was practically the same.

Even so, that one fierce stare had caused Jill's stomach to shrivel into a hard, throbbing nugget of tension. She was supposed to be the Good Daughter. Her mother had trusted her, and the disapproving glare her mother had given her after Melissa had exploded out of the bathroom wailing like a police siren announced: *You have deeply disappointed me.* Jill stood two inches taller than her mother, but her mother could still make her feel small. Small and crappy.

She'd chosen the dining room for the family meeting because it contained the fewest distractions and because the table—which she'd covered with fresh linen and a centerpiece of silk flowers she'd wound up buying from the Prairie Wind catalogue, thanks to the irresistible blurb she herself had written for the item—could hold cups, saucers and her father's rugelach. She'd boiled water for Melissa's tea and brewed a pot of Starbucks House Blend for everyone else, filled the Waterford creamer and sugar bowl she and Gordon had received from his cousin Roberta as a wedding present, and arranged a platter of grapes and sliced Jarlsburg.

She'd also downed two cans of Diet Coke before ten a.m. That had been purely medicinal. She was sure she'd need another can once this meeting was over. Maybe two more cans. Maybe six. She'd climb back on the wagon tomorrow.

"Do you have any wine?" Melissa asked, her gaze circling the table. Her eyes glistened, as if she were a nanosecond away from erupting in tears. How the hell were they going to persuade their parents to forget this silly divorce idea if Melissa was falling apart?

It was possible her falling apart would keep their parents together. Histrionics might work, especially histrionics from Melissa, who was, after all, their precious baby.

"No wine," Jill said, then added for Doug's benefit, "No scotch, either. We're doing this sober."

"Shit," Melissa muttered before plucking a raspberry-patch tea bag from the straw basket in which Jill had stacked an assortment of teas.

"Who is that man?" their mother asked Melissa as she carried a steaming cup of coffee to one of the dining room chairs and sat. So casual, so relaxed, as if she hadn't ordered Jill to assemble everyone for the purpose of announcing the dissolution of her marriage—and as if she wasn't thoroughly pissed at Jill for having pre-announced the announcement.

"Lucas Brondo," Melissa answered, compulsively bobbing her tea bag in and out of her cup. He'd been introduced to Jill's parents when they'd arrived, but with everyone crowded in the hallway and Noah performing an elaborately choreographed hand-shake-hand-slap with his grandfather while the twins babbled simultaneously and Abbie wrapped her grandmother in a much more enthusiastic hug than she ever gave Jill, Melissa's guy had faded into the background.

Obviously he hadn't faded completely. Her mother had noticed him.

So had her father. "Brondo? That doesn't sound Jewish. Is he Jewish?"

Melissa sighed. "I have no idea."

"Brondo," her father pondered aloud. "Like that actor, what was his name? Marlon Brondo. He wasn't Jewish."

"Brando, not Brondo," her mother corrected him. "Look, Jill got you that rugelach you love."

"You're a sweetheart. Thank you." Jill's father slung an arm around her shoulders and squeezed. Evidently he didn't mind that she'd revealed the truth to Doug and Melissa. She tried to gauge his mood. On a cheerful scale of one to ten, he seemed somewhere between a four and a five. The prospect of a divorce apparently hadn't crushed his spirit. Either that, or the rugelach had taken the edge off his despair.

At sixty-four, he was still a handsome man, his face lined but not pruny, his hair silver but not thin. Dressed in khakis and a polo shirt—a golfing outfit nearly identical to Doug's—he looked fit and sturdy. If he was cheating on her mother, Jill would smash the plate of rugelach over his head.

"Those grapes look nice," her mother commented, scrutinizing them as if searching for insects on their curved maroon surfaces. "Did you get them at Whole Foods?"

For God's sake. She didn't want to discuss where she shopped for grapes. "Everyone sit down," she said. Someone had to take charge. As usual, Jill would wind up being that someone. "Get something to drink, sit and let's talk."

"There's nothing to say," her mother remarked stiffly. "You've already told everyone."

Jill dropped onto the chair at the head of the table. She studied her mother, seated halfway down the table to her left. Like her father, who was seated halfway down the table to her right, her mother looked fine. Her hair needed work; smudges of gray marked her temples and streaked through the chin-length strands. She ought to color it like Melissa's, which looked truly spectacular—not just its feathery cut, with a hint of bangs grazing her eyebrows, but its color. A blend of dark and light browns with glimmers of gold, it reminded Jill of the variegated hues in the golden oak sideboard standing against the wall behind her mother. Her mother's hair was variegated, too, but its drab brown and gray reminded Jill more of a rotting log than varnished oak.

Her mother's face sagged a bit and her figure had reached the elasticized-waistband stage. For the most part, though, she wasn't aging badly. Her mood seemed more angry than sorrowful.

The room had grown silent. Everyone was seated and gazing expectantly at Jill—except Doug, who slouched in a chair next to his father and swirled a teaspoon through his coffee in a lazy circle.

"All right. As we all know, Mom told me she and Dad were getting a divorce."

Melissa, who'd taken her place at the opposite end of the table, emitted a tiny sob-like sound. "I can't believe this. I just can't believe you'd do something like this."

"What don't you believe?" Jill's mother asked. "Half of all marriages end in divorce, isn't that the statistic?"

"Half of *all* marriages, maybe. Not my parents' marriage," Melissa argued.

"We're not getting a divorce," Jill's father said, surprising her—and, if their stunned expressions were anything to go by, Melissa and Doug. They all gaped at their father, who helped himself to a slice of the honey-coated rugelach and took a bite.

Since he was chewing, Jill's mother took over. "What he means is, for now all we're doing is separating. I'll be moving into my own place. Nobody's talking to any lawyers at this point."

"Your own place? What place? Where are you moving? Why is Dad getting the house?" The questions shot across the table in all directions, like bullets at Normandy.

Swallowing, her father held his hand up to silence everyone. A few crumbs stuck to his fingertips. "I'm getting the house," he said, "because she's the one who wants to do this. It's her idea. She wants us to separate? Fine, she can move out. That rugelach is wonderful, Jill. Not as good as my mother's, but . . ."

"Nothing is as good as your mother's," Jill's mother muttered, which made Jill wonder whether her father had been unfavorably comparing her mother's cooking to his mother's for the past forty-two years. Could that be her reason for walking out on him?

"Where are you moving?" she asked her mother.

"I found a nice little apartment," her mother said.

Her father rolled his eyes, as snide as Abbie on a hormonal day. "Nice," he snorted. "What can you find for less than a million dollars that's nice?"

"I don't need a mansion," Jill's mother retorted. "I don't need lots of space. It's just going to be me."

"Overlooking a highway."

"It's not a highway."

"Not to be crass or anything," Doug said as he tore a sprig of grapes from the platter, "but how are you going to afford this nice little apartment? You're a one-income couple, and Dad's probably thinking about retiring in the next few years or so—"

"I'm not ready to hang up the stethoscope yet," Jill's father said.

"Still, this isn't the time to be squandering your money. You should be preparing for the future. You know how much Grandma Schwartz's nursing home costs. What if one of you became incapacitated?"

Jill's mother glanced at her husband. "He's already diagnosing us with Alzheimer's." She turned back to Doug. "I'll pay for the apartment out of my earnings. I have a job."

"A job." Jill's father snorted, punctuating his words with more sarcastic eye-rolling. "You call that a job?"

"What job?" Melissa asked, her voice still tremulous with unshed tears.

"Did I mention I like your hair?" Jill's mother said. "Very breezy. Very pretty."

"Tell her about your job," Jill's father said.

Jill's mother sat straighter. "I'll be a clerk at a First-Rate. You know, the discount chain."

"A clerk?" Doug was clearly appalled. "A clerk? You're going to wear one of those ugly red bibs?"

"It's more than a bib. It's more on the order of an apron. You could call it a smock," she said. "Or a pinafore. Like the Gilbert and Sullivan opera."

"Mom." Doug sounded indignant. "You're an educated, cultured woman. A musician. You shouldn't be running a cash register."

"I won't start on the register. That comes after I've been there a while," she explained. "Lots of educated, cultured women are clerks. As for my music, it's not as if anyone's going to pay me to analyze the *Goldberg Variations* for them."

"But a discount store clerk?" Melissa chimed in. "Couldn't you be a secretary instead? It would be easier on you. You could sit at a desk."

"I've been a secretary," Jill's mother reminded them. "When your father was in medical school I worked as a secretary. I don't know if they still call that job secretary anymore. Administrative assistant." She shrugged. "I don't want to do that. It's all about serving the interests of others, making everyone else look good. You knock yourself out and your boss gets all the credit. Forget that. Anyway, I'll meet more people at First-Rate. It'll be fun."

"Fun?" Doug shook his head.

"I want to earn money," she said. "I don't want your father paying my rent. That would defeat the purpose."

"What purpose?" Jill asked, lowering her voice in the hope of defusing the tension that churned the air. "The hell with the job, Mom. We want to know why you're doing this."

"Yes," Jill's father agreed, giving her mother a pointed look. "We'd all like to know that."

She scowled at him. "You and I have discussed this, Richard. I've told you. It's . . ." She considered her answer, then sighed. "It's nothing in particular."

Jill's father gazed at his children, eyebrows raised and his hands spread palm up, as if to say, *See? She's nuts.*

More silence. Shocked silence. *Nothing in particular?* "You can't just end a marriage because of nothing in particular," Jill said.

"It's lots of things," her mother explained, sounding less defensive than thoughtful. "Big things and little things. The remote, for example. He sits in front of the TV with the remote and channel-surfs. Every two seconds, this channel, that channel. Click, click, click. It drives me crazy."

"Dad," Melissa whined, "for God's sake, can't you stop channel-surfing?"

"I like to channel-surf," he argued. "You never know, there could be something good on another channel. Anyway, she's not watching the TV," he added. "She's usually reading. What does she care if I channel-surf?"

"You can't read in another room?" Doug asked Jill's mother.

"I like my recliner. I like to be comfortable. And he's going click-click-click. I ask him to stop, but he won't."

"I work hard all day, saving lives. In the evening I'm entitled to channel-surf," Jill's father declared.

"Okay, so he channel-surfs," Doug said. "Big fucking deal."

"Doug," Jill's mother scolded.

Doug shrugged an apology. "You don't break up a marriage over something that trivial."

"To you it's trivial. To me it's a thing that drives me crazy."

"So you're going to wear a red smock and work for minimum wage at First-Rate?" Doug faked a contemplative expression. "I think it *has* driven you crazy."

Jill's mother refused to back down in the face of his derision. Though Jill opposed the divorce—correction: the separation—she was proud of her mother for standing her ground.

"It's not just the channel-surfing. That was one example." She folded her hands on the table in front of her. Her nails were short and unpolished, giving her fingers a stubby appearance. If she intended to venture out into the world as a single woman, she ought to get a manicure.

Oh, God. A single woman. Would she be dating? Dating men who weren't Jill's father? Where would she meet these men? She wasn't a bar type. She often lectured Abbie about all the sleazeballs lurking on the internet, so Jill couldn't imagine her trusting an on-line dating service. And who was she going to meet as a clerk at First-Rate? Sprightly geezers who resented their wives for sending them out on stupid errands to stock up on paper towels or mouthwash when they'd rather be home channel-surfing?

"There's his beard," her mother said.

"What beard?" Melissa asked as she, Doug and Jill shifted their gazes to their clean-shaven father.

"He shaves every morning and leaves beard hairs in the sink. Why he can't rinse them down the drain, I don't know. I've asked him a million times but he leaves this mess for me every morning."

"Oh, yes, a huge mess," Jill's father snapped. "A massive mess. Hours to clean up." He shook his head. "I'm rushing to get out every morning—unlike some people, I've got to get to work by a certain time. I've got patients waiting for me, people whose lives I'm trying to save. And I'm supposed to take the time to scrub the sink before I leave. It's not like you've got so much else to do that you can't wash a few little hairs down the sink."

"I've been scrubbing the sink since the day we got married," she shot back. "Forty-two years, Richard, and have you ever once said, 'Thank you for scrubbing the sink'? I'm tired of cleaning up after you. It would take you two seconds to rinse your beard hairs out of the basin, but you won't do it. Even though I've asked. Even though it would make me happy."

"I do plenty to make you happy!" Jill's father roared.

"You do things you think would make me happy. You buy me earrings. Earrings are nice, I like earrings fine. But what would *really* make me happy is if you'd clean the sink after yourself. I've told you this and you just ignore me."

Jill closed her eyes and reconsidered her decision not to serve liquor. She could use a drink right now. Diet Coke with rum. Rum with a splash of Diet Coke. Rum, hold the Diet Coke.

Listening to her parents bicker about something so petty yet so intimate made her feel like a voyeur. She eyed her mother's hands again and wondered if her short nails and the dry white skin of her cuticles reflected all the years she'd spent scrubbing sinks. Jill also tried to remember whether as a child she'd ever thanked her mother for scrubbing the sinks. Or whether anyone in her own family ever thanked her. Gordon left beard hairs in the master bathroom sink all the time, and she always washed them down the drain. She had never thought about that before now. Maybe you had to scrub sinks for forty-two years before it drove you over the edge. Jill had twenty-six years of sink-scrubbing to go before she snapped.

"It's more than just beard hairs and the remote," her mother continued.

"It's the bed," her father muttered.

Melissa clapped her hands over her ears. "I don't want to hear this," she moaned. "La, la, la, la—"

"The mattress, Melissa," her mother cut her off. "He wants to rotate the mattress."

Doug frowned. "You're supposed to flip the mattress every year or so."

"Flip it, sure. But we got that pillow-top mattress a few years ago—"

"Almost ten years ago," her father interrupted. "And it's never been rotated."

"Because you're not supposed to flip it. The pillow-top has to stay on top. So he says he wants to rotate it to even out the wear and tear. His side is getting wear and tear. My side isn't. He weighs forty pounds more than me."

"I'm a perfect weight for my height," Jill's father pointed out.

"I didn't say you were fat. I said you weigh forty pounds more than me, which you do. So we're supposed to rotate this mattress and I get stuck with the worn-out side. My side isn't worn out. Why should I have to sleep on the side you wore out?"

"Can we move on?" Melissa begged, her hands still clamped to her ears. "Enough with the bed. La, la, la, la . . ."

"All right. Just wait until you've been married for forty-two years to someone who weighs forty pounds more than you and he wants to rotate the mattress. That's all." Jill's mother circled the table with her gaze. "I've never lived alone in my life. I grew up, I went to college, I met your father. We graduated in May and got married in June. Then we had children. And now, here we still are, side by side, rubbing up against each other all the time. I've never been alone in my life."

"You want to be alone?" Jill's father asked. "I could leave you alone. Melissa, darling, how much fun is it living alone?"

Melissa shifted in her seat. "I've been living alone for years, Dad. And sometimes I love it." She shifted again, eyeing their mother. "Sometimes it's lonely," she warned.

"That's a chance I'm willing to take. We all have our dreams, right? Well, this is my dream: to do something without first thinking how it's going to affect someone else. To decide what I want for dinner without thinking, 'Richard doesn't like having chicken two nights in a row, so I'd better make lamb chops.' To go to a movie without thinking, 'Richard hates subtitles so we can't see that foreign film.' To not have to check everyone else's schedule first. To not have to worry that what I want interferes with what someone else wants."

"That sounds kind of selfish," Doug observed.

"Yes. It's selfish. That's my dream. For once in my life, I want to be selfish. I want to put myself first."

"You're still going to have to scrub the sink," Jill reminded her. "I assume this apartment you're moving into has a sink."

"But I'll be cleaning up my own messes," her mother explained. "No one else has ever cleaned up after me. I always clean up after everyone else. It used to be all of you I cleaned up after. Now it's just him—" she gestured across the table at her husband "—but I'm still cleaning up other people's messes. No one has ever cleaned my mess out of the sink. Not that I shave, but I spit out toothpaste. And I clean up my spit toothpaste. I'm already cleaning up after myself, so I'll keep doing that. But no longer will I have to think, 'I clean up after everyone else and no one cleans up after me.'"

More silence.

Jill avoided her siblings' faces. She wondered if they were all stewing in guilt the way she was. They should be. They had more reason to feel guilty than she did. She'd cleaned the sink in their shared bathroom when they'd been growing up. Doug couldn't, of course, because as the oldest he'd always had the most homework. When she'd been in sixth grade and he'd been in eighth, he'd complained that eighth graders had tons more homework than sixth graders so she should clean the bathroom. Once she'd reached eighth grade and had just as much homework as he'd had in that grade, he'd been in tenth grade and still had more homework.

And Melissa had never cleaned the bathroom because she'd been a spoiled little princess.

Jill shouldn't feel so damned guilty. But she did. She couldn't recall ever thanking her mother for all the other things she'd done. Mothers were taken for granted. Jill knew that better than anyone else at the table—except, of course, for her mother.

"So, look," she said quietly. "You'll live in the apartment for a while, and you've always got the option of moving back home. As you said, you and Dad aren't talking to lawyers. So you'll live by yourself and clean up your own messes and go to foreign films."

"You could go to foreign films without moving into an apartment,"

Doug noted. "You could go during the day while he's at work."

"That's not the point," Jill argued. "The point is, she's tired of the fact that Dad never says, 'Okay, if you want to see that new French film, we'll go see it.'"

"Why should he, if he doesn't like subtitles?"

"They could see a dubbed version," Melissa suggested.

"I don't like dubbing," Jill's mother announced. "The actors' lips never match the sounds coming out of their mouths." She sighed. "We didn't get together with you kids so you could tell us how to not do what we're planning to do. We've already decided. I'm moving out. Your father is staying in the house. We're keeping the same cell phone service for now, so you can reach me. I'll let you know once I've got a regular phone."

"Where is this apartment?" Doug asked.

"Ten minutes from the house. Fifteen if it's snowing."

"Overlooking a highway," Jill's father muttered. "Like a slum."

"It's nothing like a slum," Jill's mother protested. "It's very nice. Clean, secure, ample parking. I'm taking a few pieces of furniture from the house, and I ordered some things at Ikea. It's a small apartment. I don't need much."

"What about the piano?" Jill asked, swallowing the tremor in her voice. Her mother was the only pianist in the family. She'd tried to teach all three children how to play. Each of them, starting at age six, had spent two years working through piano books with names like "I Can Play" and "Beginner's Song Book" without showing the merest glimmer of talent. Jill's mother always said they'd inherited her lack of a mere glimmer, that she was at best a mediocre player and that was why she'd majored in music history rather than performance. But she sounded good to Jill. She played not for glory but for her own sweet pleasure.

If she moved the piano to her new apartment, that would seem final, some sort of statement.

"I don't have room for it in the apartment," her mother said. "It's going to stay in the living room for the time being."

For the time being. What did that mean?

Jill's head hurt from thinking too hard and analyzing too much. She could just picture her mother's new residence: one of those three-story complexes scattered throughout the suburbs where divorced people lived. Usually fathers, wanting to be within reach of their children, who remained with their mothers in their houses.

There was no need for Jill's mother to move into a divorce village.

The house was big enough that her mother and father could share it and manage to avoid each other. They could even sleep in separate bedrooms. One of them could eat in the kitchen and one in the dining room. They could divide the refrigerator right down the middle.

Except that in her own apartment, her mother wouldn't have to rinse beard hairs down the drain of her bathroom sink.

It was stupid, really. Yet in some small, dark corner of Jill's brain, she understood.

Chapter Six

Doug wasn't in the mood to play golf, but he'd rescheduled his and his father's tee time and arranged to have his mother drive Brooke and the girls home so he could take his father with him to the club after the family powwow. He would have preferred to return home with Brooke, where he could share with her all the thoughts buzzing inside his head like angry mosquitoes. Better to let them escape than have the little demons suck all the blood out of his mind and leave it itching and inflamed.

But he and Brooke wouldn't have been able to chat quietly over a drink—a double scotch neat would suit him perfectly right now. Private discussions were impossible when the twins were in the vicinity, bouncing around and babbling. When he and Brooke wanted to have an extended conversation, they waited until after the girls were in bed for the night.

Should he raise the subject of his parents' marital situation with his dad during the drive to the golf course? The old man didn't seem eager to talk. He gazed out the windshield, watching grand suburban houses, knee-high stone walls and fiery autumn foliage blur silently past, and kept his mouth firmly shut, leaving Doug to his own ruminations.

Instead of contemplating his parents' foolishness, he contemplated Melissa's.

Lucas Brondo. Jesus. The guy resembled a model in an advertisement for a tacky cologne. The only way his tan could have looked phonier was if he'd spray-painted himself with Krylon. A guy who spent time in an ultraviolet coffin in a tanning salon was seriously afflicted with vanity issues—and might eventually find himself seriously afflicted with skin cancer, too.

What did Lucas Brondo do? Whom did he do it with? Whom did he do it *to*? If he was a lawyer like Melissa, he sure didn't look like a laced-up associate bucking for partner. He looked more like a *consigliere* for the mob, or maybe one of those shysters who negotiated Hollywood contracts and represented movie stars with DUI arrests. That was it: he looked like the sort of shark who would step up to a bank of microphones and assure the gathered paparazzi that his client had checked herself into a discreet rehab facility and hoped her fans would respect her privacy during this difficult time.

Nearing the club's parking lot, Doug glanced toward his father, wondering what he had thought of Lucas Brondo. Not much, probably. That Melissa's new boyfriend wasn't Jewish was enough to earn Richard Bendel's undying disapproval. Whether or not Brondo represented starlets with substance-abuse problems or paunchy guys from New Jersey named Nicky the Nose didn't matter. The guy was a goy. End of discussion.

Ironically, the first thing of substance his father said, beyond such trivial comments as, "Did you bring extra balls?" and "I hope we're not stuck playing behind a bunch of schmucks," was, "What did you think of Melissa's friend?"

They were climbing out of the cart at the first hole when he raised the question. Ordinarily, Doug and his father walked the course, but they'd gotten a late start today, and they lacked the time for leisurely strolls along the gravel paths. So Doug had rented a cart.

He would rather have talked about the far more important topic of his parents' imminent divorce, or separation, or whatever the hell they were doing. He would have liked to ask his father why he wasn't fighting harder to keep the marriage intact, why he didn't seem terribly upset by the prospect of Doug's mother moving into a shabby little apartment and working at a First-Rate franchise, of all places. As long as he and his father hadn't been talking, Doug could waste mental energy trying to psyche out Melissa's new boyfriend. But if they were going to talk, damn it, they ought to talk about the main event.

Perhaps it would be better if they eased into that subject. They could start with bronze-boy Brondo and gradually maneuver themselves into the issue of the Bendels' trip to Splitsville. A golfer couldn't play the second hole before playing the first.

"I don't know," he said, squinting through his sunglasses and then removing them. The sun sat at an angle he wasn't used to, since they usually started their game earlier in the afternoon, before shadows started to slant across the fairway. "He struck me as kind of superficial. I hardly had a chance to talk to him, but first impression, he seemed shallow." And much too tan.

"I thought he was a little *faygela*," Doug's father said. "Not that I'm saying. I mean, your sister's a wonderful girl, Ivy League education, a terrific job with a prestige law firm. She wouldn't get involved with a guy who likes boys better than girls. But the guy seemed a little light in the pants." Doug's father shrugged, then pulled his one-iron from his bag. "Not that I'm saying," he repeated, fishing a tee and a ball from the pockets of his bag. "And he isn't Jewish."

"They probably aren't serious enough to worry about religion," Doug said.

"Not serious? She brought him to a family affair. How many times does she bring a man with her to family affairs?"

"I got the impression she brought him with her because he had access to a car and she didn't want to take the bus."

"Hmmph." His father teed up and stared down the fairway. "He's meeting her family, the least he could do is shave."

"If he doesn't shave, she doesn't have to worry about washing his beard hairs down the sink," Doug said, then winced as his father sliced his shot.

His father pressed his lips together and stared in the direction his ball had vanished, his gaze hard. Doug was familiar with that look. He'd seen it dozens of times: when he'd convinced a three-year-old Melissa to rub petroleum jelly in her hair. When he'd devoured the chocolate chips his mother had bought to bake cookies for his cub scout troop's cake sale. When he'd gotten his first speeding ticket. Whenever he let his father down.

Doug hadn't let his father down this time, though. If anyone was letting anyone down, Doug's parents were doing the letting, and Doug was the one being let. So what if the old man had blown his damned swing? All he had to do was rinse his fucking whiskers down the drain and none of this would be happening.

Doug sighed. His mother wasn't leaving his father because of the beard hairs. She wasn't leaving him because of foreign films or the remote control or the mattress. When asked the reason for her decision to break up her marriage, she'd said, "Nothing in particular."

"I don't think Mom really cares about the sink," Doug said, doing his best to sound conciliatory. He really hated his father's disapproving expression. It made him feel as if he were sixteen again, or six. "She's upset, so she's come up with a laundry list of things to complain about."

"Laundry. That's another one," his father told him. "She's leaving because I sometimes put my whites in the colored-laundry hamper, and vice-versa. I'm in a hurry. I don't remember which hamper is which. She should count her blessings I don't leave my dirty socks on the floor.

Instead, she's walking out on me because I don't sort my dirty clothes properly."

Doug always left his dirty clothes on the ottoman in the dressing area of the master bedroom suite. He wasn't even sure where Brooke kept the laundry baskets. He simply piled his laundry on the ottoman, and a short time later it reappeared, clean and folded, in his bureau. Did this make him a bad husband? Would Brooke someday divorce him because of that?

The possibility sent a tide of anxiety crashing through him. He shook it off, teed up, shrugged to loosen his shoulders and swung, hitting his ball in a clean arc down the fairway. "So Mom's got her gripes," he said. "I'm sure you've got gripes with her, too."

His father remained silent, his gaze lingering on the grassy acreage in front of them.

"What I didn't hear today, when we were all at Jill's house," Doug continued as they climbed into the cart, "was either you or Mom mentioning the word love."

His father snorted. "Love has nothing to do with anything."

"How can you say that? If you and Mom loved each other, you wouldn't be separating."

His father continued to stare grimly after his poorly hit ball. "Couples who don't love each other stay together all the time. And couples who love each other get divorced because they can't live with each other anymore. Love is irrelevant."

"So what's the deal? You love each other and can't live with each other anymore?"

"I can live with her fine," his father muttered. "She's the one who's leaving." His father crossed to the cart, climbed into the passenger seat and glared at the path in front of him. Doug couldn't tell whom he was pissed at. His son? His wife? His errant golf ball? The whole world in general?

Doug had started this conversation. He'd wanted it. As the eldest child, he felt responsible in some intangible way. He ordered himself to stick with it, to keep pushing for some answers from his father.

He took his place in the cart behind the wheel and steered down the path to where their balls awaited them.

"All right. She's the one who's leaving," he said. His father didn't move. He didn't even blink. "What I haven't heard you say is that you wished she would stay. I haven't heard you say you'd try to remember to rinse out the sink for her."

His father gave him a quick look, then sighed. "Right. You haven't heard me say those things."

They'd reached their balls, Doug's sitting in a fine spot with a clear shot to the green, and his father's nestled beneath a clump of shrubs.

"You *do* want her to leave?" Doug pressed his father.

"Of course not."

Doug ignored his ball. He refused to accept his father's evasions. "You want her to stay but you won't rinse your beard hair out of the sink?"

"I don't want to fight with her. I don't want to negotiate. I don't want to drop to my knees and say, 'Whatever you wish, sweetheart. Whatever you say. Just don't leave me.' I've got my pride, Doug. I'm not going to beg. Forty-two years we've lived one way. Now, all of a sudden, she decides we're rubbing up against each other too much and she wants to live another way. Why should I have to rearrange my life for her?"

"Because you're her husband?" Doug suggested.

His father marched over to the bushes and nudged his ball out from beneath a tangle of branches and rusting leaves. Doug observed his stroke, thought about reminding him to plant his right leg a little more firmly and decided now wasn't the time for a tutorial. They played out the hole in steely silence.

Back in the cart, Doug tried a new approach: "Won't you be lonely if she's gone?"

"I'll work more hours. I'll spend less time at home."

"Are you going to date?"

That jolted a response out of his father, who turned so sharply in his seat he nearly fell out of the cart. "Date?"

"You're a good-looking guy," Doug pointed out. "A doctor. Women will line up for a chance to be with you."

Doug's father twisted back in his seat and muttered something unintelligible. "Why should I date? I might wind up with some other crazy lady who'll torture me if I don't rinse out the sink."

"Couples who separate see other people," Doug said, as if he was any kind of expert. He had some defiantly single friends, mostly from college and med school, and plenty of married friends in the social circle Brooke did such an excellent job of cultivating. Divorced friends, no. When people divorced they left the social circle. They left the neighborhood and moved to Phoenix or Tallahassee, where, he assumed, they dated.

"I've been approached," his father admitted.

"Approached?" This time it was Doug's turn to spin toward his father in shock. His hands followed his body and the cart veered off the path. Doug swiftly steered it back onto the gravel and refrained from gaping at his father. He just gaped in general. "Approached by a woman, you mean?"

"Women. Plural."

Doug might have expected a woman here or there to come on to his father, but *women? Plural?*

"I get someone's blood pressure under control and she's grateful. Or someone's husband has cardiomyopathy, he's probably not going to make it, she's scared and looking for comfort. Or the nurses. They come, they go, they flirt. You know what it's like, Doug. You're a doctor."

"My patients have lousy vision," he reminded his father, hoping he didn't sound as peeved as he felt. Why were women coming on to his father and not him? He had a busy practice, and he was a hell of a lot younger than his father. Not that his father wasn't in great shape, but come on. Doug was in his prime.

Maybe women *did* come on to him, and he just didn't notice. His antennae were retracted. He had Brooke at home; why check out other women?

Had his father ever felt that way about his mother? Ruth Bendel was nice enough looking for a woman in her sixties, but she wasn't Brooke. Had his father ever felt, as Doug did, that it couldn't get any better than this?

What if Doug was wrong? What if it *could* get better?

"It's been so long since I went on a date," his father said. "I wouldn't know what to do. Am I supposed to pay, or does everyone go Dutch these days?"

"I think that's a little un-PC," Doug said.

"What is? Paying for a date?"

"The phrase 'going Dutch.' It's offensive to people in Holland."

His father huffed. "God forbid I should offend anyone in Holland. I don't want to date," he said, sounding oddly fatigued. "I'm figuring with your mother, one month at First-Rate and she'll be ready to come home. She's going to be bored. She's going to panic the first time her coffee maker doesn't work or her tires need air in them. Or when she tries to connect the DVD player to her television. Or any time she has to do one of the things I always do for her while she's busy cleaning the sink. She'll say, 'Well, that was fun but now I'm going home.'"

Doug wasn't so sure. He could imagine his mother freaking out if an appliance stopped working—but he could also imagine her phoning him or Gordon and asking for assistance more easily than he could imagine her giving up and returning to her husband in defeat. His mother was a stubborn woman.

And forty-two years was an awfully long time to be washing someone else's beard hairs down the drain without a word of thanks.

HE DIDN'T GET HOME until after seven. He and his father had played all eighteen holes, then retired to the club house for a drink. Doug had nursed a scotch while his father had knocked back two whisky sours. By the time his father had swallowed the liquor-soaked maraschino cherry from his second drink, Doug had learned that his father was panic-stricken about having to prepare his own dinner every night—"I could do take-out, but that gets expensive over time, and all those fast-food places use too much sodium, I'll wind up with blood pressure problems"—and irritated when he thought about the one-carat-total-weight diamond stud earrings he'd given his wife for her birthday some years ago, and worried when he thought about how the separation might affect Abbie's bat mitzvah. "That's eight months away," he'd lamented, sounding more maudlin the more he drank. "I hope to God we're back together by then. Abbie shouldn't have any sadness on her special day."

Brooke had left the outside lights on for Doug. Four post lamps stood in intervals along the curving driveway that led from the street to the garage. Two matching wall lanterns flanked the front door, and two more hung above the outer two garage doors. He slid his car into the middle bay and directed a prayer of thanks toward the ceiling that he had a wife waiting for him, one who cared enough about him to leave the lights on when he rolled in later than expected.

He'd phoned her from the club to let her know he and his father would be having a drink and he'd be home late. He'd implied that his father needed something strong and wet more than he did, but that wasn't exactly true.

He pulled his clubs from the trunk, stood them in their nook in a corner of the garage near the Range Rover, and turned off the garage lights before entering the house. The spotlights above the center island glowed in the kitchen but the room was empty.

He headed up the stairs, following the sound of voices, and found Brooke reading *Harry Potter* to the girls. Doug had mentioned that he thought Madison and Mackenzie were too young for *Harry Potter*, but Brooke had argued that if she was going to read to them, she might as well read something she found entertaining, and chances were the girls didn't understand most of the scary stuff, anyway. Doug supposed he'd feel the same if he'd spent as many hours reading to his daughters as Brooke had, so he didn't argue.

The girls were in their nightgowns, tucked into their beds—five bedrooms in the house, and they insisted on sharing one, though Doug assumed that would change when they got older. They hollered a shrill greeting as soon as they saw him filling the doorway. "Daddy! Daddy!"

Brooke tucked a finger into the book to hold her place and smiled at him. "I made bowties for them," she said. "I figured you wouldn't mind missing that."

Bowties were just mutated spaghetti, as far as he was concerned. "Did you eat?"

She nodded. "If you want to throw together a sandwich . . ."

"Maybe later." Contemplating his parents' screwed-up marriage had pretty much killed his appetite. He waved to the girls, then sauntered down the hall to the master bedroom to wash up. He didn't want to breathe booze on them when he kissed them good-night.

He paused for a moment at the entry to the master suite. It was, he had to admit, the most spectacular area of a spectacular house. The main room was big enough to hold a king-size bed, Brooke's triple dresser, Doug's bureau, a small sitting area with a sofa and coffee table facing a fireplace above which hung a flat-panel TV. Two walk-in closets opened off the main room, separated by a dressing area at the end of which was a bathroom larger than the bedroom he'd had growing up. Another room off to one side served as an exercise room, equipped with a treadmill, a rowing machine and another TV so he could watch DVD's of "St. Elsewhere" while he worked out. Brooke had decorated the entire suite with superb taste. The carpet was a plush cream shade, accented by a few Oriental area rugs. The furniture was Shaker—simple and elegant—and the bed was a four-poster with horizontal beams connecting the four posts, the purpose of which Doug couldn't fathom. Sometimes, when he was in bed, he felt as if he'd gotten shut up inside a carton with invisible walls.

Brooke's voice drifted down the hall in a gentle murmur. The hall light glinted off the three-way mirror above the little vanity table she'd tucked into a corner of the room, spraying the walls with trapezoids of light.

It all seemed so . . . *right.*

Had there been a time in his father's life when everything had seemed right? Had he come home to Doug's mother every evening and believed she was as content as he was, as satisfied with the world they'd created? Had he entered his bedroom confident that she loved him and was devoted to him and her feelings would never change?

Jesus fucking Christ. What if, thirty years from now, Brooke decided to walk out on Doug?

He raced into the bathroom, took a quick piss, splashed water on his face and gargled a capful of mouthwash. Then he jogged back down the hall to his wife, needing reassurance. When he saw the light off in the girls' room and Brooke gone, he had to pause, take a deep breath and convince himself that she was somewhere in the house. Probably in the kitchen fixing him a sandwich. Just because she wasn't where he'd last seen her didn't mean she'd left him.

He tiptoed into the girls' room, bent over each bed and kissed each daughter on the forehead. "Today was fun," Mackenzie said in a sleepy, happy voice.

"Aunt Melissa's friend was so nice," Madison added.

"He fixes hair," Mackenzie told him.

"He was wearing boots."

"I'm glad you enjoyed yourselves," Doug murmured.

"Uncle Gordon played a video. *Pocahontas.* It was good," Mackenzie reported.

"Noah kept making snorting pig sounds, though," Madison said.

"He's a boy," Mackenzie pointed out, as if that explained everything.

"I love Grandma and Grandpa," Madison said, then yawned.

"Me, too." Mackenzie's voice overlapped Madison's, as if she'd known what Madison would say and wanted to express her agreement immediately.

I love them, too, Doug almost said. But he was angry and unsettled, and a little scared. So instead, he said, "It's bedtime now. Good-night, girls."

"Good night," they chorused with a final burst of energy before burrowing under their matching yellow blankets.

Leaving their bedroom, Doug contemplated the fact that the girls had no idea what was going on with their grandparents. Maybe they'd never have to know. Maybe the bickering Bendels would get back together again before their separation registered on their grandchildren.

Maybe his mother's coffee pot would break or his father would overdose on salty take-out dinners and they'd apologize to each other and vow to accommodate each other's wishes and moods a little more.

Brooke wasn't in the kitchen, although she'd left an empty plate, a package containing half a loaf of pumpernickel bread and a jar of mustard on the center island's granite counter. Did she expect him to eat a mustard sandwich? It wasn't even Dijon mustard, just the usual yellow stuff. He wondered whether she had cold cuts or cheese stashed in the fridge.

Not that it mattered. He still wasn't hungry.

"I'm in here," her voice drifted to him from the family room. "I didn't know what you wanted to eat."

What he wanted was to drink, not eat. He filled a glass with Chivas and abandoned the bread and mustard for the family room.

Brooke lounged on the couch, a goblet of white wine in her hand and her bare feet propped on the teak table. The TV was off, the windows filled with a sky halfway between blue and black. The lamp on the end table beside her spilled amber light over her hair, turning it gold. She looked so much better than he felt.

He dropped onto the couch next to her, leaned over and planted a kiss on her lips. He tasted wine on her mouth, and also a vanilla undertone. He wondered if it was her lipstick or her lips that were vanilla-flavored.

"How's your father?" she asked.

He sipped some scotch. "His game was so bad, he asked me to tear up the score sheet."

She opened her mouth, then closed it and gazed toward the window, as if unsure what to say. After a minute, she turned back to him. "Do you think I should get bangs?"

He nearly choked on the scotch in his mouth. She wanted to get *banged?*

"You know, like Melissa has. Bangs." She brushed her fingers over her forehead.

"Oh. Bangs." Hairstyle. "I don't know. Your hair looks great the way it is."

"Bangs might soften it a little. I was talking to her friend, Luc?" Brooke's voice rose into a question. "He said he thought bangs might soften the lines of my face."

"You don't have any lines," Doug said, floundering. Was she fishing for compliments? Worrying about non-existent wrinkles? And why the hell had she been discussing this with Bronze Brondo?

"Not lines like old-age lines," she clarified. "Lines like the line of my nose or my cheeks. He had some really good ideas."

"Why would he have good ideas about bangs?" It would never have occurred to Doug—or to any man Doug knew—to discuss hairdos with a woman he'd just met. For that matter, it would never occur to him to discuss hairdos with a woman he knew well. He couldn't believe that today, after having spent an hour and a half listening to his mother calmly explain why she was leaving his father and what she was leaving him for—a job at First-Rate, for God's sake—and another three hours listening to his father say things that left Doug with the clear impression that the old man was simmering with a combination of rage and fear, he should find himself cuddled up on the family room sofa with his wife, discussing hairdos.

"He's a hairdresser," Brooke explained.

He fixes hair, Mackenzie had said. *He seemed a little faygela,* his father had said. Holy shit. "The guy's a hairdresser?"

"Stop thinking like that," Brooke said, frowning and poking his forearm, almost causing him to spill his drink. "Now you're going to assume he's gay."

"I didn't say that." *I only thought it.*

"He's your sister's boyfriend," Brooke reminded him. "They're a couple. He works at Nouvelle, an exclusive salon in Manhattan. I assume you don't get to work at a place like that unless you know what you're talking about."

"When it comes to bangs, maybe." Why couldn't Melissa find a normal guy? An attorney like her. An Ivy Leaguer. Someone who made lots of money and talked about baseball.

"Anyway, he thought I should consider bangs. What do you think?"

"I think you're gorgeous," Doug said truthfully. "Whatever you want to do to your hair is fine with me."

She smiled, kissed his cheek and cushioned her head against his shoulder. "So, about your parents."

"My father's trying hard not to be a wreck," Doug told her. "My mother—God knows. Did she say anything when she drove you and the girls home?"

"What could she say with the girls in the back seat? She asked them about school and they wouldn't shut up. They spent the entire drive telling her about the ashtrays they made out of clay in art and the class's pet turtle. Its name is Shelly and it likes to eat lettuce and crickets."

"Ashtrays? They made ashtrays?" He scowled. "Nobody smokes anymore."

"But first-graders make ashtrays out of clay. It's what they do. They can't master a pottery wheel at that age."

He managed a tentative smile. As long as his daughters weren't smoking, they could make any damned thing they wanted in art. "So my mother didn't tell you anything?"

"No," Brooke replied, adding grimly, "Your parents promised to watch the girls when we go to Nevis. How is that going to work out if they're divorced?"

"Oh, Christ. Nevis."

"I know it sounds selfish, Doug, but we booked that trip months ago and your parents *promised*."

"Shit." His mother would be living in some dingy apartment somewhere. Were his daughters supposed to stay in that dingy apartment with her? Or at the house with his father, unsupervised because his father would be at work? Hell, his mother would be at work, too. "My mother's got a job," he told Brooke.

"She mentioned that during the drive. You'll have to convince her to take that week off."

A week's vacation seemed doable. Maybe he could cajole his mother. For the sake of her two beloved granddaughters, who adored her so very much. Maybe the girls could make clay ashtrays for her at school. That would melt her heart. "This whole situation is so stupid. I don't know why my mother is moving out on my father. She always seems happy."

Brooke pulled away and gave him a look that said, *Are you insane?*

What had he missed? He saw more of his father than his mother, thanks to their golf games and occasional lunches when Doug found himself in the Longwood district of Boston, home of Beth Israel Deaconess, the hospital where his father's practice was located. But whenever he saw his mother, she seemed happy enough to him. She always gave him a hug and a kiss and fixed meals she knew he'd enjoy, and she asked him about his work and then fussed over the girls. Wasn't that the definition of happiness for a grandmother? A chance to cook and spoil her precious granddaughters?

"How do you know she's been unhappy?" he asked.

Brooke opened her mouth, then shut it again and leaned back into him, her hair stroking his chin and her shoulder digging pleasantly into his chest. "She never glows. She always looks tired and drab."

"That's just the way she is. She's never been a glamour queen."

"It's not about glamour," Brooke said, sounding a touch impatient. "It's about having energy and enthusiasm. Maybe you didn't notice because you're always with your father." She shrugged. "Maybe it's just a matter of people only seeing what they want to see."

Was that what Brooke thought of him? That he saw only what he wanted to see? He had perfect vision, damn it—thanks to the skilled surgery of Barry Steinmetz, one of his closest friends since their med-school days and one of the finest Lasik surgeons Doug knew, other than himself. If his mother had been drab or unenthusiastic, his 20/20 vision would have picked up on it.

Certainly his 20/20 vision would pick up on any drabness or lack of enthusiasm in Brooke, wouldn't it? He didn't have to worry about her not being happy. She glowed all the time.

"You would tell me if you were unhappy, wouldn't you?" he asked, aware of the anxiety filtering through his voice.

Brooke nestled closer to him and sipped her wine. "Of course I would," she said. "I think I might be happier if I had bangs."

He wasn't sure if she was joking, but he decided to pretend she was. "If you want bangs," he murmured, "get bangs."

Chapter Seven

Jill lay in bed, contemplating whether she needed to pee again. She'd consumed a whole damned six-pack of Diet Coke today, and for most of the past two hours her bladder had felt like a water balloon, stretched and sloshy and ready to burst.

Six twelve-ounce cans. All that caffeine. She was never going to fall asleep.

Gordon wasn't asleep, either, but that was because he was trying to get her in the mood. He nuzzled her neck and caressed her breast. He had always operated under the assumption that an erect nipple was the equivalent of an erect penis, and if he rubbed her breasts enough to get her nipples hard and swollen, that meant she was ready for sex. She'd tried to explain to him that her nipples got hard and swollen every time she left the steamy shower stall in their bathroom and stepped into the cooler air of the bedroom, and every time she went outdoors in sub-freezing weather. "Sometimes my nipples do that because I'm cold, not because I'm hot," she'd explained.

She was neither hot nor cold at the moment. Jittery, yes. Blame the caffeine. Blame the fact that Melissa and Luc were cozying up in Abbie's room just down the hall, while Abbie camped out in the family room. Blame her failure to persuade her parents not to go their separate ways and live separate lives. Blame the fact that, although she loved Gordon and he was a wonderful man and a terrific father and all the rest, he'd left a blob of pale green toothpaste on the surface of the sink ten minutes ago, and she'd wound up washing it away.

Did that mean her marriage was doomed? Twenty-eight years from now, would she be moving into a seedy little apartment and working at a convenience store because of that wart of toothpaste?

Shit. She was thinking too much. Thinking about toothpaste and her parents was not going to get her turned on, no matter how perky her nipples happened to be.

Maybe she shouldn't have let Melissa and Luc spend the night. Abbie—clearly a better hostess than her mother—had insisted that they stay. She'd argued that Jill couldn't send Aunt Melissa off to a motel when Aunt Melissa was so sad and really, Abbie didn't mind unrolling her sleeping bag on the couch downstairs, and besides, wasn't Luc cool?

Jill wasn't so sure about Luc, but she had to concede that Melissa was sad. She'd whimpered through dinner—an assortment of take-out dishes Gordon and Noah had picked up from Bangkok Palace. Wielding her chopsticks and stuffing her face with pad thai and chicken with lemon grass, Melissa had sniveled about how children of divorce had so much more trouble maintaining their faith in love, and maybe she should just give up on true love, and while she was at it maybe she should forget about ever having children because she would never want to cause another human being the pain she was suffering right now.

When she'd confessed her doubts about true love, Luc had glanced at her, looped an arm around her shoulders and given her a squeeze. Then he'd winked at Noah—he did have strikingly pretty blue eyes—and whispered, loudly enough for everyone to hear, "Girls can be a little dramatic sometimes."

Noah had nodded knowingly. "You're telling me?"

Gordon had laughed, and Jill had sublimated the urge to throw the container of sticky rice at his head by grabbing her can of Diet Coke and chugging enough soda to make her eyes tear from the carbonation.

After dinner, Abbie had retreated to her bedroom to text her friend Caitlin, and the guys had retired to the family room to watch something suitably manly on television, leaving Jill and Melissa to clean up the dinner things. Not an onerous task, given that Jill hadn't even bothered to empty the waxy white cartons from Bangkok Palace into serving bowls. All she had to do was stack the plates in the dishwasher. Melissa's help had consisted of gathering the cartons, napkins and chopsticks and depositing them in the trash.

Melissa had poured herself a glass of wine—Jill foolishly had stayed with Diet Coke; if she'd had some wine instead, she might be asleep by now, or at least not fretting over the engorged state of her bladder—and leaned against the counter near Jill's desk. "Do you think Dad's having an affair?" she'd asked.

Jill had mentally reviewed the family conference at her dining room table that afternoon. She'd sensed undercurrents, but not an adultery undercurrent. Her father's hair had been as gray as always, no sign that he was coloring it to look younger. No updated fashion sense. No cockiness, forgive the pun.

She'd shaken her head. "How about Mom?" she'd asked. "You

think *she's* having an affair?"

Melissa had winced. "Mom? Are you kidding?"

"No, I'm not kidding. Why can't Mom have an affair?"

"Because she's . . . Mom." Melissa's eyes had welled up. She'd pulled a paper napkin from the popsicle-stick napkin holder Noah had made last year at summer camp and blown her nose into it. "She's in her sixties, Jill."

"Women can't have sex in their sixties?"

"I don't know if they can't. But why would they want to? I mean, their bodies are all . . . you know. *Old.*"

"There was a time I thought thirty was old," Jill had remarked pointedly. Melissa might be the baby of the family, but she'd celebrated her thirtieth birthday more than a year ago.

"It is old," Melissa had said glumly. "I feel old. All I do is work. Then I come home, open a can of soup and spend the evening juggling numbers to see if there's any way in hell I can afford to buy an apartment. You and Doug own your own homes. I want to own property, too."

"You're earning a fortune," Jill had pointed out.

"Not a big enough fortune."

"Maybe you need to hook up with a guy who earns a fortune, too. Two salaries are better than one." As if the money Jill earned writing catalogue copy represented the difference between her family's being able to live in a house in the Boston suburbs and a cardboard box on a street corner in Mission Hill.

Melissa's gaze had drifted toward the door to the family room, through which the guy she was currently hooked up with had disappeared not long ago. "Luc earns a salary," she'd said. "I'm not sure exactly how much, but I think it's pretty good."

"He's a hairdresser." Jill had learned this over dinner and had done an estimable job of pretending she thought that was terrific.

"At one of the city's top salons."

A top salon. Jill had supposed she ought to be impressed. "Is it serious, you and him?"

Melissa had sighed. "We haven't known each other long enough to be serious. But he's gorgeous and sweet, and the sex is fabulous. And look at my hair. He's a magician."

Jill had shaken the excess water from her hands and reached for a dishtowel to dry them. "Is the sex so fabulous you'd still want to be sleeping with him when you were sixty-four?"

"My body's going to be disgusting by then," Melissa had moaned.

Jill had inspected her sister's figure. Not a perfect ten, but at least an eight. Maybe a nine. She'd inherited their mother's round hips and sloping shoulders, which some men loved. Jill used to despise her own physique, which she believed resembled a tootsie-roll more than an hourglass. After two pregnancies, though, she'd decided to be grateful she weighed only five pounds more than she had when she'd met Gordon. There were things in life worth stressing over—like your parents' marital woes, or your daughter's bat mitzvah, or whether writing catalogue copy was *really* a job—and things not worth worrying about—like whether your shoulders were too square or whether you weighed five pounds more than you used to.

Of course, once she quit Diet Coke, she'd probably gain more weight. Unless she drank only water.

"I always thought you'd wind up with a fellow lawyer," she'd told Melissa as she'd lifted the dishwasher door and clicked it shut.

"Ugh. Lawyers are boring." Melissa had wrinkled her nose.

"You're not boring."

"I am. I worry about when Luc's finally going to realize how boring I am. I could never have a relationship with another lawyer. If we had a child, it might wind up inheriting boring lawyer genes from both of us. Like Tay-Sachs disease or something." She'd sighed and glanced toward the ceiling. "What's the point, anyway? I mean, you can be together for forty years and suddenly decide you're sick of each other. Maybe I should just skip the whole falling-in-love thing. I could have a baby through artificial insemination and the hell with marriage."

Jill hadn't known how to respond. Should she lecture Melissa on how much work a child was—and double the work if you didn't have a husband to share it with? Nah. Even in these enlightened times, most husbands didn't come close to shouldering a full half of the childcare burden. They changed a diaper and spent the rest of the day boasting about how helpful they were. They coached the kids' soccer teams but left their wives to oversee the kids' baths and take them shopping for shoes and check their homework.

Instead, she'd said, "Do you think Mom and Dad still love each other?"

"Can you love someone if you're sick of him?"

Jill had thought for a minute before answering. "Probably."

She wasn't sick of Gordon. He was sweet and smart and adorably dense, and he'd even taken Noah shopping for shoes once. The two of them had come home beaming over their purchase of a one-hundred-nineteen-dollar pair of sneakers that Noah had outgrown in less than three months.

She wanted to believe she would still be not sick of him in thirty years, but right now the sex thing just wasn't working for her. "I'm sorry, Gord," she said, gently nudging his hand away from her breast. "I have to pee."

When she returned to the bedroom, Gordon was sprawled out on his back, his tousled hair circling his face like a wavy brown halo. He wore it too long, but Jill liked it that way. So did his students, a few of whom got crushes on him every year. Not because he was gorgeous. Not because, like Melissa's new friend, he was fashion-spread handsome and polished to a glossy sheen. But he was tall and lanky and had a warm, genuine smile that made him approachable.

Jill had never been drawn to the best-looking guy in the room. She'd fallen for Gordon because, not in spite, of his long nose and chronically messy hair. In her experience, perfect-looking guys were always either dull or egotistical or, well, hairdressers.

"Better?" he asked, sending her what he undoubtedly believed was a seductive smile as she rejoined him in bed.

"Emptier." She slid under the blanket, cuddled up to him and rested her head on his naked shoulder. It was bony, not very comfortable, but she thought it best to behave affectionately while she told him he wasn't going to get lucky tonight. "I'm sorry, Gord."

She didn't have to elaborate. He knew. He twined his fingers through her hair and said nothing.

She ran her hand down to his crotch. He was still raring to go, and she gave his erection a wifely stroke. "How about a cheap thrill?" she offered.

He nudged her hand away. "That's all right," he said.

He was so good-natured. So accepting. She simply couldn't imagine walking out on him, even if he did leave globs of toothpaste in the sink. "I can't stop thinking about my parents," she explained.

"Now there's a real turn-off."

"I know."

"Your parents," he said, stroking the nape of her neck and lulling the caffeine jitters out of her, "are nuts."

"I know."

"But they probably don't pose a danger to others. So let them be, Jill. Don't try to fix things for them."

He might as well tell her to stop breathing. She was a Good Daughter. When her parents were troubled and in pain—and she was convinced they were—it was her responsibility to make things better. "If I wait for them to come to their senses, it might never happen."

"So they'll be senseless. It's not the end of the world."

Easy for him to say. His parents were happily married. Tall and raw-boned like him, they were partners in an insurance agency in suburban Maryland, spending all day together in their office and all night together at home, and they never seemed to get sick of each other. But who knew? Maybe next week, they'd be the ones announcing the end of their long, stable marriage.

"It's not something I can shrug off," she explained. "I can't just say, 'They're nuts,' and forget about it. I love them."

"They drive you crazy. You tell me all the time that they do."

"I don't tell you all the time."

"Your mother calls you when you're trying to work, and she asks if you have a free moment, and you tell her no, and she keeps on talking anyway," Gordon reminded her.

She couldn't deny it. Her mother did do that a lot, and she complained to Gordon about it whenever it occurred.

"Your parents always want you to solve their problems for them. How much should they give to their synagogue this year? Should they buy the sofa they fell in love with at list price or drive out to the discount furniture place in Gardner and see if they can find something cheaper? Should your father add that new young hotshot from Johns Hopkins to his practice? All this stuff that's not even your business, and they're asking you for advice. Well, this separation is their disaster, Jill. Not yours. Let them deal with it."

He was right. He was absolutely right. Except. "My sister is heartbroken."

"Your sister is fucking her brains out with her hairdresser." He sounded a little envious.

"But she's still heartbroken. And Doug. He's shaken by the whole thing. I know him. I know when he's upset, and he was really upset when he left the house today."

"You're upset, too. Big deal. Leave it alone, Jill. Don't try to fix it."

She could have written off his brusque words as a result of frustration about the fact that he and Jill weren't fucking their brains out like Melissa and Luc. Or she could have accepted them as sound counsel.

Instead, she rolled away from him, settled her head into her own pillow, which was much softer and more malleable than Gordon's shoulder, and closed her eyes. And thought about the toothpaste mess he'd left in the sink.

Chapter Eight

Richard ate his sandwich in the den. The kitchen was too empty to eat in; the drone of the refrigerator motor sounded like an inflamed bumblebee. The dining room, forget it. Too grand and formal. The table was long and imposing, its glossy mahogany surface now filmed with a thin layer of dust, and the chairs surrounding it had stiff, straight backs and damask seat cushions no thicker than a slice of rye. The chandelier scattered the light in all directions, making it impossible to see what you were eating. And Ruth never put anything on the table without first covering it with pads that were felt on one side and waterproof plastic on the other, and then draping a tablecloth over the pads. Richard had no idea where she stored those pads. Or, for that matter, her tablecloths.

In the den, no pads, no refrigerator motor, no formality. He could sit on the leather couch, legs kicked up onto the coffee table and a plate balanced on his knees, and watch TV while he ate. And he could channel-surf all he wanted. Unfortunately, he needed both hands to hold his sandwich, a six-inch-long torpedo roll stuffed so full that shreds of lettuce and blobs of mayonnaise kept leaking out of it. If channel-surfing was necessary, he'd have to push the channel button with his chin or else put down his sandwich. Neither option appealed to him, but he'd still rather eat in the den than the kitchen or the dining room.

Besides lettuce and mayo, the torpedo roll was crammed with turkey, tomato slices, thin, rippling circles of sweet pickle and a couple of slabs of provolone. He'd purchased it at a deli just down the block from Beth Israel Deaconess. Last night he'd brought home two large rectangles of Sicilian pizza topped with pepperoni from a pizzeria five minutes away from the house, and the oil, cheese and sausage were enough to short-circuit an EKG. The night before, he'd opened one of the cans of soup Ruth had left behind—low sodium, he was pleased to note, although it still tasted damned salty to him. The turkey in his sandwich tasted salty, too. God knew what eating like this was doing to his health.

On the television, a blowhard pontificated about corrupt

politicians. *So, what's new?* he wanted to say, but there was no one around to say it to.

She'd been gone one week. Seven bleary, dreary days. Richard couldn't live on pizza and sandwiches and cans of soup for the rest of his life. Maybe he should hire a housekeeper, someone to dust the dining room table, vacuum, wipe down the counters, scrub the bathroom sinks and have a hot meal waiting for him when he got home. How much would someone like that cost?

A sharp pang seized his chest. Not a heart attack. He was a cardiologist, he knew heart attacks. Nor was this indigestion, although the turkey seemed a little greasy along with the salt.

This pain was emotion. It was the sort of throbbing ache a man felt when his wife walked out on him and he found himself calculating in dollars and cents how much it would cost to hire someone to replace her.

How much had Ruth cost? She'd been his partner. His wife. She'd dusted, vacuumed, wiped the counters, cleaned the sinks and had a hot meal waiting for him at the end of the day. Had she felt like a housekeeper? Should he have given her a raise? Diamond earrings weren't enough?

Damn it—a marriage was supposed to be about compromise. You give a little, you take a little. You meet each other halfway. But Richard couldn't see the compromise in his current situation. She wanted a change. He didn't want a change. She got exactly what she wanted: a change. He got exactly what he didn't want: a change. He'd given and she'd taken. It wasn't fair.

His appetite gone, he set the sandwich down and sank back into the sofa cushions. After licking his fingers clean, he thumbed the channel button on the remote. *Click*: a weather report. *Click*: gales of laughter from a sit-com rerun. *Click*: a view of an ancient desert city, accompanied by the ponderous voice of a public-television narrator explaining the Israeli-Palestinian conflict, as if such an explanation existed. *Click*: a woman dancing around a kitchen with a mop in time to a bouncy rock tune.

So many rock musicians sold out, he fumed. Back when he was in medical school, too busy with his studies to storm the ramparts, he'd counted on rock stars to fight authority and overturn the government on his behalf. *There's something happening here. All you need is love. Come on, people now. I can't get no.* He'd expected musicians to end the war—thank God as a medical student he'd received a deferment and hadn't wound up in

Vietnam. He'd expected rock stars to end hypocrisy, undermine authority, overturn the social structure. He'd expected them to serenade a new era of love. Free love. Peace and flowers.

Nowadays, rock stars sold mops.

With a few more clicks, he located a Red Sox pre-game show. He tossed the remote onto the coffee table next to his sandwich and lifted the bottle of beer he'd taken for himself. Ruth would give him hell for drinking beer straight from the bottle during a meal. *You don't like my table manners?* he silently asked his absent wife. *Come home and I'll eat like a mensch, with a fork and a knife and a napkin in my lap. If you're not coming home, you lose the right to nag.*

One entire week. Some days he felt nothing but sorry for himself. Some days he felt nothing but angry. Today he felt defiant. *Shut up, Ruth. You're not here. I can drink my beer any damned way I want.*

The cashier at the deli had flirted with him. He always acted friendly toward her when he stopped in for a coffee-to-go on his way to work, or for a bagel with a schmear if he had time for a quick lunch. He hadn't expected to find her at her register in the evening—did she work all day? Did she own the place? An owner didn't run the register, did she? Anyway, this woman looked too young to own a thriving business.

Not that she was a kid. Late twenties, maybe—he could guess the age of a naked patient, but not a fully clothed cashier. With her soft face, wide cheekbones, dark eyes and olive complexion, she probably had some Latina blood in her arteries.

"Hello, doctor," she'd greeted him today. "Kind of late for you to be stopping by, isn't it?"

"I'm just grabbing some dinner to take home. My wife . . ." What? What should he say? Who was this girl that he should be telling her his marriage was on the rocks? "My wife is out of town."

"You ought to spend the evening with your buddies, then," she said. "When your wife's away, you should enjoy a night on the town with the boys."

What boys? he wondered. Doug was his only boy, and he'd undoubtedly arrived at his own house an hour ago. He kept banker's hours, tweaking the eyes of the vain. And unlike Richard, Doug had a wife waiting at home for him. A lovely girl, Brooke, and she made his son happy. Doug had Brooke, a clean house, a hot meal. He had love waiting for him at home.

Nothing was waiting for Richard. "It's a weeknight," he told the smiling cashier. "How can I go out on the town? I've got work in the morning."

"Well, then, I guess you're stuck with the sandwich. Next time your wife is out of town, you ought to make a plan with a friend. A man like you shouldn't have to eat dinner alone."

How right she was.

He leaned over his knees to put down his beer and pick up his sandwich. He still felt defiant and exceedingly pissed off, but thinking about the cashier caused him to smile. If he could find himself married to a cashier at First-Rate, which apparently was what Ruth was these days, then why shouldn't he flirt with a cashier at the Longwood Deli?

Tomorrow, he'd get another sandwich. Something other than this greasy turkey. Maybe they had a nice brisket. And he'd ask for a dill cut into spears, not sugary pickle slices that resembled soggy, green ridged potato chips. And when he paid, he'd chat with the cashier for a minute or two.

It wasn't dating. Regardless of Doug's insinuations, Richard didn't want to date.

But a man like him definitely shouldn't eat dinner alone.

All you need is love, he thought, settling back into the upholstery and listening to the sportscaster announce the Sox line-up.

Chapter Nine

Ruth adjusted the waist ties of her First-Rate pinafore and scrutinized her reflection in the bathroom mirror. It was the only mirror in the apartment, other than the shiny surface of the wall oven, which provided a ghostly impression of her appearance from her shoulders to her knees. The bathroom mirror reflected her from the chest up. She'd just have to trust her own eyes in judging how her shins and ankles looked.

The lip of the porcelain sink dug into her belly as she leaned in toward the mirror to get a closer view of her face. Not bad, she decided. Foundation couldn't hide the faint lines that laced the outer edges of her eyes and crimped her upper lip, but she wasn't one of those women who got "work" done, as they euphemistically put it. Her friend Myrna had undergone an eye lift a few years ago, and Ruth hadn't even noticed. All that pain, the expense, the exposure to possible infection, and the procedure had left Myrna looking like the sixty-year-old woman she was.

And Lenore from the B'nai Torah Sisterhood received regular injections of Botox. The thought of injecting poison into her forehead made Ruth ill. Moisturizers, sure. A little foundation, why not? But *work*? Not for Ruth.

Not even now, when she was practically single.

She certainly felt single whenever she wandered through her apartment. Sure, it was small, but to her it was a palace. She'd lived there a week and hadn't once felt claustrophobic. She hardly even noticed the rancid-taffy color of the carpet anymore. Her platform bed was like a private island when she lay in it—at the very center of the mattress, which would get rotated only if and when *she* decided to rotate it—and she'd managed to fit her sweaters and pajamas into the drawers underneath.

She'd purchased a futon couch for the living room, in case she ever had an overnight guest, and it wasn't the most comfortable seating in the universe, but no matter. She'd also bought a recliner so she didn't have to sit on the futon if she didn't want to. She'd taken the little TV from the kitchen at the house, and Doug's old stereo system, which had been sitting on a shelf in his bedroom since he'd left home for college twenty years ago. The house he lived in now was wired for sound, with camouflaged speakers in most of the rooms and, hidden in a closet off the family room, a control panel that resembled the cockpit of a space shuttle. He didn't need his old receiver and CD player and the three-inch speakers anymore.

So she'd brought them with her when she moved to the apartment. And she'd brought her beloved Corelli CD's and all her other classical music. Last night over dinner—a can of tuna and a sliced tomato, a meal Richard would never have considered a real dinner but she'd found perfectly adequate—she'd listened to Corelli's Concerto Grosso in B-flat major. She'd written her senior thesis on Corelli's use of suspended seconds, the tension of two adjacent notes sounding at the same time and the catharsis the listener felt when the suspended second resolved and the tension eased. Richard found Corelli boring and he didn't understand what a suspended second was even after she'd explained it to him a million times, starting when they'd still been in college. Because he didn't care for classical music, she'd listened to pathetically little Corelli for the past forty-two years.

From here on in, she was going to listen to as much Corelli as she wanted. And all her other favorites: Handel, Bach, Vivaldi and Mendelsohn, who composed later than the Baroque period but was her favorite of the Classicals. Her breakfast that morning—a soft-boiled egg broken over a piece of toast so it was sort of like French toast, but not really—had been accompanied by a Scarlatti piano sonata. Scarlatti wasn't big on suspended seconds, but his music still filled her with joy.

She felt as excited today as she used to feel as a child on the first day of school. Back then, her mother would have prepared her egg and toast for her, and smoothed the collar of an outfit that was brand-new because it had been purchased in August just for school. Her mother would have scrutinized the weather through the window above the deep-basin sink—"overcast but not raining," she'd announce, "maybe you should wear galoshes, just in case"—and remind Ruth to brush her teeth. She would have braided Ruth's hair tight enough to stretch her scalp, and packed a sandwich, an apple, a chocolate chip cookie and a nickel for milk into a crisp brown paper bag for her. Isaac always got two cookies in his lunch bag, but Ruth was given only one. "He's a boy, he needs to eat more," her mother would say. "You're a girl, you've got to watch your figure." When Ruth was eight years old, she didn't have a figure, but her mother had ordered her to watch it, anyway.

Into her sixties, Ruth's figure had started to resemble that non-figure she'd had at eight. Her waistline had thickened, diminishing her curves, and her breasts, never big to begin with, had shrunken and grown wrinkly like deflated balloons. Thank you, menopause.

But if she wanted to eat two cookies, she would. She was single. She was free. She could eat as many damned cookies as she liked.

She left the bathroom, checked to make sure the laces of her sneakers were double-knotted, grabbed her purse and paused in the entry to don her fall-weight jacket. Her apron hung below the jacket's bottom hem, but she wasn't going to wear a long coat just to hide it. Maybe tomorrow she'd wait until she'd crossed the street and entered the First-Rate store before putting on the apron.

Having lived only a week in the new apartment, she still felt strange when she left it. The hallway smelled of lemon. Her apartment door clanked when she shut it; unlike the pretty oak front door with the leaded glass window in it at home, this door was metal. And it felt weird to exit her home and still find herself inside. She'd bought an inexpensive rubber welcome mat and laid it in front of her door. If anyone visited her here—and she was sure she'd have visitors eventually—she wanted them to feel welcome. Wiping off their feet before they entered her apartment wouldn't be such a bad idea, either.

In time this place would feel like home, she promised herself. If it didn't, she'd move somewhere else. She could do that. She was free. She could do whatever she wanted.

Amazing to think that what she wanted right now was to leave the building, stroll across the parking lot and down the sidewalk to the corner, wait for a red light to halt the flow of traffic, cross to the other side and march through the mini-mall's parking lot to the First-Rate store. She could think of nothing, not even spending time with her grandchildren, that she wanted to do as much as that.

Francine Thorpe, the First-Rate manager who'd hired Ruth, had told her to show up fifteen minutes early for her shift, which would begin at 8:30 a.m. She entered the store twenty-five minutes early. Years, decades, might have passed since she last had a paying job, but she knew nobody ever lost points by showing up early for work.

She was used to shopping at a First-Rate closer to the house, but this First-Rate appeared almost identical to the First-Rate she knew. It had bluish fluorescent ceiling lights and a dry, almost minty smell. Cosmetics, hair products, "feminine products" and the like to the right. Books, wrapping paper, stationery and greeting cards toward the back.

Seasonal wares at the center of the store—as Ruth surveyed the store from the doorway, she saw it was set up for Halloween, the center shelves filled with jumbo bags of miniature candies, stacks of cone-shaped black witches' hats and orange plastic trick-or-treat buckets that were obviously supposed to resemble pumpkins but didn't really. Further left, small housewares. Along the far left wall, snack foods and refrigerator cases filled with milk, orange juice and ice-cream novelties. Way in the rear, the prescriptions counter. Anyone who came into the store to get a prescription filled would have to walk past shelves filled with all kinds of merchandise, tempting the customer to pick up, to buy.

Ruth crossed to the staff door at the rear of the store and pressed the buzzer to be admitted. Francine Thorpe's office was located behind that door. Ruth had seen it the day she'd been hired.

The staff door was opened by a skinny young man with hair twisted into thick strands—what was that style called? She was sure she'd heard Abbie call it…what? Deadlocks? Deadbolts? The style looked better on black boys than white boys, and this boy was white. His head looked like the business end of a dry mop. A metal rivet adorned his left eyebrow, and his cheeks bore faint traces of acne scarring.

He greeted her with a squinty scowl, but his face relaxed a little when he noticed her red apron. He was wearing a red First-Rate apron himself.

"I'm new here," she said, struggling not to stare at that piece of metal skewering his eyebrow. Why would a nice young man mutilate himself like that? At least he hadn't pierced his nose or lip. God help him if he had a pierced tongue. She'd read an article about tongue-piercing a few years ago. Terribly unsanitary. And wouldn't it affect eating? Wouldn't the metal conduct the cold if you were eating ice-cream? You might wind up with frostbite inside your mouth.

He was still staring at her, so she added, "This is my first day. I'm a little early." *I sound like an idiot. Or maybe like I think I'm talking to an idiot. Take your pick.*

He stared at her apron for another few seconds, then opened the door wide enough to let her in. "I guess you need to talk to Francine," he said.

"I guess I do."

"Okay," he said, as warm an invitation as she could hope for.

Francine had given Ruth a hasty tour of the employees-only area of the store the day she'd been hired, and she remembered it all: the floor-to-ceiling metal shelving crammed with inventory, the painted concrete floor, the lavatory, the staff room, and finally Francine's office. The mop-headed young man tapped on the door and nudged it open. "Francine?"

Burnt coffee fumes wafted from the small, windowless office. Ruth figured her boss was drinking either French roast or else coffee that had sat in a carafe on a hot plate for days, condensing until it had reached the consistency of melted asphalt. Francine stood behind her desk, dressed in a long-sleeved red smock—were sleeves a symbol of superiority, like a general's stars?—gripping a cup nearly big enough to hold a family of four in that Disney World mad-tea-party ride. Francine's skin was the color of root beer and her hair was pulled severely back from her face and held in a flat barrette at the nape of her neck. Most of the hair was straight, but stray strands that had escaped the barrette fuzzed in tiny curls. Ruth wasn't sure how old Francine was, but she was clearly younger than Ruth. Taller, too. And not given to smiling, at least this early in the morning.

"I thought you were starting yesterday," she said to Ruth.

"No. Today," Ruth said as calmly as she could. She hadn't screwed up her first day. She was positive. She'd marked the starting date in bright red ink in her little pocket-size date book, which she'd bought at the First-Rate near the house last December. She'd marked it on the wall calendar she'd hung in the kitchen, as well: *FIRST DAY AT FIRST-RATE.* Also in red ink.

Francine gulped some coffee. Ruth realized that if she'd been scheduled to start yesterday, Francine would have telephoned her when she didn't show up. She'd gotten a land-line installed in her apartment the same day her platform bed had been delivered, and she'd supplied Francine with that number as well as her cell phone number.

Phones or no phones, this was not a mistake Ruth would make. After raising three children, she knew how to organize things so everyone got where they were supposed to be when they were supposed to be there.

Francine seemed dubious, but she put down her cup, yanked open a drawer on one of the four-drawer metal file cabinets that consumed nearly half the office's space, and pulled out a folder. "All right," she said, as if her accusation had been some sort of test and Ruth had passed. "Here's your staff ID card." She handed Ruth a laminated card which had Ruth's name printed in block letters on one side and a magnetic strip on the other. "Wade will show you the time clock in the staff room. You can leave your coat and purse in a locker there. Did you bring a combination lock?"

Ruth shook her head.

"You can buy one in the store. Five-seventy-nine less the employee discount. Go buy one, and then you can clock in and lock your things up. Wade will show you what to do. Wade—" Francine shifted her gaze to the mop-head "—show her what to do."

He nodded and led Ruth out of the room, then beckoned her to accompany him into the staff room, a stark, well-lit cubicle with two round Formica-topped tables surrounded by molded plastic chairs, a sink, a coffee maker which was apparently the source of the burnt coffee, judging by the smell, a mini-fridge and a row of lockers lining the far wall. Near the door was a compact machine, its screen displaying the time digitally. "Swipe your card," he whispered. "Clock in."

"But Francine said—"

"Swipe it. The first thing you do when you get here is clock in. You're on her time, not yours, even if you're buying a fucking combination lock. Excuse me," he added, flashing her a sheepish smile. She caught a glimpse of his tongue, and it didn't seem to have any metal attached to it. "You want to get paid for every minute you're here."

"Okay," she said warily. He was right—she did want to get paid, and she was on the store's time. She didn't want to get in trouble, though. She hadn't totally recovered from Francine's accusation that she was supposed to have started yesterday, and now she was being urged by this boy young enough to be her grandson to disobey her boss.

Francine had put him in charge. He was showing Ruth what to do. If worse came to worst, Ruth could always say she was simply following his instructions.

She swiped her card.

He grinned. "Ka-ching."

"I'm Ruth Bendel, by the way," she said, extending her hand.

He shook it. His fingers were long and thin. A pianist's fingers, she thought. She wondered if he played. Boys with pierced eyebrows didn't play the piano, did they? Maybe they played rock. Not Rachmaninoff, though. "Wade Smith," he introduced himself.

Wade Smith? What kind of name was that? Wade was odd enough, but *Smith*? She had never met anyone named Smith in her life. She'd always assumed Smith was the ultimate pseudonym, the false name adulterers used at sleazy motels, or possibly the name some idiot at Ellis Island might have attached to an immigrant at the turn of the last century, when he couldn't deal with the immigrant's Slavic name that was spelled with only consonants. Smith was such a common name, nobody had it.

Wade Smith apparently did, unless he was an adulterer. He didn't look like one. Who'd cheat on her husband with a guy with hardware poking through his face like Frankenstein's monster?

She shouldn't think poorly of him. Thanks to him, she was clocked in and ka-chinging. Thanks to him, a minute later, she was standing in front of a rack of combination locks in the housewares section, and a minute after that she was at the front counter, paying for it, presenting her employee card at Wade's urging so she could receive her ten-percent employee discount. Fifty-eight cents was fifty-eight cents. And since she was now supporting herself, she had to watch every penny.

"Always keep your employee card with you," Wade said once they were back in the staff room and Ruth had her coat and purse stored safely inside a locker. She'd been about to slip the card inside her purse before setting it on the locker shelf, but he'd stopped her in time. "The card opens the staff door so you don't have to buzz in. And if you want to pick up something, like for lunch, you need your card to get the discount."

The food First-Rate sold didn't qualify as lunch in Ruth's mind. Chips, pretzels, cookies, soda, mixed nuts that looked like mostly peanuts . . . The most nutritious edible they sold was processed American cheese. She'd figured that if she had enough time, she'd buy lunch at the sandwich shop three stores down, and if she didn't she'd skip lunch and make up for it at dinner.

She didn't want to be a snob, though. If all the other employees ate First-Rate junk food for lunch, she'd do her best to fit in. Maybe she could buy a cup of yogurt and some crackers. Or she could bring her own lunch in a brown bag, just like when she was a schoolgirl, only with two cookies.

"Today you'll just do stock," Wade informed her. "By next week Francine'll have you doing check-out. But everyone starts with stock."

"Is that how you started?" Ruth asked, once again following him out of the staff room. "You must be, what, the assistant manager?"

"Who, me?" Wade snorted.

"Well, since you were assigned to train me—"

"Until this morning, I was the most recent hire," he said. "Now you're the most recent hire."

So training the new arrival was a task for the staff member with the least seniority. Ruth wondered how long she'd be working here before she'd be responsible for training the next new hire. She liked the idea that she'd soon know enough about First-Rate to train another rookie.

"With stock," Wade explained, "what you do is wander up and down the aisles, and when you see we're out of something or running low, you come back here—" he gestured toward the shelves of inventory "—and ask Frank or Carlo to get it for you. They're the stock guys, and they're . . ." He peered around for a minute, then wandered around one of the shelves and spotted an open door leading to another parking lot outside, behind the store. "Yeah. They're unloading a truck right now. But, okay, so you ask them to get you the athlete's foot ointment or the toothpicks or whatever. By the end of the week you'll know where all the stuff is on these shelves, but Frank and Carlo flip out if anyone touches their precious inventory without their permission. Trust me—you don't want to get on their bad side. They're, like, nuts."

Ruth nodded. Nuts she could handle. The world was filled with nuts.

"So Frank gets you the toothpicks or the candy corn or whatever, and you bring it out on one of these trucks." He pointed to a couple of wheeled carts parked near the door into the store. "The trick is, you don't want to go back and forth a million times, so you do a few aisles and then come back and get a bunch of stuff at once. Or if you don't have anything going on in the store, you come back here and find a truck already full of stuff—" he gestured toward one of the carts, which was stacked with bottles of vitamins, calcium supplements, and assorted other nutritional pills "—and you wheel it out into the store and restock the shelves."

The weird hair and eyebrow hardware notwithstanding, Wade seemed like a nice boy. If only he were a little older and better groomed, and had a better job and a more believable last name than Smith and no metal puncturing his face, she could introduce him to Melissa. A sales clerk at a convenience store didn't exactly sound like someone on the fast track, but Ruth was a sales clerk at a convenience store, and she was a fine person. And that guy Melissa had brought to Massachusetts with her last week, Lucas Brondo, was a beautician, which in Ruth's estimation wasn't that many rungs above a convenience store clerk. Even if he was a Manhattan beautician. Even if he was a good-looking Manhattan beautician who'd worked wonders on Melissa's hair.

A First-Rate clerk could buy Melissa all kinds of hair gels and mousses and conditioners and use his employee discount. Manhattan beauticians weren't the only route to pretty hair.

Not that Wade Smith was the boy for Melissa. He was too young. Too scruffy. And she'd bet good ka-ching that he didn't play the piano. A waste of those long, graceful fingers.

"So, let's do this truck," Wade said, pushing the cart with the nutritional supplements out into the store. Ruth trailed behind him. En route to the pharmacy corner of the store, he introduced her to several clerks whose names blurred and blended together. One had a Spanish-sounding name—Rosita or Rosalita or something—and one reminded Ruth of a gym teacher Jill and Melissa had had at high school. The pharmacist looked like something out of a magazine ad, youthful and clean-scrubbed and smiling as if to say, "I can sell you great drugs," which was pretty much what he did.

One clerk was a man past retirement age, balding and short, with bits of white hair growing out of his ears like lint, and thick-lensed bifocals, the top halves of which magnified his eyes in a creepy kind of way. Ruth hoped he wouldn't decide they should be friends because she was closer in age to him than to the rest of the staff. Everyone else appeared on the young side of forty.

Maybe they weren't so young. Maybe they just looked good because they gobbled vast quantities of the pills on the cart she was pushing. Ginseng. Echinacea. St. John's Wort. Ginkgo Biloba. So many products, and Ruth had no idea what any of them were used for. She hoped a customer wouldn't ask her. What could she say to someone who approached her in her official-looking apron and inquired about what to take for a failing memory? Ruth would have to answer, "I don't remember. My memory's going, too."

The hell with all these herbal things, these mysterious elixirs and their miraculous promises, she thought as she surveyed the contents of the cart. She'd stick with her plain, old-fashioned multivitamin. A multivitamin and homemade chicken soup could cure just about anything, as far as she was concerned.

Wade set her up in the aisle near the pharmacy and told her to replenish the supplies of pills. "Put the newer bottles in back and pull the older bottles forward so we can sell the older bottles first," he instructed her.

She suppressed a smile. Whenever she shopped, she always checked the expiration dates of the items stashed in the rear on the shelves. For the same sixteen-ninety-nine—geez, the black cohosh was expensive, so much money for such a small bottle—why should she buy an old, stale item from the front of the shelf if a more recent, fresher item lurked behind it?

He watched her place a couple of bottles of garlic extract on the shelf, then backed up a step, and another step, as if he wanted to leave but was hesitant to take his eyes off her.

"I can handle this," she said, hoping she didn't sound overconfident. She *could* handle it. For decades, she'd been unloading bags of groceries and organizing the cans of pureed tomato and boxes of corn flakes inside her cabinets. She knew how to put things on a shelf.

Wade nodded, tucked a clump of stringy hair behind his ear and shuffled off, calling over his shoulder, "Find me if you need anything."

Abruptly she discovered herself alone in the nutritional supplements aisle. What if she did need something? What if she couldn't find him? Was she really ready to fly solo?

For God's sake. Of course she was. She was a competent woman. She'd purchased a platform bed and a futon couch without any input from Richard. She'd bought a coffee maker, read the instruction manual and set the clock and timer up, all by herself. She'd been living alone for a week and hadn't discovered anything she couldn't handle.

It took her only a couple of minutes to find the area on the shelf for flaxseed oil gel caps. She pulled out the older bottles and started loading the new bottles at the back. A rumbling voice reached her from behind: "The pills are easy. Wait 'til you've got to do the beach toys. Bend, stretch, bend, stretch—it's like an aerobics workout."

She turned to find the short, balding man standing behind her. What was his name? Barney? Harvey? Five minutes ago she'd been introduced to him and she couldn't remember. She ought to take some of that cohosh stuff, or the ginko biloba.

Smiling politely, she said, "I guess they're starting me slowly. They'll get to the aerobics my second day."

"Beach toys are gone for the season, anyway. The Halloween stuff is out, and the day after Halloween, we'll have to pull whatever is left and set up the Christmas stuff."

"No Thanksgiving merchandise?"

"Oh, yeah, some. Not much. That area is for toys. We sell lots of Halloween paraphernalia, lots of stocking stuffers, but what kind of toys would you sell for Thanksgiving?"

"Stuffed turkeys?" she joked.

He laughed.

His smile pleased her. She tried to remember the last time she'd become friends with someone new and came up empty. The same old friends, ladies from the neighborhood, from the B'nai Torah Sisterhood, from her volunteer work, from the tennis club she'd joined because Richard had wanted her to get exercise, even though she was the world's worst tennis player . . . Friends she knew as Richard's wife. This man, like Wade and Rosita and the others, belonged to her alone. They were *her* friends—or they would be, if she decided she liked them and they decided they liked her. They would befriend her as Ruth, not as someone's wife or mother or grandmother.

"I'm sorry," she said, realizing this was not a good way to start a friendship. "I don't remember your name."

"Bernie," he said. "Bernard O'Hara to the police and the tax man, Bernie to everyone else. And you're Ruth, right?"

"That's right."

"You retired?" he asked, gathering a handful of bottles labeled Calcium Citrate and carrying them to the calcium area of the shelf.

"Retired?" She remained busy with the flaxseed. "No. I just started working here."

"I meant, retired from another job. Like me. The accounting firm I worked at had a mandatory retirement age, but I wasn't done yet. I wasn't ready to get sent out to pasture. Not me, no sir. I worked for a year as a bagger at the Stop & Shop up the street but hated it. So I came here. First-Rate is much better."

"What did you hate about Stop & Shop?" she asked, surprised to find herself genuinely curious.

"All that food. All that gluttony. You'd see a young mother buying candy and soda and sugary cereals for her toddlers and want to lecture her. Or someone using food stamps to buy potato chips. It drove me crazy. Besides, bagging is dreary work. Here you get to do a little bit of this, a little bit of that. And what a great group of people you get to work with."

Yes. New friends, Ruth thought. She wasn't going to have time to see her old friends now that she was working full time. No more luncheons. No more kaffeeklatches that were supposed to focus on fundraising for the synagogue but instead were mostly just excuses to gossip: *Did you hear about Edna's father, with the Alzheimer's? They found him in his underwear Sunday morning, walking along the shoulder of the Mass Pike. And Marsha's granddaughter, the bassoonist? She got accepted into the New England Conservatory's after-school program. And that rumor I heard about Lillian and Al getting a divorce? True.*

Now Ruth's old friends were probably having kaffeeklatches and whispering about her and Richard, saying, *True.*

"I guess I am retired," she said as she straightened out the Vitamin C. All the bottles were white, their labels featuring a large red C. When she lined them up evenly, all the C's extended across the bottles like links in a chain. "I'm retired from being a housewife. It was time to try something new."

Bernie laughed. "Tell that to my wife. She's the one who pushed me into finding a new job when the accounting firm handed me my gold watch. My pension pays for our expenses and First-Rate pays for our vacations. Last year we went on a Caribbean cruise."

"How lovely." Ruth had never been on a cruise, but some of her old friends went on cruises almost every year. Myrna had celebrated her eye lift with a cruise to the islands, and she came home eight pounds heavier. So much for the beautifying effects of the plastic surgery. She said she and Morty spent the entire six days eating and drinking and gambling in the ship's casino—"Oh, and we visited Nassau and St. Thomas and shopped like maniacs," she'd added. It was wonderful, she'd insisted. She would do it again in an instant.

Ruth had asked Richard if he'd like to go on a cruise and he'd said he'd rather rent a place on Sanibel Island for a week in the winter. They'd gone, eaten sensibly, he'd played golf and she'd sat in the shade of a cabana on the beach and read three novels. No gambling, no fancy evening wear, no maniacal shopping. Maybe it wasn't glamorous, maybe it wasn't adventurous, but they'd had a good time.

They could go again this winter, she thought. They could pay for it with her earnings. She'd wag the airline tickets in front of Richard's face and say, "This trip's on me."

No, she couldn't do that. They were separated. And she couldn't really see the point of going to Sanibel Island without him.

Not this winter but next. She could save as much as possible and then treat the twins to Walt Disney World. Or Noah and Abbie, although Abbie would probably think she was too old for Mickey Mouse and a ride in a teacup like Francine's.

But Madison and Mackenzie would be the perfect age for the Magic Kingdom. They'd love the rides and the Mickey-Mouse shaped ice-cream pops. They'd get a room at one of the Disney hotels and have breakfast with Snow White. They'd spend a day at the water park. They'd stay up late and watch the fireworks.

And the best part was, Ruth could plan the trip without any input from Richard. She could do it all herself. She was flying solo.

Chapter Ten

"I'm sorry," said Gloria, sounding not the least bit sorry. "It's just a three-dollar-a-person increase."

"*Just* a three-dollar increase?" Jill fumed. "*Just?* We've got more than a hundred people on the invitation list." And if Jill and Gordon had let Abbie have her way, there would have been more than two hundred. Bar-mitzvah and bat-mitzvah receptions at her middle school were extravaganzas with extensive invitation lists.

One of Abbie's classmates had invited the entire seventh grade to his bar mitzvah a couple of weeks ago—two hundred-seventy-eight kids running amok for four hours at the Westin Hotel in downtown Boston. According to Abbie, at least half of them didn't even like Toby Klotzenberg, the bar mitzvah boy. Abbie had reported that she, Caitlin and Emma Tovick had grown bored with the party—the DJ had been obnoxious, and the boys had taken to sticking pencils up their noses and competing in belching contests while most of the girls holed up in the bathroom and experimented with one another's lipstick—so Abbie and her friends had wandered down the hall to a wedding reception with better music and excellent pastries, where they'd remained unnoticed for an hour and left ten minutes before Emma's mother was scheduled to pick them up.

A reception at a downtown Boston luxury hotel for the entire seventh grade wasn't in Abbie's future. Unlike Toby's father, who owned a chain of sneaker stores, Abbie's father was a high school English teacher and her mother brought in a little spare change writing enticing descriptions of things people didn't need for catalogues created to convince people they really did need those things. Just that morning, Jill had emailed some tankini text—"Make him wonder what's under this luscious suit! Removable cup pads give your bustline a rise; adjustable side ties lift the bottoms as high on your thighs as you dare to go"—to Sabrina Lopez at Velvet Moon. Sabrina was sure to love the assonance. Wonder, under. Rise, side, ties, high, thighs. Jill had found her groove.

The caffeine from the Diet Coke she'd guzzled—one and a half cans by the time she'd settled in front of her computer at the kitchen desk—had energized her that morning. It had slaked the thirst of her muse. How could she wean herself from the stuff when it helped her to assonate?

Swimsuit text finished and sent, she'd driven to the Old Rockford Inn, which she and Gordon had booked for Abbie's bat mitzvah reception. Gloria, the inn's events manager, had sent her an email mentioning that the inn had made a slight change in its catering menu.

Jill had assumed that "slight change" meant a few new appetizers or side dishes. She hadn't expected a price hike.

"We signed a contract," she reminded Gloria, deciding she didn't like the woman, who was too thin and whose face was the same shape as an olive, a perfect, shiny ellipse. She was irked by Gloria's phony smile and the burgundy polish on her nails, which were also olive-shaped. She even disliked Gloria's title: events manager. It sounded athletic, as if she were a gym teacher who coordinated the beanbag throw and the three-legged race at Noah's school's annual Carnival Day.

Abbie's bat mitzvah wasn't an event. It was an *affair*. One of Jill's mother's favorite jokes, repeated on the occasion of every family wedding or bar mitzvah, went: Mrs. Cohen runs into Mrs. Goldberg and says, "Sadie! I hear you're having an affair!" Mrs. Goldberg grins and says, "It's true. I am." Mrs. Cohen says, "So? Who's the caterer?"

"The contract includes a clause explaining that we may impose price adjustments on the food up to one month before the event's date." Gloria managed to recite this through her fake smile. She could be a ventriloquist. Her lips barely budged.

"Why? I mean, why are the prices going up, not why does your contract have a clause explaining that you can—" *rip me off*, Jill almost said. "Raise the prices." She scanned the updated menu. The offerings appeared to be exactly the same as what she and Gordon had seen when they'd signed the contract in August. Prime rib. Poached salmon. Dijon-crusted chicken breast. Steamed green beans, which Jill knew damn well would be boiled, not steamed, and no one would eat them anyway. Fresh fruit cup—which would be canned, not fresh. A salad of mixed greens, including but not limited to spinach, romaine, bibb lettuce, arugula, radicchio, cress and iceberg, depending on availability—tossed with a delicately herbed vinaigrette which, Jill was willing to bet, would not be delicate.

"Gas prices have gone up," Gloria responded to her question, still smiling.

"We're not serving our guests gasoline at this affair."

"Food has to be trucked in. We have to factor in the shipping costs."

Jill pressed her lips together to keep from shouting, "Bullshit." If she lost her temper, Gloria might tear up their contract and re-book the place for some other affair on their date, and then where would Abbie's reception be? Much as Jill wanted to pound Gloria's offensively tidy desk with her fist, she had to be a Good Mom.

"How about if you charge us the original amount per plate and provide us with a separate bill enumerating the shipping costs?" Jill asked, modulating her voice so she sounded utterly reasonable.

Gloria's smile was so brittle, Jill half expected it to crack and then shatter, spilling tooth and lip splinters across her desk. "We find it easier just to add a fuel surcharge to each plate."

"Easier for you," Jill said.

"Well . . . yes."

They'd reached an impasse. Either Jill could yield on the higher price or she could void the contract. And she couldn't do that to Abbie, who was already pissed that she'd been limited to inviting only forty of her best-friends-forever to the reception.

Good Mom, Jill cautioned herself. Good, but not a complete pushover. "I'll discuss the new rates with my husband," she said, folding the print-out of the menu Gloria had given her and tucking it into a pocket of her purse. She wouldn't commit to the new price yet. Let Gloria sweat for a few days before Jill got back to her.

She left the inn, resenting its charming clapboard façade, its sloping roof, the beautiful landscaping—sugar maple and oak foliage just reaching the peak of color, evergreen junipers and powder-puff-shaped white and rust chrysanthemums flanking the slate front walk and the perimeter of the parking lot. In the spring, when Abbie's affair would take place, the mums would be replaced by tulips and crocuses, and the azaleas and rhododendrons bordering the front porch would be in full bloom. It was a lovely facility, even if it treated its clients like shit.

"Shit," she said aloud. She was alone in the parking lot. She didn't have to be a Good Mom anymore.

She slumped into the driver's seat of her Subaru wagon and sighed. She couldn't phone Gordon; right now he was—she glanced at her watch—teaching his fifth-period class on Greek and Roman classics. He was probably explaining the Iliad to his students. Some girl was probably asking him whether Achilles really looked like Brad Pitt in the movie, and he was trying not to laugh.

Nor could she call her mother to complain. Jill didn't lean on her mother. She was the leanee, not the leaner. Her mother called her, sounded her out, asked her to solve problems, and Jill did.

Unfortunately, this problem didn't spark any ideas in her mind. She saw no logical solution. She knew there had to be one; she just couldn't imagine it. She felt exploited and resentful and upset. For once, she wanted to call her mother and lean. Maybe adding a fuel surtax to the catering bill had become a common practice. Maybe all her mother's friends in the B'nai Torah Sisterhood had been discussing this very subject at their last meeting, and someone was filing a class-action suit, and her mother could tell her how to become a member of the class.

But Jill couldn't phone her mother. Her mother was working as a clerk at First-Rate. Ruth Bendel wasn't a Good Mom.

Jill pulled out her cell phone and punched in Melissa's number. Melissa would be at work, too, but lawyers spent lots of their time sitting at their desks, pretending to be engrossed in on-line Lexis Nexis searches when they were in fact reading relationship blogs. Melissa wouldn't calm her down—calming people down wasn't a particular talent of Melissa's—but at least she'd be a friendly voice, a receptive ear.

Someone who wasn't Melissa answered Melissa's phone. "This is Melissa Bendel's sister," Jill said. Feeling guilty for her craven desire to lean on someone, she added, "It's not important."

"Oh, wait," the voice said. "Here she comes. Hang on." Jill heard a thump—the woman clamping her hand over the receiver—and then her muffled voice: "Melissa? Your sister's on the line."

Not very professional. Jill concluded that the woman who answered was a fellow lawyer, not a secretary. Secretaries knew how to answer phones.

A few seconds elapsed, and then Jill heard Melissa's voice: "Oh God," she groaned. "This trial is going to kill me."

"What trial?"

"Counterfeit handbags." Melissa groaned again. "The shit-for-brains paralegal who typed up my brief misspelled 'counterfeit' I don't know how many times. I was up until two-thirty last night, or I guess it was this morning, retyping the freaking briefs. Remember '*I* before *E*?" She paused dramatically. "They lied. In counterfeit it's *E* before *I*."

Jill felt disoriented. This seemed so normal—Melissa whining, Jill listening. Jill wasn't a whiner, any more than she was a leaner. But Gloria and the damned Old Rockford Inn had twisted everything around. Jill felt a profound urge to whine.

She wasn't sure she could. She and Melissa had shaped their thirty-one-year relationship around a certain dynamic: Melissa-whiner, Jill-listener. Much as she wanted to reverse the equation, she found herself sliding into her standard listener role. "So this is a case you're on?" she asked. "This counterfeit handbags case? Who do you represent?"

"The good guys, of course," Melissa said, not that there was any *of course* about it. "Not the counterfeiters. Their lawyer is such an asshole. He thinks he can win this case on his dimples. He just kept smiling at the judge this morning, and she fell for it. 'Motion to suppress? Sure thing,' she said. 'You need another continuance? No problem-o. Whatever you want, Mr. O'Leary. I'm yours." Yet another groan. "I swear to God, I'm surrounded by shit-for-brains."

"Mr. O'Leary, huh," Jill said.

"What?"

"The opposing lawyer's name is O'Leary?"

"Aidan O'Leary. A one-man St. Patrick's Day parade. I think he should be forced to wear one of those green plastic derby hats into the courtroom, you know the kind people wear to the parade? And a button reading, 'Kiss me, I'm Irish.' The damn judge probably *would* kiss him, too. She'd probably vault right over the banc and give him a big wet one. Do I sound racist? I'm not against all Irish people, I swear. I'm just against Aidan O'Leary."

"I understand," Jill said gently, although the urge to whine continued to rise up in her like lava boiling toward the cone of a volcano. "Forget about him," she erupted. "I need legal advice."

"Like I'm an expert," Melissa muttered. "About what?"

"Abbie's bat mitzvah. We signed this contract with the Old Rockford Inn for the reception, and now they want to up the price per plate by three dollars."

"What? They're charging you for the plates?"

"That's what they call an entrée. Actually a whole meal. They've decided to charge us three dollars more a person."

"Breach of contract," Melissa said, her anti-Irish bigotry set aside, along with her bleating self-pity. "You want me to draw up the papers?"

"They said the small print in the contract says they can adjust the price."

"And you signed it?"

"If we didn't sign it, Abbie wouldn't have a reception."

"Then you're stuck." Melissa fell silent for a minute. "What the hell. You can still fight it. I could write something threatening on the firm's stationery. It's got a scary-looking letterhead."

Melissa's offer tempted Jill. She shook her head, even though she was sitting in her car and Melissa couldn't see her. The shade of a maple tree draped across her windshield and an empty waxed-paper cup with a straw poking through the lid sat on the floor in front of the passenger seat, evidence of a Diet Coke she'd snuck a couple of days ago when she'd found herself with fifteen minutes to kill between dropping Noah off at his soccer practice and picking Abbie up from her Science Olympiad team meeting. She hadn't been actively looking for a McDonald's, but one had suddenly loomed before her like an oasis in the desert, and she'd been unable to keep herself from steering to the drive-through window and ordering a Diet Coke. She'd sipped it like a closet alcoholic, slouching behind the wheel and sucking the drink in with an enthusiasm bordering on desperation. Wasn't there some rule that if you drank something in the car it didn't count? Or if you downed it in under ten minutes? Or if it didn't come from your own refrigerator?

"Let me think about it," she said, remembering Melissa's offer to help her with the Old Rockford Inn. "I didn't call you to ask you to write a threatening letter. I called you because I wanted to sound off and Mom isn't available. She's working at First-Rate."

Melissa groaned. "I can't believe she's doing that. Why couldn't she find a classier job?"

"Why couldn't she stay with Dad? Then she wouldn't need a job at all."

"First-Rate. God. I can't believe she's working there." Melissa fell silent for a minute, then asked, "Do you think they're really going to get a divorce?" She sounded suspiciously whimpery, as if a sob was clogging her throat.

"Not if I can help it," Jill declared. But could she help it? Or was this one problem Jill couldn't solve? Here she was, whining to her sister and aching to lean on her mother. Did that mean she'd lost her position in the family, her ability to be the peace-maker, the moderator, the stable center of the Bendel clan?

Her parents were separated. Nothing was the same, not even her role. "How can we get them back together? Brainstorm with me, Melissa."

"My brain is stormed out from dealing with this stupid case. The counterfeiters should go to jail and my clients should win a gazillion-dollar settlement. But there's this tiny part of me that keeps wondering, if no one can tell the difference between a real Prada bag and a fake Prada bag, why should Prada be charging thousands of dollars for the exact same bag some sweatshop in China can make for fifty bucks and change?"

"Because the Prada people originated the design, and they should be compensated for their creativity," Jill reminded her. As someone who wrote for a flat fee, she felt grossly undercompensated for her own creativity. But then, she wasn't Prada. She was just Black Pearl's text writer, and Prairie Wind's, and Velvet Moon's.

"You're so smart." Melissa sighed. "You're absolutely right. Honoring creativity. That's why I'm handling this case—that plus the billable hours. So what are you going to do about Mom and Dad? How can you get them back together?"

"Why are you saying *you*? Why can't we both do this?"

"We just established you're smart," Melissa argued. "Doug's smart but . . . You know the way he is. He's a doctor. He can't be bothered. It's up to you."

"I don't want it to be up to me," Jill complained. "I have no idea how to get them back together."

"You always get everyone together," Melissa reminded her. "Go visit Mom at her First-Rate store."

"And do what?"

"I don't know." Melissa fell silent for a moment, then said, "Tell her Dad's dying."

"He's not dying."

"Lie. If she thinks he's dying, she'll realize how much she loves him."

"She'll realize how much she hates me for lying to her."

"She'll forgive you once she sees that you were lying only to force her to admit how much she loves him."

Jill wasn't sure how smart she was, but if that was Melissa's best idea, Jill was a hell of a lot smarter than her.

Still, the suggestion that Jill visit their mother at the First-Rate outlet where she was employed had possibilities. Seeing her at her job might give Jill some ideas. The woman was probably running a cash register eight hours a day, constantly on her feet, and she had to wear one of those ugly red aprons. Maybe she was miserable, and eager for an excuse to go home. Maybe if Jill could get her to recognize that she'd made a mistake . . . or not even admit it. All Jill had to do was make her acknowledge that rinsing her husband's beard hairs down the sink was preferable to wearing that icky First-Rate apron.

As if those were the only options a woman had in life: clean up after a husband or take a boring minimum-wage job and wear an icky apron. But if Jill could convince her mother that those were her only options, maybe she'd return to Jill's father.

She checked her watch again. If she left this minute and encountered no traffic, she could get to her mother's First-Rate, spend fifteen minutes there and drive home, pulling into the garage before Abby's bus dropped her off. Not that it would be the end of the world if Abby came home to an empty house, but Jill was a Good Mom, and whenever possible a Good Mom should be waiting for her children with open arms and Granny Smith apples when they got home from school.

"All right," she told Melissa. "I'll visit her at the store. Maybe something there will inspire me."

"They sell scented candles, don't they?" Melissa said. "Scented candles inspire me."

They probably inspired her to jump into bed with her hot beautician—assuming she and the hot beautician were still an item. Jill didn't have time for a detour into Melissa's love life, not if she was going to make it to the First-Rate and home before Abby's bus turned the corner and wheezed down her block.

She said good-bye to Melissa and started the car. The drive took less time than she'd anticipated. Not much traffic on the road, and she tended to drive faster when she was angry. Honestly, three dollars more per plate? Because of fuel prices? Maybe she should run the contract through a shredder and host Abby's reception herself. How much trouble could it be to prepare hors d'oeuvres, dinner, dessert and a sheet cake with "Mazel tov, Abbie" written on it, along with a torah created out of colored frosting?

And drinks. An open bar for the adults, and for the kids enough soda to float Noah's Ark.

Could she use paper plates? Or would she have to rent dishes and flatware? Shit. Those rental places probably tacked on a fuel surcharge, too. The dishes had to be washed, didn't they? And dishwashers required electricity, which was powered by coal or natural gas or something else that cost more than it did two months ago.

The strip mall where her mother's First-Rate store was located looked like dozens of other strip malls within a ten-mile radius of Jill's house: First-Rate on one end, Fashions For Less on the other, and a typical assortment of retail outlets—sandwich shop, bank branch, Nails By Lia, and one of Toby Kotzenberg's father's sneaker stores—lining the sidewalk that spanned the two anchors. Jill parked near the First-Rate, shut off the engine, closed her eyes and took a few deep breaths.

She had to be calm before she went into the store. She had to be ready to face the shock of seeing her mother in a First-Rate apron without letting that shock register on her face. She had to come up with a better explanation for why she was there—and why her mother should get back together with her father—than to claim her father was dying.

Because we're a family, Mom, she rehearsed. *Because we count on each other, we rely on each other, and our family has always been a solid unit, and you can't just break it apart on a whim.* No, that sounded too scolding, too judgmental.

Because Abbie's bat mitzvah is going to be a disaster if her grandparents aren't reconciled, sitting side by side, kvelling together over their magnificent granddaughter. And if I have to pay three goddamn dollars more per person, my parents had damned well better sit side by side and kvell.

Not great, but better than calling her mother's whim a whim. And definitely better than *Dad's dying.*

She swung out of the car, locked it and crossed the lot to First-Rate. The hinged doors accordioned open automatically and she entered.

Every First-Rate looked like every other one, she acknowledged as her gaze circled the store. The racks, the shelves, the flooring and the glaring ceiling fixtures were identical to her local First-Rate. The only thing different about this store was that Jill's mother was standing behind the front counter at one of the cash registers, ringing up a customer's purchases.

A tall, skinny kid stood behind her, his hair a mess of white-boy dreadlocks and a piece of silver jewelry perforating his eyebrow. Like Jill's mother, he wore a First-Rate apron over his street clothes. He nodded as Jill's mother removed item after item from the customer's basket and slid them under the scanning gun, which rested in a bracket beside the register. The customer was apparently schizophrenic: everything in her basket was either a weight-loss aid or candy.

Jill's mother looked the same as she had last week, when the family had gathered around Jill's dining room table for Ruth and Richard's big announcement, and she also looked different. She had the same chin-length, shapeless salt-and-pepper hair, the same narrow face, the same warm brown eyes. Probably the same body, too, although who could tell when she was wearing that stupid apron? Red was not her color, at least not *that* red.

Her posture was straighter, however. Her chin was thrust forward, although whether that was a sign of confidence or pugnaciousness Jill couldn't say. Her mother's hands looked different, too. Specifically, her left hand. Specifically that hand's naked fourth finger, where she used to wear her wedding ring.

Her lips were pursed, tense with concentration. Checking out a customer's purchases evidently required deep concentration. But the scanner gave a friendly beep each time she passed an item through its beam, so she must have been doing her job correctly.

Being a Good Daughter, Jill ducked down the shampoo aisle, remaining out of her mother's line of vision. She wouldn't want to distract her mother and make her ring up a candy bar or an Atkins Diet milkshake incorrectly—although if her mother made a mistake, maybe the store would fire her and she'd go home.

Not likely. She'd only be discouraged, her self-esteem punctured. Returning home a failure wouldn't do. Her mother had her pride, and that pride could be Jill's entry. She could convince her mother she'd made her point, proven she had the right stuff, had a grand adventure and emerged a better person. Only then would she willingly put her wedding ring back on.

From the shampoo aisle, Jill could see the front door. She pretended to be fascinated by the selection of super-hold styling gels while watching for the diet-conflicted customer to leave. As soon as the woman passed through the folding doors, Jill emerged and approached the counter.

"Jill!" Her mother broke into a huge smile. "Jill! Oh, my God!" Before Jill could answer, her mother turned to the lanky kid behind her. "Wade, this is my daughter Jill. She never shops here—she's got a First-Rate in her own town. Jill, what are you doing here?"

"Obviously, I'm here to see you," Jill said, eyeing the kid warily before returning her mother's smile. "If I wanted to shop, I've got a First-Rate in my own town, just like you said."

"Jill—" Why did her mother have to keep repeating her name? Was she afraid that now that she'd embarked on her new life as a single woman, she might forget her children's names if she didn't say them over and over? "—this is Wade. He's been breaking me in." Her mother giggled. "That's what they call it, anyway. You'll never guess what his last name is, Jill."

Her mother seemed oddly hyper. Jill humored her. "Okay," she said pleasantly.

"Go ahead, guess."

"You said I'd never—"

"Smith," her mother declared. "His last name is Smith. Can you believe it?" Once again, she didn't give Jill a chance to comment. "And this—" she gestured toward the woman at the next register, who took a moment out from ringing up another customer's order and gave Jill a friendly nod "—is Rosita. And that's Bernie, straightening out the Halloween candy. Bernie, come and meet my daughter!"

Jill hadn't traveled all this way so her mother could show her off. Nor had she come here in order to meet her mother's new playmates. But before she could react, a short, spunky gentleman who appeared old enough to have celebrated his twentieth anniversary as an AARP member bounded over and clasped her hand in his. "Ruth, you didn't tell us you had such a beautiful daughter," he exclaimed.

If Jill were Abbie, she would have rolled her eyes and made retching noises. If she were Noah, she would have said, "Later, dude," and run out the door. Instead, she shook the gentleman's hand and said, "That's very sweet of you. Mom? Can you spare me a few minutes?" *Dad's dying,* she wanted to add, if only because those two words would probably scare the effusive Bernie away.

Her mother glanced at the kid, who glanced at the woman named Rosita, who nodded. Did it bother her mother that she had to get permission from people so much younger than she was if she wanted a break? As if the apron wasn't humiliating enough.

"We'll go to the staff room," she said, sauntering the length of the counter to the end, where a gate allowed her to escape into the store. "You want something to drink?"

"No, thanks—"

"I'll get you a drink. I get an employee discount." Before Jill could stop her, she'd crossed to the refrigerator case and removed a can of Diet Coke.

"No, really, Mom, I've already drunk my daily quota."

"Nonsense. My treat." She returned to the dreadlocked kid's station, scanned the can herself, and then scanned a laminated card. "I have an account," she explained to Jill. "If you buy things in the store, they keep track and deduct the cost from your paycheck. Discounted cost, of course." She strode down an aisle and Jill followed, unnerved by the certainty of her mother's steps. Not that her mother had ever minced or teetered when she walked, but there was a purposefulness in her gait today, as if she were training to hike the Appalachian Trail from end to end.

At the back of the store, she slid her laminated card into a slot and pushed open a door marked "Employees Only."

"The staff room is pretty shabby," she warned Jill as they walked past some shelves full of inventory and into a room that was, indeed, shabby. "After I've been here a while, I'll ask Francine if I can put up some posters, maybe bring in a plant or two to liven the place up."

Jill had no idea who Francine was. Another person half her mother's age to whom her mother had to answer, probably. The more pertinent part of her mother's statement was *after a while*. How long a while was she planning to work here?

Jill surveyed the dreary little lounge. Lockers lined one wall; a countertop with cabinets above and below, reminiscent of the cabinets in Jill's dentist's office, lined another. A microwave oven, its window smeared with ancient splatters of food, stood on the counter, beside it an empty coffee maker. A minifridge sat on the floor.

"There are no windows here," she pointed out. "Plants need sunlight."

"So I'll get some plastic plants," her mother said. She popped open the can of Diet Coke and placed it on a small, round Formica-topped table. "Sit. Drink." She dropped onto one of the chairs at the table and gestured to another chair for Jill. "You look worried. That's not like you, Jill. You're my one child who never worries."

"I always worry," Jill retorted, then took a sip of soda to steady her nerves. "Doug's the one who never worries. He's rich, he's successful, and he's got Brooke hanging off his arm."

"He's got twins," Jill's mother said, as if that was a cause for chronic panic.

"Okay, so I'm worried," Jill said. "The inn where we're having Abbie's bat mitzvah reception is trying to rip us off."

"They all do that," her mother muttered.

"I wanted to call you for advice, but I couldn't." Jill wondered if her mother could hear the resentment underlining her tone. "You were here, at work."

"Oh, you don't need advice from me," her mother said. "You're my rock, Jill. You're the one I depend on. The idea of you coming to me for advice . . . . That's crazy."

Maybe it was crazy, but it was also true. Jill could be a rock as long as the rest of the family stood on terra firma. But if they were drifting out to sea, what good was a rock? A rock would only sink.

She felt the pressure of tears at the back of her eyes and blinked furiously. She would not cry in front of her mother. Crying was Melissa's job, not Jill's.

Dad's dying, she longed to say. Or, more accurately, *We're all dying. The Bendel family is dying.* Instead, she said, "How is it going to work if you and Dad aren't together at Abbie's bat mitzvah?"

"What has to work?" her mother replied. "It's not like your father and I can't stand each other. We were married a long time. We can get along."

"Don't you miss him? Aren't you lonely?"

"Lonely?" Her mother shrugged. "Who's got time? I'm working, learning. Today's my first day on the register. Nobody's promising anything, but if things work out they may teach me how to run the one-hour photo machines. Just as a back-up, though. That wouldn't be my primary job. They've got two ladies who work there, Gina and Brandi with an *i*. That's her real name, B-R-A-N-D-I. Who would do that to a child, give her the name of a hooker? But she seems nice enough. A little stand-offish, both of them. They think they're special because they run the film department." Jill's mother shook her head. "I'm talking too much. Tell me, how's everything with you? How are the kids?"

"The kids are fine," Jill said, not wanting to waste what little time she had on trivial matters. "Mom . . . Okay, so you're not lonely. What about Dad? What if he's lonely?"

Stupid move. Her mother straightened in her chair and her smile vanished. "He's going to have to figure out how to fix that himself. I'm done living my life around him. He's a big boy. He's lonely? Let him pick up a phone and call a friend."

"What if the friend he calls is a woman?" Jill asked.

"We're separated. If he wants to call a woman, he can call a woman."

"That wouldn't bother you?"

"He isn't living his life around me, either." Another shrug, this one a bit more emphatic.

"You haven't . . ." Jill swallowed. "You aren't seeing another man, are you? That guy Bernie—" She gestured in the direction of the store, where she'd met the effusive older man.

Her mother laughed. "Bernie is a character, isn't he? He's married. And full of baloney, and he's old. I'm not seeing him. I'm not seeing anyone. If I wanted a man in my life, I'd stay with your father."

"Don't you want—I mean, what about sex?"

Her mother laughed louder. "Sex? If I miss it, I'll start worrying about it. Right now, I'm not worried."

That was cryptic. "It's a normal, healthy part of life, Mom."

"I'm sixty-four. I'm not the same person I was thirty years ago." She rested her folded hands on the table. Jill tried not to wince at the sight of that unadorned ring finger. "Now, my girlfriends? Them I miss. I don't have time for coffee with them anymore. No time to put together fundraisers for B'nai Torah, or to visit patients at the hospital. No time for a game of bridge on a Wednesday afternoon. But sex?" She held her hands palm up, as if to say sex was nothing, it was empty.

Unsure what to think, Jill drank some soda. Its blessedly familiar taste would have soothed her if soothing her were at all possible. She hadn't discussed sex with her mother since she'd gotten her period at the age of eleven and her mother had explained the mechanics to her, making them sound generally awful. *That thing he uses to pee with goes where? Yuck!*

So her mother didn't miss her father and didn't want a boyfriend. At that rate, if Jill said, "Dad is dying," her mother would likely say, "Poor guy. I'll say a prayer for him next time I can free up a few minutes."

"Mom," Jill said, opting for honesty, "we all want you to get back together."

"Who's we?"

"Melissa and Doug and me. Gordon, too. Abbie and Noah. I'm guessing Brooke, too. The twins are probably too young to care."

"Change is hard," her mother said gently. Jill realized her mother was giving her advice, after all. "If this separation doesn't work out, we'll get back together. So far, it's working out."

"For you," Jill conceded. "What about the rest of us?"

Her mother sighed. "That's the point, sweetie. I'm done living my life for the rest of you." For a moment she looked wistful, even lost. How could a woman who'd spent her whole life living for her family make such an abrupt U-turn? Shouldn't she have whiplash?

Then she smiled, a brighter smile than Jill could recall seeing on her mother's face in a long time. "I should get back out to the store. But listen, you and Abbie should come to dinner. I've got my new apartment set up now. We could have a girls' night, just the three of us."

Jill didn't want a girls' night with her mother. A family night with both her parents would satisfy her just fine.

"I'll schedule an early night off," her mother said. "I'll make a pot roast. Abbie loves my pot roast. Call me when you can figure out a good day for you and her. I've really got to go. This isn't my break time." She hurried toward the door, where she waited for Jill to join her.

Jill contemplated leaving the can of soda behind, but her willpower failed her. Clasping its cold, damp surface, she rose from the table and followed her mother out of the room.

"And don't you worry about Abbie's bat mitzvah," her mother added as they strode past a shelf stacked with four-packs of toilet paper en route to the door back into the store. "Your father and I will be fine. Just tell the folks at that fancy inn you booked that they'd better not try to cheat you."

"Right." As if anything in life—getting a fair price per plate or getting your parents back together—could be accomplished just by telling someone something.

Chapter Eleven

Melissa couldn't get into it. Luc was enthusiastically doing his thing, but her mind-body disconnect kept her from responding to his efforts. Her body should have been in ecstasy, but her mind was in the courtroom, where that son of a bitch O'Leary had played the judge like Itzhak Perlman playing a Stradivarius.

O'Leary hadn't been the original opposing lawyer. The counterfeiters had started out with Melvin Woo, a small, solemn attorney who lapsed into Cantonese when he conferred with his client. That they spoke a language she didn't understand had irked her. It had also irked Judge Montoya, a fact Melissa had seen as good news for her client. All the legal strategies in the world weren't as effective as having an opposing attorney who rubbed the judge the wrong way.

But Melvin Woo had disappeared that morning—what was supposed to be the first day of the trial—and Aidan O'Leary had appeared in his place, tall, confident and smiling like a quarterback who'd scored the winning touchdown, even though in fact he'd only just walked onto the field. And Judge Montoya, who, Melissa knew for a fact, was a huge fan of designer handbags and therefore should have been in Melissa's pocket, looked instead as if she wanted to be in O'Leary's pants. A continuance? No problem. If O'Leary had asked Montoya to strip off her robe and do a pole dance, she probably would have complied. With a smile.

Luc was pumping harder, his lean, muscular body rocking hers with an intensity that signaled he was nearing his peak. Melissa closed her eyes and moaned to encourage him. The sooner he finished, the sooner she could get some sleep.

Not that she expected to sleep when her mind was gridlocked with intersecting thoughts. Not just about the trial, not just about O'Leary, but about her sister. Jill had sounded awful on the phone. Well, not exactly awful, but not like herself. She was supposed to be the together one, not the panicky one.

Melissa sensed that the reason Jill was freaking out was because their parents' marriage was falling apart. And Melissa couldn't blame her sister, because she was freaking out, too. And she was doubly freaking out because Jill was the Bendel sibling who was supposed to put things back together, not fall apart herself.

If Jill couldn't fix the rift between their parents, why couldn't Doug? He was the oldest. The doctor. The hot-shot. Why couldn't he just step up and get the job done?

Luc shuddered and groaned, and Melissa remembered to shudder and groan, too. She rarely had to fake it with him, but it wasn't his fault that she was distracted by concern about her sister and fury with Big Irish Aidan. If she could give Luc the satisfaction of thinking he'd satisfied her, she'd do it. He was such a nice guy, after all, and so handsome, plus he wasn't a lawyer. For that alone, she owed him a fake-O.

She still didn't know if he was The One, if she was in love, if this thing was going to last. She felt more or less comfortable with him, but whenever she talked to him about buying a bigger apartment, he acted as if it was all her decision. Which it was, but that implied that he wasn't anywhere near ready to discuss sharing an apartment with her. Plus, he didn't have any money to chip in toward the exorbitant purchase prices Kathy the Realtor kept quoting her. He did get big tips, but nobody could afford a New York apartment—or even half an apartment, since Melissa would be paying for the other half—on tips.

Wasn't the housing market supposed to be in a slump? Shouldn't prices be plummeting? In Manhattan, plummeting prices meant a million dollars might buy you two baths instead of one and a half.

Luc groaned again, and Melissa sighed and gave her hips a helpful wiggle. Luc propped himself on his arms and smiled down at her, evidently quite pleased with himself. She managed to smile back at him, and reached up to brush a floppy lock of hair off his face. His hair was so impeccably styled, it looked great even when it was mussed from sex. He'd cut and shaped her hair to look good after sex, too—or at least he assured her it looked good after sex. She wasn't in the habit of leaping out of bed and sprinting over to the mirror to check out her appearance immediately after.

"You hungry?" he asked as he rolled off her.

It occurred to her that he was in her home, which made her the hostess and therefore the person who should be offering food. Did his question mean he wanted to think of her home as his home, too? If so, why was he so passive whenever she talked about real estate?

She wasn't hungry at all—she'd stayed late at the office, working until seven-thirty, and one of the other associates also working late had ordered too much Chinese, so Melissa had wound up consuming half a tub of leftover lo mein at her desk. "There's some cheese in the fridge," she offered Luc. "Cheddar—the kind you like, with the red wax."

"Great." He swung out of bed and crossed to the kitchen alcove at the opposite end of the room. Her vantage point gave her an excellent view of his broad, naked back, and she admired it in an objective way. He had a fine physique and an utterly sublime tush. She bet Aidan O'Leary's tush wasn't so sublime.

Christ. Why was she thinking about O'Leary? She ought to be thinking about Jill and the inn trying to rip her off. She ought to be thinking about her mother, drudging away for minimum wage at the kind of store where people bought stuff they didn't need because they wanted to make use of some discount coupons they'd cut out of the newspaper. For crying out loud, Melissa ought to be thinking about the gorgeous, sexy, bare-ass man pulling a brick of cheddar cheese out of her fridge.

"So, guess who made an appointment for me to rescue her from her hair today," he called over his gorgeous, sexy shoulder as, back still to her, he sliced the cheese into domino-size chunks and pared away the wax rind.

Eager to shove notions of O'Leary's butt out of her head, she actually put some thought into guessing. "Someone from show-biz? Or politics?"

Luc shook his head. "Someone from Massachusetts."

Jill? No, she would have told Melissa when she'd called her earlier that day. Their mother? What would she be doing with a two-hundred-fifty-dollar haircut when the only people who'd see her were those coupon-clutching bargain hunters?

"Your sister-in-law. Dr. Doug's wife."

"Brooke?" Why would she travel all the way to New York for a haircut? Surely she could spend just as much money, and a lot less time, patronizing a Newbury Street salon in Boston.

"We talked hair that weekend at your sister's house," Luc told her. "She asked for some suggestions, and I gave her a few ideas. I figured she'd just take them to her stylist and see what he could do. I didn't expect her to make an appointment to travel to New York just to get a more dimensional coloring."

How many stylists actually thought about dimensional coloring?

Luc was one of the very few. For that reason alone, people might be willing to travel two hundred miles for the privilege of having him work on their hair.

Still, the notion of Brooke coming to New York for a hair appointment with Lucas Brondo of Nouvelle disconcerted Melissa. "Could you pour me a glass of wine while you're up?" she asked.

"The white?" He pulled a green bottle from her fridge, removed the cork and filled the goblet that had been balanced upside-down on the drying rack beside the sink. He carried it and a plate of cheese and crackers to the bed, then hopped on beside her and handed her the glass. She thought briefly of cautioning him not to spill cracker crumbs onto the sheets but decided such a comment would make her seem shrewish and petty. The guy had brought her a glass of chardonnay, after all. And he'd just made love to her skillfully enough that she'd had no trouble convincingly faking an orgasm.

She sipped the cold, dry wine and settled back into the heap of pillows propped against her headboard. "So Brooke's coming to New York?"

"Next Tuesday."

"Funny that she didn't call me, given that you and I are . . ." She didn't finish the sentence, because she wasn't exactly sure what she and Luc were. "Not that Brooke and I are the closest of sisters-in-law," she continued. "I always feel as if there's a barrier separating us. She's kind of aloof."

Luc shrugged. Melissa wondered whether that meant he agreed, disagreed or had no opinion.

"She's coming to New York. The least she could do is let me know," Melissa continued, deciding after brief consideration that she was mildly pissed. Brooke didn't merit becoming severely pissed over. "What are you going to do with her hair?"

"I'll see what she wants," he said, then popped a Wheat Thin topped with a slab of cheese into his mouth.

Melissa tried to figure out what she found so troubling about this. Luc worked on women, and a few men, all day long. He gave them what they wanted, just as he gave Melissa what she wanted. Melissa wasn't jealous. She was pleased about his success. It meant he earned more, which in turn meant he might eventually want to go in on the purchase of an apartment with her, if their relationship was fated to last. It also meant that her family might not act so subtly disapproving about her being involved with a hair stylist—a beauty professional, a grooming expert, a tress *artiste*. His level of achievement would reflect well on her.

But still . . . Brooke. Melissa had never felt wholly comfortable with her sister-in-law. She'd been in college when Doug had gotten married, and Brooke had considerately included her and Jill in her bridal party. But there was always that wall. That barrier. Brooke was so pretty and polite and polished and freaking *perfect*. Not only had she created a proper nuclear family by having two children, but she'd been efficient enough to have them both at the same time. And she'd chosen such chic, androgynous names for them. Mackenzie Bendel? Madison Bendel? That whole branch of the family acted as if they were super-rich WASPs, which, except for the Anglo-Saxon Protestant part, they were.

"Next Tuesday, huh," Melissa said.

Luc eyed her quizzically. "What's the problem?"

"No problem. It's just that if she's coming all the way to the city, she could at least give me a call and asked if I'm free for lunch, or a drink, or something. She's my sister-in-law, for God's sake."

"Do you want me to have her call you when she's in the chair? The coloring takes a while. She's just going to be sitting around."

Melissa shook her head. "If it's not her own idea to call me, what's the point? Anyway, I'll probably be in court with Kiss-Me-I'm-Irish."

Luc's expression grew bemused, but he didn't question her. She wondered whether that meant he respected her privacy when it came to her work or he just wasn't interested. Either way, she was kind of glad he didn't ask. She didn't want to discuss Aidan O'Leary with him.

To be sure, she was hesitant to discuss her work with him at all. Partly because she was a lawyer and he was a tress *artiste* and talking about her career might emphasize the difference between them in educational level and professional stature—not that that difference mattered to her, not that it *should* matter, but she'd hate for him to feel inferior to her. And partly because . . .

She sipped some wine and turned to gaze at the window. Dots of light slipped into the room between the slats of the Venetian blinds, the reflections of headlights and streetlights and flashing red tower lights, warning low-flying airplanes of skyscrapers and antennas. Even in this residential Upper East Side neighborhood at nine p.m., the city was alive with lights.

She didn't want to discuss her work with Luc because she'd been thinking about Aidan O'Leary while Luc had been making love to her. And that was more unnerving than her parents' divorce or Jill's anxiety on the phone that afternoon, or the price of real estate in Manhattan. Or Brooke's New York City hair appointment.

Chapter Twelve

Richard had always admired Gert's abruptness, her determination, her take-no-prisoners approach to life. These traits made her an excellent office manager. She oversaw Richard and his partners, the nursing staff and the paper-pushers. She massaged insurance companies, strong-armed labs and found beds for Richard's patients in Beth Israel's various cardiac units even when the hospital swore no beds were available. She'd once browbeaten a CICU nurse at St. Elizabeth's into allowing a patient with an atrial valve problem to fast over Yom Kippur, even though the nurse claimed that the hospital had ultimate authority over the patients' diets. "God has authority over you," Gert had argued, "and God says this patient can fast on the Day of Atonement, even if St. E's is a Catholic hospital."

Gert was tough. Richard admired toughness, especially when he himself was feeling tough. But he was much too fragile these days. Ruth had been gone two weeks, and he was suffering cravings for baked potatoes, grilled tuna steaks, someone to talk to when he got home from work and a warm, familiar body in his bed at night. Channel surfing could take a man only so far.

So he was not thrilled when Gert swept into his office like General Patton storming Europe and said, "All right, what aren't you telling me?" She was clearly on a mission and would settle for nothing less than total victory.

He hadn't informed the office staff about the situation with Ruth. His partner Stan, yes, but not his partner Eric, whom he and Stan called The Kid because he was forty-three and had a full head of strawberry blond hair. The Kid had joined their practice five years ago, when their elderly third partner had retired and Richard and Stan had acknowledged the need for fresh blood. That had been their joke: a cardiology practice needed fresh blood. Eric was fresh, all right—smooth of cheek, fleet of foot, a bit aggressive in his treatments, but a fine addition to the practice.

That said, Richard still viewed him as something of an apprentice, not an equal, and an arrogant, vaguely rebellious apprentice at that. He wasn't about to confess to him that his wife had left him for a job clerking at a store one step above a schlock-house.

"I'm not ready for the world to know about this yet," Richard had confided to Stan last week, when he'd revealed the news about Ruth's departure. "I'm hoping it'll resolve itself before anyone else has to know. Like a pediatric heart murmur. God willing, Ruth will outgrow this nonsense and come home."

But now, if he was reading Gert's assertive posture and accusing glower correctly, his secret had leaked. She bore down on his desk and leaned toward him, her fisted hands resting on either side of the fancy leather blotter his mother had given him when he'd started his practice thirty-odd years ago. Gert's reddish-brown hair was smoothed severely back from her face, held in place by a semicircular piece of black plastic that arched from ear to ear across the top of her skull, and her thin, red-glossed lips were pressed into a stern line as she regarded him.

Should he tell her? Pretend he had no idea what she was talking about? Or just skip over all that and apologize? Her behavior informed him she'd already tried him and found him guilty.

Guilty of what? Channel surfing? Failing to keep everyone in his practice abreast of the current state of his marriage? Shouldn't he have the charges read to him before Gert pronounced her sentence? And wasn't he entitled to a lawyer? He wondered if Melissa could scoot up to Boston and handle Gert for him.

"What?" he asked noncommittally. He would have liked to tell Gert to go back to her own office and do what he was paying her to do, but he was a bit afraid of her.

"Your wife? Your marriage?"

He sighed and slumped in his ergonomic leather desk chair, his gaze resting on Myron Kupferman's lab report, which sat on the blotter between Gert's fists. Myron Kupferman had been eating a three-egg cheese omelet every morning of his life for the past seventy-five years, and now the bill had come due. Cholesterol readings you wouldn't wish on your worst enemy.

"Who told you?" he asked, distracting himself—and hopefully Gert—from the subject at hand. If Stan had betrayed Richard's trust, Richard could feel indignant instead of guilty. Indignant was better than guilty.

"Nobody told me," Gert replied. "My eyes told me. Your shirt is wrinkled. Ruth would never let you leave the house in a shirt so wrinkled."

He slumped deeper into the chair. Gert was right. He'd run a load of laundry over the weekend—darks and whites together, because he hadn't produced enough dirty laundry by himself for two loads even though he'd run out of underwear. The only darks he'd washed were his socks, and they didn't bleed. But everything had emerged a little bit dingy. And ironing? What was he, a miracle worker? He could install a stent with his eyes closed, but ironing was beyond him.

Maybe he should have thanked Ruth more often for ironing his shirts. Maybe a pair of diamond earrings, to say nothing of all the other gifts he'd given her over the years—to say nothing of the fact that he kept a roof over her head and her refrigerator full of food, and he provided the money to pay the bills, including electric and water, so she could do the laundry—wasn't enough of a thank-you.

"So my shirt's wrinkled," he said to Gert.

She straightened, only to strike another threatening pose by crossing her arms sternly across her chest. "What did you do to Ruth?"

"Nothing," he insisted.

"You were cheating on her?"

"Of course not!" Indignant was definitely better.

"You just left her, for no good reason?"

"She left me," he snapped. "For no good reason."

Gert regarded him dubiously. "I find that hard to believe."

"I'm still not sure I believe it myself," he admitted.

Pursing her lips and jutting one hip out slightly, she assessed him. "Have you ever heard of dry cleaners?"

"Of course I have." Impatience nibbled at him. Myron Kupferman's blood work demanded his attention, and Gert already knew more than she needed to know—which probably meant everyone in the practice was bound to know more than they needed to know in the not too distant future.

"Take your shirts to the cleaners," she ordered him. "When you pick them up, they'll be ironed."

"Thank you for that helpful tip," Richard said sarcastically. "Any advice on how to prepare a pot roast so it's cooked and waiting for me when I get home?"

Gert had an answer. She always had an answer. "Put a loin roast in a crock-pot, add some onions, a cut-up potato, a carrot, a little water and seasonings, and set the timer. When you get home, the pot roast will be cooked."

He wondered if he had a crock pot. It sounded like a handy item.

To his surprise, Gert's posture relaxed. She lowered herself into one of the visitor chairs facing his desk and leaned forward again, this time solicitous rather than accusatory. Her hands remained unfisted, settling in her lap. "When did this happen?" she asked.

"Two weeks ago." He pretended to glance at the Kupferman numbers, but his eyes strayed back to Gert. He wasn't used to her acting solicitous and concerned, at least not in her interactions with him. With the patients she was always a soft touch. Only with the folks she managed—including Richard, Stan and The Kid, who paid her salary, for God's sake—was she a tyrant.

She was displaying her with-the-patients demeanor now, her features gentle, her usually grim mouth curved into a sympathetic smile. "Richard," she murmured, but firmly, demanding his full attention. He obediently closed the Kupferman file and met her gaze. "You should have told me. This kind of thing can affect your work."

"What, wrinkled shirts? I don't think any of my patients have noticed."

She smiled, but her amusement didn't reach her eyes. "This is a huge adjustment. A stressful event. Traumatic, even."

"I'm not traumatized," he declared. And really, he wasn't. Annoyed, impatient, all those things he'd been with Gert just minutes ago. But not traumatized. He was still working, still eating, still chatting with that round-cheeked girl at the deli. Still saving lives. Still golfing with Doug on Saturday afternoons, although the golf season was winding down. Last weekend, they'd played eighteen holes, lubricated by glasses of bourbon Doug had bought from one of the drink girls at the tenth hole. The bourbon had warmed them, just the way it had warmed them when he used to meet Doug at the Harvard stadium for home games when Doug was in medical school. Godawful seats they had in that stadium, just concrete ledges, hard enough to bruise a tush. He used to bring a cushioned stadium seat with him, but Doug would sit directly on the cold, unyielding surface. They'd shared nips of bourbon from the silver flask Richard kept tucked in an inner pocket of his jacket. The liquor had warmed them from inside. Just like last week at the golf course.

"So everything's all right?" Gert sounded skeptical.

"Except for the lack of a good pot roast," he said. "And the wrinkled shirts."

"You're not lonely?"

"Of course I'm lonely," he said, then mentally kicked himself. How had she gotten him to reveal that truth? He hadn't even told Doug that.

Then again, Doug hadn't asked.

"I know just the woman for you," Gert said, and the warmth Richard had begun to feel in this conversation, the friendship bordering on kinship, evaporated.

"I don't need a woman," he said.

"Of course you do. Look at your shirt," Gert said. "Shari Bernstein. A dermatologist, right here in this building. She performed a miracle with Matthew's port-wine stain on his neck. When it comes to laser treatments, she's an artist. She's divorced. Very smart."

Once again forgetting to censor himself, Richard asked, "Is she pretty?"

"Gorgeous. The most radiant skin you've ever seen." She leaned across Richard's desk and snagged his prescription pad. *Shari Bernstein*, she wrote, all in capitals, followed by a phone number. Tossing down the pen, she stood and grinned, her work done, the battle won, Western Europe safely back in the hands of the Allies.

Richard stared at the pad, panic roiling his stomach. Gert was already at his door when he said, "She's a doctor. I bet she doesn't iron shirts."

"She's a doctor," Gert replied. "So who cares?"

He watched Gert leave the office, then tore the sheet off his prescription pad and tossed it into the trash can beneath his desk. Then he doubled over, dug through the trash can and pulled the paper back out.

Shari Bernstein. As if she were a prescription, her phone number the dosage.

He stared at the white square of paper for a minute, then tucked it under his blotter and sighed.

What was he supposed to do? Call her? Ask her out? On a date? The last time he'd asked a woman out on a date he'd been in college, and the woman had been Ruth.

So long ago. He ought to be more confident now, more self-assured. Back in college, he was a skinny egghead. That he'd had any social life at all he credited to the fraternity he'd joined at Cornell. Most of his frat brothers had heralded from the New York City area, but there had been a few, like him, from other parts of the country: Boston, Philadelphia, Chicago. If any of them hadn't been pre-med, Richard couldn't think of who it might have been. They were all eggheads, studying too hard, squeezing parties and mixers in around their exam schedules.

Ruth had arrived with a group of Ithaca College students for one of those mixers. With her straight, shiny hair and her curvy legs exposed beneath the hem of her minidress, she hadn't been the most beautiful of the group, but she'd been pretty. Kind of shy, like him, but smiling. Approachable. So he'd approached. And when she'd said hello, he'd heard a familiar accent. "You're from Boston?" he'd exclaimed, and she'd told him Brookline, and he'd told her his parents were still living in the house where he'd grown up in Dorchester, and that had been that.

They'd danced. She'd informed him she liked the Beatles better than the Rolling Stones and didn't care much for the Beach Boys. "Surfing just doesn't mean anything to me," she'd admitted. "Beaches are for lying on, getting a tan and reading a good book."

Why should he ever ask anyone else out after that night? Ruth had seemed fine. She played the piano. She could teach their children to play—because yes, there would be children. He'd be a doctor and she'd be his wife, and they'd remain together until death did them part.

And now he was supposed to ask someone out on a date? It was one thing to flirt a little with the cashier at the deli, but a dermatologist? Someone who had performed miracles on Gert's son's port-wine stain? A *divorcee?*

Richard wasn't divorced. He couldn't do this.

Doug had implied that maybe he could. Or, more accurately, maybe he should. Of course, Doug was younger. A different generation. Besides, he was married to a woman so lovely, the whole issue was moot.

What if Shari Bernstein was like Brooke, pretty and petite and blond? With a name like Bernstein, she couldn't be a *shiksa*—unless Bernstein was her ex-husband's name. But then, Brooke wasn't a *shiksa*, either. She just looked and acted like one.

From the moment Richard had picked Ruth out of that gaggle of Ithaca College girls who'd arrived at Alpha Epsilon Pi for the mixer, he'd known she was safe. Solid. Not glamorous, like Brooke. Not brainy and disorganized, like Melissa. He'd sensed that Ruth would be reasonable, prudent, reliable—kind of like Jill. His middle child had that same dependability about her.

Was Jill going to walk out on Gordon someday? Announce that she was tired of some habit or idiosyncrasy of his and move into an apartment? Should Richard warn his son-in-law now? Should he tell Gordon—a good man, a loving husband—to prepare himself for the possibility that someday he'd find himself spending his nights in an empty bed and wondering whether he had enough chutzpah to telephone a divorced dermatologist who could work miracles with a port-wine stain?

Richard lifted the blotter, stared at the sheet from his prescription pad and lowered the blotter, hiding Shari Bernstein's phone number. When had he lost his nerve? How had he wound up so cowardly? He was a doctor, for God's sake. A successful man who saved lives and pulled down a comfortable six-figure income. Not too bad looking, either. Ruth always said he was as handsome as the day they'd met.

He lifted the blotter again and pulled the sheet out. Coffee, that was all. He'd ask her to join him for a cup of coffee after work. No big deal.

Tomorrow. He'd call her tomorrow. Maybe he'd have a little more courage by then.

Chapter Thirteen

Abbie sat beside Jill in the car, scrutinizing her fingernails with the intensity of a lepidopterist examining the color patterns on the wings of a rare moth. She slouched in such a way that it appeared her spine had been replaced by a rubber band. Jill wondered whether, in an accident, she would slide right under the seatbelt and wind up in a puddle on the floor mat beneath the glove compartment.

Best to avoid an accident so she wouldn't have to find out. "Your grandmother is really looking forward to this," she addressed her daughter's left ear. She tried to infuse her voice with enthusiasm, even though she wasn't any happier than Abbie was about her mother's "girls' night." But if Jill and Abbie were both grouchy when they arrived at her mother's apartment, the evening was going to be even worse than Jill was anticipating, so she forced herself to pretend joy-filled revelry awaited three generations of Schwartz-Bendel-Sackler women.

"Girls' night." Abbie snorted. "Grandma isn't a girl."

"She feels like one these days," Jill explained, suppressing a shudder as she recalled her mother's bubbly—okay, there was no other word for it—*girlishness* at the First-Rate when Jill had visited her there. She remembered her mother's easy banter not just with the geezer with liver spots on his scalp but with the kid with the dreads and the eyebrow bolt. Ruth Bendel was definitely in the throes of her second girlhood right now.

"The three of us have never gotten together without a bunch of menfolk around," she pointed out to Abbie. "Grandpa, Dad and Noah are always a part of it."

"Yeah, and they're in the den watching TV while we're stuck in the kitchen. Isn't that girls' night? You and Grandma yakking about family gossip while I get stuck clearing the table."

"You don't get stuck," Jill argued. She was diligent about making sure of that. "Noah always helps you clear."

"And then he goes and watches sports on TV with Dad and Grandpa, and I'm stuck in the kitchen."

"You could watch sports if you wanted."

Abbie grimaced as if Jill had just suggested she could drink Drano. "So Dad and Noah are eating pizza tonight—and I bet they're eating in the den so they can watch TV while they eat," Abbie complained, her gaze fixed on some flaw on her thumb nail. It, like the other nails, was painted a glittery silver, as if she'd glued aluminum foil to the tips of her fingers. "You never let us eat in the den, but you aren't there and I bet they're going to eat on the couch and slobber melted cheese all over the upholstery." She paused to allow Jill the opportunity to envision the mess Gordon and Noah would undoubtedly make, then added, "Anyway, girls' night would be me and Emma and Caitlin. Not me and my mother and my grandmother."

"She's making pot roast. You love her pot roast."

"I love lots of things, and I wouldn't want to eat them for dinner."

Jill was tempted to question her about what multitude of things she loved. She suspected that at the moment, Abbie would be hard-pressed to name a single thing she loved, and that would include her mother, her best friends, that pricey, skimpy cotton-ramie sweater Caitlin had convinced her to buy at the mall—using Jill's credit card, of course—and her grandmother's pot roast.

She contemplated discussing her own misgivings about her mother's current living situation with Abbie, then thought better of it. A Good Mom didn't involve her children in the ridiculous dynamics of other branches of the family.

Shit. She had to be both a Good Mom *and* a Good Daughter this evening. The strain might just cause her to snap.

She could use a Diet Coke right now, preferably one diluted with copious amounts of rum. Didn't girls' nights include a certain amount of alcohol consumption?

Only when they didn't also include a twelve-and-a-half year old child. Jill had to remain sober, calm, in control. One petulant, sulky, selfish female was more than enough, and tonight Jill might find herself in the company of two petulant, sulky, selfish females. Who knew if her mother would be as ebullient now as she'd been when she'd invited Jill and Abbie for dinner?

"This place is the pits," Abbie opined as Jill steered into the parking lot of her mother's apartment complex. She didn't think it looked that awful, unless you compared it to the lovely suburban house on a manicured half-acre plot where Jill's father was currently residing in solitude. The apartment complex had a kind of college quad look to it, half a dozen bland three-story red brick structures with evenly spaced aluminum-framed windows, bargain-basement landscaping and outdoor lighting that reminded Jill vaguely of old World War Two movies about stalags.

Jill's mother had told her to look for Building 4, the one nearest the corner by the crosswalk. Her mother had also warned her not to park in a numbered spot, since those were reserved for tenants. After meandering around a figure-eight of driveways, she finally looped to Building 4. The nearest unnumbered spot she found was by Building 6. Not that it mattered; with the glaring spotlights making the parking lots brighter than Fenway Park when the Red Sox were hosting a night game, she was sure she and Abbie would be safe walking to Building 4.

The air contained a wintry nip. Or maybe the chill Jill felt creeping down her spine as she and Abbie walked along the paved path, passing undersized yews and dormant rhododendrons, was a result of panic. This wasn't like the first time she'd visited Grandma Schwartz after her move into the assisted-living facility. For one thing, Grandma Schwartz lived alone because Grandpa Schwartz had died, not because she'd grown tired of his channel-surfing. For another, Grandma Schwartz spent large swatches of time talking to people who didn't exist and conducting an imaginary symphony orchestra.

Jill didn't want to believe her mother was senile, although if she was, it would simplify things, or at least explain them. But she'd visited her mother at the First-Rate across the street just a week ago, and her mother had seemed sane. Worse, she'd seemed extremely happy.

At the entry to Building 4, Jill pressed the button next to her mother's apartment number and waited to be buzzed in. Next to her, Abbie stared at the cellulite-textured ceiling. The vestibule smelled of lemon-scented furniture polish, although it contained no furniture. Just a row of metal mailboxes, an intercom and an inner door, which like the outer door was glass with chrome trim.

"This place sucks," Abbie said less than a second before the buzzer sounded, releasing the inner door's lock.

"It's where your grandmother lives these days," Jill commented, hoping she sounded nonjudgmental. She considered reminding Abbie to exercise tact and keep her opinions about the place to herself in front of her grandmother, but decided not to. Abbie knew how to behave. And if she opted for blunt honesty over courtesy and told her grandmother what she thought of her new home, well, that wouldn't be the worst thing in the world. Jill's mother might respect opinions from her beloved eldest grandchild more than she respected opinions from her children.

Together they climbed the stairs to the second floor. Jill's mother stood in an open doorway halfway down the hall, beaming as if Jill and Abbie were soldiers returning home from battle. Jill wondered whether she'd deserve a Purple Heart before the evening was done.

"Welcome!" her mother bellowed as they neared the door.

Jill noticed her mother had placed a door mat in front of the sill, a vestigial reminder of her former life as a suburban homeowner.

Abbie scampered into her grandmother's embrace, her sullenness miraculously vanishing as the rich, heavy aroma of pot roast wafted into the hallway. After a quick peck on Jill's cheek, her mother looped an arm around Abbie's shoulders and ushered her inside.

"Come, let me show you around," she said grandly, as if she were about to lead them on a tour of Versailles.

Jill hesitated on the threshold, preparing herself to be disappointed and adjusting her expression to hide that inevitable disappointment. Then she entered the apartment and closed the door behind her.

"This is the kitchen," her mother was saying.

Jill followed the voice into a cramped, narrow, windowless space with ugly metal cabinetry, unfashionable white appliances and brown linoleum tiles on the floor.

"Not too big, is it," her mother said, stating the obvious. The room wasn't wide enough for her and Abbie to stand side by side, so she released Abbie and led her through to the living room. "I don't need a big kitchen. I'm cooking only for myself. When I even bother to cook. Some days, all I want is a bowl of soup, a can of salmon, some fruit and cheese. For that, the kitchen is the perfect size. Now, here's my living room . . ."

Jill followed a few steps behind them, pausing to survey the kitchen. It was so dark. So dreary. But fragrant with the scent of seasoned roast.

"Oh, cool!" Abbie exclaimed.

Jill hurried into the living room to see what Abbie was crowing about. The room didn't strike her as particularly cool—shag carpeting the color of faded mud, windows draped with generic beige curtains, boxy prefab furniture and a view of the parking lot. And a television set. A small one, perched on a shelf.

"Mom, see?" Abbie's smile was bright and challenging. "Some people *do* have TV's in the living room. Mom always says you shouldn't have a TV in the living room," she explained to her grandmother, "because the living room is for living in and watching TV isn't living. So we have to go to the den to watch TV. I wish we could have a TV in the living room."

Sure, Jill thought churlishly. *And then Dad and Noah could be dripping melted pizza cheese all over the fancy furniture in the living room instead of the sturdy old furniture in the den.*

Jill's mother laughed. "I put the TV in the living room because I don't have any other place for it. I thought maybe the bedroom, but then if I have a guest over and we want to watch TV, where would we sit? On the bed? So I put it there. Is there something you want to watch?"

"No. I just think it's cool." Abbie pranced to the windows and inspected the view, poked her head into a closet, bounced her butt on the couch and sprang back to her feet. "Cool! It's a futon."

"So if you wanted to sleep over, you could," Jill's mother said. "Or Noah. Or the twins. All my favorite people."

Jill noted that she, Melissa and Doug were not among her mother's favorite people. Nor did her mother indicate any interest in inviting her bridge ladies or her synagogue sisterhood friends for a pajama party.

"Mom, isn't this cool?" Abbie's enthusiasm seemed genuine. She darted down a short hall, announcing each highlight—"The bathroom! The bedroom! A linen closet!"—as if these features were actually special. What was it about this ghastly little apartment that had her so excited? During the drive, she hadn't used the word "cool" once, although "cold" would have aptly described her mood.

"It's very nice," Jill lied.

"It's all hers," Abbie said, waltzing around the living room and ending her dance by hugging her grandmother. "It's all yours, Grandma. You can put the furniture wherever you want. And it's all your stuff."

"I like that part," Jill's mother agreed.

"I want a place like this when I grow up," Abbie announced. "I want a place like this now, but Mom would never let me." She sent Jill a grin. "But when I grow up, I want to live all by myself, without Noah's dirty sneakers all over the place."

"They're not all over the place," Jill defended Noah. "He's got only two sneakers. How can they be all over the place?"

"I'm always tripping on them," Abbie complained. "And he never hangs up his towel in the bathroom. If I had my own place, I could hang the towels however I wanted. God, this is so cool."

Jill did not think it was cool. She thought it was just what Abbie had called it in the car: the pits. That her mother was living here instead of in her spacious, comfortable house, with its lovely, familiar furnishings and a kitchen more than one person could fit into at the same time, struck her as appalling.

Every time Abbie uttered the word *cool*, Jill wanted to scream. Didn't Abbie understand that they were supposed to be nudging Jill's parents back together again? Telling her grandmother her new residence was cool was not the way to get her grandmother to consider moving back home.

Jill's mother asked Jill and Abbie to carry the tiny table from the corner of the kitchen into the living room so three chairs could be placed around it. While Jill set the table, her mother led Abbie to the window and pointed out the First-Rate store where she worked. "It's a nice little shopping area, and I can walk. Think of all the gasoline I'm saving by walking to work."

She might save even more gasoline if she didn't work at all, but Jill didn't say that. She couldn't, not while Abbie was babbling about how ecologically enlightened her grandmother was.

"And I get home so quickly, I can even host a dinner party after work," Jill's mother continued, abandoning Abbie by the window and returning to the kitchen. "I'll slice up the meat. Do we have room on the table for a candle?"

"Ooh, candlelight," Abbie murmured.

Jill shook her head. "There's barely room for three plates," she said.

"Oh, well. We can pretend a candle," her mother said. "Jill, there's a salad in the fridge. And I bought some pretty glasses—" she motioned toward a cabinet with her chin; her hot-mitted hands were busy pulling the roast from the oven "—so we can drink grape juice and pretend it's wine."

Grape juice was not Diet Coke. Jill was finding it harder and harder to hide her displeasure.

Within a few minutes, they were all seated around the table. Crowded around it, actually. The serving platters had to remain on the kitchen counter since, as Jill had observed, three dinner plates pretty much filled the table. The cheap stemware glasses looked festive, even if Jill had to force herself to drink the grape juice. It reminded her of all those seders when she was little and the children weren't allowed to drink wine. She'd never understood why not. The kosher wine her mother used to serve at Passover tasted like cough syrup, and Jill and her siblings wouldn't have consumed enough to get drunk.

But this was girls' night at Ruth Bendel's cool apartment, and since Abbie had miraculously transformed from a whiny brat to a good sport,

Jill had to be a good sport, too. She had to sit placidly, eating her pot roast—which was as delicious as always; evidently the tiny kitchen hadn't cramped her mother's culinary ability—while her mother described her job to Abbie.

"They're training me how to run the photograph machine," she boasted. "Not that I'll work there very often. They've got these two ladies who basically run the photography department, and one of them is pretty bitchy, pardon my language. But my boss likes everyone to know the basics, in case someone is out sick or there's a big line or something. Everybody has digital cameras nowadays. It's not like film and negatives. Just pushing buttons on computers. Not that I'm a computer whiz like my brilliant grandchildren, but I can push buttons."

I'm a computer whiz, too, Jill wanted to declare. She, after all, was running a career from her kitchen computer, if you could call writing enticingly about raisin-and persimmon-hued bra-and-panty sets for Velvet Moon's catalogue a career.

"So, how's school?" Jill's mother asked Abbie. "What are you learning these days?"

Abbie grinned and shrugged. "Nothing."

"You're in honors pre-algebra," Jill reminded her.

"Yeah. I'm learning pre-algebra," Abbie told her grandmother. "My soccer team is four-two so far this season. I'm one of the top scorers . . ." And on she babbled, about soccer and Toby Klotzenberg's bar mitzvah—"in downtown Boston, at the Westin? He invited the whole seventh grade!"—and how if it were up to him, Noah would shower only once a month, he was such a pig.

It wasn't until dessert—do-it-yourself sundaes that were delicious, but Jill would have been better off, for a lot of reasons, with a Diet Coke—that Abbie raised the subject of her grandparents' separation.

"Are you pissed at Grandpa?" she asked, then apologized and said, "I mean, are you angry at him?"

"Angry? No," Jill's mother said as she dug into her heaping bowl of butter-pecan ice-cream drowning in chocolate syrup, M&M's and a lopsided dollop of canned whipped cream.

Abbie swallowed a spoonful of M&M-flecked chocolate ice-cream. "Well, you're like divorcing him, right?"

"We're separated right now. Where we go from here, who knows?"

"But it's like, what did he do? He showers every day. He has to, he's a doctor."

"A very good doctor," Jill's mother said. "The thing is, at different times in your life you need different things. Look at your mother." Abbie obediently turned her gaze to Jill, who didn't want to be looked at. She hadn't volunteered to be Exhibit A for her mother's lecture on good doctors and failed marriages. "When she was your age, she had needs like yours."

Jill shifted uncomfortably in her chair. "I'm not sure—"

"She wanted to be pretty, she wanted boyfriends, she wanted to go to Paris, she wanted a bosom . . ."

"Mom." Jill took a slug of grape juice and wished with all her heart it was something else.

"I didn't know you wanted to go to Paris," Abbie said.

Jill dismissed that old fantasy with a shrug. "I thought it would be exotic. And romantic. And the food would be great."

"So why didn't you go?"

"I was twelve years old," Jill replied.

"I mean later. When you were older."

"When I was older . . ." She sighed. She'd become Exhibit A, after all. "When I was older, I went to college. Then I met your dad, and we got married and had children, which seemed more important than Paris. I'll go someday," she insisted, because Abbie looked so sad for her.

"Exactly," her mother chimed in. "When she reaches a different time in her life, she'll go."

"With Dad?" Abbie asked.

"Of course with Dad," Jill said, hoping to reassure her daughter that she and Gordon would never do to Abbie what Jill's parents were doing to her.

"What if Dad doesn't want to go?" Abbie pressed her. "He always says insulting things about French people. He calls them frogs."

"He's joking," Jill said, even though when Gordon went on one of his anti-France tears, he seemed pretty serious.

"When I grow up," Abbie said thoughtfully, "I'll get married and have kids and have a fantastic job that pays a lot, but I think I want to go to France by myself. I think you should go by yourself, too, Mom. You don't want Dad there making stupid jokes."

Jill busied herself with her sundae, which was melting into thick, multicolored soup. She stirred the syrup into the liquefying ice cream, turning everything the same blah brown color as the carpet.

To go to France alone . . . what a scary thought. What an exhilarating idea. What if she never did it? What if she dropped everything and did it tomorrow?

She couldn't, of course. Abbie's bat mitzvah was just months away, and now that the Old Rockford Inn was ripping her off for an extra three bucks a guest, she couldn't afford a jaunt to Europe. And once Abbie's bat mitzvah was over, she and Gordon would have to start saving for Noah's bar mitzvah.

What had her mother said? At different times in your life you need different things.

She didn't need France. She certainly didn't need an ugly little apartment overlooking a major roadway and a strip mall.

Time alone, though? Did she need that?

Don't even think about it.

NOAH WAS ALREADY IN BED when Jill and Abbie arrived home around ten. "It's a school night," Jill reminded Abbie as they entered the house. "I didn't mean to keep you out this late."

"Wow, like it's *so* late," Abbie argued with the requisite eye-rolling and lip-curling.

Jill didn't take Abbie's sarcasm personally. Of course Abbie would be more affectionate with her grandmother and more snide with her mother. A Good Mom accepted the mood swings of an adolescent daughter without fussing, and she understood that it was her job to be the prime target for whatever snarkiness her daughter chose to spew. She'd spewed her own share of snarkiness at her mother when she'd been Abbie's age.

Gordon greeted them as they entered the kitchen through the garage door. "Daddy!" Abbie hollered loud enough to wake Noah up, except for the fact that nothing short of a seven-on-the-Richter-Scale earthquake could wake him up once he was asleep. The alarm on his clock was pitched about as shrilly as a police siren—and even then, he sometimes slept through it.

Abbie wrapped her father in a big embrace, and Jill, still in Good Mom mode, refused to resent the fact that Abbie hugged her father and her grandmother a lot more exuberantly than she hugged her mother, on those rare occasions when she deigned to hug her mother at all.

"So, how's Grandma's new apartment?" Gordon asked. His hair was tousled, his eyes glazed as if he'd been watching too much TV. The kitchen smelled of olive oil and oregano, and a square, grease-stained pizza box sat on the counter beside the sink. Evidently, discarding the box hadn't been on his or Noah's to-do list. Nor, for that matter, had wrapping the two leftover slices that remained inside the box, the cheese congealed and the circles of pepperoni starting to shrivel.

Abbie babbled about the apartment, answering all Gordon's questions—as if he actually cared what color the bathroom was or whether Grandma had hung any paintings on the walls. He just wanted to keep Abbie talking, to enjoy a few minutes of happy chatter with his princess before she headed upstairs and vanished into her bedroom to text Caitlin.

Jill lifted Abbie's jacket from the chair where she'd tossed it and hung it and her own jacket up in the coat closet. Then she returned to the kitchen. Still immersed in conversation, Gordon had steered Abbie out of the kitchen and up the stairs. Their voices drifted down the hall to Jill, growing fainter.

She wrapped the leftover pizza and stashed it in the refrigerator, then pulled a can of Diet Coke from the door shelf and snapped it open. A cola-scented wisp of mist rose from the opening and she took a few sweet swigs. By the time she lowered the can, Gordon and Abbie were out of earshot.

She gazed around her. She'd never considered her kitchen huge, but compared to her mother's kitchen it was monstrous. All those work surfaces, those cabinets, the full-size appliances, the table and chairs. The windows, now dark but usually filling the room with natural light. The counter-top desk with her computer humming and the screensaver spitting stars at her like the opening moments of the original Star Trek TV show, when William Shatner ponderously intoned, "Space, the Final Frontier." Gordon had Trekkie tendencies. Jill had watched a lot of those old episodes with him over the years.

She watched his shows. She put away his leftover pizza and flattened the empty box for the paper recycling bin. She sponged off the counters, which were speckled with crust crumbs, and moved his and Noah's dirty dishes from the sink to the dishwasher.

She swore to herself that she wasn't turning into her mother. It was just that she hadn't been home when the guys had been feasting on their pizza, and now it was late—too late to nag Gordon about leaving the kitchen a mess, too late to get angry and resentful about having to clean up that mess.

She absolutely wasn't her mother. Look at the computer. She hit a key to kill the screensaver, and the bra and panty text she'd composed earlier that day for Velvet Moon shivered to life on the screen.

See? She had a job. A real job, more creative than running a cash register at First-Rate. Her mother was probably earning minimum wage, whereas Jill . . . well, she didn't want to calculate her earnings per hour, and her compensation didn't include benefits, but still. She got to write things. She got to come up with new, edible names for colors, and she could drink Diet Coke while she worked, which she really did have to cut back on, but . . .

France. Imagine being alone in France rather than alone in her kitchen.

The sting of her drink's carbonation caused her eyes to water and she closed them, which liberated her imagination to conjure a stereotypical Parisian scene. A café beside the Seine. A glass of wine and a plate of cheese and fruit and crusty bread. Cute, skinny men in berets. Gorgeous, skinny women in haute couture. Edith Piaf's nasal voice wafting into the air, accompanied by tinkly accordion music. The vision was pathetically clichéd and corny, but Jill reveled in it. No eye-rolling, lip-curling daughter; no rowdy, rambunctious son. No husband. No pizza crust crumbs and dirty dishes.

Just France.

Gordon's hands alighted on her shoulders and she flinched and blinked herself back to the kitchen. "Seems like someone had fun tonight," he said.

"Yeah." Jill took another gulp of soda—nothing like an icy can of Diet Coke to jolt a person back to reality. "She whined the whole drive over there, then freaked out about how wonderful my mother's place was."

"Was it wonderful?"

"No. It's tiny and ugly."

"But your mother's happy there."

"At the moment."

She shook free of Gordon's hands and turned to face him. She didn't really want to go to France without him. He was still tall and handsome and had that crooked smile she'd fallen in love with the first time she'd seen him, when she'd been an undergraduate and he'd been in his first year of Brandeis's MAT program. She'd just settled at an empty table in the student center with a sandwich and a Diet Coke—her addiction dated back many years—and Sarah Levine's battered copy of *The Awakening*, which Sarah had already marked up with highlighter and marginal comments, sparing Jill the need to do so since she had the same prof for post-Civil War American Lit that Sarah had had the previous year. And then Gordon had dropped onto the empty chair across from her, set his sandwich and coffee down on the table and said, "You are far and away the most beautiful girl in this building, so I hope you don't mind my sitting here."

She'd been dumbfounded. She'd never considered herself particularly beautiful, and she'd never heard such a blunt come-on line before. At the time, she'd been sort of going with Marty Fischbein, but he'd been getting on her nerves, acting like an asshole when he drank too much beer—something he did on a regular basis. And this man, this totally unsuave stranger, had had the cutest smile. So she'd told him she didn't mind his sitting across the table from her.

She wrapped her arms around him, almost dumping soda down his back, and kissed his cheek. This was the man she'd married, the man she'd chosen to build a life with. She never, ever wanted to picture herself living by herself in a tiny, ugly apartment like her mother. She wanted to love Gordon always, even if loving him meant cleaning up his damn pizza. Even if it meant tolerating his channel-surfing and washing his beard hairs down the sink. She never wanted to reach a point where going to France alone seemed more romantic than going to France with him, even if he called French people frogs.

But they'd been together only sixteen years, married only fourteen. Who knew how she'd feel twenty-eight years from now? Who knew how many leftover pizza slices it took to wind up where her mother was?

And to be in France, alone in that café, with the wine and the music and the Seine flowing past . . .

Shit. She did want that. France. All by herself.

Chapter Fourteen

Brooke's bay was empty when Doug pulled into the garage. Six-fifteen. Where could she be? Were the girls home? With a baby-sitter? Which one? Ashleigh had gotten really bitchy now that she was a senior in high school—she clearly believed she was too mature and sophisticated for baby-sitting, but she loved the money so she condescended to work for Doug and Brooke when she was in the mood—but the new one, Megan, was kind of young to be left alone with the girls when they were awake. At night, once they were both in bed, they were easier to take care of. God, how Doug loved his daughters when they were asleep.

At six-fifteen in the evening, they weren't asleep.

He climbed out of the car, rolled his shoulders to loosen them—performing delicate incisions on corneas could tie knots in a person's muscles—and entered the house. Brooke had probably left a note somewhere, explaining their absence. Maybe she'd also left a nice, well-balanced meal on the kitchen's center island for him, something that would require five minutes in the microwave to be fully cooked. His empty stomach rumbled in anticipation. He wouldn't mind eating dinner by himself, as long as the food was good.

Brooke's culinary skills hadn't progressed all that much in the years they'd been married, though. "Good" was still a bit beyond her capabilities. And she'd left neither a meal nor a note.

What if she was gone? Really gone, packed-up-the-kids-and-disappeared gone?

Christ. Why would he even think such a thing? Just because his parents, two halves of the most solid, sturdy, unshakable marriage in the world, had split, didn't mean Brooke would leave him. Just because the inconceivable had happened didn't mean it would happen again.

He would not race upstairs to check Brooke's closet, her drawers, the guest-bedroom closet where they stored their luggage. He would not panic. He would not assume—

"Doug? Hi, we're home!" her voice sang out in the mudroom, accompanied by the clamor of multiple small feet that sounded nothing like pitter-patter. Maybe he and Brooke ought to enroll the twins in ballet classes so they'd learn how to walk without clomping.

At that moment, of course, Madison and Mackenzie's clomping was the sweetest sound he could imagine, short of Brooke's lilting voice as she followed the girls into the kitchen.

The girls were babbling, as usual. "Hi, Daddy!"

"We were at Stephanie's house!"

"Stephanie's mother gave us oatmeal cookies."

"I picked out all the raisins!"

"I ate her raisins!"

He nodded and automatically reached down to pat the girls' shoulders as they wrapped themselves around his legs, but his gaze was glued to Brooke. She looked . . . *different*.

Gorgeous, as always. Maybe even more gorgeous than always. Her hair was changed, though. A little darker, with lighter streaks and fluffy locks and playful strands dancing across her forehead.

Jesus. What had she done? Sure, she looked spectacular, but she looked so fucking *different*.

"Sorry we're late," she said, as if she hadn't transformed from the beautiful woman he loved into this other creature with altered hair. Her arms hugged a wilting paper bag. "We stopped at Colonel Ping's and picked up some take-out on the way home."

"Lotus Garden is better," he said, then shook his head. What was the matter with him? His wife had undergone this profound mutation, and he was quibbling over which Chinese restaurant he preferred.

"Colonel Ping's was on our way," she said breezily as she set the bag on the island.

"We got egg foo yong," Mackenzie announced.

Shit. He hated egg foo yong. Well, not hated, but honestly, all it was a glorified omelet with salty brown sauce and no cheese. For breakfast, maybe, but egg foo yong was not his idea of dinner.

"Don't worry," Brooke said, giving him a tolerant smile and a light kiss on the cheek. "We got chicken with cashews, too."

"And fried rice!" Madison crowed.

He nodded absently, too distracted by Brooke's scent to pay attention to the evening's menu. When she'd leaned in and kissed him, he'd smelled something as unfamiliar as her appearance. Whoever had done this thing to her—added infinite shadings to her hair and cut it all those different lengths—had sprayed something onto it as well, or conditioned it, or . . . something. Something that included spices a person didn't find in egg foo yong.

He felt disoriented. The knowledge that he was overreacting wildly to his wife's new hairdo made him feel even more disoriented. For God's sake, it was just a few snips here and there, and some coloring. Back in the old days—for instance, that morning—when she was blonder, he knew that a skilled hairdresser at a salon had contributed to the blondness. He wasn't opposed to cosmetic enhancement. Hell, he earned a fortune surgically enhancing patients' eyes so they could jettison their eyeglasses.

But Brooke hadn't told him she'd be doing this. She hadn't even hinted that she intended to transform her appearance. Maybe it had been a spur-of-the-moment decision; maybe she'd gone to the salon planning on the usual, and she'd impulsively changed her mind.

Her next statement informed him that it hadn't been impulsive or spur-of-the-moment. "I had your sister's friend do my hair. What do you think?"

"Jill has a friend who does hair?" Then why did Jill's hair always look so uninspired?

"No, silly." Brooke began to unload lidded plastic containers from the Colonel Ping bag. "Melissa's friend Luc."

That guy Melissa had driven up to Massachusetts with, the day Doug's parents had announced their separation. That guy Melissa shouldn't have brought with her, that guy Melissa shouldn't be dating, that guy who screamed *inappropriate* in so many varied ways.

He'd done this thing to Brooke's hair, this thing that made her look stunning, but not like his beloved Brooke.

"You went all the way to New York to get your hair done? Why?"

"Doesn't she look pretty?" Madison asked.

"I think she's beautiful," Mackenzie added.

"Of course she's beautiful. She's your mom." At Brooke's perplexed glance, he clarified. "You'd be beautiful even if you weren't their mom. I'm just saying, you're the same beautiful person now that you were this morning." *Aren't you?*

Steam rose from the containers of food, an oily fragrance laced with soy and ginger. His hunger had vanished, however. He considered pouring himself a glass of scotch, but if he did that he'd have to drink it. Right here, in his house, with his yammering daughters and his transformed wife, in a world where the earth kept shifting beneath his feet and people defied expectations and nothing was the way he expected it to be.

"Listen, honey . . . I've got to go," he said.

Brooke glanced at him again, looking even more puzzled.

"I got a call earlier today from my father," he lied. "He asked me to stop by after work."

She accepted his explanation with a nod. "I'll go ahead and feed the girls, then. Will you be long?"

"I'm not sure. You eat with the girls," he urged her. "I'll be back as soon as I can." Still in the dress shirt and tie he'd worn to the clinic, he started toward the mudroom.

"So, you like my hair?" she asked, prying off the lid of the egg foo yong and then sending him a beaming smile as the girls clamored for food.

"You look fantastic," he said, managing to return her smile before he ducked into the mudroom and out to the garage.

He didn't take another breath until he was safely ensconced behind the wheel of his Mercedes. He wasn't sure what was wrong with him: accelerated pulse, icy hands—Reynaud's, maybe? He was so far removed from his med school classes. Spend enough time doing Lasik surgery and your basic diagnostic skills began to erode.

He backed out of the garage, tore down the driveway and steered away from their subdivision, speeding along winding, tree-shaded roads bearing cloyingly picturesque two-word names that had little to do with the actual topography: Rippling Brook, Silver Hill, Blossom Boulder. By the time he hung a left off Rolling Meadow Lane, past a ghastly Tudor house designed for someone entertaining serious British-nobility delusions, and onto Route 30, his respiration was almost normal.

He pulled into the parking lot of a Dunkin Donuts, braked to a halt and took a deep, cleansing breath. And tried to figure out what was so disturbing about Brooke's new hair style.

The newness of it, for one thing. The fact that she hadn't told Doug she was planning this. Most of all, the fact that she'd traveled all the way to New York City—three and a half hours each way—just to have Melissa's boyfriend do the job.

He tugged his tie loose, unbuttoned his collar and pulled his cell phone from his pocket. He ought to call Melissa and find out what she knew about this.

No, he couldn't call her. He couldn't admit he had so little awareness of his own wife's plans that her jaunt to the boyfriend's salon had taken him completely by surprise.

He fingered the buttons on the phone. Jill, maybe. She was sensible.

She was grounded. She was the rock in the family, the one they all turned to in a crisis. But Doug wasn't prepared to admit to her that he could be thrown into a crisis by his wife's new hairdo.

Besides, Jill was a woman.

He'd never before longed for a brother—he'd liked being the only male child in the family; it was a position of privilege—but right now he could use one. He had buddies, but this was too personal to confide to them about. How could a man say, "My wife cut and colored her hair and I feel as if I'm losing her" to a buddy?

Why? Why did he feel he was losing Brooke?

Because if his father couldn't hang on to his mother after forty-two years, how the hell could Doug hang onto Brooke?

He hit the speed-dial for his parents' home number. His father's number now—he'd programmed his mother's new number into his phone, but he hadn't assigned her a speed-dial number because he hoped this phase of hers wouldn't last and she'd be back at the old number before too long.

His father answered on the third ring. "You're home," Doug said.

"I answered. Of course I'm home."

"Can I come over?"

"Now? Sure. What's wrong?"

"Nothing's wrong," Doug lied, but at least he'd turned the lie he'd given Brooke about where he was going into the truth. "I'll be there in fifteen."

It took him less than fifteen minutes to get to his father's house. He drove fiendishly. If a cop stopped him, he'd say he was having heart palpitations and was on his way to see a cardiologist. Not that he *was* having heart palpitations, but his fingers were still icy, which clearly meant he was suffering some sort of medical emergency involving his circulatory system.

As it turned out, no cops intervened, and in ten minutes he pulled into the driveway of his parents' house. He knew the driveway's dips, its frost-heaves, the crack spanning the asphalt just beyond the front walk. How many times had he cruised up this driveway since getting his license more than twenty years ago?

He still remembered steering up the driveway in his first car—actually, his mother's car, but once he'd gotten his license he'd used it more often than she did. Unlike his mother, he'd had places to go—school, cross-country practices, parties, Lynette Baker's house. He and Lynette had been quite the couple most of senior year. She'd been his first, and even though she'd been kind of narcissistic and given to the annoying habit of finishing other people's sentences for them, he'd always remain grateful to her for what he'd learned on the worn tweed sofa in her finished basement.

He hauled his tie over his head and tossed it onto the passenger seat before leaving the car. What was he going to say to his father? At their respective ages, they'd reversed the advisor-advisee relationship. His mother walked out on his father and his father turned to Doug for advice. Doug's wife hadn't left him, although her familiar blond hair had, and he'd turned to his father for . . . what? Comfort? Scotch? Definitely not advice.

His father looked frazzled when he answered the door. He had on a pale gray warm-up suit which didn't flatter him, and his hair stood out from his scalp in tawny, gray-streaked tufts. "I'm glad you came," he said, ushering Doug inside. "Maybe you can help me. I'm trying to iron some shirts."

"Why?" Doug asked.

"They're wrinkled. Gert said I look wrinkled."

Doug had met his father's office manager many times. He considered her snotty, which wasn't exactly a negative for someone with her job. "Who cares if you look wrinkled?" he asked as he followed his father down the hall to the den, where his father had set up an ironing board in front of the television. "You wear a white coat over your shirt, anyway."

"I'll tell you who cares," his father said as he shook out the extremely wrinkled shirt sitting on the ironing board. "You want a drink?"

Doug spotted an open bottle of beer on the coffee table. No coaster, he noticed. If his mother were here, she'd be infuriated. Maybe his father was leaving moisture rings on the table deliberately, out of spite.

Doug really wanted a scotch, but a beer made more sense. He'd been lucky not to get a ticket driving over. He didn't want to risk getting a ticket—or worse—driving home. "A beer looks good," he said. "I'll help myself. Who cares about your shirts being wrinkled?" he asked again as he ducked into the kitchen.

The room hadn't changed much since he'd left home for college so many years ago. Fewer notices and schedules attached to the refrigerator with magnets, less clutter on the counters, no huge bowl of fruit serving as a centerpiece on the table. His mother had always had bushels of fruit in the house, a fair assortment of which she'd heaped into a tinted glass bowl and left on the kitchen table every day. He'd thought nothing of detouring into the kitchen and grabbing a peach, a banana, a twig full of grapes on his way somewhere else.

No fruit on the kitchen table now. No piles of school books. No phone book left open to the page of an orthodontist or a Little League coach. But this room was the kitchen he associated with home, even more than the arena-sized, superbly appointed kitchen in the house he shared with Brooke, a kitchen full of top-of-the-line everything, most of which Brooke had no clue how to use.

Doug knew this room in a way he still didn't know that other kitchen. He knew the yellow walls, the scallop-edged curtains, the pine cabinets, the four-burner electric stove with the dent near one of the dials, from when he'd been practicing his swing with his brand-new 29-ounce adult bat, the year of his bar mitzvah, and he'd swung a little too wide and slugged what would have been a home run if he'd hit a ball instead of the stove.

His parents' kitchen looked the same as always . . . only different.

Like Brooke.

Wincing, he helped himself to a beer from the door of the fridge, popped it open with the church-key opener in the utensil drawer—he still knew what was in every drawer—and returned to the den.

"Shari Bernstein," his father said.

"Who?"

"Shari Bernstein cares if my shirts are wrinkled." His father ran the iron back and forth across an expanse of shirt, but the wrinkles remained.

Doug sipped his beer, wishing it was something stronger. He wasn't sure he wanted to hear the answer, but he asked anyway: "Who's Shari Bernstein?"

"She's a dermatologist. Why isn't this iron working? When your mother does this, the shirt comes out smooth." He held it up to give Doug a better view of the wrinkles.

What was his father doing with a dermatologist? The only reason Doug could think of was skin cancer. "Are you having something biopsied?"

"No. I'm having a cup of coffee," his father said, then smoothed the shirt across the ironing board once more. "What am I doing wrong here? Should I call your mother? I don't want to call her."

Doug's eyes had strayed to his father's bottle of Sam Adams

sweating condensation onto the coffee table. He pondered whether he should put his bottle down, too. Were two water rings worse than one, or once one was formed and the damage done, more didn't matter?

His mental debate temporarily blocked his brain's ability to process his father's words. "Call her," he said, opting to place his bottle atop the TV Guide rather than directly on the table. Once that decision was made, he could respond to his father's statement. "Ask her how the iron works. I think steam's supposed to come out of it."

"I have it set on steam."

"Is there water in it? You need water to make steam."

"Water. Of course." His father shook his head. "Gert said I should take my shirts to the dry cleaner. I don't have time to do that, though. The coffee is tomorrow."

"What coffee?"

"The coffee I'm having with Shari Bernstein."

"The dermatologist? You're having coffee with a dermatologist?" Doug sank onto the sofa as relief crashed over him. No biopsy. No funky-looking nevus, no irregular lesion. Just coffee.

Coffee. With someone named Shari Bernstein. "You're going on a *date?*"

"Not a date. Just coffee." His father shoved the iron across his shirt energetically but futilely. "She's divorced."

"You're not."

"I'm separated." He balanced the iron on its edge, gazed across the ironing board at Doug and sighed. "What the hell am I doing? It took me hours to get up the nerve to call her. We're meeting in the staff cafeteria at five-thirty. God forbid my appointments run late tomorrow—I'll never get there by five-thirty. She's a dermatologist, she probably never runs late. They don't have emergencies like we do."

"Someone could charge into her office at the last minute with a humongous zit," Doug pointed out, then laughed. His father on a date.

He'd been the one who'd raised the idea of his father dating a few weeks ago, the afternoon his parents had announced their separation to their assembled children. But now that it was actually happening . . . His fingers started going icy again, practically numb. He took a few long gulps of beer, but that only chilled him even more.

"So, who is this woman? This dermatologist. Have you met her?"

"Gert gave me her number." His father struggled mightily with the iron. Without water in it, his efforts were bound to be in vain, but Doug didn't know where the water went, how to inject it into the appliance.

His mother hadn't taught him how to iron. She'd done all the laundry tasks for the family when he'd been growing up.

"I'm meeting her tomorrow," his father said. "Gert knows her. She says she's pretty." His father put down the iron again, flat on his shirt, and sighed. "I don't know how to do this."

"Don't leave the iron that way," Doug said, rising from the couch and standing the iron on end. At least he knew that much—that if you left an iron hot-surface down, you could scorch the garment you were trying to press. "Maybe the water goes in here," he noted, pointing to an opening built into the handle.

"If you're wrong, we could short-circuit the damn thing."

"If I'm right, you could have an ironed shirt to wear tomorrow."

His father thought for a minute, then left the room.

Alone, Doug circled the den with his gaze. The TV was on, the volume low enough to be ignored. The screen showed devastation somewhere. A storm? A battle? An attack from outer space? Given the way Doug felt—that the earth had somehow tilted slightly, that nothing was quite what it was supposed to be—he'd bet money on the third option.

His father returned carrying a measuring cup full of water. "In here?" he asked, pointing to the opening on the iron's handle.

"Give it a try."

His father poured some water in. The iron hissed like a venomous snake. "That sounds good," his father said. Doug didn't think he was being facetious.

"If Mom can do this, you can do this," Doug cheered him on. "Give it a try."

His father rubbed the iron across his wrinkled shirt. A cloud of steam wheezed out of the vents. Doug and his father exchanged a triumphant look across the ironing board.

"So, does Mom know about this date?"

"It's not a date. It's just coffee. And why should your mother know about it?"

Good question. His parents were separated. Maybe his mother was dating someone, too.

No, Doug couldn't imagine that. Not possible. Even if space aliens had attacked the planet. "If she knew, she might get jealous," he said.

His father peered up from his shirt. He appeared intrigued. "You think that's a good idea?"

"If she's jealous, maybe she'd come home." On the other hand, if the dermatologist was spectacular, maybe Doug's father wouldn't want Doug's mother to come home.

Scratch that possibility. Doug's parents belonged together. No dermatologist, regardless of how pretty, should come between them. Ruth and Richard Bendel were a couple. A pair. United unto death in the eyes of God, not that Jews were as rigid about divorce as Catholics. And if Doug's parents remained apart, who would baby-sit for the twins when Doug and Brooke went to Nevis?

His father rested the iron flat, then remembered and balanced it on end. He held up his steam-ironed shirt. The sleeves were still a mess, but the back was a smooth expanse. "Look at that. A little water was all it needed. I wish the cuffs were cleaner, though. Your mother always got them so clean." He sounded wistful. Doug hoped his rueful mood arose from thoughts of his absent wife, not his dingy cuffs.

"So, you're meeting this woman for coffee," Doug said, crossing to the ironing board and taking the shirt from his father. He spread the cloth on the silver padding covering the board. It was warm, the back of the shirt hot. He smoothed a sleeve out on the board and lifted the iron, which sighed and sputtered as he pressed the sleeve smooth.

Brooke never did this, he realized. He wasn't even sure they owned an iron. They probably did, since they owned just about every consumer item a person could buy. But Brooke never ironed anything. He suspected their cleaning service took care of the dirty clothes, and what they didn't launder Brooke brought to the dry cleaners.

He felt an odd surge of pride performing a domestic task Brooke didn't know how to do. She was no homemaker—he'd known that when he married her, and he'd been okay with it. But he liked acknowledging that at a crucial moment he could figure out a steam iron.

"You really think I could make your mother jealous?" his father asked as he circled the ironing board and grabbed his beer. "I'd have to let her know I was meeting Shari. How do I do that? I can't just call her and say, 'Guess what? I'm having coffee with another woman.'"

"I could tell her," Doug said, then grimaced. He didn't want to get caught in the middle. "Or I could tell Jill and Jill could tell her." Much better. Jill was a daughter. She'd be more likely to call their mother and sound alarms about their father's flourishing social life. Not that meeting a fellow doctor for coffee in the staff cafeteria of the hospital qualified as a flourishing social life.

"And you think your mom would get jealous?" His father sounded awfully eager.

Doug scrutinized the sleeve he'd ironed. He'd exercised a degree of care and precision that wouldn't be foreign to his operating room, and it showed. No accidental pleats, no crumples along the shoulder seam. He arranged the other sleeve on the board and applied the iron. "It wouldn't be fair," he said cautiously, "to meet this doctor for coffee if the only reason is to make Mom jealous. That would be using her, you know?"

"It's just coffee," his father insisted. "It's not like I'm sleeping with her."

"Good."

"I can't even imagine . . ." His father shuddered, as if the very idea of sex with the dermatologist disgusted him. Then he seemed to reconsider. "Gert did say she was very pretty."

"Just take it slow," Doug warned him. "If you walk too far down that path, it may be impossible to retrace your steps."

His father blinked a couple of times as he digested Doug's metaphor. "How would you know? You're an expert on having sex with people who aren't your wife?"

"I was thirty when I got married," Doug said. "And I wasn't a virgin."

His father's dark eyes flashed, not with disapproval but with competitive fire. He probably hadn't been a virgin when he'd gotten married, either. But he'd gotten married right out of college. Forty-two years was a long time to be having sex with the same woman.

Yet Doug could imagine nothing he'd like more than to have sex with Brooke for forty-two years. The Brooke he knew, though. Not the Brooke with feathery hair in layers of gold and bronze and copper, and probably a few other metals, all done up by a Manhattan-based pretty-boy who might, God forbid, wind up becoming his brother-in-law.

"So," his father broke into his thoughts, "what's up with Mackie and Maddie? How are my two little angels?" He took the iron from Doug and arranged the shirt on the ironing board so he could press the front.

His ironing services no longer needed, Doug flopped onto the sofa and drank some beer. His digestive system was empty—better than full of egg foo yong from Colonel Ping's, he consoled himself—and the lager's bitter, yeasty bubbles sloshed inside his stomach with nothing solid to absorb them. Thinking about Brooke's hair stole his appetite, though. Not even pretzels or beer nuts could tempt him. Not even a sprig of grapes or a banana from his mother's fruit bowl.

"The girls are great," he said, wondering whether they would someday grow up and journey all the way to New York City to change their hair styles. These days, they both wore their hair straight and shoulder length. Madison liked to clip brightly colored barrettes shaped like flowers and butterflies into her locks, and Mackenzie sometimes insisted on having a single narrow braid woven from the hair beside her left ear, but otherwise their hair was a sweet, honey-blond color, the color genetics had given them.

"What a pair," Doug's father said, shaking his head and smiling fondly. He lifted his shirt, scrutinized it and draped it on a hanger, evidently satisfied that it would pass muster with the dermatologist. "I can tell them apart all the time, now. It takes me a minute or two sometimes, but I'm usually right. How does Melissa tell them apart so well? You and Brooke, of course you don't need a minute or two. But Melissa sees them only once in a while, and she can always tell one from the other, right away. How does she do that?"

Melissa's name dragged him back to thoughts of Melissa's boyfriend. "So, Melissa's still with that hairdresser," he said experimentally. His father's reaction would inform him as to whether this was a subject they could discuss.

"The goy? Marlon Brando?"

"Brondo," Doug corrected him. "Something Brondo." *Lucas Brondo*, he knew damned well. Since his father didn't veer back into mushy grandpa comments about the girls, Doug decided to share his uneasiness about the situation with Brooke. "It's the weirdest thing, Dad—Brooke arranged to have this Brondo guy do her hair."

"Brooke? Your Brooke? What, she couldn't find someone with a scissor and a mirror closer than two hundred miles away?"

"That was exactly what I thought. Why the hell would a woman travel all the way to New York City to get her hair done?"

His father settled on the sofa next to him, lifted his beer and snorted. "You're asking me why women do what they do? I know a lot, Doug, but not about that."

"It just . . . shook me up," Doug said. "The whole thing. Her going so far away for a haircut."

His father twisted to study him. "You're having problems? You and Brooke?"

"No. Not at all," Doug insisted. "We're fine. It just . . . ." He shrugged. "She went all that way, and she never even told me she was going. And it's . . . Melissa's boyfriend." Another shrug. He didn't want to come across as desperate. He *wasn't* desperate. Shaken up, that was all.

"So? Was it worth the trip? Does she look two hundred miles better?"

"I don't know." Doug sighed and stared down into the small-bore opening of the bottle in his hand. "She looks great," he conceded.

His father didn't miss his glum tone. "You like her hair better the other way? Let her know. Tell her to let her hair grow back out the way it used to be. Communication is important. Like I should be giving anyone marital advice."

Doug managed a smile. Back when he was a teenager, when he was schtupping Lynette Baker every chance he got, he'd never asked his father for advice on his social life. Nor had he confided in his father during his college years, when he'd squeezed a semi-decent social life into his pre-med schedule. Certainly not in medical school, when he'd had a bizarre relationship with Jennifer Zelnik, a fellow med school student who disliked him as much as he disliked her but, Christ, they were good in bed together, so they'd fucked and fought throughout the four-year slog and then gone their separate ways. Not once, in all those years, with all those women, had Doug turned to his father for guidance on how to survive a relationship. The last time he'd discussed women with his father, as he recalled, was shortly after his bar mitzvah, when his father had bought him a package of condoms and said, "God forbid you should use these. They expire in three years—see the expiration date?—and I expect you to throw them out because you're too young to need them. But better you have them and don't need them than you need them and don't have them."

Doug admitted that that was pretty wise counsel, actually. "The fact is," he said, "Brooke's new hair looks really good."

"Well, of course," his father said. "She's so pretty, that wife of yours. Not that pretty is everything. There was a popular song when I was in college, about how if you want to be happy you should marry an ugly woman. Calypso. That was very big then, Calypso music."

"I know that song," Doug muttered. It was one of those catchy, bouncy tunes that, once lodged in your mind, plagued you like tinnitus. "Mom was pretty and you married her."

"And look at me now. Ironing my own shirts."

"Making a coffee date with a dermatologist. Who's also pretty, according to Gert."

"I shouldn't have called her. I should have asked Gert to introduce me to some ugly women." His father laughed. "So, this is why you came here? To tell me about Brooke's new haircut?"

When his father put it that way, it sounded remarkably stupid. "I just wanted to see how you were doing," he said. "Maybe I had a premonition about your struggles with the iron."

"It was good timing, your coming here. You want something to eat? I picked up some cold cuts and torpedo rolls. Sliced turkey, low-salt. And some lettuce and tomatoes, and a couple of pickles. I'm eating terribly since your mother left."

The cold cuts didn't sound as terrible as anything from Colonel Ping. Doug would have eaten take-out from Lotus Garden. But Colonel Ping, and Brooke's hair, and the girls spending all afternoon at a friend's house because their mother's tresses were being ministered to by Melissa's boyfriend . . .

"Nah. I'm not that hungry," he said, which was true. He was actually kind of queasy. "Anyway, Brooke's got food waiting for me at home."

"Then go home, eat her food and count your blessings. I don't care what the song says—if you've got a pretty woman who cooks you dinner, count your blessings."

Doug didn't bother to mention that Brooke hadn't cooked his dinner, that in fact she was an unenthusiastic, uninspired cook. Truth was imbedded in his father's statement—he had Brooke, and he ought to count his blessings.

Really, everything was perfect between them, hairstyle notwithstanding. It was as perfect as it had ever been, wasn't it? It would be even more perfect if he could get his parents back together so they could baby-sit for the girls in February. Brooke would be so grateful if he accomplished that. He'd be her hero—more heroic in her eyes than he already was.

"Do me a favor, Dad," he said as he drained his beer bottle and stood. "Don't fall in love with the dermatologist. Work things out with Mom."

"We'll see," his father said, sounding both cryptic and weary. He rose, too, and ambled with Doug to the kitchen to drop off their empty bottles. From there he accompanied Doug to the door. "Do *me* a favor, Doug. If you hear anything about your mother having coffee with some other man, let me know, okay?"

"Sure." As if his mother would share such news with him. With Jill, perhaps. Doug ought to give her a call.

"And let me know if she changes her hair, too," his father added. "I like it the way it's always been. I don't want her to change it."

Doug thought about handing his father's advice back to him, telling the old man he ought to communicate with his wife. But they'd been communicating when they'd decided to separate, hadn't they?

Jealousy might bring them together again a hell of a lot faster than communication.

Chapter Fifteen

The morning air was gray and clammy as Ruth waited for the traffic light to change so she could cross the street. Francine had yet again asked her to do the pre-opening set up. All this meant was setting her alarm clock a half-hour earlier than usual. Not a big deal; she lived just across the street, so getting to the store earlier was easy. And Francine was so prickly—Ruth still wasn't sure Francine believed that she'd started work the day she was supposed to—that Ruth didn't like to say no to her.

She turned up the collar of her jacket and shoved her hands into the pockets. The cars speeding down the street left cold, swirling gusts in their wakes, and she turned her face away from the wind as she waited for the light to change. When it did, she hesitated before stepping into the crosswalk, just in case some jerk chose to run the red light. The street was too busy, especially at rush hour.

But Ruth felt a kinship with the drivers. They were all commuters traveling to work, after all. *I'm a commuter,* she thought. The novelty hadn't worn off yet.

The first time Francine had asked her to do the pre-opening set-up, she'd been excited. Making sure the shelves were neat and well stocked, the cash registers humming, all the lights turned on and functioning had seemed like a huge responsibility. Now, her fourth time, the task was routine. Open the staff room, hit the light switches, ascertain that the public trash cans had been emptied overnight, position the portable displays correctly, make sure the end-caps were neat, and generally spruce up the store before Francine arrived and unlocked the front door for customers. Arriving early meant Ruth had to enter through the rear of the building, where either Frank or Carlo would already be hard at work, supervising deliveries. God knew when they had to arrive to do this, but whichever one handled the morning deliveries got to leave by three in the afternoon, so Ruth didn't feel sorry for them.

An impatient driver revved his engine as she crossed in front of it. It was like an automotive leer, the car lurching aggressively into the crosswalk, stopping just inches from her leg. She turned and glared. Part of being a member of the family of commuters meant being allowed to glare at jerks. Even flip them the bird, if Ruth felt particularly daring.

After arriving safely on the strip-mall side of the street, she walked around the parking lot to the rear of the building. An eighteen-wheeler, its sides adorned with the fluffy-teddy-bear logo of a toilet paper company, was being unloaded by a driver as Carlo watched. Ruth waved, then turned toward the back door and noticed the young man leaning against the cement wall. She immediately recognized his lanky build, the woolly hair tumbling around his face, the red apron extending below the edge of his battered leather jacket and the glint of silver at the outer corner of his left eyebrow.

He was smoking.

"Idiot," she muttered, stalking across the asphalt to confront him. "Wade Smith, what the hell are you doing?"

He gave her a crooked smile, then eyed the cigarette in his hand. "Smoking?"

"Do you know how unhealthy that is?"

"Hey, come on," he said amiably. "Don't give me a hard time."

"You think this is a hard time? You should hear my husband." She never talked about Richard with her coworkers, but this morning the statement slid out easily, without thought. He was still her husband. She could still use his expertise to make a point. "My husband is a cardiologist. He treats people who smoke cigarettes. Their arteries are a mess. Their hearts, their lungs, their throats, their gums and teeth, they get strokes, they get cancer, they get phlebitis—"

"Okay, okay." Wade's smile hadn't been big to begin with, and now it was gone. He turned away and took a defiant drag on his cigarette.

Ruth wasn't that easily silenced. "It's a terrible habit."

"It's not a habit. This is the first smoke I've had in six months."

"Second," Carlo noted with a smirk. Apparently he'd been eavesdropping from his post near the truck. "First one was five minutes ago."

Ruth clicked her tongue in disgust. She'd gotten used to Wade's hair and his facial jewelry. She'd grown fond of his low-key personality, his patience, his surprisingly unsarcastic humor. She was not going to stand by while he sucked poison into his body. "Put that thing out, Wade. Let's go inside and get you some nicotine gum. Or one of those patches. With our employee discount, it won't be that expensive."

"A lot cheaper than cigarettes," Carlo added.

Ruth sent him a grateful look.

"Get off my back, all right?" Wade snapped, more at Carlo than at Ruth. He turned to her, obviously seething with resentment. "You're not my mother."

Ruth had raised three children. A little backtalk didn't faze her. "You're practically done with it, anyway," she said, gesturing toward the shrunken cigarette. "Put it out and come inside."

She might not be his mother, but he obeyed anyway, lifting his foot and snubbing the cigarette out on the thick black sole of his shoe. Scowling, he accompanied her into the building. She noticed that he deposited the butt in a trash can en route to the staff room. Defiance and backtalk notwithstanding, Wade didn't litter, at least not in front of her.

Neither of them spoke while she turned on the staff room lights, set up the coffee maker and pressed the brew button. Not until the room was filled with the rousing scent of coffee—strong enough to overtake the cigarette smell that clung to Wade's hair—and she'd filled two cups did she confront him. "You quit six months ago? Only an idiot would start smoking again after quitting for six months."

"So I'm an idiot," Wade shot back before taking a swig of coffee. "Shit," he said appreciatively. "Your coffee tastes so much better than what we used to have here."

"That's because I'm not an idiot," Ruth explained—a non-sequitur, but she didn't care. "Now tell me what's going on with you. And don't use the s-word."

Wade sighed. "Nothing."

She glared at him.

"Okay," he relented. "My girlfriend and I had a fight last night, that's all."

Wade had mentioned his girlfriend once or twice before. Ruth recalled that she had an old-fashioned name—Bertha or Ernestine or something. "What did you fight about?" she asked.

"The fact that she was breaking up with me."

"Ah." Her stern-mother attitude melted slightly. Poor Wade, suffering from a broken heart. Not a valid excuse to resume smoking after half a year, but a little sympathy might be in order. "You're better off without her," she said.

Wade opened his mouth, then shut it, then gave her a dubious look. "How do you know that?"

"I know these things. I know how to make a good pot of coffee and I know smoking will kill you. I'm a smart lady."

"If you're so smart, what are you doing working here? You're married to a doctor. You don't need the money."

"We're not . . ." It was Ruth's turn to sigh, hesitate, then grin. "Let's just say he and I had a fight."

"He broke up with you?"

"I broke up with him. But that's neither here nor there," she said, busying herself at her locker, removing her employee ID card from her purse and letting the building's warmth seep into her. She scanned the card into the time clock, because even though she was married to a doctor, she did need the money.

It wasn't as if she was broke. She'd always been frugal, and she could manage on what she earned. But the thing she'd so looked forward to—supporting herself, paying her way, not depending on Richard and feeling obligated to him—required extra attention and diligence. She was a working woman now. Self-supporting. Self-sufficient.

"You broke up with your husband? No shit? Sorry," Wade mumbled as the s-word slipped out. "Why?"

Ruth's automatic reply was that the subject was none of his business. She didn't say that, though. Here she was, making his smoking and his girlfriend—or ex-girlfriend, as the case might be—her business. She owed him a little reciprocity. "It's hard to explain," she said, then sipped some coffee. He was right, her coffee was tastier than anyone else's. Maybe that was why she didn't mind doing the pre-opening set-up. Whoever came in early wound up making the first pot of coffee in the staff room, and better she did that than anyone else. Especially Bernie, whose coffee put Ruth in mind of raw sewage. "Really, it was nothing in particular."

"You left your husband over nothing in particular?"

"I left him because it was time for a change."

"That's what Hilda said," Wade muttered. "It was time for a change. What kind of crap is that? Hey—" he held his hands up defensively, before she could criticize "—I said crap, not shit."

Hilda. That was the girlfriend's name. "Maybe Hilda's right," Ruth suggested. "Maybe it *is* time for a change."

Wade shook his head. "We change all the time. She's tired of Mojo's, we go to The Hut. Those are clubs where we hang out," he clarified. "She's tired of pizza, we eat sushi. She's tired of beer, we drink bourbon."

"Could it be . . ." Ruth struggled for a gentle phrasing, then gave up. "She's tired of you?"

Wade appeared more shocked than insulted. "How could she be? I love her."

"Did you try making up with her?"

"I don't know what I'm making up for. She wants a change. That makes as much sense as nothing in particular." He slumped into a chair and gazed up at Ruth, his eyes pleading. "You think I should send her flowers?"

"Flowers are a cliché," Ruth pointed out. "If she wants a change, maybe you should send her something different. Something she would really like."

"Weed?"

"Why would you send her weeds? Oh, you mean pot?" She pursed her lips. "That's illegal."

Wade snorted.

Ruth sat across the table from him, ignoring the tasks that awaited her out in the store. Right now, Wade was more important than turning on the lights and straightening out the end-caps. "When a woman says she wants a change, it means she's not happy with things the way they are. Men—and I'm not saying you specifically, but in general—it doesn't take much for a man to be content. He likes his recliner, and as long as he can sit in his recliner he's happy. He likes his TV, he likes his car, he likes pot roast—that's pot *roast*, not pot—and if he has those things, he can't see what the problem is. Whereas women—and again, I'm speaking in generalities—spend the majority of their lives making sure men have all those things that make them happy. And no one does that for women. No one makes sure *they* always get to sit in their favorite chair and eat their favorite dinner. Unless the women make that dinner themselves, of course. What's Hilda's favorite dinner?"

Wade frowned. "I don't know. She was on that sushi kick for a while, but she's over it now."

"You don't even know what her favorite dinner is. I bet she knows what your favorite dinner is. I bet she prepares it for you all the time."

"It's Big Mac's," he said. "She doesn't have to prepare anything."

"I bet she agrees to go to McDonald's with you all the time."

Wade considered, then smiled sheepishly and nodded. "So that's what your husband did? Made you eat at McDonald's all the time?"

"My husband is a cardiologist," she reminded him. "He would never eat at McDonald's." Though, God knew, maybe he was eating at McDonald's now. She couldn't picture him coming home after a long day with his patients and colleagues and whipping up a healthy vegetarian stir-fry for himself. Or even a steak. In all the years they'd been married, his grand contribution to meals had amounted to shaking the bottle of salad dressing or filling a pitcher with milk. And carving the turkey at Thanksgiving. He claimed that as the family's expert in anatomy, he ought to be the one wielding the carving knife.

So what was he eating now that she wasn't there to fix him his meals? Cold cereal in the morning, she'd bet. Eggs, toasted bagels, pancakes or even oatmeal would be beyond him, but pouring Cheerios into a bowl he could manage. For dinner, sandwiches, probably. Maybe a salad. He had such talent when it came to shaking a bottle of salad dressing.

"What would he have to do for you to make up with him?" Wade asked.

"Don't compare your situation to mine," she said. "My husband and I have a long history. We were too close for too long, rubbing up against each other."

"That can be fun," Wade pointed out, then apologized again.

"I'm not talking about *that*," Ruth clucked. Discussing sex had never embarrassed her, not with her own children and not with Wade, who could have been another child of hers. Of course, if he was, she wouldn't have let him pierce his eyebrow. "In music, there's this thing called suspended seconds," she began, then sighed. Surely he didn't want to hear an explanation of her college honors thesis.

Yet how else to describe what she was talking about?

"One note in a chord is dominant," she continued. "The other note gets too close and the chord becomes unstable. So that other note has to move, to stabilize the chord."

Wade gave her a blank look.

"Never mind. I know what I mean." She smiled and sipped her coffee. "In any case, you and Hilda couldn't possibly have been together long enough to become dissonant, the way Richard and I did."

"Six months," he protested. "That's pretty long."

"You met her and stopped smoking?"

"She made me."

"She's a good woman." Ruth ruminated.

"She's the best," Wade said sadly, soulfully. Then he brightened. "Would you talk to her?"

"Me?"

"Woman to woman. Woman who walked away from her guy to woman who walked away from her guy."

The very idea of talking to some young, pierced, female version of Wade unnerved Ruth. She was from another generation, another world. She hadn't had Hilda's options when she'd met Richard. She'd come of age on the cusp of the feminist revolution, and she'd endured a long, fruitful marriage which, for the most part, she'd enjoyed. She hadn't had a job, but she'd done volunteer work. She'd tried to learn tennis. She'd kept busy.

But she'd never been self-sufficient. Her decision to leave Richard had been about *her*, about wanting to live on her own and be her own person.

Hilda, like Ruth's daughters, was from a generation where those things were a given. She was born being her own person. What could Ruth possibly say to her?

"You could ask her why she broke up with me," Wade answered her unvoiced question. "If it's something real, maybe I can fix it. Flowers, weed, whatever. You could find out what she wants me to do—if there's anything I *can* do. If not, if we're just an unstable chord . . ." He sighed. "Well, at least I'd know that much."

Ruth had serious misgivings. "I've never even met this girl."

"You'd love her. She's so cool." Wade's eyes glowed. He actually seemed to think a meeting between Ruth and Hilda was a great idea. "We could go over after work today. She gets off work at five-thirty. We could catch her when she leaves."

"Where does she work?"

"She's a dental technician. Yeah," he said, sitting taller. "That's practically like being a doctor. Maybe she broke up with me because I didn't finish college."

"You started college?" Ruth asked. At his nod, she patted his hand. "Then you should finish. Finish college, quit smoking, and the world is your oyster."

"Who wants an oyster?" Wade made a face. "If I had to eat that shit—I mean, that crap—I'd rather eat sushi."

WADE SEEMED TO THINK Ruth was wise. But as she bounced in the passenger seat of his ancient, rusty Corolla at five-fifteen that afternoon, she questioned her wisdom. The car's interior smelled like kitty litter, the floor at her feet was carpeted in Big Mac wrappers, a few loose CD's and an apparently unpaid parking ticket, and the car's shock absorbers were on strike.

Behind the wheel, Wade looked more cheerful than he had all day.

His hair echoed the bouncing of the car, the stringy locks vibrating with each bump and pothole in the road, and he chatted about Hilda the entire drive. "She's really beautiful," he told Ruth, as if that was her most important attribute. Ruth supposed that to a single guy in his twenties, it was. "And we like exactly the same music," he added, as if to prove that he loved Hilda for more than her looks.

Ruth refrained from asking what kind of music that might be. She doubted it was Corelli. Then again, Richard hadn't been a huge Corelli fan, and she'd gone ahead and married him.

And look at them now.

All right, so maybe Ruth wasn't wise. She understood suspended seconds, but what good had that ever done her? If she was so wise, why was she letting Wade send her on this fool's errand? What was she going to say to Hilda, the beautiful dental technician? What if she asked Hilda why she'd broken up with Wade and Hilda said, "Nothing in particular"?

Why, when she'd finally resolved to stop worrying about taking care of everyone else, was she trying to take care of Wade?

It was all her fault for scolding him about the cigarette. She'd acted like a mother to him, and now he was expecting her to continue acting like a mother. Just as she'd knocked herself out to help Doug, Jill and Melissa through their assorted struggles when they were children, she was now on a mission to help Wade.

Once a mother, always a mother, she thought glumly. Even living by herself, taking a job, paying her own rent and eating dinner blissfully alone every night, accompanied by a book and a baroque concerto spilling out of the compact speakers of Doug's old stereo, she couldn't stop being a mother.

All right, so she'd talk to Hilda. Maybe she'd discover a kinship with the girl. Maybe Hilda had learned, as Ruth had, that a woman needed more than the comfort of familiarity. More than doing the same thing every day. More than the joy that came from making other people happy. More than Big Macs, or even sushi, which Ruth had never really understood at all. She'd tried to eat it once when she and Richard had spent a long weekend in New York City, visiting Melissa and taking in a Broadway show. Melissa had insisted on bringing them to her favorite sushi place, and Richard had mumbled something about whether eel was kosher—as if he'd ever given a damn about kosher when presented with a steamed lobster or a ham-and-cheese on rye. That evening with Melissa in New York, Ruth had gamely downed a few pieces of something wet and slimy, then ordered the beef teriyaki and enjoyed the rest of the meal.

If Hilda liked sushi . . . well, Ruth liked Melissa and she liked sushi. Ruth shouldn't hold this sushi thing against Wade's ex-girlfriend.

That she'd broken Wade's heart, that she'd driven him to start smoking again . . . Those things Ruth could hold against her if necessary.

Wade steered into the parking lot of a strip mall that looked uncannily like the strip mall where their First-Rate was located. No First-Rate here, no manicure shop or athletic footwear store, but there was a bank branch, a sandwich joint, a boutique specializing in bird feeders and bags of seed, and Miles of Smiles, For All Your Dental Needs, Dr. Hiram Showalter, D.D.S.

"That's where she works," Wade said.

Ruth reviewed everything Wade had told her about his girlfriend: beautiful, loves the same kind of music he loves, college graduate, got him to quit smoking, sushi, wants a change. He'd also mentioned that she read romance novels, that she shared an apartment with a girlfriend who was a total head case, and that she collected elephants. "Statues, drawings, toys. Those freaky kiddie books about the elephant who wears the green suit, you know which ones I mean?"

"Babar?" Ruth guessed. Doug had adored the Babar books when he'd been a child. The girls hadn't been such big fans, but Doug had always preferred stories about powerful characters. An elephant who was a king and wore a green suit seemed pretty powerful.

"Yeah. She collects Babar books and Babar dolls. She's got plates with elephants painted on them, and elephant stationery. I gave her a gold elephant on a chain for her birthday this year."

Elephants. Swell. Was she a Republican? Ruth couldn't imagine Wade being involved with a Republican—or, more accurately, she couldn't imagine a Republican being involved with Wade. But who wanted to collect donkeys?

"There she is," he whispered, as if the woman emerging from Miles of Smiles could hear him.

Actually, two women emerged together, and Ruth wasn't sure which was Hilda. They were both cute in a bland sort of way, but neither of them would Ruth consider beautiful. Not like her daughters, for instance. Or Brooke, who could stop traffic, she was so pretty.

"Which one?" she asked.

"The blonde." He had parked his car in front of the bank, as far from Miles of Smiles as he could, and slumped down behind the wheel. "I can't let her see me. Go—talk to her." His voice was edged in desperation.

"I'll see what I can do," Ruth said dubiously. "Don't expect a miracle."

"I know, I know. I really appreciate this." He slid lower and leaned toward his door, as if he could hide behind the steering wheel.

Ruth got out of the car and closed the door. Walking toward Miles of Smiles, she realized she should have removed her First-Rate apron. It was mostly hidden under her coat, but still, she looked like a colleague of Wade's, which might not be such a good thing.

Well, she *was* a colleague of Wade's, and that fact was going to emerge within the first few seconds of her conversation with Hilda, assuming Ruth got that far. Drawing closer, she heard the two women making arrangements to go somewhere for mojitos. The dark-haired woman checked her cell phone, then shook her head and said she had to go. As she headed toward a car, Hilda turned and spotted Ruth. She must have sensed that Ruth was approaching her and not the dental clinic, because she backed up a step and smiled hesitantly.

Not beautiful by Ruth's standards—Ruth's standards being Jill, Melissa and Brooke, to say nothing of her breathtakingly gorgeous granddaughters—but beauty was in the eye of the beholder, and Wade's eye obviously beheld this young woman as beautiful. She wore white slacks, white sneakers and a scuffed leather jacket that looked like a female cousin of Wade's. No jewelry punctuated her face, but her ears—visible because her hair was pulled back in a ponytail—were adorned with multiple earrings, two gold dots and one hoop per lobe. And along the crooked part of her platinum-blond hair, dark roots showed.

"Hilda?" Ruth called to her.

The woman's smile grew even more tentative, and she backed up another step.

"My name is Ruth Bendel," Ruth said. She had such an unthreatening name, she hoped hearing it would reassure the girl. "I just want to talk to you for a minute, okay? I'm a friend of Wade's."

Hilda emitted a laugh so abrupt it sounded almost like a cough. "You're his *friend?*"

Ruth squared her shoulders. All right, so she was almost old enough to be Wade's grandmother. But age was in the eye of the beholder, too. "We work together. And yes, we're friends."

Hilda stopped laughing. "Sorry. It's just, most of his friends are . . ."

"Young," Ruth finished, figuring they may as well get the awkward stuff over with.

"I was going to say slackers. You don't look like a slacker."

"Well, we work together, so I guess I'm not a slacker. He's very sad," Ruth added. It was chilly; her hands crawled into her pockets, seeking warmth. "He said you broke up with him because you wanted a change."

Hilda raised one eyebrow. Ruth was always impressed when someone did that. The muscles in her own forehead seemed bonded for symmetry.

"He told you that?" Hilda seemed incredulous. "He told you why we broke up?"

"It's the sort of thing friends tell each other. Is there someplace we can sit and talk? Someplace warmer than out here."

Hilda eyed the Miles of Smiles door, then the door to the sandwich shop. She motioned toward the sandwich shop with her head and they both went inside. "You want a cup of coffee?" Ruth offered. "My treat."

"Sure." Hilda settled at one of the small round tables crowding the narrow café. "Black."

Not even a "please." So far, Ruth wasn't bowled over by this girl. Wade might be better off without her.

Then again, she hadn't been bowled over by Melissa's latest boyfriend, either. Maybe she was too critical. And maybe Hilda was a better match for Wade than the hairdresser was for Melissa. All she needed was to say "please" and "thank you." And to do a better job of bleaching her hair, although the dark roots were probably her answer to Wade's eyebrow jewelry.

At the counter, Ruth ordered a black coffee for Hilda and a decaf latté for herself, then carried the thick paper cups to the table. Once Hilda had finished sweetening her coffee, stirring it with a little red-and-white striped plastic stick and taking a sip, Ruth decided it was safe to talk. "I know, you're thinking, who is this lady? What business is it of hers if I want to break up with Wade?"

"Well, yeah," Hilda agreed.

They agreed on something. It was a start.

"The thing is," Ruth ventured, "I saw Wade smoking a cigarette this morning."

"Oh, shit." Hilda scowled.

Ruth thought it best not to complain about her language. Now wasn't the time to lecture Hilda. "I gave him hell for it, too," she said. "He started smoking again because he's really upset."

"Well, he's got to grow up," Hilda said. "I mean, he's a great guy, don't get me wrong. Maybe breaking up with him is dumb. Like maybe I won't meet anyone better and I'll spend the rest of my life alone and wind up an old lady with a bunch of cats." She frowned again, as if this potential future was as horrid to her as the idea of Wade smoking. "But you know? It was just like the same old same old. I want to try new things. I'm too young to get stuck in a rut. Every day I scrape tartar off people's teeth. I don't want to spend every night doing the same thing, too. I need variety."

"You want a variety of men?" It was Ruth's turn to frown. Not that she was a prude, not that she was judging, but her idea of freedom was no men, not lots of them.

"I don't know." Hilda drank some coffee and sighed. "All I know is that I *don't* want what I've got right now."

"So maybe it has nothing to do with Wade. Maybe it's just you need a change of pace. Instead of going to—" what were the names of those clubs Wade had mentioned?— "the Shack, you want to go to the Old Rockford Inn."

"The what?" Hilda looked bewildered. "What's the Shack?"

"Some club you went to with Wade, I thought."

"The Hut." Hilda nodded, her eyes narrowing on Ruth. "You and he really are friends, huh."

"He's a sweet boy."

"You want him? He's all yours."

Ruth laughed. So, to her relief, did Hilda. "What do the movie stars say? We're just friends. And the last thing I want is a boyfriend. Especially one with a silver *tchochke* in his eyebrow. Not that there's anything wrong with it," she hastened to add. "It's just not my taste."

"I think his eyebrow stud is sexy," Hilda said, then pursed her lips, as if annoyed that she'd admitted to liking something about Wade.

"To each his own," Ruth conceded. "So Wade asked me to talk to you. He's willing to do things differently if that's what you want. You've just got to tell him."

"I don't know." Hilda raised her hands, palm up, as if she was trying to lift the air in front of her. Those hands spent hours every day inside people's mouths, fussing with their teeth. Ruth reminded herself that Richard's hands often wound up inside people's chests, but for some reason removing plaque from teeth struck her as more disgusting than removing plaque from arteries. "I don't even know what different things I want."

"Maybe a different club," Ruth suggested. "Instead of the Shack, or the Hut, or whatever it's called."

"What was that place you mentioned? The Old Something Inn?"

"The Old Rockford Inn." Ruth smiled. "I wouldn't recommend it, actually. My granddaughter's having her bat mitzvah there next spring, and they're giving my daughter a hard time on the pricing. It's wrong, changing their prices in mid-stream. Anyway, it's not really a club. It's an inn with banquet facilities."

"There's this club I want to try," Hilda told her, hands back on her cup as she leaned forward. "It's in the city, and Wade hates driving in the city. Well, not driving. Parking. Like, the parking costs a lot? But this club I think has valet parking, which would also cost, but at least you don't have to go cruising for a space, or else go to a garage and hand over your life savings. But when I suggested we try this place, Wade got all, like, freaked out about some valet driving his car."

What could a valet do to Wade's car? Add more garbage to the floor? Make the seats even lumpier?

"So, if Wade was willing to go to this club with you, you'd get back together with him?" Ruth asked.

Hilda mulled over her answer. She drank some coffee, gazed past Ruth toward the service counter, spent several long seconds studying the checkerboard tiles on the floor. "If I just made up with him, he'd be like, 'Well, that was easy.' I want him to put a little effort into it."

"Letting a valet drive his car would be an effort for him," Ruth said.

"Here's an idea." Hilda's eyes brightened, and Ruth conceded that they were, in fact, quite pretty. The rest of her face wasn't all that special, but her eyes, large and hazel and fringed in long lashes assisted by a generous application of mascara, were lovely. "You could come to the club with us."

"Me?" Ruth laughed and swiped the idea away with a wave of her hand. "Don't be silly."

"No, it'd be cool. We could double-date."

"Me? Double-date with you and Wade?" She laughed again.

Hilda was smiling, but she wasn't laughing. "I don't want to do everything the way I've always done it. This would be different. And you're Wade's friend, so why not?"

"First of all, I'm too old," Ruth said, then frowned. Why was she too old? Who said there was an age limit on going out to clubs?

Hilda's steady stare conveyed that she was thinking the same thing.

"Okay, so I'm not too old. But I don't have a date."

"Oh, shit." Hilda clapped her hand over her mouth. "You're not one of those old ladies who lives with a bunch of cats, are you?"

"No. But I'm separated from my husband."

"Well, cool," Hilda said happily. "Maybe you'll meet someone at the club."

Ruth was rendered momentarily speechless. She didn't want to meet someone. She was enjoying her life alone. If she wanted to be with a man, she'd be with Richard. He was good-looking and she already knew all his faults.

But if she refused to go to the club, would that mean she was too old? Would it mean she was afraid of doing something different?

"Tell you what," she said. "I can be the designated driver."

"Oh, that's no fun," Hilda argued. "Besides, Wade is always the designated driver. He doesn't drink at clubs. He says drinking makes him dance funny."

Ruth would bet he and Hilda would consider her a funny dancer, drunk or sober. But she wasn't too old. She'd been brave enough to leave Richard, move into her own apartment, buy her own furniture, get a job and figure out how to set the alarm clock so she could open the store. Surely she could be brave enough to go to a club.

"Okay," she said. "Count me in."

Chapter Sixteen

Jill huddled inside her coat and watched the soccer players as they charged up and down the field in front of her. They managed to stay warm—some were even sweating—by running non-stop across the crisp grass, but the devoted parents—mothers, mostly—standing motionless on the sidelines were bundled in parkas and scarves and clutched insulated travel mugs filled with coffee or cocoa in the hope that hot beverages might stave off frostbite.

The hell with hot beverages. Jill hankered for a Diet Coke. Four o'clock on a late October afternoon was a lousy time to be watching a soccer game, not only because of the cold and the waning light but because her energy was at low ebb and her body cried out for caffeine. Noah's games were usually played on Saturdays, but this was a make-up game, originally scheduled for September but postponed due to a nor'easter that had blown through New England that weekend. Why the game couldn't have just been forgotten, Jill didn't know.

She picked Noah out in the crowd of oatmeal-colored jerseys, his dark hair flying and his skinny pre-puberty legs pumping hard as he raced up the field. The opposing team wore radish-hued jerseys. For some reason, they seemed to outnumber Noah's team. Jill knew they didn't really. It just looked that way. In fact, it looked as if Noah himself was surrounded by nothing but radishes.

And if she was thinking of soccer uniform colors as oatmeal and radish, she was spending too much time writing catalogue copy. Why couldn't the kids' jerseys be beige and red? Why did she have to think of their colors in terms of food?

She stood stoically, feeling the tip of her nose tingle in the biting autumn wind, and tried to keep track of the oatmeal jerseys, number eleven in particular since that was Noah's. She noticed that the elastic in his knee-length uniform socks was stretched out, causing the socks to sag around his shin guards. The soccer season was nearing its end, so she wasn't going to buy him new socks at this point. If the old pair died, they died. Only three more weeks and she'd be done with soccer until next spring.

Only four more weeks and she'd be dealing with Thanksgiving.

How was the family going to manage that holiday? Jill's parents always hosted the big turkey feast. But now . . . Her mother couldn't possibly prepare turkey, yams, turnips, cranberry mold, string beans almandine and celery stuffed with cream cheese and chives in that puny little apartment kitchen. For that matter, she couldn't possibly fit the entire family into the apartment, unless they set up a table for the children in the bedroom. At her parents' house, the expanded dining room table was long enough to accommodate everyone, all three generations.

But Ruth and Richard Bendel were separated. How could they co-host a family Thanksgiving at the house Jill's mother had abandoned? Where could a broken family give thanks, and what were they giving thanks for?

Jill realized with a twinge of something—regret, grief, supreme annoyance—that she would get stuck hosting the family's Thanksgiving dinner. Melissa couldn't do it; the whole family wasn't about to trek down to New York City when it was so much easier for her to travel to Massachusetts. Brooke wouldn't do it because, as best Jill could tell, Brooke didn't cook. She and Doug always contributed the wine to the annual Thanksgiving feast. Jill traditionally baked the pies and brownies, and Melissa got a pass because she had the burden of traveling two hundred miles.

A cheer erupted among the mothers standing on her side of the field, dragging her attention back to the game. She leaned forward to see a group of boys in oatmeal jerseys jumping up and down near the goal. Apparently someone on Noah's team had scored. She hoped it wasn't Noah, because if it was, Gordon would demand a second-by-second description of how the play was set up, who had passed the ball to Noah, which part of his foot—or God forbid his forehead—he'd used to power the ball into the net and exactly how he'd felt when the ball had blown past the goalie. It was up to Noah to report on how he felt, but Gordon would be expecting Jill to supply the other details. "Noah couldn't see what was going on behind him," Gordon would point out. "You had a view of the entire field. Where was the rest of his team? Where was the other team's defense? How did he get around them?"

She could make something up. She was creative. Noah could amend her narration if necessary. Of course, that was based on the assumption that Noah had kicked the goal, which, if she was lucky, he hadn't.

Did thinking that make her a Bad Mom?

The teams gravitated back to midfield. The woman standing next to Jill, one of those loud, energetic jock types who actually loved standing in the cold and watching kids kick a ball around, grinned and said, "These boys are *fabulous*, aren't they?"

"Yes," Jill agreed, despite her belief that winning a soccer game played by ten-year-olds fell a bit short of *fabulous*.

"The Revolution ought to send their scouts this way. I'm telling you, these boys. The talent. The *heart*."

Jill nodded vaguely. As far as she was concerned, *fabulous* was when Noah aced a math test. *Heart* was when he gave her a hand-made Mother's Day card. Soccer was just a game.

A muffled trill emerged from her purse. Her cell phone. The woman beside her eyed her purse, then scowled. Clearly she disapproved of anyone who'd leave her phone turned on during something as *fabulous* as a town-league soccer game.

Jill didn't care what the woman thought. She'd left Abbie home alone, and if Abbie had set the house on fire or cut herself and was hemorrhaging into the kitchen sink or was bored, she had to be able to reach her mother. Jill might be a Bad Mom when it came to paying attention to Noah's game, but she wasn't bad enough to turn her phone off when her twelve-year-old daughter was home all by herself.

She dug frantically through the clutter in her bag to find the phone, even though she doubted Abbie had set the house on fire or cut herself. Abbie was calm, sane and generally responsible. Jill had called her at the end of the game's first quarter and Abbie had rhapsodized about how much she loved having the entire house to herself. "It's so peaceful," she'd said. "There's so much space. When I grow up I want to live all by myself, just like Grandma."

Jill had refrained from suggesting that Abbie might seek a better role model than her crazy grandmother, who at that very moment was undoubtedly wearing her ugly red First-Rate pinafore and ringing up a box of tampons for a PMS-ing customer.

Her fingers closed around the phone and she pulled it from her bag. The ringing sounded much louder out in the air, and several mothers glared at her. *Bad Mom*, she muttered to herself, forcing an apologetic smile before she moved away from the sideline. Noah had better not score a goal while she was on the phone.

"Hello?"

"Jill? It's your mother. Have you got a minute?"

Jill sighed. "Actually, I don't. I'm watching Noah play soccer."

"I know. I called your house and Abbie told me where you were. She said you had your cell phone and you wouldn't mind my calling you. I'll be quick. I've only got a ten-minute break, anyway. I have to ask you to do a big favor for me."

Jill sighed again. "What?"

"I need some clothes from the house. When I moved out, I took only the clothes I thought I'd be wearing for work, because I just don't have the closet space here. I'm not complaining, the apartment's fine, but the closet space is on the less than ample side. So I tried to be practical and take only what I would use."

Jill's mother seemed determined to expend her entire ten-minute break on this phone call. Jill glanced toward the game, wondering if she was missing anything significant.

"So, wouldn't you know? I need something I didn't bring with me," her mother continued. "I was thinking that turquoise V-neck sweater, the cashmere, you know which one I mean? And the off-white shell, it's a silk knit, not machine-washable but I love it, so if I have to, I'll hand-wash it in the sink. Can you pick those things up for me?"

"Why can't you get them yourself?" Jill asked, hoping she didn't sound too impatient.

"How can I? I work."

"I work, too," Jill pointed out.

"You're not working now."

"Because someone had to attend Noah's game, and Gordon's . . ." *Working*, she thought peevishly. He couldn't possibly have left the school building as soon as he was done teaching his last class so he could attend this game, but Jill could put aside the copy she was composing for the open-toed canvas espadrilles, available in a delectable fruit-salad of colors—blueberry, lemon, lime, plum and mango—that would be featured in Prairie Wind's catalog next summer, and stand outside at the Howland Street Parks-and-Rec complex, freezing her ass off, while Noah's team played its rescheduled game.

Her mother didn't wait for her to finish the sentence. "And I can't go over after work, because your father'll be home then, and I just think it would be easier if he didn't have to watch me enter the house and pack some more clothing and take it with me. Oh, and I need shoes, too. Those low-heel black pumps. The high-heeled ones hurt my arches. Can you get me those things?"

Jill's mother thought it would be easier. For her, yes. Not easier for Jill. "Why do you need this stuff?"

"I'm going to a club this weekend. In Boston."

"You joined a club? What kind of club?" Now that her mother was working, she could no longer enjoy bridge afternoons with her friends. Maybe she'd found a bridge group that met weekends, although why she had to go all the way into Boston to find a foursome, and why she needed her cashmere sweater—

"A club, where they play music and people drink."

Jill's mouth clamped shut as she tried to digest this. Her mother was going to a *club*? "Do you have a date?" she asked, forcing the words around a strangulating knot in her throat.

"Don't be silly. If I wanted a date, I'd be living with your father. I'm going with friends, that's all."

"What friends?"

"Wade Smith from work. You met him that day you came to First-Rate, remember? With the thing in his eyebrow?"

Jill recalled a skinny white kid with dreadlocks. "You're going to a club with him?"

"And his girlfriend. His ex-girlfriend. Not exactly ex. It's complicated. Wade wanted to invite Bernie to join us, but I said absolutely not. He's married, and he's always flirting, and it's bad enough he flirts at work, but what if he flirts while he's at a club? Unless he flirts with his wife, but I got the impression Wade wanted to invite him without his wife. Forget about it. I've got my hands full with Wade and Hilda."

"Who's Hilda?" Jill didn't bother to ask who Bernie was. From her mother's tone, she assumed she was supposed to know that already.

"Wade's girlfriend. Ex-girlfriend. Almost. I don't want to take up your time, Jill, I know you're busy watching the soccer game, so if you could just pick up those few things for me. You can bring them here, to First-Rate. I've got a locker I can store them in. I showed you the staff room, didn't I?"

Jill didn't care about her mother's locker in the staff room. She cared that here she was, worrying about how the family was going to survive Thanksgiving, and her mother was gallivanting off to a club with a guy Jill wouldn't leave alone in the same room as her daughter, and someone named Hilda.

"Are you sure you want to do this?" she asked.

Her mother laughed. "It's like I'm their chaperone. And just because I specialized in Corelli doesn't mean I can't enjoy some rock-and-roll every now and then. I was a Beatles fan. I didn't jump up and down and scream when they played, but I loved their music."

"Rock today is a little different from the Beatles."

"You think I don't know? I've got grandchildren. I've got a TV. So can you get those items for me before Saturday? I'd really appreciate it. You don't want your mother going to a club in Boston wearing her First-Rate apron, do you?"

Jill didn't want her mother going anywhere in her First-Rate apron. "All right," she said.

"You still have your key to our house, right? I don't think Dad changed the locks."

Not if he wanted Jill's mother to come home. But maybe he didn't. Maybe he enjoyed life as a single as much as she did. Maybe he'd already done a pub crawl or two. He had access to his full wardrobe, after all.

"I'll get to it before Saturday," she promised her mother, even though she knew damned well she'd get to it tomorrow. She'd set aside the Prairie Wind espadrilles again and run her mother's errand for her. She was, after all, the person who took care of everything.

THE KEY HER MOTHER had given Jill when she was a ten-year-old still unlocked all the outer doors to her parents' house. She was accustomed to coming and going through the back door. The front door was used mostly by company, parcel delivery people and the occasional Jehovah's Witness passing through the neighborhood. So once she'd parked in the driveway, she circled around to the back of the house, passing the flower bed her mother always planted with chrysanthemums. None there this year; Jill's mother had obviously been planning her escape in early September, when she would otherwise have put in the mums.

Jill entered her parents' kitchen.

She wasn't sure what she expected. With her mother gone nearly a month, would the place be a wreck? Unwashed dishes piled up on the kitchen counters? A three-inch carpet of dust covering the floor? The master bathroom sink clogged with beard hairs her father had neglected to rinse down the drain?

What she found was the house she remembered. The atmosphere felt a little stagnant. Since her father was at work all day, no one was around during the sunlight hours to throw open a window and let in some fresh air, but she didn't smell rotting food or the stale, musty fragrance of dirty socks that always emanated from Noah's bedroom. Sections of that morning's *Boston Globe* lay scattered across the kitchen table, but the only unwashed dish was a coffee mug in the sink. Was her father eating breakfast? If so, where was the plate, the bowl?

Maybe she should have run this errand in the evening, when he would be home and she could check up on him. But the thought of explaining her mission to him made her queasy. How would he take the news that his wife hadn't just abandoned him but had also apparently abandoned her senses? Going club-hopping with pierced twenty-somethings in Boston? The news might give him a heart attack, and unlike him, Jill wasn't a cardiologist. She'd taken a CPR course when she was pregnant with Abbie, determined to be prepared for every emergency her precious firstborn might encounter, but that was twelve and a half years ago. If her father keeled over, she wouldn't know how to revive him.

She peeked through the doorway into the dining room, the table lightly filmed with dust and truncated without the leaves inserted in it. Not ready for Thanksgiving, she thought dolefully. All right, so she'd host the damn dinner. Would both her parents come? Would they insist on sitting at opposite ends of the table, and would they growl and snap at each other?

With a shudder, she turned and headed down the hall to the stairs. If she hosted Thanksgiving and her mother showed up wearing her turquoise cashmere sweater and low-heeled pumps, would her father wonder when she'd gotten hold of those garments? Or wasn't he even aware of which clothes she'd taken with her when she'd moved out? If Jill ever left Gordon, he wouldn't notice which clothes she'd packed and which she'd left behind. As it was, he hardly noticed her clothing while she lived with him. Every now and then she would catch him staring hard at her and frowning. "Where did that shirt come from?" he'd ask, and she'd answer that she'd owned the shirt for years, and she wore it frequently, and he'd give her a bewildered shrug and, if he was thinking fast enough, mention that she looked nice.

He just didn't pay attention to things like her wardrobe. Her father didn't pay attention, either. She was willing to bet most men didn't.

Melissa's boyfriend, the hairdresser, probably did.

She felt like a trespasser moving through the empty house. The soles of her sneakers muted her footsteps as she prowled up the stairs. It was silly, really. She wasn't breaking any laws. She didn't have to tiptoe around. Besides, no one was home to hear her.

She tiptoed anyway, because logical or not, she felt like a trespasser, grabbing her mother's clothing behind her father's back.

At the top of the stairs, she paused. What was it about returning to your childhood home that caused you to regress? Standing at the top of the stairs, gazing down the narrow second-floor hallway, she could have been seventeen again, wishing she had the nerve to tell her parents she was going out and it was none of their business whom she was going with or where they'd be. In her case, she would only have been going out with her girlfriends—Lucy Shapiro or Marianne Delmonica or a group of fellow staff members from the school newspaper—and where they'd be would likely have been the roller rink or the movie theater at Shopper's World, or maybe swimming at Walden Pond, which besides being a historical landmark also had a cute little beach. They would not have been going somewhere to get drunk or stoned. They would not have been searching for guys to pick up. Sure, they might check out guys, but they wouldn't have wound up at the house of someone whose parents weren't home, where everyone could pair off and vanish into various bedrooms. Jill had always been a Good Daughter.

Doug had been a boy, so her parents hadn't been overly protective of him. They'd tried to be protective with Melissa, but she'd shrugged them off and they'd let her. By the time Melissa had been old enough to get into trouble, Jill had been in college, Doug in medical school, and her parents no longer had the energy to be vigilant. Their two older kids had survived adolescence, so maybe they'd felt less of a need to police Melissa, and she'd had the guts to take advantage of her freedom. And look at her now: a lawyer, with degrees from two Ivy League schools.

And a boyfriend who colored and cut women's hair for a living.

Scolding herself for being such a snob, Jill stalked down the hall, passing Doug's and Melissa's bedrooms, both of which remained essentially untouched since they'd moved into adulthood. Through the open door of Doug's bedroom Jill glimpsed the shelf holding all the model airplanes he'd built from kits as a boy. Lots of precision work on them, delicate painting and gluing of miniature decals. Good practice for slicing and rearranging people's corneas.

She also glimpsed a sliver of Melissa's pink bedroom through her open door. Melissa had been awfully feminine as a child. She'd insisted on the pink walls, the pink bedspread, the pink curtains. Strawberry, Jill corrected herself. Or Pepto-Bismol. Did that count as a food?

Jill's childhood bedroom had been converted into a study, the bed replaced by a sofa, a small television sitting on a wheeled stand where her desk used to be. The shelves that had once held every Judy Blume book ever published, along with a teeming menagerie of stuffed animals and a milk-glass piggy bank that was usually heavy with money because she never did any naughty stuff—like buying pot or sneaking into bars with a fake ID—that cost money, now contained the obsolete family encyclopedia and rows of *Consumer Reports* magazines in chronological order.

If Jill hadn't already felt like a trespasser prowling through the house, entering the master bedroom would have done the trick. Guilt seized her as she stepped over the threshold into the room her parents had shared until her mother's departure a month ago. The bed was made, barely. The blanket lay haphazardly across the mattress and both pillows looked mashed and misshapen.

Both pillows? Were two people sleeping in this bed?

Oh my God.

No. Jill refused to believe it. If her father was sharing a bed with someone, it wouldn't be *this* bed, the bed he'd shared with her mother. Jill simply couldn't accept that possibility.

He must be doubling up the pillows under his head. Or punching Jill's mother's pillow to sublimate his rage at her mother. Or alternating sleeping on her side of the bed and his own, since her mother had refused to rotate the mattress.

She paused at the foot of the bed, debating whether she should sniff her mother's pillow, just to see if it smelled of some other woman's perfume, and then decided she couldn't bear the possibility that it might.

Turning resolutely from the bed, she marched to the closet. Her mother's side looked slightly depleted, but she had apparently left most of her clothing behind when she'd moved out. Jill quickly found the turquoise V-neck and the white silk-blend shell. She pulled them out and hung them on the doorknob, then dropped to her knees and rummaged through the shoe boxes lining the floor. Her mother was no Imelda Marcos, but she did have a surprising number of shoes, including some Jill had never before seen. A pair of pumpkin-orange satin pumps—they must have been dyed to match a dress. Women used to do that for formal occasions—buy white satin shoes and dye them to match their gowns. Did her mother have a pumpkin gown? If so, Jill was relieved never to have seen her wearing it. Pumpkin was definitely not her color.

A pair of thong sandals with plastic daisies glued to the straps. A pair of boat shoes, for a woman who claimed boating was for rich *goyim*. A pair of black pumps with three-inch heels. She'd specifically said she wanted her low-heeled pumps, though. If she was going to be dancing at this club in Boston . . .

Jill shuddered again. The last time she'd seen her mother dance had been at Laurie's wedding last year. Laurie was Jill's cousin, her Uncle Isaac's youngest. A while back, she'd spent a year studying Buddhism and ingesting hallucinogens in Katmandu, and she'd returned to the states with an extremely hirsute Californian whose name was either Chandaka or Ernie, depending on his mood. They'd had a vegetarian wedding—Jill's parents had muttered profusely about the abundance of bean dishes and the absence of anything resembling meat in the buffet, and the wedding cake's frosting had tasted suspiciously like tofu—but Uncle Isaac had insisted on hiring a DJ who'd played regular music for the party. Jill recalled that her parents had danced a sprightly fox trot to Neil Diamond's "Song Sung Blue."

She hadn't been wearing a pumpkin dress then. Nor had she worn those shoes with the three-inch heels. Why had she even bought them? She was such a pragmatic woman. She'd never wear shoes that could cause bunions.

Leaving her husband of forty-two years hadn't been pragmatic, Jill reminded herself as she peeked into another shoe box, and another. Four boxes later she found a pair of low-heeled black leather pumps. She hoped those were the shoes her mother wanted, because she was tired of searching.

She lifted the box, stood and draped the two tops over her arm. Refusing to spare her parents' rumpled bed another glance, she hurried out of the room and down the hall. At the top of the stairs she heard a noise.

Someone entering the house. A door opening, then shutting. Footsteps.

She froze, told herself not to panic and remembered that she'd left her purse, with her cell phone in it, on the front seat of her car. She contemplated racing back to her parents' bedroom, where she could use their phone to dial 911, but before she could move she heard her father's voice hollering up the stairs. "Jill? Are you here?"

She almost would have preferred to confront a burglar. With a burglar, she could scream, kick, try to flee. With her father, she'd have to explain her presence, and the sweaters and shoes she was carrying. Getting robbed had to be easier than that.

"Jill?" he called again.

"Yeah, Dad, it's me." Jill might not have Melissa's chutzpah, but she'd brazen her way through this. The man was her father, for God's sake. Home in the middle of a workday. He had some explaining to do, too.

She descended the stairs to find her father standing in the hall below, gazing up at her. "I saw your car in the driveway," he said. "What's going on?"

Since she didn't have Melissa's chutzpah, she resorted to honesty. "I had to pick up some things for Mom. What are you doing home?"

"What do you mean, what am I doing home? It's my house. I live here."

"It's the middle of the day. What about work?"

"Oh." He wilted, his shoulders curving downward, his entire posture melting into limpness. "I'm not feeling so good."

Concern swamped Jill, washing away her worry about justifying her mission. She descended the stairs, scrutinized his wan face and touched the inside of her wrist to his forehead, as if he were one of her children. Actually, much to Abbie and Noah's disgust, she often tested their temperature with her lips, not her wrist. But her father was a doctor. She couldn't just kiss his forehead and force Tylenol into him.

Not that he needed Tylenol. His forehead felt cool.

He tilted his head away from her hand. "It's a stomach thing," he told her. "Maybe I ate something I shouldn't have."

He didn't look particularly nauseated. Pale, sure, but not green. Well groomed and steady on his feet. Although his tie was loosened, his shirt was surprisingly crisp-looking.

"What did you eat?" she asked.

"Who knows? Without your mother here, I scrounge."

Scrounging didn't sound particularly healthy, but Jill decided not to give him a lecture on nutrition. "What about your patients? Were you able to clear your schedule?"

"Stan and The Kid are covering for me." He turned and walked down the hall to the kitchen. Jill followed. Not a wrinkle in his shirt, she noted. Was he sending his clothes out to the cleaners now that her mother wasn't around to handle his laundry? Surely he wasn't washing his shirts himself. If he was, they wouldn't look so fresh.

"Would you like me to make you some soup?" Jill asked as he settled heavily onto a chair, propped his elbows on the table and rested his chin in his hands. "Or some ginger ale? Do you have any? That can settle an upset stomach." She draped the sweaters over the back of another chair, set the shoe box on the seat and crossed to the refrigerator. She should have expected it to be nearly empty, but seeing the interior light reflecting harshly against the bare shelves jolted her. "You want me to run out and buy you some ginger ale?" she asked, doing her best to mask her dismay. Maybe her father's stomach thing was starvation.

"No, but if you brought me some of that rugelach I love, I wouldn't object. What's this stuff of your mother's? Shirts and shoes? How come she couldn't come here and get these things herself?"

"She's working," Jill said. *Unlike me,* she added silently. Of course, she *should* be working. If she didn't get that copy sent in by the end of the day, Lois Forman might show up at her house and kick her in the butt with one of Prairie Wind's mango-hued espadrilles.

Jill's father snorted. "Working? Your mother is standing at a cash register. It's crazy that she'd rather do that than be my wife. So, she couldn't come and get her things in the evening?"

Jill closed the refrigerator door and stared at her father. He really didn't look sick. "I don't want to be drawn into the middle of anything," she said. "Mom asked me to do this favor for her, so I'm doing it. You want me to bring you rugelach? I'll do that favor, too. I live to do favors for you two."

He must have heard the sarcasm filtering through her tone. "Invite me to dinner and I'll eat the rugelach at your house."

"Fine. When would you like to come to dinner?"

"Anytime. Tonight."

"I thought you weren't feeling well."

"I'm already feeling better. Just thinking about eating dinner at your house makes me feel better."

"Then you should go back to work and see your patients."

He winced, as if suddenly seized with pain. "I can't go back," he confessed. "Not today."

Jill lowered herself into one of the empty chairs and scrutinized her father. Whatever pain he was suffering appeared to be psychic, not abdominal. "What's wrong?"

"What's wrong? You want to know what's wrong?" His eyes flared with anger. "My wife walks out on me, and she won't even come home to get her own shoes. She sends our daughter to run and fetch for her. What, she's afraid to look at me? She's afraid if she sets foot in this house, she'll never be able to escape? I'll lock her up and throw away the key?"

"You should talk to *her* about that," Jill said primly. Listening to her father gripe about her mother was almost as embarrassing as seeing two indented pillows on a bed her father was supposedly sleeping in alone. "What's with your stomach?"

"My stomach was supposed to have coffee poured into it this afternoon."

"Decaf, I assume," Jill said.

He made a puffing sound, impatient or disgusted, Jill couldn't tell. "I was supposed to meet another doctor for coffee. A dermatologist." He hesitated, then cringed and spat out the words: "A female dermatologist." Sighing, he shook his head and let it rest deeper in his cupped palms. "I canceled. I called her office and said I wasn't feeling well, and we'd have to do it another time. I couldn't go through with it, Jill. I just couldn't."

Jill decided this wouldn't be a good time to tell her father her mother was planning to go bar-hopping in Boston on Saturday night. "A female dermatologist, huh."

"Gert set us up." He shook his head without lifting his chin from his palms. His arms rocked back and forth from the motion. "I can't do this. It's practically like a date. I'm a married man."

She was touched by his rectitude. But the sad fact was . . . "You and Mom are separated. I think it's allowed."

He raised his hangdog eyes to her. "You think I should have coffee with this woman?"

No. "I think you and Mom should get back together and work out your problems, but nobody listens to me."

"I listen to you." He lowered his eyes again, briefly distracted by something on the *Globe's* front page. "There were no problems to work out. Your mother just wanted to be by herself, that's all."

"The remote control?"

"That bullshit," her father retorted. "What does she care if I channel-surf a little? That's enough to destroy a marriage?"

"You're very stubborn," Jill pointed out. "If Mom agreed to come home if you stopped channel-surfing, would you stop?"

"It's unfair for her to make unilateral demands like that. She wants me to stop channel-surfing? She should lose five pounds. Not to be picky, but she doesn't get enough exercise. When was the last time she played tennis? She should make an effort."

"Have you ever discussed this with her?"

"What am I, crazy? I'm supposed to tell her to lose five pounds?"

"You know," she said, not willing to dwell on her mother's weight, which was within the healthy range, "if you don't want to have coffee with the dermatologist, you don't have to fake an illness to get out of it. You could just phone her and say you want to cancel."

"Doug thinks I should do it," her father told her. "He even helped me iron my shirt. He agreed I should look nice for this dermatologist."

"Doug is a guy. What does he know?"

Her father actually smiled. Then he grew solemn. "I want your mother to come home, Jillie. If she wants something from this house, I want her to get it herself, not send you so she can avoid me. What, does she hate me so much she's afraid to talk to me?"

"I don't think she hates you," Jill assured her father. "I just think she's trying some new things. Breaking out of her rut."

"Some rut. She's free all day here. She wouldn't even have to make my breakfast for me if she didn't want to. Or dinner. We can scrounge, I'm getting good at it. She wants to work at First-Rate, she can live at home and work at First-Rate. She can still be my wife."

"You should tell her this," Jill said. "Not me. It's between you and her."

"She won't talk to me. She won't even come here to grab a sweater and a pair of shoes. Two sweaters," he amended, glancing toward the chair.

Jill ached to call her mother right now, hand the phone to her father and force the two of them to talk. She wanted them back together. She had not just Thanksgiving but Abbie's bat mitzvah to think of. And her family. Tradition. The foundation beneath her feet. Bendels didn't divorce.

But her mother was at work. If she took Jill's call while she was supposed to be working, she might get fired. Which wouldn't be the worst thing in the world, as far as Jill was concerned, but her mother would never forgive her. As a Good Daughter, she wouldn't risk it.

"I'll tell her to talk to you," she promised instead. "I'll tell her you want her to come home. But you have to do your part, too."

Her father gave her an eager look. "What's my part?"

"Stop channel-surfing."

Chapter Seventeen

Melissa locked herself into one of the bathroom stalls and hit the speed-dial for Jill on her cell phone.

This was not a good day. This was not a good bathroom. The sinks were ancient, the ceiling lights glared, the air smelled like Lysol and lemon cut with a cloying floral air freshener, and the floor was constructed of tiny square tiles that had probably started their lives white but were now a cloudy yellow that made Melissa think too many people over the years must have missed the toilet and peed on the floor. And this was a ladies' room. It wasn't as if women had to aim to use the damn toilets.

That her lovely leather shoes—three-hundred-ninety-five bucks at Bloomie's, and worth every penny because despite their high heels and narrow toes they'd never given her blisters—were touching the suspiciously stained floor disgusted her. So did Judge Montoya, who'd decided there was no reason Melissa and Aidan O'Leary couldn't hammer out a settlement that would satisfy everyone. Melissa had been shut into a tiny, dreary conference room with the Lord of Dimples for over an hour and she sure as hell wasn't anywhere close to satisfied.

Montoya had shot down her attempt to turn the case into a class-action suit. She'd shown the judge persuasive evidence that the factory in China that was producing counterfeit bags for sidewalk vendors in New York City was also producing counterfeit bags for sidewalk vendors in San Francisco and Seattle, and counterfeit belts from the same factory had shown up in Boca Raton, La Jolla and Winnetka, Illinois. This was obviously a huge racket. Designers were getting screwed left and right. But O'Leary had argued that her client's suit was only against his client—the distributor of the counterfeit bags in New York City—and if she wanted to sue the Chinese manufacturer, she'd have to deal with international law and extradition. Montoya had given O'Leary a lovesick smile, tossed out Melissa's motion and shut them up inside that ghastly little cell of a room with orders to "work things out, you two." As if they were children arguing over a toy.

They'd been circling each other for the past hour. More accurately, Melissa had been circling O'Leary and he'd been subjecting her to a charm assault. "Let's split the difference," he'd suggested, although they hadn't even established what difference they were supposed to split. "Then I'll take you to lunch."

After a while, she'd realized she was starving. Forget about his taking her out, though. She'd told him to order her a chicken sandwich off a deli's take-out menu they'd obtained from a court stenographer, and she'd ducked into the ladies' room and called Jill. She could have phoned her office, could have phoned her client, but no. When her life was a mess, Jill was the person she called.

"Hello?"

"It's me." Melissa spoke quickly, softly, hoping with all her heart that no one would enter the ladies' room for the next few minutes. "I can't talk. I'm standing in an icky toilet stall in the courthouse downtown. My life is a mess."

"Is this about the phony purses?"

"Yes. No. I mean, we were supposed to have a hearing but the judge told us to try to negotiate a settlement our clients could live with. I'm stuck dealing with Obnoxious O'Leary, the Irish-American Lawyer-God. But that's not why I'm calling you. Last night I fell in love with an apartment. It's in Murray Hill. I don't know why anyone would want to live in Murray Hill. It's right by the UN, so the next time the city gets attacked by terrorists this building would probably be in the line of fire. Tell me I'm crazy to love this apartment."

"What's it like?"

"It's a two-bedroom." Melissa closed her eyes and the entire floor plan appeared in her memory. The adorable kitchen. The rococo grillwork covering the radiators. The parquet floors that would require area rugs so her footsteps wouldn't bother the people in the apartment below. Why would anyone build apartments with hardwood floors when you had to cover those floors with carpets to muffle the sound? "The second bedroom . . ." She sighed as that square, cozy room materialized in her mind. "It would make a perfect nursery. As soon as I walked into that room, I thought, 'I want to have a baby and I want this to be the baby's room.' Tell me I'm crazy."

"You're crazy."

"I can practically afford it. I just need a little extra for a down payment."

"I haven't got any extra, Melissa, so—"

"No, of course not, that's not why I'm calling."

"You aren't pregnant, are you?"

"No!" Jesus, why did Jill have to be so fixated on reality? "I'm not pregnant. But I want a baby. My family is falling apart, I'm a child of divorce—"

"Mom and Dad aren't divorced," Jill argued.

"They're separated, okay? I'm a child of separation. I want to make a family of my own, one I can count on. The way Mom and Dad count on you."

"Not the way they count on you," Jill clarified.

"Right. I want a child like you. A smart, well-behaved, reasonable child. A daughter, if I have any say in the matter."

"You don't."

"And here's the thing, Jill—when I picture this daughter? She doesn't look anything like Luc."

In the silence that followed, Melissa heard the buzz of the restroom's fluorescent ceiling lights. She wondered whether her sister wasn't talking because she was busy Googling "mental illness" right now, searching for a diagnosis for someone who wanted to buy an apartment in Murray Hill, for God's sake, a dowdy, WASP-y neighborhood near the freaking United Nations, because she wanted to have a daughter but not with the guy she was supposedly in love with.

"I think Luc and I are breaking up," she added, hoping to offer Jill some guidance.

"Okay," Jill said cautiously.

"It's all so weird. I don't know. Ever since he did Brooke's hair—"

"What?"

"Brooke came down to New York just so Luc could do her hair. I thought that was weird. He said she was very pleased and wants him to do her hair again. You didn't know about this?"

"I haven't talked to her since the day Mom and Dad announced their separation."

"Right. The day she met Luc. Don't you think that's weird?"

"He must have made quite an impression on her."

"Yeah. We were all in the dining room listening to Mom and Dad announce that they were destroying our family, and he was off in the rec room, impressing Brooke." Melissa smothered a groan. A ribbon of toilet paper was dangling from the molded plastic case, distracting her. She tugged on it and several feet of toilet paper unspooled into her hand. She tore it off, tossed it into the toilet and leaned against the wall, which was gouged with graffiti. All those messages about Trina and Darren 4-eva and Anna sucks—only the S looked like a backward Z because digging curved lines into the wood was so much harder than digging straight lines, so maybe it said Anna zuckz. How did people carve these messages, anyway? How did they smuggle sharp objects past the metal detectors in the courthouse entry?

"I know he spends his time with his hands in other women's hair," she said. "That's his job, to do other women's hair. But Brooke isn't just some other woman. She's our sister-in-law. I bet she looks fabulous."

"She always looks fabulous."

"If I have a baby," Melissa said resolutely, "I'm not going to have it with someone who gives my sister-in-law scalp massages. That's just too weird. You probably think I'm crazy."

"I didn't say that."

Melissa continued before Jill could elaborate on Melissa's mental health. "I just need a small loan for a down payment on the apartment, but I don't see how I can ask Doug for a loan when Luc is massaging his wife's scalp. I know Doug can afford it, and I could pay him back as soon as I got my bonus check in December, but I can't ask him for a loan when my boyfriend—who I guess is actually my ex-boyfriend now—is doing Brooke's hair. I just can't."

"All right." To Melissa's amazement, and relief, Jill sounded as if she understood. At least she wasn't calling her crazy.

"So I was thinking about asking Dad for a loan. But I don't know what's going on with him, with Mom gone. I don't want to make things worse. How is he doing?"

"Not good," Jill said. "He tried to ask a dermatologist out and it made him sick."

"A dermatologist? That would make me sick, too."

"It wasn't even a real date. Just a cup of coffee. He couldn't do it. He wants to get back together with Mom."

"How's she doing?"

"She's planning to do a pub crawl in Boston tomorrow night."

"You're shitting me."

"I'm not. She's going out with some new young friends of hers."

"Oh, God. Now *I* feel sick."

"I wish they would grow up," Jill said wearily.

"So I can't ask Dad for a loan, either, can I."

"Do you really not have enough funds for a down payment? I thought the firm paid you a fortune."

"You don't know what apartments cost in this town. And the economy sucks." *It zuckz,* she wanted to say. "But rumor has it we're getting bonuses this year, and my bonus check would cover it. I just don't think this apartment is going to be around in two months. Murray Hill," she muttered. "What am I thinking?"

"You fell in love with it," Jill said.

"Yeah." Melissa glanced at her watch. "Shit. O'Leary thinks I just came in here to pee. I've got to run."

"You're really calling me from a public bathroom?"

Melissa didn't bother answering. "I'll talk to you later. Maybe I'll try Dad tonight. Thanks, Jill." Snapping her phone shut, she unlatched the stall door and sprinted lightly to the exit, trying to minimize her shoes' contact with the discolored tiles.

The corridor was nearly as dreary as the bathroom, yet she felt better. Jill hadn't thought her reaction to Brooke's having Luc do her hair was nuts—or if she did think it was nuts, she was kind enough not to say so. She was also kind enough not to suggest that Melissa's instant infatuation with an apartment in Murray Hill was nuts. And most of all, she hadn't laughed when Melissa had said she wanted to have a baby.

It wasn't as if the idea had never occurred to her. She was a thirty-one year old woman; the idea occurred to her with each tick of her biological clock. She'd always assumed that, like Jill and Doug, she would have children someday. She'd assumed that her brilliant, beautiful, magnificently well-behaved children would play with their cousins at big, multigenerational family gatherings hosted by her parents.

She'd always assumed her parents would remain alive and healthy and married, hosting these gatherings together.

She felt the sting of tears in her eyes and batted them. God, it was embarrassing how she got all weepy every time she thought of them living apart, contemplating a divorce. Luc didn't understand. His parents had been divorced for so many years. Maybe she'd thought that would make him more sympathetic, but it didn't. To him it was just the way things were.

She might have expected her parents' dissolving marriage to make her less susceptible to mommy-lust. And really, she hadn't felt such a visceral craving for a baby until she'd seen that second bedroom in the apartment for sale on East 38th between First and Second, and the plain white walls had suddenly seemed eager to embrace a crib, a mobile with painted butterflies dangling from it, a toy chest with a big stuffed teddy-bear perched atop it and wallpaper flocked with butterflies. Her nursery would have a butterfly motif.

Jill hadn't said it, but Melissa was thinking it: she was certifiably deranged.

That thought vanquished her tears and prompted a faint smile. All she had to do, she resolved as she strode down the hall to the cramped conference room where Aidan O'Leary and—she hoped—a grilled chicken sandwich awaited her, was to convince him she was sane long enough to hammer out a settlement that left her satisfied.

Whether or not he was satisfied was his own problem.

FOUR HOURS LATER, she was as satisfied as she'd ever be. Which wasn't very, but what the hell.

"Okay." O'Leary sighed, evidently as exhausted as she was. Or at least he faked exhaustion well. His tie was loosened, the jacket of his slate-gray suit draped over a chair and his shirt sleeves rolled up. His dark hair was mussed and his cheeks were just beginning to show stubble, which had the unfortunate effect of emphasizing his dimples. "You've got an apology—"

"Some apology," she complained. "Your guy says he's sorry the purses he was selling bore a resemblance to my client's purses. Big whoop."

"He'll say he's sorry and he'll desist. And he'll toss in some good-will money."

"Nowhere near enough money. Do you have any idea what good will costs? A hell of a lot more than this." She waved at one of the papers in front of her. "Your guy's paying for the cheapo generic good will, not the top-of-the-line good will." She fell back in her chair and glowered at O'Leary. Her jacket was also off, but she hadn't rolled up the sleeves of her blouse. It was a silk-linen blend, prone to wrinkling, plus the sleeves belled out and then were nipped at her wrists by elegant cuffs. They looked much prettier with their delicate pearly buttons fastened.

She'd bet her hair was as tousled as O'Leary's, though. Not that she cared. Luc had styled it so it looked great even if it was messy.

If she broke up with him, she'd still have to use him to do her hair. He was fabulous in bed, but even more fabulous with a color, cut and blow-dry. She'd give up the former if she had to—surely there must be other men in the world as adept at finding her G-spot—but not the latter. Hair was too important.

O'Leary jabbed his finger at one of the long sheets of lined yellow paper spread across the table between them. "As I've explained to you—"

"—a million times," she muttered.

"—at least five times," he corrected her, "your client lost no money due to my client's business. Zero. Zilch. The ladies buying eighty-dollar bags on a street corner in Flatbush were never going to waltz into Saks Fifth Avenue and buy the eight-hundred-dollar version. My guy's sales never put a dent in your guy's sales."

"But there should be a bigger penalty," she argued. "Your guy did something wrong."

"And he'll say he's sorry." O'Leary groaned, tilted his head back until he was staring at the ceiling, then straightened and presented her with an overwhelmingly charming grin. "So. We'll take this settlement back to our clients and convince them this is the way to go, and Judge Montoya will get her happy ending. Now, what do you say I buy you a drink?"

"You will *not* buy me a drink," Melissa retorted, although she could think of nothing she'd like more right now than a margarita. Sweet and tart and salty, heavy on the tequila.

"Fine. Then *you* can buy *me* a drink."

"Not in this lifetime."

"Then we'll pay for our own drinks. Come on. If nothing else, we've got to go somewhere and exchange gossip about Montoya."

He had a point. She would love to hear juicy gossip about the judge. Plus she could practically taste the first icy sip of a margarita.

They packed up their notes, the compromises they'd wrestled over. They shut off their laptops and zipped them into their padded laptop bags. She donned her jacket without help from him—a good thing; if he added chivalry to that ridiculously sexy smile of his, she'd probably have to smack him—and he donned his. Then they left the room, she first, only because she'd been seated closer to the door, not because he'd held the door open and waved her through.

The day had slipped away while they'd been shut up inside, and the skyscrapers lining the streets blocked the evening's faded light from reaching the sidewalk. Melissa felt as if she were wading through a cool river of shadow.

"Let's head uptown," O'Leary suggested. "The bars around here are all filled with lawyers."

"God forbid." Melissa allowed herself a tiny grin.

They started walking, Melissa once again grateful that her chic shoes were so comfortable. All around them, people filed out of the office towers and government buildings, the first wave of rush hour. Were all these weary workers heading for bars and cafes in search of liquid refreshment, too? Would she and O'Leary wind up in some noisy, crowded place filled with thumping music and twenty-year-olds dressed like hookers?

She decided even that would be preferable to going home. She had no plans with Luc tonight. The last time they'd spoken—by phone—had been two days ago, and neither of them had mentioned getting together. It had been a friendly enough conversation, but Melissa hadn't been able to ignore her mental image of Luc standing behind his chair at the salon, and Brooke sitting in that chair, and Luc digging his long, skilled fingers through her tresses while they watched each other in his mirror. Remembering that phone conversation and the icky vision Luc's voice evoked in her mind chilled her in a way the late-October evening couldn't.

She knew she was being unreasonable. She knew nothing besides hair was going on between Luc and her sister-in-law. She knew jealousy was a petty, worthless emotion.

But she was currently the child of a broken home, and she was allowed to indulge in petty, worthless emotions.

The blocks they walked grew progressively more crowded as workers spilled from the office towers and joined the parade of pedestrians. The growing density of the throngs on the sidewalk spared her the need to talk to O'Leary. He was awfully tall, his strides so long she had to trot to keep up with him. Maybe instead of a margarita, she should order a Gatorade.

Gatorade and tequila. It had possibilities.

Eventually they reached TriBeCa, where the bars would be expensive but filled with artists and bohos instead of lawyers. They entered the first one they came to, a narrow, not-too-busy establishment with soothingly dim lighting and some sort of atonal music playing—the singer sounded as if she was rhythmically hiccupping. At least it wasn't so loud they'd have to shout to be heard. Spotting an empty table, O'Leary charged ahead of her to claim it.

Pushing her aside and storming across the room was the antithesis of chivalrous. But racing to grab a table *was* chivalrous, kind of. She really wished he didn't have that dazzling smile. She was not in the mood to be dazzled. Especially not by him, after he'd worn her out arguing about the amount of the good-will settlement money his client would have to pay her client.

A terminally thin waiter with close-cropped green hair that molded to his skull like moss on a rock appeared almost as soon as they were seated. Melissa requested her margarita, O'Leary a Guinness draft.

"Drinking in company is better than drinking alone," he said once the waiter departed. "Either way, I'd be having a drink right now, but I appreciate your having one with me."

He appreciated her. She tried to recall the last time she'd been appreciated and came up empty. But she refused take his words as a genuine compliment. He was just saying nice things so she wouldn't feel so bad about the crappy compensation she was supposed to convince her client to accept.

The bar's lighting had a blue cast to it, making O'Leary's hair look unnaturally black. It was a little too long. Okay, not really too long, just not shaped very well. Luc preferred working with women—probably because men didn't have G-spots—but she'd bet he could do wonders with O'Leary's hair. It was thick and slightly wavy. A snip here, a snip there, and Luc could turn him model-handsome.

As if he needed to look any better than he already did. "All that winking and smiling at Montoya," she said. "What was that all about?"

He chuckled. "This is your first time in her courtroom, huh." At Melissa's nod, he said, "Mine, too, but one of my partners told me she's easy to play. So I played her."

"All I knew about her going in was that she's partial to Prada bags."

"How do you know they aren't fake Pradas?"

"She's a judge. Do you think she'd buy contraband?"

O'Leary's response was a cynical smile.

"Okay," she conceded. "She probably buys them from the same sleazeball who supplies her with fake Rolexes."

"I don't get why anyone would spend thousands of dollars on a handbag," he said. "I mean, come on. There are children starving in Africa."

"And in China, where your client pays the parents of those starving children pennies a day in a dingy, dirty factory, piecing together counterfeit bags."

He laughed. Even in the bar's murky light she could see his dimples. Unlike Judge Montoya, however, she wasn't easy to play. He could smile and wink at her all he wanted. She refused to melt into a puddle at his feet.

The waiter arrived with their drinks. Hers was lusciously pale, with crystals of salt glinting along the edge of a glass as big as a minivan's headlight. Just looking at it caused the knotted muscles at the base of her neck to relax.

O'Leary tipped his glass toward hers in a silent toast before drinking. "So," he said as he lowered the glass. "Come here often?"

She would have scowled, but her first sip of margarita tasted too good. She smiled instead. "I've never been here before."

"Me neither. This isn't my neighborhood."

She hated herself for being curious. "Where do you live?"

"Inwood."

"Inwood? Isn't that halfway up the Hudson River?"

"It's as north as you can go and still be in Manhattan," he confirmed. "I moved there before gentrification hit. Got a cheap rent, and when the building went co-op the insider price was unbelievable. I could easily sell my place for ten times what I paid for it."

"Why don't you?"

"Why should I?"

"Because it's halfway up the Hudson River."

He shrugged and lounged in his seat, stretching his legs alongside the table so his feet wound up next to her chair. Lucky for him they didn't wind up under her chair. If they had, she would have had to stomp on his instep. As it was, he was encroaching too much on her space. "If I sold my place, where would I live?" he asked.

"Murray Hill," she said, then pressed her lips together and closed her eyes. Why had she said that? She'd had only two sips of her drink so far, so she couldn't blame her statement on alcohol.

O'Leary's smile grew quizzical. "Murray Hill? Why the hell would I want to live there?"

Screw it. She was tired, she wasn't drunk but wanted to be, and she'd spent too many hours today fighting with O'Leary. She didn't want to keep thinking of him as her adversary. And her brain was crammed to overflowing with all sorts of painful thoughts, anyway, so she might as well let one out. "Last night I saw this apartment for sale in Murray Hill. The minute I stepped inside, I wanted it."

"Why?"

"I don't know. It wasn't breathtaking. It wasn't spectacular. It was just a bunch of square rooms with decent closet space and a kitchen that could use major updating. But the second bedroom . . ." No, she wasn't drunk enough to share with him her visions of a nursery in that bedroom. As enormous as her margarita was, she didn't think there was enough booze in it to get her as drunk as she'd have to be to tell him that.

"The second bedroom . . ." he cued her.

"Really spoke to me," she said lamely.

"What did it say? 'Hey, lady, buy me!'"

"Something like that, yes." She smiled and sipped her drink. Flecks of lime-flavored ice cooled her tongue.

"So, are you going to buy it?"

"If I can scrounge some money from . . . Shit. I can't scrounge money from anyone. If I could get my year-end bonus tomorrow, I could swing it, but my firm doesn't calculate the bonuses until the end of December. And I don't know who to hit up for a loan. My brother's rich but he's—I don't know, in the middle of something he probably doesn't even know about, but it feels to me like it's going to be bad, and my parents are in the middle of something that's definitely bad, and my sister's trying to budget for her daughter's bat mitzvah with this inn that jacked up the price on her after she signed the contract."

O'Leary's smile grew bemused. Apparently he hadn't been expecting her to enumerate all the crap going on with her family. She hadn't been expecting to enumerate it, either. But she had. He'd just have to deal.

"If your bonus is going to cover the shortfall," he suggested, "maybe you could sign a short-term bridge loan with a bank. They could probably come up with a reasonable rate for a two-month loan on the down payment."

"On top of a mortgage? In this economy?" Yet she was touched that instead of telling her she was crazy he'd come up with a decent suggestion.

"You might be able to negotiate something. You're not bad when it comes to negotiating." He grinned.

She was not going to let him play her. "Sure," she snorted. "Your guy should be paying my guy a hell of a lot more than we negotiated. Seven figures."

"Six figures isn't shabby, considering your guy didn't suffer any monetary damages."

"Wait 'til he sees my bill," she grunted. "That alone will count as monetary damages."

"He's shutting my guy down in New York. If that's not good enough for him, he's a schmuck."

Everyone in New York City knew a smattering of Yiddish, and the word *schmuck* was universally understood. Yet hearing a Guinness-drinking guy named Aidan use the term struck her as hilarious. Somehow she managed not to laugh out loud.

He wasn't laughing. Evidently he didn't think he'd said anything funny. "So, your family is all screwed up, huh?"

She felt a pang of embarrassment over her earlier rant. "Forget I said any of that."

"I won't forget it. Things are going bad for your brother and your parents, and your sister is getting ripped off by an inn. You must be feeling a lot of pressure."

She shrugged. "I'm not in the middle of their *tsorris*," she said, although her amusement was gone, replaced by a wobbly bleakness. "They're all up in the Boston area. I'm down here." And sometimes Doug's wife Brooke was down here, too, which might well cause more *tsorris*.

"But they're your family and you're upset."

"Well . . ." She attempted a smile. "They're my family."

He angled his head and scrutinized her. "You're not just trying to rouse my sympathy so I'll agree to go to my guy with a bigger settlement, are you? Because it's not going to work."

"I wouldn't do that," she said, meaning it. She was a good lawyer, she worked hard, she deserved to make partner, but unlike O'Leary, she didn't play judges. And she wasn't going to play him. Not out of scruples, but because he would have her pinned to the mat in seconds if she tried. He was clearly much better at playing his opponents than she was.

"So you fled the family—what was that word you used? Circus?"

"*Tsorris*. It means heartache, problems, that kind of thing."

"*Tsorris*," he repeated like a diligent language student. *Schmuck* he could pronounce easily, but not *tsorris*. He'd probably never experienced *tsorris* in his life. As a lawyer, he undoubtedly encountered schmucks all the time, so the word sounded more natural when he said it.

"And I didn't flee the family. I got my law degree from Columbia and decided to stay here."

"Because your family was driving you crazy?"

"No," she said emphatically, then succumbed to a reluctant smile. "Yeah. They're good people. I love them. But . . ." She sighed, feeling tears press against her lower eyelids. God, she'd already said too much to O'Leary. She damn well wasn't going to cry in front of him, too. A couple of deep sips of margarita helped her to recover. "My parents are getting a divorce."

He chewed on that and frowned. "Now?"

"Well, not this minute, but my mother moved out a month ago."

"I mean, they're your parents. If they're just getting a divorce now, they must have been married—" he did a quick calculation "—what, thirty years?"

"Forty-two. I'm the baby of the family." Tears were rising again, bubbling up toward her eyes like lava, threatening to erupt. "I don't understand it. Forty-two years, and they want to throw it all away. And it's not what you're thinking."

"What am I thinking?"

"That my father's having an affair or something? No one's having an affair, as far as I know. My mother just decided she wanted a change, and my stubborn-ass father refuses to change."

He ran a hand through his hair, leaving it adorably unkempt. The hiccupping female singer had been replaced by a growling male singer and the bar was beginning to fill up. Melissa glanced around, but in the bluish gloom the other patrons were mere silhouettes. When she turned back to O'Leary, she found him gazing at her with unnerving intensity. "You aren't going to cry, are you?"

That was all she had to hear. Her vision went blurry and she gulped in a breath. Damn. She looked so wretched when she cried, her eyes swelling, her cheeks blotching, her nose running like a leaky hose.

"I'm sorry," she mumbled, her voice thick with a suppressed sob. "I'm breaking up with my boyfriend and I can't talk to anybody about it, because my parents are already broken up and I don't know what's going on with my brother and his wife, and my sister's husband is sweet but he's just so . . . I mean, he's a teacher, for God's sake, and he and my sister are so much like my parents, I bet they wind up getting a divorce in another twenty-five years, and I can almost afford that apartment in Murray Hill except almost doesn't count, and I have to go to my client tomorrow and say, 'This is all we're getting out of that scumbag who's been ripping off your bag designs,' and you know, some days just suck." The last word came out *zuck* and she didn't care.

O'Leary sighed, dug into a trouser pocket and pulled out a linen handkerchief, which he handed to her. She didn't know men still carried handkerchiefs. Men of her generation, anyway. Her father always had a fresh square of linen folded and tucked into a pocket of his slacks. Maybe that was why her mother left him—she was tired of laundering and ironing his handkerchiefs, in an era when Kleenex could be sneezed into and then discarded.

She waved off O'Leary's gesture and wiped her face with one of the cocktail napkins the green-haired waiter had placed on the table with their drinks. The white paper square was damp with condensation from her margarita, but that moisture felt cool on her fevered cheeks. By the time she was done wiping her eyes, the napkin was a lot damper, and it also had faint traces of mascara on it. She'd paid a fortune for the stuff, too, because it had been guaranteed not to smudge.

Maybe she'd sue the cosmetics company. She could probably get at least as much out of them as she'd gotten out of O'Leary's asshole client.

She dabbed her eyes one final time, hoped the mascara wasn't striping her cheeks with smeary black rivulets, and risked a glimpse of O'Leary. He didn't look alarmed, the way most men looked when the woman they were with began weeping. He didn't look helpless or annoyed. He actually looked kind.

"I wish I could solve your problems," he said. "I can't, but I can think of a way to take your mind off them for a little while."

Not kind. He looked seductive, or at least he looked like what he thought seductive would look like. Slight smile, plenty of dimple, eyelids slightly lowered, head angled in a beckoning manner.

She sat straighter. "If you're implying what I think you're implying, the answer is no. No way in hell."

He chuckled. "No way in hell? That sounds pretty definitive."

"I'm not Judge Montoya."

"And I would never offer to take her mind off her problems." He held up his hands in surrender. "Okay. All I'm saying is, once we've gotten all the parties to sign on to this settlement, let's have dinner."

Skepticism reared up inside her. What did he want? She wasn't going to lower the settlement amount one penny. And his client was going to have to make the apology, too. Maybe she'd add that he had to make a video of his apology and post it on YouTube, just so the entire world could see him expressing regret for his dishonorable behavior.

If he didn't want to influence the settlement, why would he want to have dinner with her? She'd already blubbered like a baby in front of him—terribly unprofessional, to say nothing of embarrassingly immature. She hadn't let him treat her to this margarita. She hadn't done anything to indicate any interest in him. She hadn't even officially broken up with Luc, for what that was worth.

"Dinner?" she asked dubiously. "You and me?"

He made a big show of searching the area around their table. "Is there anyone else here?"

"I thought you didn't like lawyers." When he arched his eyebrows in a question, she reminded him, "You didn't want to go to any of the bars downtown because they'd all be filled with lawyers."

"True." He contemplated her charge and shrugged. "You're right. I don't like lawyers."

"And my life is full of *tsorris*."

"A definite negative." His smile widened.

"So why on earth would you want to have dinner with me?"

"I'm not really sure," he admitted, still sending her that mischievous smile. "I think it's because your hair turns me on."

Chapter Eighteen

Jill stood in front of the sink, trying to avoid her reflection in the mirror, which was impossible to do. Whose brainstorm had it been to place mirrors right above sinks? A person had to use a sink to wash her face and brush her teeth, even at those times when she absolutely didn't want to look at herself.

Thanks to the mirror, she had no choice. There she was in the silver glass, her eyes weary, her complexion pallid, not a trace of summer color left in her cheeks. The skin at her neck wasn't quite crepe-y, but it wasn't silky-smooth, either. Then again, she'd never had silky-smooth skin. Doug and Melissa had inherited her father's coloring: tawny hair, honey-brown eyes, peachy skin. Jill was definitely her mother's daughter: hair the color of wet pine bark, eyes the color of raisins and skin with a khaki undertone.

Someone, break this mirror, she thought, although she couldn't think of who in her life deserved seven years' bad luck. Well, actually, she could: Noah, for forgetting to remove the half-eaten granola bar from his pocket before he'd tossed his jeans into the wash. Abbie, for pretending her cell phone battery was dead when Jill had called her at Caitlin's house to tell her to come home for dinner. Her father for considering having coffee with another woman. Her mother for planning to hit Boston's night spots with a couple of punks barely out of high school. Melissa for phoning Jill from a bathroom and telling her Brooke was salon-cheating on Doug with Luc. Doug for phoning her during dinner. Brooke had fed the twins spaghetti at five, he'd told her, and he and she were planning to eat later in the evening, and it hadn't occurred to him that normal families like Jill's might be gathering around the table for the evening meal at six-thirty. He hadn't even apologized for interrupting her meal; he'd just asked her if she'd be willing to take his daughters for a week in February, because he and Brooke were booked at a resort in Nevis and Mom and Dad were no longer available to baby-sit.

Gordon was probably the only person in her family she wasn't pissed off at, although he wasn't completely pure of soul, either. He'd left several congealing blobs of toothpaste in the sink. Not beard hair, thank God. If it were beard hair, she just might threaten to leave him if he didn't break the damn mirror for her.

But that was the thing about Gordon. If she asked, he would tell her she was insane, he'd resist as long as he could, but ultimately he'd break the mirror. He'd take seven years' bad luck upon himself, even though he thought superstition was silly. Perhaps this was why, unlike her parents, unlike Melissa and Luc, and possibly—who the hell knew?—unlike Doug and Brooke, Jill and Gordon were still together.

She should have donned a sexier nightie. She was wearing one of her old flannel nightgowns—Gordon was delaying turning on the furnace as late into the fall as the family could tolerate an unheated house, to save money and the environment. But with October winding down, the nights were getting awfully chilly. Yesterday morning when she'd awakened, the thermostat in the upstairs hall had read sixty-two degrees. Bright sunlight warmed the house up during the day, but it was bound to cool off again overnight. She needed flannel.

Besides which, she wasn't feeling the least bit sexy.

She rinsed her mouth, washed away her toothpaste residue and the dried blobs Gordon had left blemishing the porcelain bowl of the sink, and averted her eyes as she reached for a towel. If she didn't look into the mirror, she wouldn't notice her dowdy nightgown, her dowdy hair—untouched by the likes of Luc Brondo—her unpolished nails and the way the tendons in her neck protruded when she was tense. No doubt they were forming two strident ridges right now.

She flicked off the light and left the bathroom. Gordon was sprawled out in bed, wearing gray sweatpants. He didn't believe in pajamas—as if pajamas were a religion you were supposed to believe in. During the coldest stretch of winter, he would usually wear a sweatshirt as well as sweatpants, but late October wasn't cold enough for that.

He had a nice chest. Sometimes just gazing at it was enough to turn her on, but not when she was anxious and harried and wishing seven years of bad luck on her parents, siblings and children. Gordon's upper torso was lean, not muscle-bound. He wasn't buff, but he wasn't too fat or too skinny. And he wasn't too hairy.

And really, of all the people in her life, all the people she cared about, he was the only one who'd break a mirror if she asked.

She wished, for his sake, that tonight had been one of those times when gazing at him turned her on.

She climbed onto her side of the bed and slid under the blanket. He reached over, arched his arm around her and drew her against him, cushioning her head against his bare shoulder. "Come here often?" he asked, wiggling his eyebrows like Groucho Marx.

"Pretty much every night. I'm a regular," she joked.

Gordon knew her well enough to sense that, despite her playful words, she was in a glum mood. He could have tugged down her nightgown, watched her nipples harden at their sudden exposure to air and claimed that as proof she was aroused. But he spared her, just running his hand up and down her arm. "Any chance I'm gonna get lucky tonight?"

No. "Depends on your definition of lucky," she said tactfully, hating that she couldn't muster even a smidgen of romantic interest for him at the moment. "It's been a long day."

"This weekend it'll get longer," he noted. She thought he was referring to her mother's impending night on the town, which would surely keep Jill fussing and fretting. But then he said, "Daylight Savings ends."

She groaned. All the clocks—in the microwave, in the oven, in the DVR—had to be reset. One more chore she didn't need.

"Do we really have to take the twins for a week?" he asked.

"You don't want them here?"

"For an afternoon, sure. For a whole week? They're five years old."

"Six," she said.

"I still can't tell them apart."

"I'll put a braid in Mackenzie's hair."

"You're going to have to drive them back and forth to school," he went on. "Their bus isn't going to cross town lines to come and pick them up."

"So I'll drive them. I'm driving Abbie and Noah all over the state, anyway. What's two more passengers?"

"Your brother is probably spending a fortune on this trip to Nevis. I don't see why he can't spend a little more and hire a baby-sitter."

"They're my nieces," Jill said, trying to ignore the logic in Gordon's words. "Why should they stay with a stranger? I don't mind, really." *I do mind,* she thought. But how could she have said no to Doug? Whether or not he knew it, his marriage might be in jeopardy. What did it mean when your wife traveled two hundred miles to get her hair cut by your sister's boyfriend? Melissa was right. It was weird.

Mackenzie and Madison had enough instability in their lives with their grandparents contemplating divorce. If taking them for a week enabled Doug to fly off to the Caribbean with Brooke and get their marriage back on track, Jill would do what she could to make that happen.

"Here's what I think," Gordon said. "Doug and Brooke should stay home with their kids and give us their tickets to Nevis."

Gordon had never expressed a desire to vacation in Nevis before. As for Jill . . . If she were taking an exotic vacation, it would be in France. Not that she'd ever mentioned that wish to him. Her dream of France was a private thing, personal, fragile. If she expressed it aloud, Gordon would remind her that given his salary as a public high school teacher, given that they had to save for the kids' college, given that the damned Old Rockford Inn was ripping them off to the tune of three extra dollars a person for Abbie's bat mitzvah, and who knew how much catering would cost by the time Noah's bar mitzvah came along, and given that France was full of frogs, a trip there wasn't really feasible.

Or else he'd say, "Fine, book two tickets and a hotel room with a view of the Eiffel Tower," and she'd have to explain that she wanted to go by herself. Even if she hadn't spoken French since her sophomore year of college. Even if she wasn't sure where her passport was, let alone whether it had expired. When was the last time she'd used it? Their honeymoon in Bermuda?

If Gordon wanted to go somewhere with her, they could go back to Bermuda. But France was for her alone—if she ever found the guts to make that dream come true.

"Nevis is too glamorous for me," she said, although she had no idea how glamorous it was. "The girls will have fun here. Abbie will love having more females in the house."

"Noah and I will be grossly outnumbered. We might have to move out when the twins move in. And take in a lot of Celtics home games to restore our manhood."

"Fine." If they wanted to flee a house full of Bendel women, let them go. Jill wasn't going to waste energy worrying about an eventuality that was months away. She had more immediate concerns. "Melissa called me today from a bathroom," she said.

"Do I want to hear this?"

"She's in love with an apartment she can't afford. She needs a loan."

Gordon groaned. "Don't tell me you said yes to her, too."

"She didn't ask. She said she wanted to ask Dad, except that he and Mom are embroiled in their marital crisis. And she wanted to ask Doug, except that he and Brooke . . ." Jill drifted off, unsure she ought to share the whole bizarre situation with Gordon. He already thought Doug was a pain in the ass. Doug *was* a pain in the ass. Her whole family were pains in the ass.

"He and Brooke what?"

"Well, it's just that Melissa told me Brooke went to Manhattan to get her hair done."

He didn't seem concerned. "Brooke has too much time on her hands."

"Not just Manhattan." Jill propped herself up so she could look at Gordon. "She had her hair done by Luc. Melissa's Luc."

Even this didn't perturb him. "Keeping it in the family. Is there a problem with that?"

"Melissa made it sound tawdry." She settled back against him and shrugged, her shoulder nestling in his armpit. "Luc isn't family. And the way Melissa was talking, he never will be."

"He was a nice guy," Gordon said, then added, "A little too suave, maybe."

Jill tried to smile. "That day, when you and Brooke and Luc and the kids were watching videos while my parents were making their big announcement, did you notice any undercurrents between Luc and Brooke?"

"You're asking *me* if I noticed undercurrents?" Gordon laughed. "Come on. If Brooke had heaped a bunch of twigs at his feet and set fire to them, I wouldn't have noticed."

True enough. Gordon was Mr. Oblivious, at least when it came to undercurrents. "It's probably nothing," Jill said. "Brooke and Doug are still planning to take this trip to Nevis in February, so I guess things are okay between them."

"What difference does it make who did her hair?" Gordon sounded genuinely perplexed. "I mean, what's the big deal?"

"No big deal." But it *was* a big deal. If her parents could be contemplating a divorce, why couldn't Brooke and Doug? Just because they looked so good together, and they were both devoted to their daughters, and they complemented each other financially—Doug made tons of money and Brooke spent tons of money—didn't mean their marriage was destined to last. Once Jill's mother had informed the family that she was ending her marriage, Jill had lost all faith in 'til-death-do-us-part.

Her own marriage was . . . good, she assured herself. Unlike Melissa and Doug, Jill hadn't dated much when she'd been single. She'd met

Gordon that day in the student union, gotten to know him and decided he'd make a good husband. When he'd asked her to marry him, of course she'd said yes. And she had no regrets.

Except that she wanted to go to France alone.

And her libido had lapsed into a coma.

And she'd lost faith in the institution of marriage.

"I think Melissa is looking for an excuse to break up with Luc," she said, remembering her sister's call from the public lavatory. "And on top of that, she wants a child. If she breaks up with him, she's got to find someone else to father it."

"She could adopt. Or go to a sperm bank." Gordon was adept at coming up with simple solutions to problems. Unfortunately, most problems weren't simple. "Your family is nuts. All of them. Excluding you." He rolled onto his side, facing her, then leaned in for a kiss.

Jill kissed him back, but she couldn't fake a passion she didn't feel. "I'm sorry, Gord. I'm just so stressed."

"Sex might de-stress you," he said, skimming his hand over her breast. Her nipple perked right up; she was sure he could feel it through the flannel. His eyes glowed.

She sighed. "You know what I'd like?"

"To be on top," he guessed hopefully.

She sat up. Her phone conversation with Melissa was still reverberating inside her mind, all that clamor about apartments and Luc and Brooke and fake pocketbooks. "I'd like you to massage my scalp."

"Your scalp." He sounded dubious.

Luc massaged women's scalps. Melissa was upset because he'd massaged Brooke's scalp. The thought of Gordon's hands in her hair, his strong fingers stroking, turned her on more than his naked chest or his kisses. "Just for a minute," she implored. "Just to de-stress me."

"I think sex would work better."

I don't. "Please, Gord."

He sighed dramatically, then rose onto his knees behind her and placed his hands on her head, molding them to its curves. "Like this?" he asked, moving his palms in tentative circles.

"Use your fingers," she said.

He probed with his fingers. He swirled them through her hair as if he was shampooing it. He must have heard her respiration deepening, because he increased the pressure, tangling into her hair, probing her skull with his fingertips.

Oh, God. This was good. Better than sex. Much better.

If he would do this every night instead of sex, she'd never leave him. Not even if he left dried toothpaste in the sink. Not even if she never got to go to France by herself. *This*—this glorious sensation, this strange intimacy—would satisfy her forever.

She would never leave him. But if she made him do this every night instead of sex, he'd probably leave her.

Chapter Nineteen

What am I doing here?

An hour ago, Ruth had been in her apartment, dabbing on make-up while Corelli's Concerto Grosso in C Minor spilled out of the speakers of Doug's old stereo. Such sweet, rich music, the familiarity of Corelli's counterpoints, the tinkly rhythm of the harpsichord almost, but not quite, overwhelmed by the strings, and of course the suspended seconds. She loved how those two notes would bump against each other, creating all kinds of tension, and then resolve themselves into a safe, solid chord.

But that was then. This was now, in a place called some number, Thirty-Two or Fifty-Six or something. The room was dimly lit and loud, and so crowded you had to walk with your arms pinned to your sides to avoid accidentally hitting someone.

Somehow Wade had managed to secure a table for them. It wasn't much bigger than a seder plate in circumference, but it was tall. They had to perch themselves on stools around it, and she had to sit between Wade and Hilda, who were barely talking. Hostility swept back and forth between them like the waves rolling in on Cape Cod at high tide.

Wade played with the straw in his club soda. He was the designated driver and promised to stick with soft drinks. But Hilda was making quick progress with her cocktail—some fashionable variation on a martini—and the white wine Ruth had ordered was so cold she couldn't taste it.

Across the room was a dance floor crammed with people. From this distance they looked like a single writhing organism, their movements in no way related to the thumping music a DJ was playing. She didn't recognize the song. She'd followed the music her kids had listened to in their youth, but this next generation, she just wasn't exposed to their music as much. Unlike Doug and the girls with their stereos, Abbie and Noah absorbed their music through iPods plugged into their ears. Ruth could never lurk in their bedroom doorways, eavesdropping on what they were playing and deciding whether she liked it.

She hoped they weren't listening to this. The singer was nasal and whiny, and the song had a robotic feel to it, the rhythm as regular as a ticking metronome and the instruments all synthesized. Somebody ought to open a club where the DJ played Corelli. Not exactly dancing music, but much kinder to the eardrums.

"Why don't you two dance?" she suggested to Wade and Hilda, motioning toward the dance floor. She wasn't sure if she was supposed to be negotiating a truce between them, helping them mend their relationship. It wasn't as if she was responsible for their happiness. But the two of them, while both speaking nicely enough to her, kept snarling and snapping at each other. A couple of bouncy dances might erode their prickliness.

"I don't dance," Wade told her.

"Sure you do. Everybody dances."

"Not me." He gave his head an emphatic shake, causing his hair to tremble. Without his red smock he looked a little less benign. Or maybe it wasn't the missing smock that gave him a mildly sinister appearance. Maybe it was the snug black shirt, the black jeans and the thick-soled black boots he had on. The thing in his eyebrow was different, too, not the usual modest strip of metal with a tiny ball on each end. Tonight's piece looked like a twisted barbell, with cone-shaped points on the ends. It had never occurred to her that a person might want to vary his eyebrow jewelry, but she supposed if a woman could have a full wardrobe of earrings for every occasion, a man could have a full wardrobe of eyebrow thingies.

Hilda looked relatively wholesome compared to him, dressed in a ribbed pink sweater and blue jeans, her brassy blond hair rippling loose down her back. Her only jewelry, besides multiple earrings, was a silver ring on her thumb which didn't seem to inhibit the thumb's movement. Of course, she was young. In thirty years, when she started sprouting knobs of arthritis in the joints of her fingers, the thumb ring would be out.

"I'll dance with you," she said to Ruth.

Ruth's mouth flopped open and she slammed it shut. She'd suggested the dance to try to get Hilda and Wade interacting, not that it made a big difference to her if they reconciled, but the evening would be more pleasant if they stopped sniping at each other. She had nothing against dancing with another woman, though. She'd done it often, starting back in her high school days, when the gym was transformed, thanks to paper streamers and cheesy murals, into Winter Wonderland or Around the World and all the boys who weren't going steady spent the entire dance climbing on the bleachers or ducking out onto the hockey field to drink booze. The girls who didn't have boyfriends wound up dancing with each other.

But she hardly knew Hilda and she had no idea how to dance to this thumping, thudding music. If you could even call it music.

"He doesn't want to dance," Hilda said, shooting Wade a lethal look. "Let's go out on the floor. I bet we can find some guys to dance with out there."

Wade scowled and Ruth suppressed a smile. Was Hilda trying to make him jealous? Maybe she wasn't as indifferent to him as she was pretending to be.

"Watch my purse," Ruth requested as she slid off her stool. Hilda didn't have a purse, unless you counted the tiny sack on a black velvet cord around her neck. It was hardly bigger than an eyeglass case. What could a woman stick in it? A credit card and keys, maybe. A tube of lipstick. Not much more than that.

She was grateful for Hilda's bright pink sweater as they wove past tables and clots of people to the dance floor. If Hilda had been dressed like Wade, Ruth would have lost her in two seconds flat.

The dance floor was as crowded as it looked. It smelled like humanity—sweat, perfume, aftershave, liquor. Blue and green lights gave the impression that this mass of bouncing people was underwater, an enormous sea monster that had swallowed her and Hilda without a burp.

Ruth glanced around her. No one was doing a dance she could recognize. They were just bouncing, flailing, swaying.

She started bouncing.

Four songs later, or maybe it was five—one song sounded like another to her—she was still bouncing. More than bouncing, really. She was waving her arms and shimmying her tush. She might have some arthritic bumps on her fingers, but her hips and knees had so far been spared that affliction, and while she didn't dance as wildly as some of the young people around her, she fit in well enough.

When was the last time she danced like this? When had she *ever* danced like this? The exertion, combined with the heat of all the gyrating bodies around her, caused her to sweat. Someone jostled her. She didn't care.

She closed her eyes and let the music's rhythm run up and down her spine. So what if it was awful? It had an infectious beat, and she let it invade her like a virus and take over her body. She was no longer a grandma, no longer a store clerk, no longer a student of Baroque concertos, no longer a wife contemplating divorce. She was no longer a woman who savored her newfound solitude. In the middle of the dance floor—well, actually more on the edge; she had no interest in muscling her way deeper into the crowd—she was alone and united with all these people, all this energy.

When she opened her eyes again, she couldn't see Hilda. Someone patted her shoulder and she kept dancing. Another pat and she turned to find Wade behind her, smiling sheepishly. "Hilda came back to the table," he shouted, although the music was so loud she barely heard him. "You tired her out."

Ruth nodded. She saw no point in straining her vocal cords in an effort to be heard over the clamor on the dance floor.

Wade started to bounce. He was not a good dancer. His movements were stiff and klutzy, lacking fluidity. His hair fluttered around his head, reminding her a little of the way the pile of her apartment's shag carpet fluttered when she vacuumed.

He shouldn't feel obligated to dance with her just because Hilda had abandoned her. She was perfectly happy to dance by herself, although it was hard to be by herself when she was surrounded by a hundred other dancers. Wade could be sitting at the table with Hilda right now, without Ruth positioned between them like the Berlin Wall. They could be talking, working things out.

But he remained with her, loosening up a little—although the more he loosened up, the klutzier he looked. Still, he didn't seem too pained by the ordeal. Maybe Hilda had been lying when she'd said he didn't dance. And what the heck—dancing with a young guy, even if they weren't touching, was good for her ego. Imagine if Myrna from the B'nai Torah Sisterhood saw her. All that work Myrna had had done on her face to make her look younger, and she was still stuck dancing with her husband Howard, who looked like a turtle.

Another song, or maybe it was two, and Ruth decided she ought to take a break. God knew how she'd feel tomorrow morning after all this boogying. If Wade wanted to remain on the dance floor, fine, but when she pointed toward herself and then in the direction of their table, he nodded and followed her.

A stranger had planted himself at the table with Hilda. He looked a little older than her and Wade, and his shirt had one too many buttons undone in front. He wasn't particularly good-looking, either. Despite the contorted little barbell puncturing his eyebrow, Wade was much more handsome.

The stranger stood when they reached the table, although he leaned possessively over Hilda, who appeared bored. "Hey, taking your mom dancing?" he asked Wade, smirking at his profound cleverness.

"She's my friend," Wade said, then turned to Hilda. "Who's this bozo?"

"Just some bozo," she replied with a shrug.

"Well, thanks for keeping her company," Wade said, nudging the guy out of the way and sitting next to Hilda. Pleased that she no longer had to hover between them like a referee in a boxing match, Ruth took her seat on the other side of Hilda, sandwiching Hilda and making clear to the bozo that there was no place for him at the table.

"Well, okay," he said with what appeared to be forced amiability. "So, I'll see you around."

Hilda shrugged again. Wade chased the bozo away with his stare. "Who the fuck was that?" he asked Hilda.

"Don't use that language," she scolded, shooting Ruth a glance. Ruth shook her head and waved her hand to show she wasn't scandalized by Wade's word choice. Hilda turned back to him. "He was just some creep. I could handle him."

"What a dork. He looked like—who was that actor? The one who made all those stupid movies about moonshiners and redneck sheriffs?"

"Burt Reynolds," Ruth said. The guy *had* looked a little like him in some of his sleazier roles. She took a sip of her wine, which had warmed up enough to taste like cleaning solvent. She ignored the flavor. All that dancing had made her thirsty.

"You really know how to move out there," Wade praised her, gesturing toward the dance floor. "You were fly, Ruthie. I didn't know you had it in you."

"You tired me out, for sure," Hilda said with a grin.

"Fly? What's that?"

"Cool," Hilda translated.

"Me? Cool?" Ruth laughed and took another sip of wine.

"We ought to take her dancing with us all the time," Wade said. "She'll keep us on our toes."

"Literally," Hilda added.

"No." Ruth shook her head for emphasis. "You're not taking me dancing all the time. In fact, I think you should go back over there and dance, just the two of you."

"Ugh." Hilda curled her lip. "What are you, a matchmaker? We're breaking up, remember?"

"*I'm* not breaking up," Wade said.

"Fine. You don't have to break up. I'll break up for both of us."

Wade sent Ruth a despairing look. If Hilda weren't sitting between them, she would have given him a firm lecture, ordering him to fight for what he wanted.

It occurred to her that she might have enjoyed doing things like this—going to clubs in Boston, drinking lousy wine and dancing until she was dripping with sweat—for years. But she'd never demanded that Richard take her dancing at clubs. She'd never even asked. He would have considered it out of character for her, and inappropriate. She'd been a suburban wife and mother, for God's sake, not someone who was fly. And so she'd never fought for what she wanted.

Until now.

Ruth couldn't say all those things to Wade, so she just gave him a stern frown. He straightened slightly, stood, and closed his hand around Hilda's. "Fine," he snapped. "You can break up for both of us. But first, we're dancing." With that, he tugged her out of her chair and dragged her back to the dance floor. Not really dragged. She wasn't resisting him, Ruth noticed.

Alone at the table, she smiled and settled herself more comfortably on her stool. Either they'd break up or they wouldn't, but at least they'd dance. And that was what tonight was about: not saving relationships, not figuring out the future. Just dancing.

Chapter Twenty

The queasiness was returning. Richard swallowed several times, tightened the knot of his tie at his throat and squared his shoulders. He'd brought patients back from the edge of death. He'd restarted moribund hearts. Surely he could have a cup of coffee with Shari Bernstein without vomiting.

He and Doug had played golf on Saturday—probably their last outing on the links until spring. They'd worn fleece jackets for warmth, and they hadn't indulged in drinks until they'd finished all eighteen holes and retired to the clubhouse to thaw out. But the ground wasn't frozen or covered with snow, so they'd played.

And talked.

Somewhere between the fourth and the seventh hole, Doug had told Richard that, according to Jill, Ruth intended to go out dancing that night. Doug might as well have swung a nine-iron into Richard's gut. Dancing? Moving to the music in some other man's arms?

Richard had been unable to conjure a picture of Ruth as he knew her, dependably familiar in her unflashy way, dressed in jeans, an old sweater and her battered leather loafers. Instead he'd visualized her with her hair swept up and her body draped in silk, her head tilted back to gaze into the eyes of a guy Richard couldn't identify but wanted to pummel. He'd visualized them swirling around on a stereotypically romantic dance floor, with gauzy lighting and a combo playing a schmaltzy tune Ruth would never listen to in real life, given her scholarly knowledge of music. He'd visualized sparks of brilliance flashing from her earlobes as the diamond earrings he'd given her caught the light.

The possibility that she'd wear those earrings with another man had made him nearly crazy.

Doug had lowered Richard's blood pressure by saying that, as far as he knew, Ruth's plan involved going out with co-workers. That she was socializing with the sort of people who worked as clerks at First-Rate didn't thrill Richard, but it was much better than his first image of her with her left hand draped on some creep's shoulder and her right hand clasped within his while they floated across the dance floor to the strains of "Strangers in the Night" or "Moon River."

Still, he'd needed a stiff belt of scotch at the clubhouse to restore his equilibrium. He'd wondered why Jill hadn't mentioned Ruth's dance outing when he'd found her in his house, collecting clothing for Ruth. If he'd taken her up on her invitation for dinner, would she have told him over a dessert of rugelach that his wife was going club-hopping with First-Rate clerks? Had she ever intended to mention this news to him?

Obviously not. She wouldn't have wanted to upset him.

Doug hadn't wanted to upset him, either. At least Richard was pretty sure that hadn't been his motive. No, what Doug had wanted to do was light a fire under Richard, to prod him into meeting Dr. Shari Bernstein for coffee.

So, here he was. Walking down the hall to a staff lounge at five-fifteen Monday afternoon to drink a cup of coffee. Or maybe tea. Or maybe ginger ale, to settle his stomach.

He entered the room cautiously, surveying it with his gaze while trying to act as if he was just strolling in. People sat at tables, some in scrubs, some in street attire. Gert had claimed Dr. Bernstein was gorgeous, but Richard didn't let that limit his search.

Forget gorgeous. Not even an ugly woman was sitting alone in the room.

All right, so he'd arrived ahead of her. Maybe that was good. A gorgeous woman shouldn't be kept waiting. Who knew—if she was gorgeous enough, someone else might swoop in and buy her a cup of coffee while she was waiting for Richard.

That wouldn't happen, because he'd gotten to the lounge first. He didn't mind waiting. It would give him a chance to relax before he had to meet her.

He sauntered over to an empty table, sat and wished he had a newspaper to flip through. Or a book. A patient's file. Something to make him appear as if he wasn't waiting.

A slap on the back jolted him. He turned to find Maury Slovisky hovering behind him, beaming. The reflection of the overhead light on Maury's bald spot was almost as bright as his smile. "What are you still doing here?" Maury asked. "Aren't you usually out the door by now?"

Maury was a hot-dog cardiac surgeon, always boasting about the punishing hours he kept and the high-risk procedures he performed. Every surgery with him was dire and rife with complications. The man was a good doctor but also a bullshit artist. Too bad he wasn't as adept at closing his mouth as he was at closing a chest.

Richard didn't care to discuss his coffee date with Maury, of all people. If Maury found out he was meeting another woman because he and Ruth were separated, everyone at Beth Israel Deaconess would know about it.

He scrambled to come up with a cover story. "I'm meeting someone to discuss some collaborative research," he said, silently congratulating himself. Not only did it sound distinctly unromantic, but it also made him seem important.

Sure enough, Maury deflated. "Research? I didn't know you swung that way, Richard. Since when are you vying for a Nobel Prize?"

"It's just something we're discussing," he said cryptically.

"What area? A new product? You know the problems patients have had with some of those stents. Problems followed by law suits. Can you say class action? You could be walking straight into a minefield."

"I'd rather not go into it now," Richard said. Even better—let Maury think this imaginary research might involve patentable products that could earn Richard millions. Maury would eat himself up with envy and curiosity.

"Well, you know my expertise, Richard. If there's anything I could contribute . . ."

And get your greedy hands on a third of the licensing fees? Not a chance, Richard thought, then reminded himself that his supposed research collaboration was a lie. No licensing fees existed for Maury to get his greedy hands on. No Nobel Prize in Medicine loomed in Richard's future.

A woman entered the lounge. Middle-aged, shoulder-length reddish-brown hair, not exactly gorgeous but even from across the room her skin seemed luminous. She was dressed rather plainly, in a tailored blouse and slacks and a colorful scarf that hung around her shoulders, serving no purpose Richard could fathom. He'd never understood the whole thing with women and scarves. In his world, you wore a scarf to keep your neck warm, or else you didn't wear a scarf.

She scanned the room, just as he had when he'd arrived. Her gaze slid right past Richard, perhaps because Maury was hovering over his table, perhaps because she wasn't Shari Bernstein. But when she did a second scan, she lingered on him for a moment. He nodded slightly. Was that how it was done? he wondered. Was that how two people who'd never before seen each other connected? Non-verbal signals had never been his forte.

She nodded back and smiled.

"My colleague is here," he said in a sharp tone, hoping Maury would take the hint and disappear. Unfortunately, he didn't. And why should he? He wanted to meet Richard's potential co-Nobelist.

Richard stood as she wove among the tables in his direction. Definitely not gorgeous, he concluded. Her eyes were close-set and her nose had the chiseled, not-quite-right appearance that indicated a rhinoplasty—an older one, probably done when she was in her teens. Plastic surgeons were much better at shaping noses now than they were thirty years ago, when all the noses sculpted by a given surgeon wound up looking exactly the same, regardless of the surrounding face. Richard recalled three classmates in high school who'd all gotten nose jobs done by the same surgeon over summer vacation. When they'd returned to school the following September, they could have passed for cousins. They all had exactly the same nose.

Shari Bernstein's nose might have qualified her for membership in their family. Her complexion really was amazing, however, smooth and creamy, an excellent advertisement for her dermatological expertise. "Dr. Bernstein?" he asked, extending his hand, hoping his palm wasn't too sweaty with nerves.

She returned his smile and gave his hand a firm shake. "Dr. Bendel?" Her gaze shifted to Maury.

"This is Maury Slovisky, also a cardiologist," Richard said quickly. "He's on his way out."

Maury's eyes shifted between Richard and Shari. "Don't leave me in the dark," he said, nudging Richard in the ribs. "You get something cooking here that I can contribute to, just let me know."

"I'm sure I will," Richard mumbled while a faint frown creased Shari's forehead. Richard glared at Maury until he shambled off toward the door. Not until Maury had left the room did he gesture for Shari to sit.

She did. "What did he mean, contribute?"

"Nothing. He's a putz. You want some coffee? Tea?"

She glanced over her shoulder, as if she needed confirmation that Maury was truly gone, and then settled in her chair. "Decaf, please. Black."

Over at the counter, where Richard filled two thick porcelain mugs from the decaffeinated machine, he realized why she'd seemed so rattled by Maury. She thought she and Richard were on a date, or at least something that might lead to a date, and there Maury had been, offering to join in. Shari Bernstein must have thought Richard was a pervert, interested in threesomes. He shuddered. Just thinking of Maury naked made him queasier than he'd ever felt while anticipating this meeting with Shari Bernstein.

They'd started out on the wrong foot, as the cliché had it. He hoped he could redeem the situation.

After paying for the drinks, he carried them back to the table. She smiled and thanked him. Very mannerly, very polite. Very stilted.

"So, you're a cardiologist," she said once he'd resumed his seat across the table from her.

What was the appropriate response? *Yes, I'm a cardiologist.* He didn't really want to talk about his work. He decided to let her do the talking. "I understand you worked miracles on Gert's son. He had a birth mark or something?"

"A port-wine stain. And it was hardly a miracle." She trilled a laugh as light as crystal, so delicate it could splinter.

"Well, Gert spoke very highly of you. I'm sure if I asked her son, he'd speak highly of you, too."

"Doubtful," she said, then took a sip of her coffee. Her fingernails were polished a startling red. Doctors didn't have red nails, did they? His daughters—a lawyer and a freelance catalog writer—didn't wear red nail polish. Nor did his lovely daughter-in-law or his magnificent granddaughters. Red nails didn't happen in his family, and thank God for that. "Gert's son is a teenager," she went on. "Teenagers never have anything good to say about anything."

"You sound like you're speaking from experience."

"I've got two teenage daughters," she said, and then that was that. For the next—by the time he looked at his watch, fifteen minutes had elapsed—he got to listen to her rant about her daughters. They spent more than the gross national product of Botswana on hair grooming products. They slammed doors rather than closing them. The older one believed that having a driver's license was the same thing as owning a car, and ever since she'd gotten her license she'd acted as if Shari's car was her own. The younger one believed that she could learn to play the piano through osmosis, and after Shari had spent a fortune on piano lessons for her, this younger daughter had decided she no longer needed to practice. But God forbid she quit taking lessons.

Richard listened as Shari told him about her daughters' cell-phone habits, their musical tastes—"when I say 'musical,' I'm being facetious," she noted—their exploits in field hockey, their apparel budgets, their bickering, their messiness, their idea of home cooking—"if it can't be zapped in the microwave, they won't make it"—and their forgetfulness when it came to walking the dog.

She eventually wound down, leaving Richard to understand that he was supposed to say something. "You've got a dog?"

That turned out to be an effective conversational gambit. Shari launched into another monologue, this one about the dog, a shih-tzu—which sounded kind of obscene to Richard—named Hayley, who had to be the stupidest dog ever to utter a "woof-woof," and her grooming cost more than the gross national product of Swaziland. Hayley refused to sleep on anything but a velvet cushion, and Shari had had her spayed despite her pedigree bloodline because, as a dermatologist with a demanding career, she simply didn't have the time to breed her. "Do you have a dog?"

"No," Richard said, feeling a toxic blend of panic and desperation bubble up inside him. What else could he say? He had to say something more than *no*. But what? He'd never had pets, and his children were adults, accomplished, a source of pride. How their spending habits compared to sub-Saharan economics, he had no idea.

Shari Bernstein had teenage daughters. She was too young for him, although she didn't seem *that* young. He'd become a father right after he'd finished medical school—he still remembered Ruth waddling around in her eighth month at his graduation ceremony—whereas Shari had obviously become a mother later in life. So she had teenage daughters. He had a nearly-teenage granddaughter. Six months and Abbie would be bat-mitzvah.

He groped through his memory in search of something to say. "There was a documentary about dog breeders on PBS the other day," he remarked. He'd caught a few seconds of the show while he'd been channel surfing, searching for something more interesting to watch.

That was good enough to get her going again.

He leaned back in his chair, sipping his coffee and letting her voice wash over him. Her hair was sleek, evenly colored, not a hint of gray in it. Ruth's hair was streaked with gray, but it looked more natural. His fingers flexed, missing the feel of her dark, ordinary hair. When was the last time he'd stroked her head? When was the last time he'd cupped his hands around her cheeks and kissed her?

When was the last time he'd lingered over a cup of coffee with her? In the morning, he was always gobbling breakfast while reading the newspaper, and then filling his travel mug with coffee and bolting out the door. If he had a cup of coffee after dinner, he drank it in front of the TV while he clicked through the channels.

Sorrow laced through him. He never drank coffee with Ruth anymore. More important, he never *went someplace* with her for coffee. If they had a cup, it was in the house. They never went on dates.

Sure, they'd go out for dinner—when Ruth was tired from tennis or a three-hour meeting of the fundraising committee at the synagogue and couldn't bear the thought of cooking, or when the potatoes in the bag under the sink unexpectedly went moldy and she didn't have a chance to run to the supermarket to buy fresh potatoes, and the menu she'd planned for that evening wouldn't work with rice.

But a date? Richard calling her from his office, the way he'd called Shari Bernstein, and saying, "Let's get together after work today." And then ironing his shirt so he'd look spiffy for her. Surprising her, treating her, making something special out of a coffee tête-à-tête. When had he last done that?

Before they were married, probably.

No wonder she'd walked out. No wonder she thought working as a clerk at First-Rate was better than staying with him. He was doing for a stranger, a doctor with porcelain skin and a phony little nose, something he never did for his wife.

She'd been gone a month. Tomorrow was Halloween, and Jill had promised to buy some bags of candy and explain what would be expected of him. He'd never dealt with trick-or-treaters before. When his own children were young, he'd been the parent to accompany them through the neighborhood in their costumes. Doug had favored superheroes until about the age of ten, when he'd decided to dress up as a doctor, which Richard hadn't thought was much of a costume, let alone a scary one, though he'd been deeply flattered that his son had wanted to dress like him. Melissa had loved flamboyant, glittery outfits—a fairy, a princess, an angel. One year, as he recalled, Jill had wanted to trick or treat as a teacher. She'd worn a cardigan, wedged a pencil behind her ear and carried a globe under her arm.

Ruth had always been the one to stay home, answer the door and distribute the candy. Once his own children were old enough to trick-or-treat on their own, he'd spent the evening in the den, watching television while Ruth had answered the constantly ringing doorbell. Over the din of the television he'd hear her exclaim, "Oh, my goodness, you frightened me! You are definitely the scariest Teletubby I've seen tonight!" and "Aaaiiee, is that a Dick Cheney mask? You're giving me nightmares!"

He'd answer the door tomorrow night, but he doubted he could charm the trick-or-treaters the way Ruth could. In all honesty, he'd be happy to skip the whole thing. Kids didn't need that much candy, anyway. Eat enough candy now, and in forty years they'd be his patients.

Shari Bernstein was still talking, he wasn't sure about what. He nodded, smiled, discovered how difficult it was to drink hot coffee from a mug while smiling, and stopped smiling.

He wanted to go home. He wanted to scrub the bathroom sink. He wanted to hand Ruth the remote control. He wanted to sleep next to her and wake up next to her and let her know, on either end of the night, that she was the only woman for him.

Shari Bernstein finally wound down, thank God. Richard realized that it was once again incumbent upon him to say something, and he truly meant to be courteous. But the only thing that came to mind was, "Well, I think I need to be getting home."

And amazingly, his queasiness vanished.

Chapter Twenty-One

Doug kissed Mackenzie goodnight first, and then Madison. He had to remember to alternate which one got the first goodnight kiss; they complained loudly if he kissed one first two times in a row. As if who got the first kiss, or the last, indicated favoritism.

They were twins. And they were female. He'd long ago quit expecting them to make sense.

He turned off their bedroom light, reminded them to go to sleep—he knew they'd whisper and giggle for another half hour at least, but the warning was his attempt at discipline—and headed downstairs. Brooke awaited him in the den nursing a glass of wine, and he poured some scotch for himself and joined her there.

She sat on the sofa, her legs tucked beneath her and her gaze on the gas fireplace. Flames flickered behind the fireplace's glass doors, but those doors prevented the fire's heat from filling the room, and the gas had no scent. Without the aroma of burning wood, without the crackling and hissing and the wafts of warmth, the gas fireplace was about as exciting as the burning yule log some television station used to broadcast for twenty-four hours on Christmas day, back when he was a child.

But Brooke loved the gas fireplace. She loved being able to start and stop a fire with the flick of a button.

He settled onto the couch next to her and she sent him a smile. "I talked to your sister today," she told him.

"Melissa?"

"Jill." She sipped her Chardonnay. "She said that since your parents are separated, she'd host Thanksgiving this year. She didn't sound too thrilled about it."

"Of course she's not thrilled about it. Our parents are separated. It's a tragic situation."

Brooke shrugged. So much for tragedy. "She's being a sweetheart about taking the girls when we're in Nevis."

"Jill's good that way. She picks up the slack." He hadn't even considered the logistics of a Thanksgiving dinner with his parents living apart. Thank God Jill had.

"I think it's the cooking and preparing she's not thrilled about."

"You could help her," Doug suggested.

"Me? Cook?" Brooke tossed back her head and laughed, causing her hair to ripple. He still wasn't used to its darker color and shaggy style.

He conceded her point with a nod. For tonight's dinner, she'd prepared soup and grilled cheese sandwiches. Soup from cans and sandwiches prepared with a gadget the sole purpose of which was to make grilled cheese sandwiches. God knew, if she'd had to make grilled cheese sandwiches in a pan on the stove, she might not be able to manage it.

"I was thinking you could help her with setting up," he explained. "We could buy the pies. And the wine. And a centerpiece for the table or something."

"A centerpiece would be nice," Brooke agreed. "I'd have to know the theme of the dinner so I could pick out an appropriate one."

Did Thanksgiving dinner have to have a theme? Other than giving thanks, of course. Harvest? Turkeys? A memorial to whoever came up with the notion of turning cranberries into a sticky sweet jelly?

"And the color scheme," Brooke went on. "Her dining room walls are such an awful green. I don't think it's a good idea to eat surrounded by green. It reminds me of mold."

"Why doesn't it remind you of salad?" he asked, then realized he didn't care about her answer. He'd never before spent a moment contemplating Jill's dining room décor. If Brooke hadn't mentioned that the walls were green, he probably would have been unable to recall what color they were.

Brooke laughed again and shook her head, clearly considering him a philistine for being so insensitive to the nuances of green walls. "Speaking of food, can you pick up some dinner at Colonel Ping's on your way home from work tomorrow? You can skip the egg foo yong if you want. Although the girls love it."

"I hate Colonel Ping."

"Lotus Garden then. I don't care. You can get those cold sesame noodles you love."

He swallowed a mouthful of scotch, feeling it numb his throat going down. For some reason, Brooke's simple request filled him with apprehension. "Why can't you get dinner together tomorrow? Where are you going to be?"

"New York. I should be home in time for dinner, but last time you got home ahead of us. If you pick up the food while I pick up the girls at Stephanie's house, we should arrive home at the same time."

"New York." More than apprehension. Apprehension augmented by dread.

"I need a touch-up on my hair," she explained, her voice calm and even, as if driving two hundred miles for a touch-up—a fucking *touch-up*—was perfectly normal.

"You just had your hair done last week."

"It was more than a week ago, and I think it should be lightened just a little bit. Don't you? I think he went a tad too dark."

The ratio of Doug's mood shifted. Now it was dread, augmented by apprehension. "You're going to New York to get your hair lightened a tad?"

Her smile was like the gas fire, visually alluring but exuding no warmth, as if a pane of glass blocked it from him. "Luc did the job in the first place. I need to give him the opportunity to adjust it. And he's so talented."

Luc. Shit. "Melissa's boyfriend," he said, just so they'd both know what was at stake—if, indeed, anything other than Brooke's hair was.

"Not anymore," Brooke told him.

Apprehension. Dread. A huge wallop of terror. "He's not?"

"When he was working on my hair last time, he said they were breaking up. Well, not exactly. More like drifting apart."

"He discussed their relationship with you?" Melissa was Doug's sister, and she didn't discuss her relationships with him. Why should her hairdresser discuss her relationships with Brooke?

"He was just talking. Stylists talk while they're working."

"He wasn't just talking. He was talking about my sister." To make sure Brooke understood, he added, "Your sister-in-law."

"It wasn't like he said anything bad about her," Brooke said defensively. "He just said they're traveling down different paths."

"That's obvious. She's traveling down the successful professional path. He's traveling down the beauty parlor path."

"It's not a beauty parlor, Doug. It's a spa. A lovely place. They've got a wonderful atmosphere there, tabletop fountains and relaxing flute music playing. Everything smells of hibiscus."

Doug thought fondly of the barbershop where he got his hair trimmed once a month. It smelled of soap, and instead of flute music, the owner usually had the radio tuned to a right-wing talk radio station. He claimed to disagree with everything the hosts said, but he found the guys' rants hilarious. Doug found nothing humorous about a couple of yahoos howling that when restaurants supplied soup kitchens with their unused inventory they were contributing to the homeless problem because why would anyone get a job and buy his own food if he could eat leftover dinners from Legal Seafood and Chez Henri? But he knew better than to disagree with a man wielding extremely sharp scissors in the vicinity of his ears.

At least the place didn't smell of hibiscus—whatever the hell hibiscus smelled like.

"Luc said Melissa was obsessed with buying an apartment. He has no interest in co-ops and condos."

"Like I have no interest in Gulfstream jets," Doug muttered. "Of course he has no interest in co-ops and condos. As a barber—excuse me, a *stylist*—he'll never be able to afford Manhattan real estate. It's completely out of his range."

"It's not about what he can afford," Brooke argued. "His salon isn't cheap. I bet he makes good money." She took another sip of wine and sighed. "It's about settling down, planting roots. Melissa is looking for a commitment. Luc isn't."

Doug took a deep breath. He took a deep swig of scotch. "Brooke," he said as gently as he could, given the adrenaline rampaging through his bloodstream. He absolutely did not want his beautiful wife having her hair done by an uncommitted New York City stud. "Why go back to the guy who botched your color? Why not have someone else fix his mistake?"

"It wasn't a mistake," Brooke said. "He didn't botch it. He just took it a little darker than I'd like."

"So you want to spent four hours driving down to the city so he can make it lighter, and then drive four hours back?"

"It's not four hours," she said, then flashed him a wicked grin. "I drive fast."

"Three and a half hours. Brooke, it's crazy. Boston is full of fancy salons with flute music. The suburbs have spas with tabletop fountains. Why do you want to kill seven hours on the road so this uncommitted schmuck can mess with your hair?"

His anger—which he was trying hard to keep under control, but apparently not succeeding—seemed to take her aback. "He's not a schmuck, Doug. He's incredibly talented."

"And no one in the entire state of Massachusetts is as talented as he is?"

She frowned, as if the possibility had never occurred to her. "Well, he was Melissa's boyfriend. And she looked fabulous after he did her. I like to have a recommendation, and Melissa's hair was quite a recommendation."

Okay. Okay. More deep breaths, and the anger began to wane. Maybe it was as simple as Brooke made it out to be: she'd loved the way Melissa's hair had looked, so she'd gone to the same person who'd done Melissa's hair.

Or maybe not. Maybe she'd been so impressed by the way Luc *did* Melissa that she'd decided to have Luc *do* her, too.

Oh, God. That possibility shifted his mood ratios once more. Less anger, but a lot more terror. A shitload of terror.

Eight years ago, he'd married this woman. He'd fallen in love with her because she'd been charming, beautiful and blessedly undemanding. She'd asked of him only security, support, devotion and a credit card with no limit—things he'd been happy to give her. He'd believed marriage was as simple as that.

Not any longer. Not since his parents, whose marriage he'd always viewed as being built on the very same foundation of security, support and devotion, had proven that such a foundation could crumble, that those elements weren't enough. Now his mother had walked out on his father, and his wife was traipsing down to New York, where people talked funny and littered the sidewalks with empty food wrappers and cigarette butts and cheered for the Yankees and booed the Red Sox, to meet with the incredibly talented hunk who'd *done* Doug's sister.

Panic seasoned the terror, anger and dread. "What would you do if I told you I really, really didn't want you going to New York?" he asked, a tamer question than the one burning in his mind: *What would you do if I forbade you to let that man near your hair?* He couldn't ask that question. Asking it would send any woman storming out the door. And it would make him sound so unreasonable, so bossy. So panicked and angry and terrified and filled with dread.

"Why would you say that? It's not like the girls don't love spending the afternoon at Stephanie's."

"But . . ." He turned to stare at the fireplace and prayed for his control not to slip. "But New York, Brooke. It's so damned far to travel just to get something you can get right here at home." Oh, shit. He'd meant she could get a *haircut* here in the neighborhood. His words hadn't come out that way, though.

She looked bemused, then suspicious. Evidently she'd figured him out. "Do you think something's going on between me and Luc?"

The accusation lay between them like a dead cod, wet and slightly smelly. No sense denying that that was exactly what he thought, and what he feared. "You were the one who said he was *doing* Melissa."

"Doing her hair, you idiot."

"He was doing more than her hair."

"Well, he isn't doing more than mine. For God's sake, Douglas."

He felt ashamed and a little ill. Brooke leaned away from him and managed to fit her downturned mouth around the edge of her wine glass so she could drink and pout at the same time.

"I'm sorry," he said.

"How could you even imply—"

"Look. I'm an idiot. Ever since my parents split, I just . . . I'm afraid to believe *anything* is forever anymore. They had the most stable marriage in the world, and it fell apart. We have the most stable marriage in the world." *I hope,* he added silently. But God only knew. If he hadn't lost Brooke to Luc's incredible talents, he might lose her because he'd insinuated that he'd lost her to Luc's incredible talents. Either way, he lost.

"He's a nice guy," she said, her tone softer, less indignant. He sneaked a glimpse and saw that she was pouting a little less. "He's got an amazing aestheticism when it comes to hair."

Doug nodded. He didn't dare to say anything. Whatever he said might land him in even deeper trouble.

"And it's New York. It's a whole different place. The trip is relaxing. I listen to an audio book while I'm driving. I don't have to think about play dates or dentist appointments or volunteering for the class trip to the animal hospital. I just drive. And then I get there, and the city is noisy and gritty and fun. And I get a fabulous haircut and color—although the color could be a little more fabulous. And I come home refreshed. And while I'm in New York, I can treat myself to one of those big hot pretzels. The New York pretzels are better than the ones they sell in Boston."

"So—it's like an outing."

"Exactly. It's a day away. And Luc is very talented."

Doug wished she wouldn't keep reminding him of that. "What, are you bored?"

"Bored? Me?" Her eyes grew round.

"Bored of being home. Bored of the usual routines. So bored you consider trekking all the way to New York City for a haircut exciting."

"I'm not bored," she said in a wavering voice.

"Sure you are. The girls don't need you twenty-four-seven anymore. They're in first grade. They've got their own lives. The cleaning service takes care of the house. There's only so much shopping you can do. You're bored." He felt his anger and panic and dread seeping away as he said this. It made sense. She was bored, and sitting in a contoured chair having a handsome guy fuss over her hair gave her a charge. That was what this was about. A change of scenery for the day. And a fat, hot pretzel.

"If you got your hair done here, the time you would have spent driving to and from New York could be spent doing something interesting. Something new."

"Like what?" she challenged him.

"Like . . . like helping Jill plan Thanksgiving. Or helping her with Abbie's bat mitzvah. The place where it's being held is putting her through the wringer. They're hiking the dinner price, they're hemming and hawing about how many hours the DJ can play—I don't know. I got an earful the last time I talked to her."

"And I'm supposed to help her how?"

"You're good at parties," he said. "You're a pro when it comes to organizing them. You could be a party planner. Isn't that what they're called?"

"A party planner?"

"Remember the party you threw for my parents' anniversary? The jukebox rock-and-roll party?"

"And now look at them," she said dryly. "They're getting divorced."

"It was a great party, though."

She contemplated his statement, sipped some wine and apparently came up with no argument. "You're right. It was."

The idea was so brilliant, Doug decided to pretend he hadn't accidentally stumbled upon it in his effort to convince Brooke to have her hair done locally. "A party planner. You'd be your own boss, work only on parties you wanted to, get paid to be creative."

"Paid? You want me to get a job?" She narrowed her gaze. Fortunately, the pout didn't return, but she was wearing an emphatic frown. "Is there something about our finances that you aren't telling me?"

"No. Our finances are fine." He leaned forward, energized. "People are vain. They want their Lasik surgery. I'm booked solid until we leave for Nevis, and people are already scheduling for next spring."

"So why do you want me to do this? Why should I get paid to be creative?"

"If you don't want to get paid, do it for free." He set his glass on the coffee table in front of the couch and reached for Brooke's hand. Her skin was velvet-soft, her fingernails pale and oval, like slivered almonds. "Look at my parents. My mother left my father not because she didn't love him, not because he betrayed her. Not even because he channel-surfs too much. She left him because she wanted her own life, her own identity. She wanted a job."

"I don't want a job," Brooke insisted.

"A hobby, then. Do it as a hobby." He sighed. "I'm being selfish, Brooke, I know. I'm asking you to consider this because I don't want to wake up thirty-five years from now and hear you tell me you're moving out and taking a job as a clerk at First-Rate."

"I would *never* take a job as a clerk at First-Rate." She wrinkled her nose. "I don't even like entering those stores. The merchandise is so cheap."

One thing Brooke detested was buying anything that wasn't overpriced, Doug thought with a wry smile. No wonder she preferred Colonel Ping to Lotus Garden: not because of Colonel Ping's overreliance on salt and MSG but because its mu-shu pork cost a buck-fifty more than Lotus Garden's.

"I don't want you to work at First-Rate," he said gently. "I want you to do something that keeps you from getting so bored you think going to New York for a haircut is an exciting adventure. I want every day to be an adventure for you."

She ruminated, her hand unmoving in his clasp, her other hand slowly lifting her wine glass to her lips. Her perfectly shaped lips. Lips he loved, lips he hoped would still be meeting his in eager kisses thirty-five years from now.

She drank, swallowed and smiled enigmatically. "You know what would be an adventure for me?"

"What?"

"Holding the remote while we watched TV so you couldn't channel-surf."

He allowed himself a tentative smile, as well. Maybe, just maybe his marriage wasn't doomed.

Chapter Twenty-Two

"Tonight?" Melissa leaned back in her chair and closed her eyes. She had her phone wedged between her ear and her shoulder, a definite no-no posture-wise, but she'd broken a fingernail and was smoothing it out with the emery board she kept stashed in her desk for just such emergencies. The manicure repair left no hand available to hold the phone.

She ought to get a headset so she could talk on the phone hands-free. But those headsets were so dorky. Using one would make her resemble a telephone operator from the 1950's. Every time she answered, she'd have the urge to say, "Your number please," in a nasal singsong.

"Yeah, tonight," Aidan O'Leary's voice rumbled through the line. "We've got everybody on board with the settlement. Case closed. We can have a dinner together without raising any ethical issues. We're not adversaries anymore."

Just because the settlement had been accepted by their respective clients didn't mean he wasn't her adversary, she reminded herself as she ran her thumb over the damaged nail, searching for rough spots. Certainly he could still be her adversary, even if they were no longer on opposite sides of a suit.

He must have interpreted her silence as resistance. "I'll treat," he added.

"No, that's all right."

"Then you can treat."

"No."

"Come on, let me treat," he said in a cajoling voice. "We can go someplace cheap if it'll make you feel better."

She laughed, then shook her head. He was her adversary because he was too damned enticing, that was why. Too clever. Too cute.

"I'm supposed to meet my realtor at the apartment in Murray Hill at six," she told him. "I want one last look before I decide whether to make an offer on it."

"Not a problem. I'll meet you there and we can go out for dinner afterward."

"All right," she said, then sighed. If he could get her to say yes over the phone, when she couldn't even see his dimples, she was in big trouble.

What the hell. She was in big trouble, anyway. She was going to torture herself by walking through the apartment one last time when she still hadn't figured out how to cover the down payment. Her hope was that giving it one final viewing would convince her she wasn't really in love with it, and that standing in its cozy second bedroom wouldn't fill her with all sorts of wistful ovarian pangs. One more look might prove to her that the place wasn't that special.

She gave O'Leary the address and agreed to meet him outside the building at six twenty, at which time he could take her someplace cheap for dinner. She'd probably be bummed out after her farewell tour of the apartment—whether because she discovered she still loved it but couldn't swing the financing or because she discovered she didn't really love it and therefore couldn't trust her instincts—so wherever he took her had better have a liquor license.

She was able to leave her office by quarter to six—early for her. Usually she worked until about six-thirty. When she'd been with Luc, he'd complained about her late hours on the days when he didn't have any evening appointments. She supposed O'Leary's schedule was similar to hers—eight-thirty to six-thirty, or thereabouts.

As if she cared whether O'Leary worked sixty hours a week like she did. They were having dinner together to celebrate the settlement, period. His career trajectory had no relevance to her. This was not a relationship. It was going nowhere. Plus, the last time she'd seen him, when they'd gone out for a drink after their marathon negotiating session, he'd made that flirty comment about how her hair turned him on. Her ex-boyfriend was her hair stylist. If she got involved with a guy who was turned on by what her ex-boyfriend did . . . well, it would be weird.

She decided O'Leary truly was her adversary when she arrived at the building on East 38th. She'd expected to see her realtor there, and sure enough, Kathy was waiting under the entry's nondescript awning, clad in a matronly blazer and pleated slacks that amplified her chubby physique. Standing beside her was a tall, dark-haired man in a business suit. The light from the lobby illuminated enough of his silhouette for Melissa to recognize him.

She'd specifically told him six-twenty. What the hell was he doing here? Discussing the apartment—*her* apartment, if she could finagle a way to buy it—with her realtor? Was he planning to bid on the apartment, too? He already owned a place up in the boonies of northernmost Manhattan. Surely he couldn't want this place, too.

No, there was nothing *surely* about that. If she lived in Inwood, she'd want to move downtown, too, even if Murray Hill wasn't the hottest neighborhood in the city. Maybe O'Leary was curious enough to want to check out the apartment for himself. Or maybe he just wanted to give her *tsorris.* She'd taught him a new word; now he wanted to make the concept come to life.

What was he up to? Why was he still trying to game her?

She approached the two, who were chattering away like old friends. No doubt O'Leary was treating Kathy to a double-barreled barrage of charm. Melissa suppressed the urge to kick him.

"Hi," she greeted him curtly, then turned to Kathy. "I told him to meet me here at six-twenty," she explained. "I guess he can wait in the lobby."

"Oh, I thought . . ." Kathy's quizzical gaze shuttled between O'Leary and Melissa.

"It's all right," O'Leary said smoothly. "I'd like to see the apartment, too. Considering."

Considering what? He was definitely gaming Melissa, pulling something on her, and she didn't like it. She didn't like it even more when he touched his hand to the small of her back and escorted her into the building, as if he were her boyfriend or something.

Kathy conferred with the doorman for a minute. The lobby was nothing special, and the doorman, who wore an ill-fitting brown suit, looked peevish, as if Kathy had awakened him from a nap. But given that the cost of the apartment upstairs was more than Melissa could afford, she wasn't about to waste time looking at apartments in swankier buildings. She was already paying an exorbitant rent for her studio apartment uptown, and a significant chunk of that rent was probably subsidizing the building's three doormen, who dressed in spiffy livery with gold-braid trim and stood in a lobby graced with black marble flooring and smoky veined mirrors, which actually seemed kind of dated to Melissa but were still more elegant than the plain cream-hued walls of this building's lobby.

"Why are you here?" Melissa whispered to O'Leary.

He was spared from having to answer when Kathy returned and

gestured toward the elevator. "Nice place," he said, as much to Kathy as to Melissa as they stepped inside the elevator. "It doesn't smell like onions."

"Is it supposed to smell like onions?" Melissa asked, her voice icy enough to freeze whisky.

"My building's elevator usually does. I'm not sure what the source is. I've complained to the super, but he says he doesn't notice it. I guess it's the sort of thing you get used to after a while."

"There's such a thing as an air freshener," Kathy pointed out. "Perhaps your super could plug one in."

"I don't think there's an electrical socket in the elevator," he mused. "What would he plug it into?"

"There's got to be an electrical source," Kathy said. "It's an elevator. It runs on electricity."

Melissa gritted her teeth as they yakked amiably about elevators, electricity and onions. After a sluggish ascent—this particular elevator didn't run, it trudged—they reached the fourth floor and exited into a hall that smelled blessedly like nothing at all.

"Have you crunched the numbers?" Kathy asked Melissa as they strolled down the hall to the unit. "Is this going to be doable for you?"

"I'm still crunching," Melissa assured her, although the numbers had so far proven themselves crunch-resistant. She smiled placidly, ignoring the light pressure of O'Leary's hand at the small of her back again as they waited for Kathy to unlock the door.

"The unit is empty," Kathy explained to O'Leary as the door swung in. "The owner is an elderly woman who's having some health issues, so her son moved her down to the Atlanta area, where he lives. From what I hear, she hates it there. She says the place is full of southerners."

"New Yorkers can be so provincial," O'Leary joked.

Kathy took him seriously. "Indeed we can be. But the move is a done deal, and her son wants this place sold ASAP. There's some kind of arrangement where the money she makes on the sale will go to the senior community where she's living down there. She told her broker her new residence is like a cruise ship, only on land. They've got activities all day long. Movies, lectures, crafts. Shuffleboard, she said. She hates shuffleboard."

Kathy switched on the ceiling light in the entry, then hurried ahead of them to turn on the few lamps that had been left behind in the otherwise barren apartment. The rooms looked small to Melissa, as if the naked walls were leaning inward, but that didn't concern her. Rooms always looked smaller when they were empty.

O'Leary abandoned her side and ducked into the kitchen. She wondered if he was an amateur chef; he surveyed the tiny work space with more intensity than she ever had.

She scrutinized the kitchen, trying to figure out what he saw that she might have missed. The cabinets were some enameled compound material, but the cooking range was gas, which she considered an asset. The fridge stood open, its bulb unscrewed and its dark, vacant shelves forlorn. O'Leary rapped a fist gently against the laminate countertop, then exited into the dining nook off the living room. "You could fit a full-size table here," he said.

"I doubt I'll be hosting any banquets."

"Still, it's a nice size. The kitchen, though . . ." He glanced behind him, then ventured into the living room. "Southern exposure. How's the air conditioning in this unit?"

"Nobody's turned it on in a couple of months," Kathy informed him. "If there's a problem, management will cover the repair costs. We can write that into the contract."

"I'm just saying, with all these windows facing south, you want to make sure the room isn't going to be hard to cool in the summer. These are double-panes, right?" Before Kathy could answer, he was striding down the hall to the bedrooms.

Kathy and Melissa shared a look. Kathy was smiling one of those aww-he's-adorable smiles. Melissa didn't smile back. She was thinking not that he was adorable but that he was asking questions she'd never thought to ask. She was a lawyer, for God's sake. She should have been thinking like a lawyer. But she'd been thinking like a woman desperate to find a halfway decent apartment that wouldn't ultimately land her in debtor's prison.

"The master bath could use some updating," O'Leary called from deep within the master bedroom.

What did he care? If he didn't have to pee right this minute, he'd never have an opportunity to use that bathroom.

What she'd noticed when she'd inspected the master bedroom was the closet. It was a walk-in—small enough that "step-in" would be a more accurate description, but bigger than what she currently had. The bathroom could be updated after she'd paid down the mortgage a bit. Like maybe fifteen years from now. As long as the toilet flushed and the shower didn't spray too hot or too cold, she was satisfied.

He emerged from the bathroom as she emerged from the closet.

"Hardwood floor in a bedroom?" he said. "You'd need to put down a rug. Who wants to get out of bed and have your bare feet touch a cold, hard floor?"

"Who wants to get out of bed, period?" she retorted, then realized, from his mischievous grin, that he'd misinterpreted her words. "I'm usually so tired when the alarm goes off," she clarified. "The cold hard floor wakes me up. Wood isn't that cold, anyway. And the bathroom is clean. I don't need fancy."

"If you say so." He winked again, and she wondered if she was going to be hearing about how she didn't want to get out of bed for the rest of her life, or at least for as long as it took to eat dinner with him.

She told herself she didn't care. His criticisms of the apartment implied that he wasn't going to enter into a bidding war with her over it. Maybe his place up in Inwood had a marble sunken tub and granite counters in the master bath. Maybe his kitchen featured a six-burner Viking range. Maybe such things mattered to him.

In any case, she didn't have to worry about his vying with her for this unit. Which was a good thing, because walking through it, wrapping herself in the atmosphere of its dowdy kitchen and its potentially steamy living room and its antiquated master bath, only reinforced her love of the place. She couldn't pinpoint *why* this apartment felt so right to her. All she knew was that it *did* feel right.

He peered into the walk-in closet, then headed for the door, where Kathy stood on the threshold watching them, her "aww" smile still plastered across her face. She stepped aside so he and Melissa could exit. Melissa braced herself for the second bedroom.

Yes, it was compact. Yes, its window overlooked an air shaft, not the street. But the instant she entered the room, which was lit only by a cheap tabletop lamp standing on the floor in one corner, throwing knee-high parabolas of light onto the walls, she felt that same maternal stirring she'd felt the first time she'd seen this room.

"This would make a nice nursery," O'Leary said.

Melissa flinched. Why would he say that? Did he feel the same vibe she felt? If the room had ever been a nursery, it hadn't been one recently, given the advanced age of the current owner. Most childless people considering the purchase of this apartment would turn this room into a den or an office.

But O'Leary saw it as a nursery. Just like her.

"All right," she said briskly, brushing past him as she bolted toward the doorway. She couldn't stand in this room, this would-be nursery, with a man who saw it the way she did. She had no idea what O'Leary's agenda was, but she was unnerved. If he hadn't already riled her suspicions, his ability to identify the room as a nursery spooked her.

She had to get back into the living room—someplace where the yearning to have a baby could fade away. No one wanted a baby in a living room.

O'Leary and Kathy sauntered down the hall to the living room at a more leisurely pace. "The place has possibilities," O'Leary was saying. "It also has flaws."

Kathy shrugged. "What apartment doesn't? I've been in luxury towers, penthouses, townhouses—they all have flaws. Still, I'd say that for the asking price, this is a real little gem."

"A flawed gem," O'Leary said, strolling across the living room to the south-facing wall of windows and then meeting Melissa's gaze. Another wink.

Would he stop with the winks already? Did he have a freaking tic in his eyelid? "I heard you," she muttered. "It's flawed."

"I'm just thinking, given the flaws, there's got to be some flexibility in the price." His voice was muted, but he'd managed to project it enough for Kathy to overhear

Then she got it. God, was she stupid. She might be able to negotiate on behalf of her clients. But on behalf of herself, she was helpless. It had never occurred to her to pretend to be less than thrilled by this apartment as a way of bargaining down the price.

"A two-bedroom apartment for under seven figures?" Kathy said. "You're not going to find a better deal, not if you want to stay in Manhattan."

Melissa almost retorted that $995,000 was barely under seven figures, but Kathy wasn't the person she had to convince. The seller was. "Tell them I'll buy it for eight-fif—" O'Leary squinted slightly and pointed his thumb downward. "Eight hundred thousand," she said, her voice wavering. Even eight hundred thousand would be a stretch for her. She'd have to give up twelve-dollar margaritas and four-hundred dollar shoes. She might even have to buy her purses from some counterfeiter running his business from a card table on a street corner in Queens.

"Eight hundred thousand?" Kathy sounded shrill. "They'll be insulted."

O'Leary watched Melissa. He was measuring her, testing her, and that pissed her off. But damn if she wouldn't pass his stupid test. "No they won't," she told Kathy, turning from him. "If they're serious about selling, they'll counter-offer."

"Well, I don't know." Kathy sighed heavily and shook her head. "Eight hundred thousand?"

"The market is soft and mortgages are hard to come by. And any buyer who wouldn't need a mortgage because he can pay cash for this place isn't going to be house-hunting in this neighborhood. He'll be looking at penthouses overlooking Central Park."

"Yes, but Melissa—eight hundred thousand? For *two* bedrooms?"

"And a kitchen with synthetic cabinets."

"The kitchen's shortcomings are all cosmetic," Kathy said.

"And they'll cost money to renovate. Bring them the offer, Kathy. Let's see just how insulted they are."

Her back was to O'Leary, so she couldn't see his smile. She could feel it, though. She could sense it.

"I'm just telling you," Kathy said with a resigned sigh. "They're going to slam down the phone in my face."

Melissa was pretty sure you couldn't slam a phone in someone's face. "Well, you represent me, not the seller," Melissa reminded her. "And I won't hang up on you."

Another deep, pained sigh from Kathy. "I'll try," she said.

"There is no 'try,'" O'Leary intoned, once again resting his hand at her waist. When Melissa gave him a quizzical scowl, he recited, "Do or do not. There is no 'try.' Yoda says that in one of the Star Wars movies."

Great. He'd gone from sensitive nursery-envisioner to Star Wars geek. "Was Yoda into real estate?"

"I think he was more a mutual funds kind of guy." He sent Kathy a dimpled grin and ushered Melissa toward the door. "Thanks for letting us check out the place one more time. You can call Melissa tomorrow and let her know what the seller has to say."

TWENTY MINUTES LATER, they were seated across a table from each other in an Indian restaurant. The walls were covered with sagging strips of cloth—uncoiled saris was Melissa's guess—and raga music whined from the ceiling speakers. The air smelled of curry and chutney and cinnamon and Melissa discovered she was starving.

"So, tell me what you think," she said after swallowing a warm chunk of *naan*, the puffy Indian version of pita, and washing it down with a sip of beer. O'Leary had ordered a beer for himself, an Indian label she'd never heard of, and she'd decided to be adventurous and try it herself. Plus she didn't want him thinking she was some sort of female-urban-professional cliché, always ordering margaritas. "Is the apartment a dive? Am I crazy to want to buy it?"

He seemed surprised. "No, you're not crazy. It's a terrific place."

"Really? You think so?" She didn't know why his opinion mattered so much to her. Hell, she *did* know. It mattered because he was smart and he was handsome, and after the first few times she'd kind of enjoyed the feel of his hand on her back. And, like her, he'd seen the second bedroom as a nursery, which was further proof that she wasn't crazy—or else that they were both crazy.

"It's not the Taj Mahal," he said, "but the Taj Mahal is a mausoleum. Who'd want to live there?"

With a sitar wailing from a speaker somewhere above and behind her left ear, Melissa was not about to speak ill of the Taj Mahal. Instead, she tore off another piece of *naan* and popped it in her mouth. Sweet and floury, it melted on her tongue. They'd already ordered meals, and she was pleased to see that the restaurant was, indeed, cheap. She didn't want O'Leary spending a fortune on her. He'd already done too much for her at the apartment. "Thank you," she said.

"You're welcome." He grinned. "What are you thanking me for?"

"For nudging me to low-ball my offer."

"Honey, in case you haven't noticed, I'm good at negotiating."

"Don't call me honey," she muttered, though she was smiling. Then she grew solemn. "Thank you for what you said in the second bedroom."

"What did I say? I don't even remember."

"That it would make a nice nursery."

"Oh, yeah. I did say that, didn't I." The glint in his eyes indicated that he'd remembered damn well what he'd said. "You have kids?"

"Me?" She nearly choked on the piece of bread she'd just bitten. "I'm not even married."

"You don't have to be married to have kids."

"If I had kids, do you think I'd be sitting here having dinner with you?"

"If you were a lousy mother, you would." He tore off a chunk of bread, popped it into his mouth, swallowed and asked, "You want kids?" as casually as if he'd asked her where the nearest subway station was.

She didn't answer casually. Having kids was generally not the sort of thing a woman discussed with a man on their first date. Assuming this was a date. She sort of thought it might be.

But he'd asked. If the subject scared him, he wouldn't have raised it.

She had the feeling very little scared Aidan O'Leary. "Yes," she answered. "Kid, singular. I don't know about kids, plural."

"But you've broken up with your boyfriend."

Had she told him that? God, she'd made such an ass of herself the last time they'd seen each other. She'd sobbed and whimpered and wound up with raccoon eyes. She'd probably mentioned Luc, too. "Well, you know, there are sperm banks," she said, sounding less nonchalant than she'd intended.

"Yeah. There are men, too." He grinned. "I think you'd look very cute pregnant."

"Oh, God. My sister looked like a walrus when she was pregnant. And my sister-in-law—sheesh. She's this adorable little thing with a twenty-inch waist and she was carrying twins. By her ninth month she looked like she'd devoured the magic pumpkin whole. I don't care what Hallmark says. Pregnant women don't look cute."

"I guess it's a matter of taste," he said with a shrug. "*I* think they look cute."

The waiter delivered their bowls of pistachio soup. Melissa took a taste. Pale and sweet and milky, delicious. If she ever became pregnant, she'd make pistachio soup her food fetish of choice. No pickles and ice-cream for her. She wanted pistachio soup. And *naan*. Maybe she ought to get pregnant just to have an excuse to pig out on Indian food.

She sighed happily and forced herself not to gobble the entire bowl of soup in five seconds. "How about you?" she asked. "Do you have any kids?"

"Not that I know of," he joked, then smiled to reassure her. "No."

"Do you have a girlfriend?" He already knew her story; she had a right to know his. And since this was more or less a date, she ought to at the very least find out if he was unencumbered.

"No."

Neither of them spoke for a few minutes. The waiter cleared away their soup bowls and returned with their entrees: chicken tikka for her, a tandoori mixed grill for him. While she smiled vaguely at the waiter and gazed at the food, and inhaled its spices and seasonings, and listened to the pounding raga drums, O'Leary's *no* hung in the air between them.

He didn't have a girlfriend; that was a plus. He was arrogant; that was a minus. He was a lawyer, which could be a plus or a minus, depending. With a name like Aidan O'Leary, he probably wasn't Jewish, which was neither a plus nor a minus as far as she was concerned. He was smug—a minus. He'd elbowed his way into her second tour of the apartment—a minus, except that he'd maneuvered her into bargaining hard on the price—a plus. He'd seen the second bedroom and thought *nursery*—so big a plus it scared her.

She was way ahead of herself, she realized. The fact was, his pushy, arrogant personality had predominated during the fifteen minutes they'd spent with Kathy in the apartment. She didn't want pushy and arrogant. She already had an arrogant brother, and everyone in her family, with the possible exception of Jill, who was probably more passive-aggressive than anything, was pushy.

"All right," she said, finally breaking the silence that had settled like a fog around their table. "Why did you insist on touring the apartment with me?"

He shrugged. "I was curious. I wanted to see how Murray Hill compares to Inwood. And what the hell." He smiled. "I figured it would make your life more interesting."

That it did. "And what was with all that pretending we were . . . something? A couple looking for a place big enough to start a family?"

"I wasn't pretending anything," he defended himself, doing a poor job of faking indignation.

"You kept touching my back."

"You've got a nice back," he said.

"I mean, you're coming on kind of strong."

He gazed steadily at her. "Is that a problem?"

Yes. No. Who the hell knew?

"I've already seen you at your worst, Melissa, and your worst wasn't bad. Although I've got to say, you should go lighter on the eye make-up if you're planning to cry."

"I wasn't planning to cry that day. I just felt overwhelmed."

"And now?"

"Now I've got to crunch numbers." She sighed. "Even at eight hundred thou—which the seller is never going to accept—I'm not sure I can make the down payment."

"Sure you can. Ask for an advance on your bonus. What do you need to put down? Ten percent?"

"Twenty, probably."

"Scrape it together. That apartment for eight hundred thou would be a steal. If you can't afford it, you can put in new cabinets and counters and flip the place for a mil, easy."

"Thanks." She scowled. "I'm not looking for an investment. I'm looking for a home. Someplace stable, where people you've depended on all your life don't suddenly announce they're getting a divorce."

"That place doesn't exist," he said gently. "Not for eight hundred thousand, not for a million."

He was right, but the thought pained her. "Are your parents divorced?"

"No, but they probably should be. They fight all the time. Maybe you should count your blessings."

"Why did you say the second bedroom would make a nice nursery?" she asked.

He drank some beer and displayed a couple of dimples. "Why else would you be looking at a two-bedroom apartment you almost can't afford? You want to put someone in that second bedroom. Given what little I know about your parents, I figured the second bedroom wasn't for them."

"Maybe it was for a boyfriend. You know, he could come into my bedroom for fun and games and then go somewhere else to sleep, so I wouldn't have to fight him for the blanket or listen to him snore."

"I don't snore," O'Leary said. Despite his smile, he sounded extremely serious. "I think you ought to know that."

Another silence settled over the table, this one surprisingly comfortable despite the aftershocks roiling the space between them. And in that silence Melissa understood that in the not too distant future, she was going to have the opportunity to find out if Aidan O'Leary truly didn't snore.

Chapter Twenty-Three

"You're sure you want to do this?" Jill asked.

Seated in the passenger seat beside her, Brooke smiled. "Are you kidding? It's going to be fun."

Jill didn't think arguing with Gloria, the events manager at the Old Rockford Inn, would be fun. But then, she wasn't Brooke.

She'd been surprised by Brooke's phone call yesterday afternoon. When the phone had started jangling at two-thirty, just as she'd made the final push to complete the text for a Velvet Moon spread on camisoles—and honestly, just how much could a person say about camisoles, other than they came in such intoxicating colors as sherry, champagne, burgundy, bourbon and crème de menthe, although what Velvet Moon called sherry actually looked more like watered-down root beer to Jill—she'd assumed the caller was her mother, who despite her job had an uncanny knack for interrupting her with a phone call just as she was trying to compose some desperately needed catalogue copy. Jill had groaned, cursed and answered the phone, fully expecting to hear her mother say, "It's your mother."

Instead she'd heard Brooke saying, "Are you free tomorrow?"

"If I can get this copy written in the next twenty minutes, yes," she answered. "Why?"

"Doug told me you're having problems with the place where Abbie's bat mitzvah is going to be. I thought I might be able to help."

Brooke? Help? Jill had taken a moment to regain her equilibrium. "What do you mean?"

"This may sound silly to you—it certainly sounds silly to me—but Doug thinks I ought to be a party planner."

"A party planner." Jill had slumped in her chair, legs spread to accommodate the printer below her desk. The words she'd typed had blurred across her monitor screen; the only one she'd been able to decipher was "intoxicating," which, given the boozy colors, had seemed appropriate when she'd written it.

"It's not that we need the money," Brooke had hastened to assure her. "We don't. But he thinks I'm bored. And you know what? He's right."

"Bored." Why had Jill kept echoing Brooke? Why had she had such difficulty imagining Brooke being bored? Brooke had twins; surely that couldn't be boring. And Brooke was beautiful. Jill had always assumed that beautiful women, especially beautiful women whose rich husbands pampered them, couldn't possibly be bored.

"I wouldn't charge you, of course. This is just an experiment. If you'd be willing, of course."

"Willing to what?" Jill had sounded mentally challenged to herself.

"Willing to let me discuss your situation with the Old Rockford Inn. Let me see what I can do."

Jill had figured she'd have nothing to lose by letting Brooke intervene—she did have a contract with the place, after all, so even if Gloria didn't like Brooke's attitude, she couldn't unilaterally erase the Abigail Sackler reception from the inn's calendar. And given that Jill hadn't done particularly well dealing with Gloria on her own, she'd seen no downside to letting Brooke conquer her boredom by toiling on Abbie's behalf.

Brooke had arrived at Jill's house the next morning at ten, dressed like a Junior Leaguer in a stylish sweater set and tailored tweedy trousers that made her look slimmer than any woman who'd given birth to twins had a right to be. Jill had felt profoundly dowdy in her Red Sox sweatshirt and jeans. But Brooke didn't order her to change into a less disreputable outfit, and today Brooke was in charge. She was the party planner, the unpaid pro.

"What's the theme of Abbie's bat mitzvah?" she asked as Jill drove her through town to the inn.

"The theme? 'Happy bat mitzvah,' I guess."

"It needs to be something more than that," Brooke suggested. "Just like the theme of your parents' fortieth anniversary party wasn't 'Happy Anniversary.'"

"Yeah, that wouldn't have worked," Jill agreed. "Two years later and they're kaput." Stopped at a red light, she reflected on the party Brooke had hosted for her parents. A juke box filled with sixties rock, she recalled. Psychedelic wall posters illuminated by black lights. A peace sign on the powder room door. A couple of strategically placed lava lamps.

"Summer Of Love," Brooke said, answering Jill's unvoiced question. "So what's Abbie's theme?"

Jill panicked. She'd signed Abbie up for Hebrew school, booked a venue for the party and sent out "Save the Date" postcards, but she hadn't come up with a theme. "Maybe you ought to ask Abbie," she said, evading the question with a twinge of shame. "She might know what the theme is."

"I'll do that." Brooke reached into her massive red-leather purse, pulled out a matching red leather folder, opened it and jotted a note to herself. "So, the inn. What are you gripes? What are we fighting for?"

"The price per plate, for one thing. They increased the price they quoted us. They said rising fuel prices are responsible for the hike. And there's some disagreement about how long the DJ will be allowed to play."

"You've already booked a DJ," Brooke said.

Jill suffered a moment's panic. Had that been a mistake? Should she have waited until she'd decided on a theme before hiring the DJ? He'd been recommended by Emma Tovick's mother, and she'd wanted to lock him in before someone else hired him for that evening.

But then she glanced at Brooke, who was merely jotting another note into her red leather folder, and her panic abated. Brooke was asking for information, not sitting in judgment. At least Jill hoped so.

"I've hired a photographer, too," she said, figuring that while Brooke had her red leather folder out, she should jot that down as well. "You have to get them under contract way in advance."

"Okay." Brooke snapped her pen shut with a decisive click as Jill steered into the inn's parking lot. "Anything else?"

Jill sighed. Her biggest worry was her parents. What if they were still separated by next spring, when the affair was scheduled? What if they were divorced? What if they were so bitter and hostile they wouldn't talk to each other?

She doubted Brooke and her little red notebook could solve that problem.

"It looks pretty," Brooke said, gazing out at the charming structure, classic New England white clapboard with black shingles and a sloping slate roof.

"It's even prettier in the spring, when all the flowers are in bloom," Jill told her. Now the driveway and front walk were lined with the shriveled brown remnants of the chrysanthemums that had been blooming the last time she'd visited—which had been when Gloria had informed her of the price increase. "I didn't want to go to one of those affair factories, with four bar mitzvahs going on at the same time."

Brooke crinkled her pretty nose. "So you'll be the only affair here on that night?"

"Other than whatever might be going on in the bedrooms upstairs," Jill joked.

Brooke gave her an indulgent smile. "Let's go slay the dragon," she said calmly. She didn't have to rev herself up with an adrenaline-producing pep talk. She was the sort of woman who could slay dragons without chipping a nail.

They emerged from the car, and Jill noticed, in the glow of the late autumn sun, that Brooke's hair was darker. She'd sensed as much when Brooke had arrived at her house, but Brooke had been standing beneath the porch's overhang then, and they'd left through the garage, and Jill hadn't gotten a good look at her hair in natural light. Definitely darker, and shaped into layers and stray wisps. The cut was actually pretty similar to Melissa's. Jill wondered whether Luc Brondo cut every woman's hair the same way, or only Bendel women's hair. If she drove down to New York, would he do her hair that way, too? No doubt it would look better than it did right now, gathered at the nape of her neck in a pale blue scrunchy.

The hairstyle looked gorgeous on Brooke. Naturally—everything about Brooke was gorgeous. But it didn't really look like *her*.

"You've changed your hair," Jill commented.

Brooke gave her an eye roll that rivaled Abbie's. Jill hadn't realized she'd said anything exasperating, but as soon as Brooke spoke she realized Brooke's irritation wasn't directed at her. "Doug hates it."

"It looks good," Jill lied. Well, no, that wasn't a lie. It did look good. It just didn't look right.

"What he hates about it is that Melissa's boyfriend cut it. Her ex-boyfriend, I guess."

Jill wasn't sure if she was supposed to be surprised by this revelation. She decided not to bother pretending. She wasn't a particularly good actress. "Melissa mentioned that Luc had done your hair. And that things weren't working out between her and Luc."

"I think Doug was jealous," Brooke admitted.

"Of your hair?"

"Of my going to New York and having Luc do it. I can't imagine what he'd be jealous about, though. I mean, Luc—he's a *hair stylist*. Not to criticize your sister's taste in men, but . . . a *hair stylist*? What would I ever want with a *hair stylist*? Other than to let him do my hair, of course."

Jill was surprised that Brooke would reveal anything so personal about her relationship with Doug. She never talked about things like that. She was so reserved, so contained, so goddamn perfect. She didn't have difficulties, with Doug or anyone else.

Except, apparently, she did. Jill slowed to a stop next to her car's front bumper and stared at Brooke. Maybe she wasn't so perfect, after all. Jill noticed a weariness in Brooke's exquisite features, the first microscopically faint lines fanning out from the corners of her eyes and a hint of tension in her pink-glossed lips.

Maybe she *was* bored. Maybe she needed to be a party planner more than she knew.

"Doug isn't a jealous-type person," Jill argued. "He's so . . ." She was going to say full of himself, but she chose a more positive phrase instead. "Self-assured. I can't imagine he'd ever feel threatened by a hair stylist." She hoped she didn't sound as snobby as Brooke when she mentioned Luc's profession.

"I couldn't imagine it, either," Brooke said, starting up the walk and forcing Jill to follow, even though she'd rather have remained out in the parking lot until they'd finished their discussion. She and Brooke had never spoken like this before, as if they were confidantes.

But Brooke was ready to slay the Gloria dragon, and Jill took a couple of skipping steps to keep up with her. "It's my parents," she said as they reached the porch.

That brought Brooke to an abrupt halt. "Your parents?"

"Doug is feeling insecure because my parents have split."

"He implied something about that."

"We're all feeling it," Jill explained. "It's like an earthquake. The ground has stopped trembling, but we're still, I don't know. Shaky. Waiting for the next tremor."

"Hmm." Brooke pondered Jill's explanation. "Doug never said he felt shaky. Mostly he was worried about who would take care of the girls while we were in Nevis. Thank God you agreed. We're very grateful."

"It's no problem, really." Okay, that was a lie. But if Brooke could get Gloria to honor the original price she'd quoted for catering Abbie's bat mitzvah, Jill would consider baby-sitting Madison and Mackenzie for a week a fair trade.

"I really don't think when your mother moved out on your father she thought about the impact that would have on everyone." Brooke sounded more than a little judgmental.

"I'm sure she didn't." That had been the point, of course. Jill's mother had decided to stop worrying about the impact of her every act on the rest of the family.

"But to tell the truth, sometimes things work out for the best. The girls adore Abbie, and they love horsing around with Noah. It'll be fun for them, even if you don't spoil them as much as their grandparents do." Brooke smiled, turned and opened the inn's door.

Once they'd strolled through the understated lobby, past the stairway leading up, past the colonial-tavern style lounge, down the hallway and beyond the main dining room to the offices at the rear of the building, Brooke seemed to have eliminated all thoughts of Doug from her mind. She walked with the posture of a ballerina, her spine straight, her delicate chin raised to display her long, slender neck, her steps graceful but purposeful. Marching along behind her, Jill felt like a schlub, a pitiful bag lady Brooke had adopted out of charity.

"Jill, hi," Gloria said, her tone unctuous as she waved them into her office. "What's up?"

"I'm Brooke Bendel," Brooke said, stepping forward and extending her hand. "I'm a party planner Jill has hired for Abbie's bat mitzvah. Here's my card." She plucked a sterling silver card holder from a side pocket of her purse and produced a crisp cream-colored rectangle, which she presented to Gloria. "As I understand it, we've got some issues to resolve. May I?" She gestured toward one of the visitor's chairs facing Gloria's desk and sat without waiting for permission. Dumbfounded by Brooke's poise, Jill dropped onto the other chair and resolved to keep her mouth shut.

It occurred to her that, for once in her life, she wouldn't have to fix everything. Brooke, with her *savoir faire* and her beauty and her business cards, had stepped into the role of the fixer.

Jill felt as if she'd just dropped the boulder she'd been hauling around all her life. Being the family fixer wasn't a job she'd volunteered for. Some unnamed force of family dynamics had assigned it to her. Doug had been busy with the demands of being the golden boy, the Phi Beta Kappa pre-med, the superlative medical student, the businessman establishing his laser surgery eye clinic, the husband, the father, the success. Melissa had been equally busy being the baby, the brilliant ditz, the legal scholar who could reduce a thirty-page contract crammed with jargon into a single English sentence but spent forty minutes every morning dithering over what to wear. Jill's mother phoned Jill constantly with crises big and small—or she used to, when she was home and had free time to make all those phone calls. Jill's father depended on her to solve her mother's crises.

But now . . . now she had a crisis with the inn's unexpected hike in catering costs. A small crisis, to be sure. Given the wretched state of the world, a three-dollar-a-plate price increase fell safely within the trivial range on the crisis scale. Jill and Gordon could afford the higher price if they had to. It wasn't as if she'd have to raid her non-existent France-trip fund to cover the added expense.

But Brooke was handling everything. Maybe Jill and Gordon wouldn't have to cover the added expense, because Brooke would fix this crisis for them.

"The plate surcharge you sprang on Jill is unconscionable," Brooke said, her voice as smooth and sweet as molasses. "To negotiate one price and then change it after the contract has been signed . . ."

"It says in the contract—" Gloria's voice made Jill think not of molasses but of vinegar.

"And I'm sure the Better Business Bureau and the state's Department of Consumer Affairs would love to hear about those tiny-print clauses in your contract, which are designed for no other reason than to confuse clients and increase your profits. As a party planner, I'm in a position to send more business your way. I'm also in a position to steer all my clients to more ethical venues, and to pass along what I know about your business practices to my professional colleagues." Brooke's voice drifted off, but she kept smiling, her gaze locked with Gloria's.

Despite her smile, Brooke's expression was icy. Yet it acted on Gloria like heat, causing her to melt into a puddle of acquiescence. "Well, I suppose in this instance we can accommodate your client," she said. "I ordinarily wouldn't do that, given what fuel costs these days, but—"

"Great," Brooke cut her off, refusing her the chance to retract her offer. "Now this price includes a dessert but not the cake. The Sacklers don't need a dessert in addition to the cake. The cake *is* the dessert. We'd like to make that substitution."

"Most people prefer to have the cake made elsewhere."

"But you *can* make a cake, right?"

"Of course. I explained that to Mrs. Sackler." Gloria flashed an anxious glance in Jill's direction. She used to be just Jill, but now she was Mrs. Sackler, thanks to Brooke. "For an additional fee, our chef can prepare a customized cake."

"We'll skip the additional fee because we're skipping the non-cake dessert. What was that standard dessert? Ice cream? Rice pudding?"

"Ice cream," Gloria confirmed weakly.

"Who needs ice cream when there's cake? And ice cream is so messy. So we'll cut the ice cream and replace it with the cake. Abbie—the bat mitzvah girl—hasn't decided on a theme yet, but once she does, we'll get back to you with the cake's specs. Was there anything else?" Brooke asked Jill.

Jill snapped out of her daze with a shake of her head. She hadn't even thought about the cost of the cake. She was stunned that Brooke had. "The DJ?" she mumbled, wondering just how many miracles Brooke could pull off.

"Right." Brooke steered her smile back to Gloria. "The DJ will play for the entire party. As long as there are no noise complaints—and there won't be, we'll do volume checks to make sure—there's no reason for him to have to shut down before the party is scheduled to end."

"We have guests staying in the upstairs rooms," Gloria pointed out.

"And the DJ will respect those guests. I assume your reception room's soundproofing is up to code?"

"Everything here is up to code," Gloria huffed.

"Then there won't be a problem. I think that's it," Brooke said, rising from her chair. Jill scrambled to her feet as well, eager to flee the office before Gloria realized how many concessions she'd made.

Brooke appeared to be in no hurry to leave, however. She shook Gloria's hand again, the model of affability, and reminded Gloria that she'd be in touch soon with a specific cake order. "It'll probably be chocolate," she alerted Gloria. "Abbie loves chocolate, and it's her bat mitzvah. But we need to confirm that with her."

"Of course. Whatever she wants," Gloria said. "We want her to be happy."

"And we want Mrs. Sackler to be happy, too, since she and her husband are the ones paying the bill. So nice to meet you, Gloria." With that, Brooke swept out of the office, the prima ballerina jeté-ing off the stage.

Jill would have liked to shout "Brava!" and toss rose petals at her, but she simply trailed her down the hall and out of the building, not daring to look back to see whether Gloria was furious or just flummoxed. Neither she nor Brooke spoke until they were in the car.

"Wow," Jill said, jamming the key into the ignition and then twisting in her seat to face Brooke. "You're good."

"I am," Brooke agreed, not a boast but a simple statement of fact.

"Doug was right. You should be a party planner. You were born to do this."

"No." Brooke folded her hands neatly in her lap. "I was born to be an object of worship." She smiled, but Jill didn't think she was joking.

"Well, I'm ready to convert to the Cult of Brooke. You've made a believer out of me." Jill started the car, backed out of the spot and steered toward the street.

She owed her object of worship. She could stop at a florist and purchase a bouquet for Brooke, but with Brooke seated right beside her, that would be kind of tacky. She could bring Brooke back to her house and pop open a bottle of champagne in her honor, except she didn't have any champagne. Diet Coke, yes, but that particular bubbly drink wasn't festive enough.

She glanced at the dashboard clock. Eleven-thirty. "Can I take you to lunch?" she asked. Lunch at her house would be limited to peanut butter or tuna fish sandwiches and Granny Smith apples. Her refrigerator lacked the ingredients for anything classy, like Salad Niçoise or cold cucumber soup or yogurt and fresh berries. Brooke definitely deserved something classy.

"Sure," she said. "Let's have lunch."

Jill so rarely went out for lunch, she had to think for a moment about what restaurants in town served the midday meal. The Old Rockford Inn did, but they couldn't very well go there. If they did, Gloria might find them drinking a toast over having finessed her, and to avenge her wounded pride she'd sabotage Abbie's bat mitzvah. Jill couldn't risk it.

She drove to the small shopping center that housed the bakery where she bought her father's rugelach. A few doors down was a gourmet café. At least Jill believed it was gourmet, since it was called "The Gourmet Café." She'd never eaten there before, but walking past it on her way to the bakery, she'd occasionally recognized the mother of one of Abbie's or Noah's soccer teammates seated with friends at a round, linen-covered table inside, eating what looked like Salad Niçoise or cold cucumber soup or yogurt and fresh berries. It seemed like the sort of place women who wore two-carat diamond rings with their blue jeans and Earth Day T-shirts would eat.

Brooke would fit right in. And they'd have to serve Jill, because she was treating.

The restaurant smelled of warm bread and sage, and classical guitar music whispered from hidden speakers. Because the kind of classy women who went out for lunch at places like this usually arrived later, Jill and Brooke were seated immediately at one of the many empty tables. "This is nice," Brooke said.

"I've never eaten here, so I can't vouch for the food," Jill warned. "But it's probably better than what we'll be eating at Abbie's bat mitzvah."

Brooke chuckled. "Affair food is what it is," she said as she opened the menu. "Oh, good. They've got wine."

Somehow, Jill ordered a bottle of Pinot Grigio to accompany their salads—Brooke wound up with a Cobb salad, Jill a Caesar with grilled chicken because the Niçoise just looked too involved. Somehow, the level of wine in the bottle kept dropping; somehow their glasses kept emptying. By the time Brooke lowered her fork and declared herself stuffed, which Jill wasn't sure she believed given that most of the hard-boiled egg, bacon and romaine remained uneaten on her plate, while Jill had managed to leave behind only a few viscous drops of dressing on hers, an hour and a half had passed and Jill heard herself say, "I've been thinking about renting office space."

"For your catalogue business?" Brooke asked.

Jill was touched that Brooke spoke about Jill's work as if it were a real job. She nodded, took a sip of wine and felt the warm flush of its alcohol content infuse her. "I work in the kitchen and nobody takes me seriously," she said. "The kids come and go. Gordon comes and goes. I may as well be cooking dinner for all anyone respects what I do."

"I don't cook dinner," Brooke remarked.

Jill laughed. She would enjoy cooking dinner a lot more if she had a kitchen like Brooke's, with all that space and those gorgeous high-end appliances. Brooke's kitchen was so huge, Jill could wall off a chunk of it and turn it into an office for herself, and no one would even miss the square footage.

"I've thought about setting up shop in the unfinished part of the basement, but . . ."

"Spiders," Brooke guessed, wrinkling her nose.

"Exactly."

"So rent an office," Brooke said.

Jill sighed. "I don't earn enough with my catalogue copy to be able to afford the rent."

"If you had an office, you might earn more," Brooke said. "You wouldn't have the distractions of home. You wouldn't have the kids and Gordon badgering you and treating you like a cook when you were trying to work."

"That's what I've been thinking."

"Your kids are old enough to come home to an empty house," Brooke pointed out. "You could set up shop, get some business cards . . ."

"You've got business cards," Jill said. "And you don't even have a business. How did you manage that?"

"I made them." Brooke reached into her purse and pulled out the elegant silver card holder. She handed Brooke one of her cards. It was simple: *Brooke Bendel, Party Planner* and her phone number. "You can create them on your computer and run them off on your printer, just like mailing labels. Doug picked up a box of card sheets at the local First-Rate. The sheets come in white and cream. I thought cream was more soothing and feminine."

"They look great," Jill agreed. She would never have thought of cream as more feminine, but she was used to thinking of colors as edible. Did the white cards look like milk?

"I can give you a couple of sheets and you can make your own cards."

"What would I do with these cards?"

"Mail them to other catalogue companies, along with a resume. Drum up some business. I don't know." Brooke shrugged. "Give them out at parties."

"You plan the parties, and I'll give out my cards."

"Listen to me, giving you business advice. *I* don't have an office."

"If you're serious about becoming a party planner," Jill counseled, "you ought to have an office, too."

Brooke ruminated, running one perfectly manicured finger around the rim of her wineglass. "I'm not sure I'm serious," she said. "But I'll admit I had fun with your friend Gloria today."

"She's no friend of mine," Jill muttered, then grinned. "But you were fantastic. You flattened her. And of course you're serious. You printed cards."

Brooke smiled hesitantly. "I guess."

"We could share an office," Jill blurted out, then reconsidered. Then reconsidered again. If she could share a bottle of Pinot Grigio with Brooke, surely they could share an office. They'd both be working flexible hours, after all. Two desks, a file cabinet, one phone line—they could take each other's phone calls and pretend to be each other's secretary. And the whole thing would be a lot more affordable if they split the costs.

Brooke's smile grew wider. She no longer looked weary. Even the lines framing her eyes—so much fainter than Jill's, despite her being a year older than Jill, but some things in life simply weren't fair—seemed to vanish.

"We could," she said.

Chapter Twenty-Four

Richard stepped out of his car and stared at the front windows of the First-Rate. They were plastered with ads, promos, announcements: a popular brand of dandruff shampoo on sale this week; Halloween candy, fifty percent off; this store will be open until midnight Thursdays and Fridays. Not that he expected a sign displayed in the window reading, "Ruth Bendel is inside," but it would have been helpful.

She might have already left for the day. He had no idea what her hours were. He could have phoned to let her know he was planning to stop by. But he'd wanted to leave himself an out in case he got queasy the way he had with Shari Bernstein and decided at the last minute not to come.

He locked his car door and assessed his physical state. Nervous, yes, but definitely not queasy. He reminded himself for the dozenth time since leaving his office twenty-five minutes ago that Ruth was still his wife, that she'd been his wife for forty-two years, that he'd slept beside her nearly every night of those forty-two years. And if worse came to worst and he started feeling nauseous, First-Rate sold plenty of over-the-counter gastrointestinal remedies.

If she wasn't there, at least he'd get a sense of the environment in which she worked. He'd view the place she had chosen over their home and their marriage. He knew she'd moved into an apartment across the street, but he didn't know which one of the drab brick buildings, with their asphalt parking lots and flat roofs and feeble landscaping, contained her apartment. Perhaps her colleagues knew, but he couldn't ask them. If he did, they might think he was a stalker, one of those deranged, possessive husbands who inevitably wound up featured in articles about homicide-suicides.

He stooped beside his car to check his reflection in the side-view mirror one final time. Shirt crisp—he'd ironed it last night and carried it to work on a hanger, so it wouldn't get wrinkled during the course of the day. Silk tie knotted neatly against his throat. Hair combed, although the silver waves drifted stubbornly out of alignment despite his efforts in the bathroom at the hospital before he'd left work, and again before he'd emerged from the car.

He looked . . . well, not great but not awful, either. Ruth had once seen something in him. Perhaps, if he was lucky, she would again.

Shoring up his resolve, he strode down the sidewalk, passing a sandwich joint, a bank branch and a shop that apparently sold only sneakers. Its front window was dark enough to afford him a glimpse of his ghostly reflection. Not awful, he assured himself. Not wretched. If Ruth took one look at him and ran screaming out of the store, it wouldn't be because of his appearance.

Assuming she was even there.

The First-Rate door opened automatically as he reached it. He stepped inside and caught the first whiff of a familiar smell—a little soapy, a little antiseptic, a little sweet. In fact, it smelled like every other First-Rate he'd ever entered.

Several people in red aprons stood behind the counter. One was a Hispanic-looking woman, another a balding older guy, the third a young punk with stringy hair and something metallic glinting in his eyebrow. A middle-aged woman, also wearing a red apron, worked an elaborate machine behind a separate counter with a sign reading, "One-Hour Foto." Evidently, the folks who ran First-Rate didn't know how to spell. Maybe they should call the store "Phirst-Rate."

No sign of Ruth, not behind the counters, not wandering the aisles. A few customers roamed through the store, either carrying plastic shopping baskets or pushing wheeled carts as they loaded up on Q-tips, cellophane tape and cans of diet milkshake. One whole aisle seemed devoted to Thanksgiving merchandise: paper plates and napkins with harvest scenes printed on them, straw cornucopia baskets and brown candles shaped like turkeys.

Jill had told him she would host Thanksgiving this year. He supposed he'd have to go, although if Ruth wasn't going to be there he wasn't sure how much he'd have to give thanks for. His grandchildren, he reminded himself. His children. His daughter Jill, who had volunteered to take over a holiday which had always belonged to Ruth. That couldn't be easy for her, but the family could always count on Jill to step in and keep things operational.

He realized he was sinking into a melancholy mood and shook it off. He wanted to be in a positive frame of mind when he saw Ruth. *If* he saw her.

"Can I help you?" the stringy-haired guy behind the counter called to him. He realized he must appear lost and befuddled.

"I'm looking for someone who works here," he said, scanning the aisle nearest him. It was crammed with sleek, sophisticated bottles of facial cream. So many products designed to make a person's face look marginally less old than it actually was. He'd bet Shari Bernstein would know what each of those products was and whether it did any good—if she ever stopped yapping about her daughters, her dog and the economies of various African nations.

"I work here," the young man said.

"No, I mean a specific person. Her name is Ruth Bendel."

"Oh yeah, Ruth's here. I think she's in the back. Hey, Rosita?" he called to the Hispanic woman. "Ruth hasn't left yet, has she?"

"I think she was talking to Francine," the woman called back.

"She's talking to Francine," the young man informed Richard, as if he was supposed to know who Francine was.

"Will she be returning to the store?" he asked.

"Well, she's in the store," the kid said. "Francine's office is in back."

"Can I go back there?"

The kid gave Richard a measuring look. "Maybe I could help you instead."

"I highly doubt it." He measured the kid right back. Tall and thin, with hollow cheeks and clothes that hung loosely from his angular shoulders. Give him a haircut and take that stupid metal thing out of his eyebrow, and he might be a pleasant-looking young man.

The kid pulled himself to his full height. "Who are you?" he asked.

Richard might have been offended, but he actually appreciated the fact that Ruth's coworkers looked out for her. "I'm her husband," he said.

"Ah." The boy resumed his slouching posture. "The famous doctor."

"I'm not famous," Richard argued, then decided he sounded too peevish and cleared his throat. "I'd really like to talk to her."

"She'll be out soon. She usually checks out around six." The kid looked at his watch, and Richard looked at his, as well. A few minutes past six.

The kid turned from Richard to a customer waiting to pay for a stack of gossip magazines. She cradled them in her arms as if they were a swaddled infant; Richard could make out *People* and *US Weekly*, but there were a bunch more in her stack, the schlockier ones at the bottom of the pile. Was she planning to compare their coverage, absorb all the news and then reach her own conclusion about whether this or that movie star had behaved badly at a party? Or was she perhaps replenishing the reading material in a doctor's office? Richard and his partners preferred to leave a higher class of magazine around the waiting area for their patients, but according to Gert, the patients generally grabbed *People* and ignored *The New Yorker* and *Business Week*.

He distracted himself by surveying the facial products. Cleansing beads—what the hell were they? Oatmeal he knew about as a way to reduce itching caused by rashes and irritations, but as a beauty aid? Sure, it could make your cholesterol numbers more beautiful, but not if you rubbed it on your skin.

"Richard?" Ruth's voice—so familiar, so welcome, so unnerving after he'd gone so many weeks without hearing it—floated down the aisle. He glanced in its direction and saw her walking toward him. She had on a coat, and her apron was rolled into a cylinder and tucked under her arm. Her hair was as flyaway as his, and her face . . .

He'd fallen in love with that face more than four decades ago. Not the first time he'd seen her—he'd always been too practical for love-at-first-sight, although he still remembered that evening at the frat house. He'd spotted her among all the other girls from Ithaca College and heard her Boston accent and thought, "That one has possibilities."

There were many more possibilities now, and some of them weren't so good. But he loved her face. Now more than ever, he loved it—so much that just seeing her made him feel slightly woozy.

He steadied himself and managed a smile. "Hello, Ruth," he said, a bit too formally, but what do you say to your wife when you haven't seen her for a month because she's walked out on you?

After a moment's hesitation, she continued down the aisle toward him. "What are you doing here?"

"I don't suppose you'd believe me if I said I needed to buy some sun block," he said, reaching for a face cream that boasted 30-SPF.

"This time of year? When did you ever worry about sun block, anyway? I always had to nag you to use it. And you're the doctor."

Was she scolding him or just bantering? He couldn't tell. He let his arm fall away from the shelf and felt the emptiness in his hand. When had he last held hands with her? He wanted to hold her hand now, but he didn't dare. "Can we talk?" he asked, aware of how ambiguous that question was. She could take it any way she wanted.

"I was about to leave. My shift is up. Come on." She didn't seem too angry—he could almost convince himself he saw a hint of a smile crossing her lips—and he followed her down the aisle to the front of the store.

"Hey, Ruth," the kid Richard had spoken with earlier called out. "Introduce us to your old man."

"He's not so old," Ruth joked. Richard was touched by her defense of him. "Richard, this is my friend Wade Smith. And Rosita Reyes, and Bernie O'Hara. That's Gina at the film counter. Everyone, this is my husband, Richard Bendel."

Richard stood stoically while they all gave him a thorough going-over. The balding older guy, Bernie, subjected Richard to a particularly intense inspection. "He doesn't look like much," Bernie said. "I still say you should run away with me."

"Yeah, sure. Let's check with your wife and see what she says," Ruth chided, even though she and Bernie were both laughing. Richard didn't join their laughter. He wanted to punch Bernie in the nose—and he wasn't a violent man. Instead, he slid his arm around Ruth's shoulders, staking his claim.

He could barely feel her through the thick insulation of her coat, but he didn't care. He was holding her. Holding her in a way he hadn't held her in too long. Just as he couldn't remember the last time he'd taken her hand in his, he couldn't remember the last time he'd wrapped an arm around her shoulders.

"We were just leaving," he said, a general announcement. "Nice meeting you." He steered Ruth gently toward the door.

"Can't blame a guy for trying," Bernie called after them.

Sure I can, Richard thought, but he didn't want to embarrass Ruth in front of her coworkers, so he kept his mouth shut. He noticed her exchange an enigmatic look with the young kid. What was his name? Something Smith.

Christ. Maybe *he* was the one she was planning to run away with.

They stepped outside into the chilly evening. "I can take you home," he offered.

"That's okay. It's just across the street." She halted under the awning of the sneaker shop and turned to face him. "So? What's up?"

"I was wondering . . ." He felt like the twenty-year-old boy he'd been the first time he'd posed this question to her. "I was wondering if we could go out."

"Go out? What do you mean?"

"For coffee? Dinner? Whatever you want."

"A date? You're asking me on a date?"

"Yes." He angled his head toward the First-Rate. "Unless you've got something going on with that married man in there."

"Bernie?" She snorted. "Not only is he married, he's too old. He just likes to flirt."

"How about the boy with the thing in his eyebrow?"

"Wade? He's my buddy," she said fondly. Her smile faded as she appraised Richard. "You look good. Spiffy. What, you're using the cleaners?"

"Huh?"

"Your shirts. You're taking them to the cleaners?"

He puffed up with pride. "I'm ironing them myself."

"No kidding?" She ran her fingers along his collar, as if trying to detect starch. He wasn't exactly sure what starch was, at least in the context of laundry, so he knew she wouldn't feel anything except cotton broadcloth.

"I'm doing okay with laundry. Cooking, not so good." He smiled and fluttered his hand in the air to indicate that his skills in the kitchen were nothing to brag about. He had become a lot less intimidated by the microwave, but . . . God, he missed her pot roast. "What do you say? Dinner out on Saturday night? Any restaurant you choose."

"Oh, Richard." She sighed, turned to stare through the adjacent store window at a pair of sneakers that appeared engineered for walking on the moon, then lifted her gaze back to him. He couldn't read her expression—but then, could he ever? Obviously, she'd been nursing grievances for years, but he'd been too dense to notice. "I don't know."

"It doesn't have to be dinner. What would you like? A movie? Bowling?"

"Bowling?" She laughed. He hoped that was a good sign.

"Sure. Why not? And ice-cream sundaes afterward."

"I'd rather go dancing."

"Dancing. Perfect." What a lie. He hated dancing. Not that there was anything particularly wrong with it, but he always felt stupid standing in the middle of a crowded floor with his arms around her and shuffling his feet in time to some song he didn't know or like. She was the music expert, so maybe the whole thing made sense to her. To him, dancing was just a substitute for sex, only sex was a hell of a lot more satisfying. "Where should we go to do that? A ballroom? Or . . ." He realized he had to put some effort into this outing. If she did all the planning, she might resent him. She might feel as if she was stuck cleaning up after him again, and he was trying to prove to her that she didn't have to do that. He could rinse his damn beard hair out of the sink, and he could figure out where to take her dancing.

"I was thinking, this club in Boston," she said. "I went there with Wade and his girlfriend—I *think* she's his girlfriend, although they're on-again-off-again. But he's not smoking at the moment, so I'm hoping they're on again."

Wade? The punk behind the counter with the eyebrow thing. "What kind of club?" he asked dubiously, picturing a seedy building full of motorcycle gang members who guzzled cheap whisky and shared a secret handshake.

"A rock club."

"I thought you liked classical music. What's his name—Corelli?" That he remembered her favorite composer might win him a couple of points.

"To listen to. Not to dance to."

"I don't know about the rock clubs today. And they probably don't play *our* music. The Beatles? Grateful Dead?"

"You're turning into an old fogy," she scolded, but he sensed a teasing undertone in her voice.

"I'm already an old fogy." He shrugged bravely. "If you want to go to your friend Wade's favorite rock club and listen to rap, fine."

"Dance, not listen. And it's not rap. They play all kinds of stuff. I don't know it. I just dance to it."

"So we'll go." He suppressed a shudder. If this was what it took to win her back, he'd do it. "This Saturday. We could have dinner together before."

"No," she said firmly. "If we're hungry for a snack afterward, maybe."

"Ice cream sundaes," he suggested, although from the sound of things, this club wouldn't be conducive to such a sweet, innocent treat. He was envisioning black leather, torn denim, the aromas of beer and sweat. He was envisioning some of the rowdier parties in his frat house basement at Cornell forty-and-then-some years ago.

"You can pick me up at eight-thirty," she instructed him, waving toward the apartment complex across the street. "I'm in Building 4. I'll wait in the entry."

"Don't be silly. I'll come to your door. You shouldn't be standing all alone in the entry."

"No, I'll meet you downstairs," she said decisively. "And I'll warn you, Richard—I don't put out on the first date. So don't get any ideas."

He stifled a laugh. He hadn't dared to allow himself that particular idea. Dancing would have to do. And really, she wouldn't have offered to go dancing with him if she didn't want him to touch her. Bowling would have been a lot less romantic.

So she wouldn't put out. They'd dance. It was a start.

Chapter Twenty-Five

Thanksgiving had been Ruth's holiday for forty-two years. Her first Thanksgiving as Richard's wife, his parents and hers had bickered and squabbled, competing for the honor of hosting the family feast until Ruth had felt like the rope in a tug-of-war. To shut everyone up, she'd announced that she would host the meal and both sets of parents would be her guests. Her brother Isaac and his shiksa wife had come, and Richard's *nudnik* brother Ben, who'd been living on a commune somewhere in the Adirondacks but had hitchhiked to Boston and shown up wearing his hair practically down to his tush and jeans that smelled like wet hay. He'd announced he was a vegetarian and then devoured three heaping portions of turkey.

Ruth hadn't even known how to cook a turkey that first year. Diligent newlywed that she was, she'd read several cookbooks, ignored the badgering phone calls from her mother—"Remember to brown the mushrooms in margarine before you mix them into the stuffing"—and her mother-in-law—"*Dahlink*, I don't mean to interfere, but I think you should know, Richard's father hates mushrooms"—and managed to concoct a delicious feast, which she'd served in the third-floor walk-up in Somerville where she and Richard had lived while he'd been in medical school. That ugly, sun-deprived flat had been smaller than the apartment she was living in now, but it had been all they could afford on her secretarial salary. Somehow, everyone had squeezed in, and Ben had remained an extra few days, devouring leftover turkey and taking full advantage of the indoor plumbing before he hitched back to the Adirondacks.

Every year she'd gotten better at preparing a Thanksgiving dinner. Year three, she'd made her own pie crusts from scratch instead of buying frozen. Year six, with a toddler son and a baby daughter underfoot, she'd tried a recipe for cranberry bread which had proven enormously popular. By the time Richard had finished his residency and they'd bought their house, no one had dared to meddle. The holiday had become hers.

This year it was Jill's, and Ruth was surprised to discover that instead of feeling bereft, she felt liberated.

Richard had persuaded her to let him pick her up and drive her to Jill's, insisting that carpooling would save gas. She wasn't so sure about that; he had to drive five miles out of his way to fetch her, the same five miles she would have driven if she'd taken her own car. But if he drove she could drink more wine, so she'd acquiesced.

She'd told him she wanted to visit her mother first, and no doubt eager to prove what an accommodating, selfless husband he could be, he said he would be happy to drive her to the nursing home. Her mother had been in fine spirits, apparently more pleased to see Richard than to see Ruth. She'd kissed him, called him *bubbela* several times and sung a Yiddish ditty that was probably obscene, given the way she kept cackling and blushing at the end of each verse, but Ruth had no idea what the words meant. Her mother had eaten three of the chocolates in the Whitman's Sampler Ruth had brought, and thanked Richard for them. Then they'd walked her to the dining room, where a turkey dinner had been prepared for the residents, said good-bye and headed off to Jill's house.

They'd talked mostly about her mother during the drive, about how well she was doing, how the nursing home seemed to be taking good care of her. What they hadn't said was that Ruth's mother was never to learn that they were separated. At this stage, she probably wouldn't even understand what a separation was. She clearly couldn't remember Richard's name—hence the *bubbelas*—but there was no need for her to think anything had changed in their marriage. Because if Ruth ever told her, and she was lucid enough to comprehend the situation, she would hate Richard and blame him and pity Ruth. The blame was Ruth's at least as much as Richard's, and she was enjoying her life too much to deserve pity.

She experienced a spike of anxiety as Richard pulled into the Sackler driveway and shut off the engine. This was the first time the family would all be together since the separation. None of the kids knew that she and Richard had gone on two . . . well, *dates* seemed like an awfully formal name for spending an evening with your spouse of forty-two years with whom you were not living at the moment. She didn't want the kids to know she and Richard had spent a couple of evenings with each other. They might regard those two outings as proof that their parents were getting back together again, and Ruth wasn't so sure about that.

Not that their dates had gone badly. The first, she and Richard had wound up double-dating—God, that sounded so high-schoolish—with Wade and Hilda at a rock club in Cambridge. A different club than she'd gone to with them the last time; Wade had said the music would be a little mellower, which might be easier for Richard to take. Wade and Hilda were still having enough ups and downs to give a person the bends, but Ruth and Richard had ignored their oscillations between antagonism and affection and had taken to the dance floor. Richard had complained that he was the oldest person out there, and Ruth had said, "So what?"

He hadn't enjoyed the dancing the way she had. He hadn't lost himself in the music, the beat, the collective energy of a crowd of people crammed together on a sticky dance floor, rocking and rolling. He hadn't talked much to Wade or Hilda. He'd claimed the room was too noisy for conversation, but Ruth suspected he just didn't feel comfortable. Wade and Hilda weren't his type, after all. His type was late-middle-aged doctors who played golf after shul on Saturdays and channel-surfed in the evenings.

Still, he'd been a good sport about the dance club. When he'd driven her back to her apartment at one in the morning, he'd assured her that he'd had more fun than he would have had bowling. But then, he'd never been much of a bowler, either.

So when he'd invited her to have dinner with him at their favorite Italian place on Route 20 the following weekend, she'd said okay. She'd been dining alone so many evenings, she'd thought she ought to dine with someone else to make sure she hadn't forgotten her table manners.

The hostess at the restaurant had greeted them like loved ones just back from paddling a canoe around the world. "Where have you been? We haven't seen you here in so long!"

They'd wound up seated at their usual table, and Richard had ordered the chicken parmesan as he usually did, while she'd ordered the shrimp scampi, as usual. They'd split a bottle of Chianti Classico. He'd told her about a new stent currently in the testing stages. He'd asked her if she found running a cash register tedious. He'd mentioned that he'd vacuumed the house earlier that day, and that he'd had the sprinkler system winterized, and did she usually pay eighty dollars for that service, because that was what the guy had charged him and he hoped he hadn't been ripped off.

When he'd driven her back to her apartment, he'd kissed her good-night. It had been more than a simple little peck on the lips, but less than a prelude to steamy sex. Ruth wasn't sure she was ready for hot kisses. She missed snuggling, but not sex, not really.

And now their third date: Thanksgiving dinner at their daughter's house. Jill had insisted that she bring "nothing but herself," as Jill had put it, but Richard had purchased a lovely autumn bouquet, brown and orange and honey-colored mums in a nest of ferns, for Jill. *That* had tempted Ruth to give him a hot kiss. She'd always been the one to remember to bring things for the children and the grandchildren when they'd visited. But Richard had thought of his daughter's efforts and come up with a sweet, generous offering. Lacking Ruth's input, he'd done the right thing on his own.

Even without the flowers Richard had brought, the house was already beautifully decorated. A willow wreath hung on the front door, and the dining room was adorned with clusters of Indian corn on either end of the sideboard and a centerpiece of pine cones and holly anchoring the beige table cloth, which was obviously new since its rectangular packaging creases hadn't been laundered out of it yet. Each place setting—and there were a lot of them; no way could Ruth have fit everyone comfortably around her tiny table in her apartment—had a crisp new linen napkin rolled inside a carved wooden napkin ring. Clove-scented candles stood flickering on the wide window sill. The living room was decorated, too, with tangy-smelling pine branches strewn across the mantel and another clove-scented candle burning inside a glass chimney on the coffee table. A little Christmasy, Ruth thought, all that pine, even though the ribbons tied around them were copper-hued rather than red. But still charming.

The house was already humming with activity when Gordon ushered them inside. He kissed Ruth's cheek, then led Richard away to get him a drink, as if afraid to allow Richard and Ruth to remain in each other's company any longer than absolutely required. After a boisterous greeting from Mackenzie and Madison, who hugged her, yanked on her hands and jabbered incomprehensibly about some video they were watching downstairs in the rec room, Ruth made her way to the kitchen, where she found Jill monitoring the temperature of the roasting bird and Brooke arranging a platter of raw vegetables, creating a floral effect with broccoli florets and slivers of green pepper. Brooke gave her a smile, but she wasn't one for big smooches, so Ruth refrained from kissing her.

"You're a sweetheart, helping Jill out with the cooking," she said. She always felt an obligation to compliment Brooke. They weren't that close—Brooke didn't seem to be close to anyone except Doug and maybe, on occasion, her daughters—but Ruth didn't want to lose what little ground she had with her. So she offered lavish praise at every opportunity.

Brooke only laughed. "Don't be silly, Ruth. I don't cook. Jill's done it all."

"Bull," Jill said as she swung the oven door shut and crossed the kitchen to hug her mother. "Brooke's my party planner. She created all the decorations. Look—she can even make baby carrots look cute." Jill gestured toward the platter.

"Baby carrots have always troubled me," Brooke confessed. "It's like they've got a pituitary disorder." She shook her head, causing the delicate blond strands of hair framing her face to shudder.

"Well, the salad dish looks very nice," Ruth praised her, even though she thought Brooke's concerns were a bit on the fussy side.

"It's crudités," Brooke said. "Jill, what did you do with that dip?"

Dip? At Thanksgiving? Ruth associated dips with potato chips and the Super Bowl. But it was Jill's party, not hers. She wasn't going to behave like her mother and mother-in-law had the first time she'd hosted the celebration. If Jill wanted to serve dip—with chips, salad or, pardon the pretension, *crudités*—by all means, let her serve dip. Ruth was a guest, not the hostess.

She experienced another swell of liberation that washed away any lingering nervousness about surviving an evening with her children when she and their father were neither here nor there emotionally. She liked the fact that she wasn't the one scurrying around, fixing and preparing and worrying that everything should come out perfect and everyone should go home stuffed to their eyeballs. She was a working woman now, a single woman, someone who had the right to expect others to cater to her.

As if Jill had read her mind, she pressed a glass of white wine into Ruth's hand. "Here. This is just to get you started."

"Thank you! A toast . . ." She raised the goblet, and Brooke raised a glass half-full of wine standing next to the vegetable platter on the counter. Jill raised a can of Diet Coke.

"To Mom," Jill declared.

"You can't drink a toast with Diet Coke," Ruth objected.

"I can drink a toast with anything I want. And I'll be drinking wine once we sit. Right now I need caffeine. Potatoes," she said, half to herself before lifting the lid of a pot bubbling on the stove. "I'm making mashed. No yams. I hate yams."

"You never said." Ruth felt a pang of guilt. Every year she made yams, and every year Jill gamely ate half a yam.

"So now you know."

"Where's your sister?"

"She called from the road. She said the traffic is awful, but they should get here by about four."

"*They*," Ruth muttered. "What do you know about this new one? He's not a hairdresser, is he?"

"He's a lawyer," Brooke told her.

"Ah." Ruth didn't want to seem snooty, but she was pleased that her Ivy-League daughter was dating someone at her professional level.

"Not Jewish," Jill warned.

"That's okay. He's a lawyer. They'll have something to talk about besides styling mousse."

"I liked Luc," Brooke said wistfully, then took a long drink of wine. "I'll go bring these into the living room for the boys to munch on." She lifted the vegetable platter, nestled the small bowl of dip beneath the broccoli blossom she'd created, grabbed her wine glass and glided out of the kitchen.

"It's nice of her to help," Ruth noted. "She doesn't usually contribute in the kitchen."

"She's helped me plan this entire dinner, Mom. I can't believe it, but she and I are really getting along well. We'll be moving into our office on December first. I think it's going to work out."

"I think you're both nuts," Ruth said, "but why not? You can afford this?"

"Not right away. We'll both be operating at a loss for a while, but the accountant said that's to be expected." Jill sighed. Obviously, she wasn't thrilled about operating at a loss. After a long slug of Diet Coke—straight from the can; why couldn't she drink out of a glass like a civilized person?—she smiled. "We're both taking a risk. The rent is cheap, at least, although God knows they wouldn't dare to charge more for this room. It's not much bigger than a closet. Actually, it's smaller than the closet in Brooke's bedroom, but she's got a humongous closet. We'll make it work. We're planning to share a desk, which is good because there's no way we could fit two desks into the place."

"And you're going to lose money?"

"Because of you, Mom." Jill placed the lid back on the pot of boiling potatoes and gave Ruth a hug. "You took a risk. You took a chance. You took a leap of faith. That's what we're doing—taking a leap of faith."

"Faith has nothing to do with me," Ruth argued. "As it is, I haven't been in touch with the B'nai Torah Sisterhood in weeks."

"I mean faith in things working out. Or faith in yourself, knowing that if they don't work out you'll still be okay." She released Ruth, and when she stepped back Ruth saw a shimmer of tears in her eyes. "If I lose money trying to expand my catalogue writing business, I'll be okay. If Brooke's party planning business doesn't work out, she'll be okay."

"Of course she'll be okay, all the money Doug makes."

"And we'll be okay, too. I thought Gordon would be opposed to this. I expected him to wave the checkbook under my nose and explain that we couldn't afford it. But he's fine. He said I should give it a try and see what happens."

"He's a good man, your husband," Ruth said, and meant it. If she'd stayed with Richard while working at First-Rate, he would have hated it. He would have seen her job as a commentary on him. He would have worried that people might think he didn't earn enough to support her. Or he would have been embarrassed that she was doing a job you didn't need a college degree for. She'd hinted for years that she wanted to get a job, and he'd always laughed off her comments or reminded her she already had a job.

Taking care of him. That had been her job. Taking care of him, the house, her children—everything and everyone but herself.

She'd had to leave. For her own sanity, for her own satisfaction, she'd had to.

Abbie bounded into the kitchen, munching on a curl of green pepper. "Hey, Grandma!" She raced to Ruth and squeezed her in a crushing hug. When had she gotten taller than Ruth? Not only had she grown an inch in the couple of weeks since Ruth had last seen her, but she'd grown in other ways. Her bosom was no longer just a couple of bumps the size of mosquito bites on her chest, and her waist seemed a little narrower. So did her face. She was losing the baby fat that had softened her cheeks and chin.

Before Ruth could comment, Abbie popped the rest of the pepper into her mouth and spoke while she was still chewing. "I didn't even hear you and Grandpa arrive. I was texting Caitlin, and the next thing I knew, you guys were here. Grandpa said he drove you. Does that mean you're back together with him? Because I think your apartment is so cool."

"I think it's cool, too," Ruth assured her. "Grandpa and I are friends. I've still got the apartment, though."

"Cool. Because if you decide to move back in with Grandpa, you should keep the apartment anyway. Like a secret hideaway or something."

"An escape hatch," Jill said.

"Kind of like Mom's office." Abbie grinned mischievously. "I know she's renting the office just to get away from me and Noah because we *drive her crazy*." She made her voice deep and spooky when she said that, and waved her hands wildly in front of her mother's face. "Noah is eating all the carrots. He's such a pig."

"Tell him to eat the broccoli."

"Oh, yeah. Fat chance."

The doorbell rang and Abbie sprang toward the door. "Aunt Melissa!" she shouted, and Ruth never had a chance to tell her how right she was about keeping the apartment.

Chapter Twenty-Six

If Jill was to believe Brooke, her Thanksgiving dinner was a huge success.

Brooke claimed that two signs of a successful party were people eating a lot and people talking a lot. Drinking, less so, because too much drinking could lead to bad behavior. But no one seemed to be drunk, and Noah swore the cider tasted hard, even though it wasn't, and Jill couldn't imagine how he would know what hard cider tasted like, anyway. Well, she could imagine it, but not in the context of Noah. He was too blessedly nerdy to be messing with liquor.

The twins thought the term "hard cider" was hilarious. "It's a liquid!" they shrieked between hiccups of laughter. "How can it be hard?"

"It would be hard if you froze it," Abbie pointed out, which quelled their hysterics.

Abbie was lording over the other children, which, as the oldest of the young, was her right. She held her water glass by the stem and crooked her pinkie—where she'd picked up that affectation Jill couldn't guess—and lowered her knife to her plate between bites, and took it upon herself to lead the interrogations of everyone at the table who had some explaining to do, starting with Melissa's new boyfriend, Aidan O'Leary.

"Are you a lawyer or an attorney?" she asked him solemnly. "Melissa is a lawyer. Which one are you?"

"Oh, I'm definitely a lawyer," Aidan said without smirking. "Attorneys are pretentious."

"What's pretentious?" Noah asked.

"Stuck-up and phony," Abbie informed him before turning back to Aidan. "Are you a Democrat?"

That got a smile out of him. Jill's mother intervened. "No politics on Thanksgiving," she said.

"Why not? I thought Aunt Melissa brought him with her so we could get to know him."

"I'm a registered Democrat," he said, saving Abbie from her grandmother's disapproval.

"Last time Aunt Melissa visited, she brought Luc," Mackenzie commented.

"Yeah, Luc," Madison chimed in.

"He did hair," Mackenzie said.

"I do intellectual property," Aidan informed her, winning points for being unflappable in the face of such tactlessness. "It's similar to hair."

"He also helped me get the price down on the apartment," Melissa added. "He's a hell of a negotiator. So—something to give thanks for!" She lifted her wine glass in a toast to herself. "My bid was accepted, and now I've just got to survive the mortgage application."

Congratulations were shouted, glasses were raised, Doug mentioned something about how the real estate market in Manhattan seemed impervious to the upheavals in other regions and Brooke mentioned the name of an interior designer she knew in Soho, if Melissa was interested. Melissa joked that by the time she was done paying the down payment and closing costs, she'd be lucky to afford an air mattress. Decorating would have to wait.

"It's a terrific apartment," Aidan assured everyone.

"How many bedrooms?" Jill's father asked.

"Two."

"Two bedrooms? You need two bedrooms?" Jill's mother tilted slightly in her chair, as if trying to glimpse Melissa's abdomen. Jill, at the foot of the table, could have told her there was nothing to see.

"I might eventually," Melissa said laconically.

Aidan was less discreet. "The second bedroom would make a nice nursery."

An uproar ensued—a happy uproar, for the most part, punctuated by the twins squealing, "What? What's everybody screaming about?"

The hubbub was silenced by Melissa's vehement announcement: "I am *not* pregnant." Jill scanned the long table and noticed more people were staring at Aidan than at Melissa. The object of their critical scrutiny was grinning. He wasn't photo-spread handsome like Luc, but he had an animated smile and sparkly green eyes. And he was demonstrating an admirable ability to take on her family without quailing.

"It's just, you two haven't known each other very long," Jill's mother said. She sounded as if she was selecting each word with care, but it was too late for diplomacy.

Across the table, Jill's father turned to Aidan, who was seated next to him, and said, "Not that this is any of our business."

"Of course it's your business," Aidan said affably. "She's your daughter."

That won him a few points from Jill. "Aidan, have some more stuffing," she offered, nudging the bowl toward him. "Doug, you look like you could use some more turkey."

Doug held up his hand in protest, but when Gordon passed him the platter of meat, he forced himself to spear a slice of breast meat and add it to his plate.

"So, you didn't want to have Thanksgiving with your own family?" Jill's mother asked.

"They live on Long Island," he said. "I see them all the time. Besides, I've got four sisters and a brother. One less mouth to feed is okay with them." He grinned and scooped a spoonful of stuffing onto his plate. "Your stuffing is better than my mother's. She ruins it by putting raisins into it."

"Raisins! Eew!" The twins erupted in giggles while Noah made gagging sounds and wrapped his hands around his neck, pretending to choke.

"Did you know," Abbie addressed him, "that Grandma is a musician?"

"No, I didn't," Aidan said, glancing quizzically at Melissa.

Jill's mother shook her head and waved her hand. "I majored in music, sweetheart. That doesn't make me a musician."

"She wrote a paper about this old composer. What was his name, Grandma? I forgot."

"Corelli."

"Right, Corelli," Abbie confirmed.

"She wrote about his suspenders," Noah added.

This elicited some confusion among most of the guests. Jill corrected him. "Suspended seconds," she said. "Isn't that right, Mom?"

"Yes." Jill's mother attempted a modest smile, but she sat straighter and a flash of pride lit her eyes. Maybe she was sort of a single woman, maybe she was destined to become a divorcée, maybe she was a clerk in a convenience store—but she'd written an honors thesis on Corelli's suspended seconds, and that was worthy of respect.

"I think classical music is boring," Noah said.

Abbie gave him a withering look. "You're probably just too immature to understand it." She turned back to Jill's mother. "Next time I visit, will you play me some Corelli?"

"I'd love to," Jill's mother promised.

"Corelli, *schmelli*. When she's not listening to Corelli, she goes dancing at rock clubs," Jill's father muttered.

"Rock clubs?" More tumult. Noah raised a fist in victory and hissed a *yes!* Doug frowned at Brooke, who turned her hands palm up in the universal "don't ask me" gesture. Jill simply sipped her wine. She'd known about her mother's club-hopping, just as she'd known Melissa had fallen in love with the apartment in New York because the second bedroom would make a perfect nursery. She knew Brooke was a lot tougher and smarter than she let on, and she knew Doug was a lot softer and more vulnerable. She knew her father was far more dependent on her mother than her mother was on him.

Everything was different, and she knew all about it.

Down at the other end of the table, Gordon caught her eye. He wasn't different, she thought with a burst of gratitude. He'd been Gordon when she worked at home, and he would be Gordon when she worked in the minuscule office she'd found for rent on the second floor above the bakery where she bought her father's rugelach. He was Gordon, the father of a little boy and a little girl, and in a few months he'd be Gordon, the father of a not-so-little boy and a young woman.

Everyone was eating. Everyone was talking. This was definitely a successful party.

"MOM?" ABBIE CALLED through the open bedroom doorway.

Gordon was already in bed, clad in his sweatpants and leaning against his pillow, which he'd turned vertical against the headboard so he could sit comfortably. He was reading the sports section of the *Boston Globe*, which he hadn't had a chance to read earlier because the house had been full of company.

Now they were all gone. Melissa and Aidan had accepted Doug and Brooke's invitation to stay with them—"We've got more room, and Jill's got her hands full dealing with dinner," Brooke had pointed out. Jill's parents had left, and Jill had watched from the front door as her father had opened the passenger door for her mother and taken her hand as she lowered herself onto the seat. Chivalry, affection . . . whatever it was, it had made Jill's eyes tear up.

Or maybe they'd teared up because of the monumental mess awaiting her attention in the kitchen. Pots, plates, leftovers, half-burnt candles. Silverware. Stemware. Picked-over *crudités*.

But things had gotten cleaned up, with assistance from Abbie,

Noah and Gordon. Noah stuffed things into the dishwasher the way professional basketball players stuffed balls into baskets, and Gordon's concept of clean counters differed drastically from Jill's, but eventually the kitchen had been restored to its usual state of semi-neatness. Jill had rewarded herself with a Diet Coke once the last of the mashed potatoes had been snapped inside a plastic container and crammed onto an already overcrowded shelf in the refrigerator.

She'd been in the bathroom when Abbie had summoned her. Noah was slumbering peacefully in his bed; ten years old meant he no longer fought her over bedtimes. He seemed to be growing an inch a day, and he needed sleep to recover from the strain. It was too early for Abbie to retire when she didn't have school the following day, but she was dressed for bed in an L.L. Bean nightshirt.

Jill was dressed in a nightshirt, too. She'd just finished rinsing her toothpaste and Gordon's down the sink. No way would she complain about his having left blobs of toothpaste stuck to the porcelain. She was in too good a mood, and he *had* wiped down the kitchen counters, sort of.

"What's up, honey?" she asked, emerging from the bathroom into the bedroom.

"Earlier today, Aunt Brooke told me I needed to have a theme for my bat mitzvah."

Jill nodded. "You don't *need* to have a theme. Aunt Brooke thinks that makes for a better party, but we had a great party today and it didn't have a theme."

"Yes it did," Abbie argued.

"What was the theme?"

"Thanksgiving," Gordon shouted from the bed.

"Family," Abbie corrected him. "That was the theme."

Jill pondered Abbie's statement and found nothing to dispute. "Okay. That still doesn't mean you need to have a theme for your bat mitzvah."

"Well, I've got a theme." Abbie lifted her chin slightly, a posture of pride. "Independence."

"Independence?"

"Yeah. That's the theme."

Jill suppressed a smile. "I think Aunt Brooke was thinking along the lines of, you know. Soccer. Or Star Wars."

"Gross!"

"Or the Red Sox. Something that would lend itself to the

decorations and the invitations."

"Independence would work. We could have the Statue of Liberty on the cake. And party favors that looked like the Declaration of Independence."

"You mean, a Colonial theme?" Jill supposed that would work. Stars-and-stripes bunting, red-white-and-blue tablecloths . . .

"No, an *independence* theme," Abbie emphasized. "Like freedom. Liberation. It's my bat mitzvah, and it means I'm taking charge of my life, and I can be anything I want to be. Anyone can, if they're willing to fight for it. Like Grandma getting her own apartment. And you getting an office. Liberation."

It sounded awfully amorphous to Jill, but she loved the idea. More important, she loved Abbie for having come up with it. "We'll talk to Aunt Brooke about it," she said. "You and she can brainstorm and figure out how to make it work."

"You too, Mom. I want you brainstorming, too."

"All of us, then."

"We can meet in your office."

Jill smiled, trying to picture all three of them squeezing into that tiny space. They might all fit if she and Brooke wound up buying a small desk. And maybe only one file cabinet, instead of two.

"Fine. We'll meet in the office."

Abbie broke into a joyous grin. "Thanks," she said, gathering Jill in a surprisingly strong hug. "'Night, Daddy," she hollered in Gordon's direction before skipping down the hall to her own bedroom.

Jill waited until Abbie had closed her door before shutting her own bedroom door and turning to Gordon. He folded the sports section and tossed it onto the floor beside the bed.

Jill considered picking it up and putting it on his dresser, then thought, what the hell. Right now his chest was more important. His naked chest. His adorable, familiar smile. His flyaway hair. His strong arms empty, waiting.

"Hey, buddy," she murmured, crossing the room to the bed and tugging open the buttons of her night shirt. "Wanna show a girl a good time?"

"Let me think about it," he joked, though his eyes were warm and those strong arms reached eagerly for her.

She had an office. Paying for it meant she might never be able to afford France. Or maybe she *would* be able to afford it, eventually. Anything was possible.

And in the meantime, she thought as Gordon pulled her closer, she had this.

Chapter Twenty-Seven

Ruth was stuffed. She didn't think she'd eaten more this year than she had at previous Thanksgiving dinners. But this year, she hadn't done any of the cooking or cleaning up, so she hadn't had an opportunity to burn off any of the feast she'd consumed: turkey, stuffing, mashed potatoes—a nice change of pace from the yams, she had to admit—Brooke's crudités, several glasses of wine and a generous slice of that banana cream pie Melissa's guy had brought.

She wasn't used to eating such huge meals anymore. She hadn't taken the bathroom scale with her when she'd moved, so she had no idea what she weighed these days. Without Richard to cook for, though, she existed quite happily on suppers of soup and salad or fruit and cheese, and recently, she'd noticed her slacks fitting her a little more loosely at the waist. She felt . . . lighter.

It could be a psychological thing. She'd shed some burdens, jettisoned some emotional stuff. Could losing psychic weight change the way her pants fit?

Beside her, Richard drove, his face settled into a relaxed smile reflecting the sort of contentment that came from spending an evening eating good food while surrounded by family.

"So," she asked, "what do you think of Melissa's new boyfriend?"

"He's not Jewish," Richard said, then shrugged. "At least he's not a hairdresser."

"I liked him," Ruth said. "I thought it was very sweet that he brought a pie."

"Who brings a banana cream pie to Thanksgiving?" Richard shook his head. "Apple pie, cherry pie, pumpkin pie, sure. Banana cream pie?"

"It was delicious." Ruth sighed happily. "The way he and Melissa were talking about nurseries . . . I think they're serious."

Richard shot her a quick look. "Did she say anything about getting married?"

"No. But she seemed awfully happy."

"She can hire Brooke to plan her wedding."

Ruth grinned. "Maybe her old boyfriend will do her hair for the event. Maybe he'll do all our hair."

"Marlon Brando," Richard muttered, glancing Ruth's way again. "Don't let him near your hair. It looks fine the way it is."

Ruth realized with a start that he'd said something nice about her appearance. She tried to recall the last time he'd given her a compliment, the last time she was even aware that he'd noticed her hair. Not that she blamed him; you live with a person for forty-two years and you stop seeing that person. "Thank you," she said.

Richard slowed the car as they neared the entry to her apartment complex. His smile faded as he steered a meandering route past the blocky brick buildings and the parking lots, in and out of pools of light from the street lamps, until he reached her building. He pulled into one of the unnumbered visitor spots and shut off the engine. Then he turned to her.

She braced herself. Was he going to plead with her to come home? Point out that the wonderful evening they'd had, not just with their family but with each other, proved their marriage was still solid and healthy and they should be together? Blubber that he missed her?

If he did, how would she respond? Would she break his heart if she told him she wouldn't come home? She adored her cozy little apartment and her simple suppers. She appreciated her newfound lightness. And while she admittedly felt affectionate toward him right now, maybe even loving—she *had* drunk quite a bit of wine, after all—she didn't miss him.

"I had a good time tonight," he said somberly. "I'd like to see you again."

Like a date. She stifled the urge to laugh at his stilted, polite request. He seemed so solemn, she didn't want to insult him by bursting into giggles.

"I was going to ask you to come back to the house with me," he continued when she remained silent. "But I realized . . . this will sound strange, but I'm not ready for you to do that."

It *did* sound strange. Her urge to laugh waned as she studied him in the uneven light. He looked bemused, as if he didn't understand his own feelings.

"I don't know how to say this, Ruth. You're my wife. I love you. But . . . I like channel surfing. I'm not sure I want to stop clicking the remote."

She did laugh then, a gentle chuckle, and he allowed himself a hesitant smile.

"Does that make me a bad person, that I like to channel-surf?"

"You're not a bad person," she assured him. "Neither of us is bad. We're just people, that's all."

"So. Can I see you again?"

She leaned across the console, planted a quick kiss on his cheek and said, "Call me." Then she swung out of the car and entered her building.

Inside the vestibule, she watched through the glass door as he started the engine and backed out of the visitor space. She followed his tail lights until they disappeared around the side of the building and all she could see in the glass was her own faint reflection. Turning away, she unlocked the inner door and climbed the stairs.

This is my home, she realized. If Richard had asked her to come home, she would have had to say she *was* home. This building, this stairway, this corridor. The welcome mat. The metal door. The tiny kitchen. The ugly shag carpeting. The old stereo and her rack of classical music CD's. The futon. The platform bed on the other side of the bedroom door, with drawers for storage built in underneath it.

This is my home, she thought. *I'm stuffed, and I'm tired, and I'm happy, and I'm home.*

About Judith Arnold

Judith Arnold can't remember a time when she wasn't making up stories. Her older sister taught her how to read and write by the time she was four years old, and she's been at it ever since. A detour in college, thanks to a charismatic professor, led her to spend most of her twenties writing plays, which were professionally produced around the United States and in Canada. But she eventually returned to her first love—prose fiction—and sold her first novel, *Silent Beginnings*, shortly before her thirtieth birthday. (She found out she was pregnant with her first son the same week she made her first sale. Both the book and the baby were October releases. She and her husband nicknamed the baby "Noisy Beginnings.")

Since that first sale, Judith has sold more than eighty-five novels, with more than ten million copies in print worldwide. She's been a multiple finalist for Romance Writers of America's RITA ® Award and the winner of *RT Book Reviews* Reviewer's Choice Awards for best Harlequin American Romance, best Harlequin Superromance, best Series Romance and best Contemporary Single Title Romance. *Publishers Weekly* named her novel *Love In Bloom's* one of the best books of the year, and her novel *Barefoot In the Grass* has appeared on recommended reading lists at hospitals and breast cancer support centers.

A native New Yorker, Judith lives near Boston. She considers her sons her two greatest creations, but she's pretty proud of all her books, too.

CPSIA information can be obtained at www.ICGtesting.com
Printed in the USA
BVOW07s0142080114

341231BV00002B/35/P

9 781611 940930